Posy: Book Four

Family

By Mary Ann Weir

Table of Contents

1: A Market ... for Fleas?

Posy

After kissing my other mates goodbye, I held Mason's hand as he led me out to his new truck.

That's right. After Garnet destroyed his truck's interior during the parasite incident, Mason bought a brand-new one. It was almost exactly the same as his other truck, which could have been repaired, according to Wyatt, but Jayden said Mason wanted an excuse to make Cole buy him a new one, and that was that.

Since their personal money was in a joint account, I didn't really see how it mattered much, but I didn't care to get involved and let them solve stuff like that amongst themselves.

"Can I help you get in?" Mason asked after watching me jump around for a bit.

"I guess you'll have to if we're going to leave anytime soon. If Ash would have made me that kissing box, I could use it as a stepping stone to get in these massive vehicles."

Chuckling, he put his hands on my waist and lifted me, then made sure I was properly buckled before closing my door and trotting around to his side. Once he was in and also buckled, he looked at me as he started the engine.

"Kissing box, huh? What's *that* story?"

So I told him about my second day here and the conversation with Ash that led to the kissing box, and Mason laughed.

"How is he so tall, anyway?" I asked. "Even with my limited knowledge of the outside world, I can tell six foot ten isn't a normal height."

"Some people grow that tall, and some people stay as short as you." He glanced at me with a smirk, and I stuck my tongue out at him. "Before he got his wolf, Uncle Jay and Aunt Denise took him to a human doctor to make sure, but he doesn't have gigantism. He's just a really tall guy."

"Gigantism? I guess it means being a giant?"

"Oh. Yeah. So, if your body makes too much of a growth hormone, it makes you grow faster than normal and keep growing, but it can be treated if it's caught when a kid is young enough."

"I like how you explain things so I can understand them," I told him.

"Thank you. I like explaining things to you. I like talking to you in general. Before we found you, I didn't talk much to anyone except my family," he admitted. "And even then, not so much. I told you before, after Willow died, I shut out a lot of people."

4

"I'm glad that's changing," I told him gently.

"Me, too. I'm— I'm happy, Posy."

And I grinned, glad to know that. I sent him a blast of love through the mate bond, and he sent one back.

"It's a little early for dinner, I guess," he said as he drove. "Should we kill some time first?"

"Well, we missed lunch, so I could eat. What about you?" I asked, then remembered who I was talking to and face-palmed.

My boys could *always* eat.

"Sure. I'm taking you to Roger's Diner, since you asked to go there the other day. Is that fine?"

Bouncing in my seat, I clapped my hands.

"Oh, yes! I'm so happy! They really did have the best chicken tenders I've ever tried, not that I've tried that many," I admitted.

"Then Roger's chicken tenders you shall have, my little flower."

Reaching across the seat, he took my hand in his and kissed my knuckles before he had to look back at the road.

"Do you have time for this?" I asked. "I know how busy you all are as alphas of such a huge pack."

"Even if I didn't, I'd *make* time. Luckily, though, I'm all yours from now until tomorrow at one."

"What happens at one?"

"I hand you off to your next date and the surprises that come with it." He grinned when my jaw dropped. "Surely you realized my brothers each planned a date with you, too."

I shook my head, feeling dumb that I hadn't.

"Would you like to see a movie after dinner?" he asked. "Wait. Have you ever gone to the movies before?"

"No. There wasn't a theater in Green River, and Alpha Briggs didn't let Mom take us off pack territory."

"Okay, now we're *definitely* going," he declared. "I can check what's playing, but I think the independent theater is showing the latest in that dinosaur series we watched. Are you interested in seeing it?"

"Yes! They're good, even though I have to close my eyes a lot," I joked, which made him laugh.

Coming to a stop, Mason shut off the engine and jumped out, and I was surprised to see that we were already at the diner. My mate opened my door, unbuckled me, and helped me down.

"I'll look up when the next showing starts once we sit down," he said as he led me into the diner.

The sign said, 'Please seat yourself,' so we found a booth in the back corner and grabbed menus from the holder at the end of the table.

"Are you getting anything else besides chicken tenders?" Mason asked me as he skimmed the menu.

"The onion rings were also tasty, but I couldn't eat all of them. Do you want to help me if I can't finish them?"

"I know I'm not Ash or Wyatt to fight over your leftovers, but I think I could manage to choke down a few extra onion rings." He rolled his eyes and I giggled.

"What are you getting? Do you have a favorite order, or do you like to try something new each time?"

"I usually get a double cheeseburger with bacon and French fries," he told me, and I treasured even that small fact about him.

My other mates didn't hesitate to share little details about themselves with me, but Mason was a much more private person. He probably didn't even realize how closed off he was, which is why I hoarded each and every detail he revealed.

A waiter came over and politely introduced himself, then took our orders. As we were waiting for our dinner, I asked Mason if I could talk to him about something important.

"Anything, Posy. Any time. We'll always listen to you. *I'll* always listen to you. Is something wrong?"

I bit my bottom lip as I considered how to bring this up, then decided to just say it.

"Not with me, but with Lark. I need to tell you now while she's asleep. She's, uh, been feeling a little, um, left out."

"Did our wolves stop talking to her?" His brows came down in a fierce frown. "Garnet says they haven't, but—"

"Oh, no, she talks to them *all* the time." I giggled. "Did you know they wake up in the night sometimes and play together? They were up before dawn playing tag the other morning! And sometimes ... *friskier* ... activities, which is why we sometimes wake up tired."

I blushed as I said that last part.

"I can't believe you sleep through it every time," he muttered, also blushing. "Then again, Ash usually does, too. The rest of us at least wake up enough to see what's going on before falling back to sleep. Anyway, what is making her feel left out? Her relationship with her wolves is solid."

"She sees how your wolves interact with me, and she would like to have that with you guys, too. I told her that she needs to reach out, but she's nervous about it. As you said, she's solid with her wolves, but is convinced their human halves aren't interested in her."

"Oh." He blinked a few times. "Why wouldn't we be?"

"She doesn't really know how to interact with humans other than me. She figured out her relationship with your wolves mostly on instinct, but humans are more complicated. And she's scared."

6

"We told her when we first met her we were enjoying getting to know her, and we talked to her a couple of other times since, but she always withdraws afterward." Mason tilted his head as he frowned in thought. "We figured she was overwhelmed, so we gave her space to feel safe. Maybe we shouldn't have."

He sighed heavily, then scratched the top of his head.

"We're acting on instinct here, too, Posy. Knowing she was badly abused, we don't want to scare or pressure her. What do you suggest?"

"Um, maybe sometime, you could ask her to shift? Tell her you miss her and want to pet her? She's never been cuddled, but I think she'd like it. It always makes her squeal when you guys cuddle me or I cuddle your wolves."

"I would *absolutely* love to cuddle her. Like Ash said, she's as small as a stuffed animal and cuter than one. I'm sorry we didn't realize she was feeling left out. She didn't say anything to our wolves, or they would have told us. Gran especially can't keep anything secret."

"She's hidden it from them." I swallowed hard as I thought of everything my wolfie had endured. "Lark has always tried to protect me, almost to an overwhelming degree. I think it's because my stepfather hurt me so badly the first time I shifted. What a welcome for her, huh? She spent her first four months healing me, so I guess it's no wonder she became overprotective."

Mason turned into a statue. I could *feel* the fury radiating off of him and hear Garnet's wild roars. With a soft sigh, I grabbed his hand and rubbed his knuckles against my cheek, knowing the touch and mate sparks would help him, and eventually he calmed down.

"Goddess, if there was ever anyone I regretted not torturing before I killed him, it's Kendall Briggs," he growled hoarsely, then vowed, "I will cuddle Lark every day if she wants me to."

I giggled a little, imagining the two of them having a time set aside for snuggles, like a child with a bedtime story at exactly eight o'clock.

"You don't have to go that far. She will be so excited if you give her even a few minutes of attention once in a while."

"My darling girl, that little wolf is about to be lavished with attention, now that we know she wants it." He drew our joined hands across the table and kissed the back of my hand. "She's *never* been cuddled?"

"No. You can be the first!" I smiled brightly, displaying my dimples.

"I'm honored." As he smiled, his eyes crinkled at the corners.

"I love your smile. It makes you even more handsome," I told him in case he didn't know.

Pink bloomed along his high cheekbones as he dipped his head and tucked his chin against his shoulder, and my heart fluttered at his unexpected bashfulness.

He's so adorable, I can't stand it! I squealed inside.

#

The movie was a fun experience. Mason bought popcorn, candy, and sodas, even though I was still stuffed from dinner, then we watched dinosaurs try to take over the world. There were several times I ended up hiding my face in his chest or neck, but he didn't mind. Far from it. He used each one of my scares to kiss me senseless.

Needless to say, by the time the movie was over, we were both ready to find somewhere more private. Our innocent snuggling had turned into something a lot more heated. Bundling me out of the theater and into his truck, he took me to a fancy-looking building, which he said was a hotel.

"I've never stayed in a hotel before!" I wiggled with excitement.

"That's why I rented a room, little flower," he said with a chuckle.

Carrying our overnight bags, he went to the front desk and checked us in, and then led me over to the bank of elevators. I've never ridden on one of those before, either, and I wasn't sure how I felt about it. Mason seemed to know that, and he put both of our bags over one shoulder so he could hold my hand.

He went to an elevator separated from the others and swiped the plastic card the clerk had given him. The door slid open and I cautiously stepped inside, clinging to Mason's hand. He pushed the only button on the wall next to the door, and it lit up soft yellow. The doors closed and the elevator began to move, but it was so smooth, it felt like riding in his new truck. Before I knew it, the door was opening with a dull ping, and Mason was leading me into a small room that had only one other door.

"Why aren't there more doors?" I asked. "I thought there would be lots of rooms in a hotel. Not that I've ever been in one. That's just from what I've read in books."

"It's a penthouse suite. We're on the top floor, and this huge space is ours for the night."

He used that plastic card to unlock the door, then pushed it open and motioned me ahead of him. I walked in and saw what he meant. There was a big open area like our living room with high ceilings, two fireplaces, and giant windows. It was still light out enough for me to see a balcony full of furniture beyond the windows.

"Wow!" I gasped. "This place is amazing!"

"You haven't even gotten inside yet," Mason chuckled. "Go look around, little flower. The master bedroom is at the end of the hall. At least, that's what the desk clerk said when I asked." He scratched the back of his neck. "I've never been in a penthouse suite, either."

"Great! A first we're experiencing together, so it's not just me all the time." I grinned, then asked, "Do you think anyone can see us through these big windows? There aren't any curtains."

"Oh, baby, you don't need to worry. You can run around naked and no one will see but me," he teased me with half-lidded eyes that sparked the heat we'd been building between us since the lights turned off at the movie.

Squeaking, I ran down the hall, hoping he'd play and chase me. Hearing his heavy footsteps coming fast behind me, I sprinted for the master bedroom in a fit of giggles. I flung open the door and found a huge, beautiful bedroom done up in light gray. There was a big bed, but not nearly as big as ours, and a comfy-looking couch that was shaped weird, a desk with a plush chair, and side tables with fancy lamps.

I kept running and went through the door on the side of the room and discovered the bathroom. One glance and I skidded to a halt in amazement. Mason said a no-no word as he wrapped his arms around me and carried me with him a few steps until he could come to a stop.

"Sorry," I said as I gripped his shirt, "but look at that tub! It has little feet! And there's a separate room for the toilet and another one for the shower! That's crazy!"

He laughed as he swung me around in a circle, then carried me back into the bedroom, where he threw me on the bed.

Instead of bouncing as I expected, I sank into the squishy mattress and my eyes widened.

"Help!" I called and held up my arms. "The bed is eating me!"

With a sharp bark of laughter, he followed me down and laid on top of me, his big body smushing me even further into the death-trap mattress.

"Mason, you're too heavy!" I squealed. "We'll sink through to the floor!"

This time, he laughed so hard, he snorted.

"Oh, baby, I love you," he chuckled.

"I love you, too."

He kissed me gently, then raised his head and stared down at me.

"Wait here for a second. I have something for you."

"You don't need to give me a gift." I frowned and held his face in my palms. "You already gave me flowers and took me out to dinner and—"

"And you deserved all of that and so much more. If it makes you feel better, though, I didn't spend a dime on it."

"Oh." Now I was curious. "What is it?"

"I'll be right back."

And he was. In less than a minute, he returned with both of our bags and set them on the little desk. Then he reached into the side pocket of his, took out a white envelope, and brought it over to me.

As he held it out, I watched him rub the back of his neck nervously and wondered why. Taking it with a confused frown, I opened the envelope and pulled out a handmade card.

"Oh!" Tears stung my eyes. "Did you— Did you make this?"

"With Peri's help. We each made you one. Sorry mine's not very creative, and my handwriting is garbage, even though I tried to write as neatly as I could. Anyway, she said my words were what mattered."

At the insecure look in his eyes, my chest tightened painfully. *Oh, my heart.*

Looking back at the card, I opened it and read his words, and my eyes lost the fight to hold the tears back. They skimmed down my cheeks and dripped off my jaw.

He grabbed the box of tissues from the side table, laid down next to me, and blotted my face dry, then handed me one to blow my nose.

"Mason, I love you so much. You never have to do anything to earn forgiveness other than be sorry and regret what you did," I sniffed as I stated into his glistening gray eyes. "Are you— Are you *really* proud of me? You didn't write that just because I told you I was proud of myself, did you?"

"My sweet girl. I *am* proud of you. We all are. We are proud to be your mates, and we're so blessed that you are ours." He pecked my forehead, my cheeks, my nose, my chin, and finally my lips. "Now my brothers want to say good night to you."

"Is it bedtime already?"

"It's just after nine, but Ash is fading fast and Cole's not too far behind. It was a stressful day for all of us."

So I linked each of my mates, blew them a kiss, and told them good night. It wasn't as satisfying as when we were all in bed together, but we made do.

After I closed the link, I stared up at Mason for a moment, then fought my way out of the body-sucking bed to grab him by the ears and pull him in for a long, lingering kiss.

10

"Hmm. Wyatt promised me a tangle of sweaty limbs tonight."
I pooched out my bottom lip. "Are you going to keep his promise?"

A sexy smirk appeared on his face and I was once more smooshed under his big, hard body.

"Of course I am," he murmured. "Any special requests?"

"Just you inside me," I said, then covered my red face with my hands.

"I can guarantee that happening." He pulled my hands away, wanting to kiss me, but I held him back.

"Wait! My card! Put it somewhere safe first," I told him. "I don't want anything to happen to it."

He did as I asked, picking it up and laying it on the side table closest to him, then settled next to me.

"Now," he growled playfully, "where were we?"

Next thing I knew, our clothes were in a pile on the floor and his face was buried between my thighs. His busy mouth had me twisting and moaning in seconds, and his harsh grunts and deep-throated hums excited me even more.

"Mason!" I cried out as I came, my fingers digging into the soft blanket beneath me.

He slid up my panting body and spread my knees wide, then braced one hand beside my head and used the other to guide himself to my dripping entrance, carefully pushing into me until he was as deep as he could go.

"What do you feel, baby?" he murmured as he hovered over me.

"You!" I gasped. "I feel you! So big and hard inside me!"

"And you're so gorgeous with me inside you," he murmured as he began to slowly thrust in and out. "Am I getting it right for you, Posy?"

"You're making me lose my mind!" I latched onto his tattooed forearms and rocked my hips in time with his. "Am *I* getting it right for *you*?"

"So good, so good, so good," he chanted. "You always feel so damn good."

Then he dropped to his elbows and buried his face in my neck, his mouth hot and greedy as it sucked my mate mark.

"Mason?" I whined.

Closing my eyes and tipping my head back, I wrapped my quivering legs around his waist and locked my ankles behind his back.

How had he brought me to the edge of an orgasm so quickly?

"Already, little flower?" he snickered.

A low moan was my only answer.

11

His hand snaked between us to massage my nub, and I fell apart at the seams with his name on my lips.

Then he picked up the pace and rode me hard and fast, and I came twice more before his big body went taut and still.

As I floated in glittery clouds for the third time, he growled and playfully gave me a couple more jerky pokes. That tickled and made me giggle, and without thinking about it, I clamped my inner walls down on his softening penis a few times, and gasped when I felt it swell and harden again.

He snarled and pulled out of me, making me worry that I did something wrong, but when he rolled me over onto my stomach, I realized what he wanted, and anticipation raised goosebumps all over my skin. He lifted my hips with urgent hands, gripped my bum cheeks and spread me open with his thumbs, then sank his diamond-hard length into me and hammered away as if he hadn't climaxed seconds ago.

He hit the right spot with every thrust, and I came continually as he pumped into me like a machine. My boy could last for a long time, to my very great pleasure, and my arms and legs were trembling like crazy before he finally lowered his chest to my back and cupped my shaking breasts in his palms.

"I'm going to come, baby," he rasped in my ear. "Do you need more or can you come, too?"

"I ... haven't ... *stopped* ... coming!" I panted, then moaned as another burst of pleasure hit me.

He roared with laughter as he finished, and his heavy body dropped and drove me deep into the mattress before he rolled onto his side. Gathering my limp, shuddering body into his arms, he placed dozens of kisses all over my face and neck, and I couldn't stop the tears as they streaked down my cheeks.

"I know, baby," he said, his chest heaving as he sucked down air. "I know. It's intense, isn't it?"

I nodded, but didn't have the wind or energy to open my mouth.

"Goddess!" he said in a husky chuckle. "I've never had back to back orgasms. Then again, my hand doesn't begin to compare with your tight, wet warmth. That was amazing, Posy. *You* are amazing!"

My face burned as I shoved it in his neck, but I was too wiped out to do more than kiss his mate mark. Shivering under my lips, he pulled me more fully on top of him, and I lay there lifelessly as I began to drift off.

"My exhausted flower." He kissed my temple and squeezed me tight in his ink-covered arms. "You've had a very long, stressful day, and we're getting up early in the morning, so get some sleep, my little baby."

I opened my mouth and a yawn came out, but I managed to push out a "K" on a puff of air.

"Good night, Posy. I love you."

"Goo nigh. Wuv oo, May."

And I fell asleep as his chest rumbled with chuckles under my ear.

#

Lark

Garnet's deep voice called my name, luring me out of sleep, and I slowly blinked and stretched.

Garnet? I murmured. *What is it, my love?*

My boy wants to see you, sweetheart.

Surprise woke me up quickly.

He does?

Yes. Will you please shift and come out to visit with him?

But Posy—

She knows, sweetheart, and approves. They talked about it yesterday. But only if you're okay with it, Garnet hurried to assure me. *If you're not, he will understand.*

Oh. No. It fine. If he sure?

He is. Garnet winked and gave me a smile. *And I'm always here if you need me, sweetheart.*

I know, my love. Thank you. I smiled back.

Hesitating, I looked around first. Now dressed in a clean t-shirt and boxers, his damp hair evidence he'd already showered, Mason lay next to Posy on the bed, propped on one elbow as he stared down at her sleeping face.

"Lark?" he said softly. "I'm sorry if Garnet woke you. I would have waited, precious."

You really *want to see me?* I asked just as softly.

"Yes. I miss you. It's been a while since we talked and even longer since I've seen you. Are you nervous with me?"

Oh. No. It just, you busy with Posy. I lowered my eyes and heard Garnet begging to know why I was sad.

"Lark, please shift." Mason sat up and moved to rest his back against the headboard. "I'm not too busy for you. Not ever."

Drawing up my courage, I put the moon magic to work and soon stood on the bed on my own paws.

"I keep forgetting how small and cute you are." Mason grinned and held out a fist for me to smell. "I'd really love to hold you,

13

precious, but only if you want that. Don't be afraid to say no if you don't. I won't be mad or upset."

Cautiously, I moved closer and put a paw on his knee. He patted his lap, encouraging me, and I hopped up onto his legs, careful of my claws so I didn't accidentally scratch him. Then I laid the top of my head on his chest and rolled it around, inviting him to pet me, and he obliged.

For nearly an hour, he rubbed my ears and petted my fur, careful to be gentle with his strong hands that were so large, he could cup my whole head in them - or I was just that small. All the while, we chatted about any number of things, just like Posy did with Quartz, and happiness hummed in my heart to experience this.

Oh, sweetheart, Garnet murmured. *I'm so glad you're happy, but why didn't you tell us you wanted this? We could have told our boys and made it happen long before now.*

Your humans so big and powerful, I told him. *Even bigger and more powerful than Alpha Briggs, and he—*

What, Lark? He what?

He hurt me, I whispered. *He hurt me so bad, Garnet. I too small and weak to do anything!*

Oh, sweetheart, he breathed. *No one will harm you ever again, not in any way, and if someone tries, we will kill them. Don't be afraid anymore.*

I love you, Garnet. Sniffling a little, I wiped my wet eyes on Mason's shirt.

I love you, too, sweetheart, more than my own life. Our boys love you, too, in the same way we love Posy, and they want to get to know you. Trust them. I swear by the moon that you won't regret it.

"Lark?" Mason scratched under my chin. "Are you okay?"

Nodding, I reared up to put my front paws on his shoulders. "Yes, precious?"

His gray eyes were as soft as rabbit fur as he looked at me, and I licked his cheek. He chuckled and ran his fingers down my back and stopped to scratch what Sid called the Good Spot at the base of my spine. Joy fizzed through my whole body, and I licked all over his face, my tail wagging frantically.

"Okay, okay," he laughed. "Don't wear out your tiny tongue! We'll do this again soon, I promise. For now, should we wake Posy? It's almost dawn, and she needs to get ready for the rest of our date."

There more to the date? What we doing? I jumped off his lap and hopped around on the bed in my excitement.

"We're going to a flea market, precious."

A market for ... fleas? I shuddered in horror and slowly shook my head. *I no want to go there.*

14

And I couldn't understand why he laughed so hard.

#

Posy

After Mason explained what a flea market was to Lark and me, we were both excited to go, but once we were there, the size of it overwhelmed me.

Thankfully, we had the place mostly to ourselves, and I understood why Mason rolled me out of bed and into the shower as early as he had. As the main building began to fill up with other shoppers, my nerves flared and I clung to his large hand with both of mine.

I knew I wasn't in danger, and even if I was, Mason would kill anyone who tried something. Still, old fears died hard.

"Let's go outside," he leaned down to murmur in my ear. "I think I know a few stalls you'll like out there."

I nodded and let him lead me to the door - and I quickly discovered he was right. I could breathe again away from the crowd.

Before we went too far, he opened the cloth shopping bag he'd brought along with us, took out my sunhat, and plopped it on my head. I rolled my eyes at him as I straightened it, and he grinned down at me.

"Where's *your* hat?" I demanded with my fists on my hips.

"I can't stand a hat," he said as he reached into the front pocket of the cloth bag. Pulling out a pair of black sunglasses, he perched them on his nose and looked down at me with a raised eyebrow. "How do I look?"

"Hmm. George-us," I teased him.

"Don't steal Reau's lines. Goddess, the two of you loose in a school together is going to give me gray hairs." He held my hand again as I giggled. "Come on, little flower. First stop: Kawaii Town."

"Kawaii Town?"

"Just the name of one of the stalls," he said with a shrug. "Kawaii means cute in Japanese."

Then he took me to a booth set up with tables and shelves full of items I found *very* cute. I went right to a rack of pretty sunglasses and picked out a pair of lavender heart-shaped ones with silver glitter in the frame. I put them on, and Mason stared down at my upturned face.

"Adorable," he murmured and kissed the tip of my nose. "You're getting this pair. Leave them on."

"Thank you!" Grinning broadly, I threw my arms around his waist and squeezed him.

He chortled as he patted the top of my head, then encouraged me to keep looking.

15

So I did and soon found a charming strawberry-shaped water bottle I could take to school with me and a pair of teddy bear soap and lotion dispensers I wanted for my bathroom. Mason bought everything and stowed my prizes in the cloth bag.

"Now I want you to find some things for your special room," he said after refusing to let me carry the bag. "This next vendor has some unusual items that might appeal to you."

As we walked hand in hand, I saw things I didn't recognize or understand their purpose, and I bit my lip, hesitant to look stupid by asking him, especially after he had to explain what the word vendor meant, so I kept quiet and contented myself to look around.

A display of cute headbands caught my eye and I pulled Mason over to it. There were unicorn horns and cat eats in all colors and fabrics, even lace and flowers, and other animal ears including—

"Bunny!" I yelped.

Grabbing a pair of grayish-brown ones that almost matched Mr. Nibbles' fur, I held them up for Mason to see. With a smirk, he took them from my hands, swept my hat off, and put them on my head.

"Sir, you can't try them on unless you're buying them," the vendor said nervously as he took in Mason's heavy tattoos, muscular body, and intimidating height. "I'm sorry. It's for health and safety."

"We're buying this pair," Mason said with the blank voice and face he used in public, and the bald little man twitched a bit.

Even though I knew the man behind the mask, Mason's cold front still made *me* shiver, so I felt bad for the guy. But my mate paid the man his full asking price and even added a dollar tip, and I figured it was all okay. Then the vendor gave me a smile that made me uncomfortable, although I didn't know why, and I wasn't sure he deserved a tip.

As we walked away, a flash of anger shot through our bond, and Garnet also stirred with a little growl.

"I don't like the way he looked at you," Mason scowled and grabbed my hand, towing me along with him. "Like you were prey or a meal on a menu. Males like that make me want to—

"What's unhealthy or unsafe about trying on headbands?" I asked to distract him.

He huffed and didn't answer, and I had to trot to keep up with his long legs. Only after I almost tripped trying to keep up with him did he realize what was happening. With a sigh, he stopped walking and gently squeezed my hand before releasing it and draping his dragon-inked arm across my shoulders.

"Sorry, Posy," he muttered and held up my hat in his other hand. "Do you want your hat back or keep your ears on?"

"Even though that guy was creepy, I like these ears," I said, "and I want to keep them on."

He nodded and slipped my hat back in our shopping bag, then finally answered my question.

"Lice, I'd guess. Do you know what that is?"

"Yep. I remember learning about it in elementary school. Don't share hats!" I chirped. Wanting to chase away this small gray cloud, I smiled up at him. "Hey, Mason, I have an idea for my special room, but I want you to guess what it is based on things I buy today. Are you up for the challenge?"

"Baby, I'm always *up* for anything with you. I thought I proved that last night, but if you need a reminder, we can go back to the hotel room and I'll prove it again."

When I realized what he meant, my cheeks lit on fire and I dug my fingers into his sides, tickling him, and he almost dropped the shopping bag.

"No! My treasures!" I wailed and stopped tickling him to grab it, but he was faster than me and moved the bag back into the crook of his elbow.

"A water bottle and two bear containers are treasures?" He slid his sunglasses down enough to stare at me over the tops of them.

"Yes, they are!" I folded my arms and glared at him.

His eyes fogged over for a second, then he got out his phone and pointed it at me.

"What are you doing?"

"Taking a picture of my little baby's cute pout. Oh, and the boys love your ears, by the way. Cole and Jay are determined to buy you a sexy outfit to match, and Ash and Wyatt want you to wear them the next time they make a Posy sandwich—"

Squeaking and red-faced, I punched him in the stomach, careful to keep my thumb on the outside like Landry had told me. It still hurt my hand, and Mason didn't even flinch. In fact, a smirk slowly curled up one side of his mouth.

"Mason Andre Price! That's private talk for the bedroom!"

"Mmm. *Aggressive* little baby," he purred and stroked his index finger down my cheek. "Forget the flea market. Let's go back to the hotel and you can show me how aggressive bunnies can be—"

"No, Mason! We're shopping!" I stomped my foot with a frown.

"Okay, little flower," he laughed. "Let's shop."

In the end, I found a pretty blue wreath made of pine cones cut into flowers, a night light made with a preserved maple leaf, and two vanilla-scented candles in vintage glass jars. We'd just returned to the

17

market after carrying a lovely rose area rug out to the truck when Mason finally caught on.

"And what are you going to do for campfire?" he asked with a little smile, looking proud of himself for figuring it out.

I wanted each of my mates to be represented in my special room, so I had been on the lookout for things that reminded me of their special mate scents. I almost gave up on maple syrup, then I saw the night light, and the fact that it was beautiful only convinced me to buy it.

"Well, I was thinking of those fake fire lights we saw at that one booth with all the Halloween decorations, but I don't want anything scary, even though you can be *very* scary."

"Scary? *Me?*"

His face was blank and I couldn't see his stormy gray eyes behind his sunglasses, but I still knew he was amused.

"Yes, you. I may have to look somewhere else." My bottom lip pooched out. "Grr! I wanted to find them all here with you today."

"Hmm. I might have an idea."

He guided me to a booth with dozens and dozens of paper and silk balls hanging from strings and wires. I didn't know what they were, but they were really pretty. They ranged from deep jewel tones to light pastels and everything in between, some with patterns and others solid colors. There were several different shapes and sizes, too, and I studied them with curiosity.

"They're called lanterns. The smaller ones fit over bulbs on a strand of lights," Mason said. "You could get a string with flicker flame bulbs and pick out lanterns to go over them. Then it would look like the lanterns have a lit candle inside."

"Oh, that's perfect!" I clapped my hands and smiled brightly. "I can hang them up over the balcony doors!"

I looked around for several minutes, but my eyes kept coming back to the same paper lanterns. Round and about the size of baseballs, they had beautiful pink blossoms on pale blue and light green backgrounds.

"Okay, we're getting those." Mason kissed the top of my head. "You've come back to them five times now."

After I agreed, he haggled with the vendor for twenty of the lanterns and two strands of flicker flame lights to go with them. I tugged the hem of his shirt and told him ten would do, but he insisted I needed twenty. Since he was paying, I shrugged and accepted his generosity with a quiet thank-you.

"No need to thank me," he said as he packed everything in our shopping bag. "It's my pleasure to set your world on fire."

"How long have you been waiting to use that line?" I quirked up an eyebrow and held back a grin.

"Since you told me what I smelled like to you." His fingers linked with mine and he reeled me in for a kiss on the lips. "And now, my little flower, let's go. We have just about an hour for lunch, then I need to hand you off to your next date."

"Oh! Who is it? Tell me! Please, Mason?"

"No."

"Can I try to guess?" I asked.

"Sure, but I'm not going to tell you if you're right."

"But Mason!" I pouted.

"All right, I'll give you a clue. Leave those bunny ears on and he'll have you pinned up against the wall in the restaurant's bathroom before you finish saying hello—"

"Wyatt!" I screeched, making several people look at me, but I ignored them as I hopped up and down.

"Aw!" Mason rolled his eyes. "I gave you too big of a clue!"

Mason's Letter:

Dear Posy,

I am truly sorry, my little flower. You were right, and we deserved every word you said. I let my fear and worry control me and made a terrible choice, and that choice cost you something you can never get back — your first feeling of accomplishment as Five Fangs' luna. I can't make that up to you, and I will forever regret it, but I hope I can earn your forgiveness someday.

I want you to know that I am proud of you. So, so proud of you! Not only for how you bravely helped Landry, but also for how you stood up to us and made us see how wrong we were.

All my love,
Mason

2: *Making Art*

Wyatt

"Did you enjoy the tea shop, cutie?" I asked, already knowing the answer from the sparkle in our girl's eyes.

"Oh, yes, so much! We had the most wonderful little sandwiches cut into tiny squares. I didn't know what some of them were. What is watercress, anyway? The cucumber ones had some kind of soft herb cheese that was delicious. And then we had— Mason, what were they called? Something that sounds like macaroni, but not that."

"Macarons, baby," Mason supplied, smiling at her rambling as we three stood on the sidewalk outside the little restaurant.

He smiles so much now, Granite noted with a wagging tail.

I know. We all do. She's our happiness.

"The ones that are piles of coconut," I asked Posy, "or the ones that are like crunchy little cookie cakes?"

"The second kind. They were pink and purple and mint green!" she squealed and bounced on her toes. "So pretty! I almost didn't want to eat them!"

This girl, I linked Mase with a big grin. *Could she be any cuter?*

I know, he linked back. *Goddess, I love her.*

Me, too, brother.

"So what are *we* doing, fifth star?" She stopped hopping around and hugged my arm.

"Thought we'd go for a walk at the park and swing by McDonald's for dinner," I teased, wanting to see her pout, but I should have known better.

"Oh, I love the park! I used to feed the duckies at the park in Green River. And I haven't been to McDonald's in years, but I think I remember liking chicken nuggies."

Aww! Gran sniffed. *Now I has a sad.*

Me, too.

Gently gathering her into my arms, I held her head against my chest with one hand and cupped her opposite hip with the other as I raised my eyes to the sky until I could speak again.

"I'm teasing, Posy. I have a great date planned, full of secret reveals." My voice was still husky, so I did what I did best and made a joke. "We're just waiting for Mr. Third Wheel here to leave."

"All right, all right. I'm going." Mase scrubbed his knuckles on top of my head, making me scowl at him, and he laughed.

He actually laughed.

Where is my big brother and what have you done to him? I demanded.

Rolling his eyes at me, he handed me her overnight bag, then leaned down, kissed our girl's cheek, and told her to have fun. She thanked him and said bye, then I led her to my Jag as he headed to his truck.

"What did you find at the flea market, cutie?" I asked after we were both buckled in and I started driving. "Besides those sexy ears?"

"Are they? I thought they were cute." She sounded unsure. "Should I not wear them in public? Are they for private bedroom time?"

"No, baby," I hurried to tell her. "They *are* cute, and you can wear them anywhere, anytime. I'm teasing you because you look adorable in them."

"Okay," she agreed in her calm, peaceful way. "What sort of secrets are you revealing?"

I wasn't ready to answer that yet, wasn't sure I had the courage to even go through with what I'd planned, so I gave her a lame answer.

"You'll have to wait and see, Ms. Curiosity." I took my eyes off the road long enough to wink at her. "Now, what did you buy?"

She spent the rest of the drive telling me about her fabulous finds. After I guessed the secret behind her purchases for her special room, she gave me a round of applause and I smiled.

"What is this place, Wyatt?" she asked as I pulled into the parking lot of the art museum. "It looks old and expensive."

"Come inside and see," I told her as I opened her door and held out my hand.

She took it and climbed out of the Jag, and we walked hand-in-hand to the front entrance. Her eyes found the golden letters that announced this was the city's art museum.

"Really?" Her eyes grew wide as she smiled up at me. "Is any of *your* art in here?"

"Hahaha! No, baby. Only famous artists have their work in museums." I laughed again at the idea.

I *did* have a few pieces in a nearby gallery, where we were going next, and Granite and I had a bet on whether or not she'd recognize the paintings as mine. He said she would and I said she wouldn't. I usually wouldn't bet against our girl, but she'd never seen any of my paintings, only my sketches, and I figured she'd be too distracted by everything to notice my signature.

"Well, they could be," she retorted, sounding upset that I wasn't represented in a museum. "You're so good! Have you tried to be a famous artist?"

"No, cutie." I rolled my eyes as I held open the door for her. "I have enough on my plate with being alpha. I don't think I could juggle being famous in the human world, too."

"Hmpf. Well, you *could*," she insisted with a little frown as she went inside. "What do you do with all your artwork? I know you must have more than those sketchbooks."

Following her, I raised my eyebrows, surprised she'd guessed that much.

Never bet against mate, Gran sang out with a smug smile.

Hush, wolf.

"I give some away as gifts," I admitted.

"Do you sell the rest? And where do you keep it? I haven't seen any around the house. And where do you create it? Do you paint? Do you sculpture?"

"It's *sculpt* as a verb. *Sculpture* is the noun. No, I don't sculpt, and the rest of your questions will be answered later."

I led her to the welcome desk, paid for our tickets, and escorted her into the first viewing gallery. I wasn't surprised that her romantic little soul liked impressionist art the best. She liked the only pointillist piece there, saying it reminded her of those photo-mosaic puzzles that her mother used to put together. Neither of us were into cubism, or any abstract art really, but she giggled her way through the surrealism gallery. The museum wasn't wealthy or famous enough to have a Salvador Dali or MC Escher or anything like that, but Posy liked a couple of paintings, including one that showed an egg cracked open to reveal the sun and another of a woman in a fancy gown being lifted into the air by harnessed butterflies.

"They're not what I'd want hanging in my house, but they're fun and interesting to look at," she said, and I agreed. "These aren't for sale, right?"

"Right. If you want to buy art, there are a couple of galleries in the city. Want to check one of them out?"

"Sure!" she chirped.

Bwahahaha! Gran rubbed his grubby paws together in anticipation. *I 'bout to win a bet, Wy!*

We'll see, wolf. We'll see.

#

On our drive to the gallery, I noticed Posy was suddenly restless in her seat and twisting her fingers around like she did whenever she was nervous.

"Hey." I reached over and laid my hand on her thigh. "What's wrong?"

"Nothing, but can I ask you something? You don't have to answer if you don't want to."

I frowned as I glanced over at her. Did she really think she had to ask?

"Sure, cutie. You can always talk to me about anything."

"Well, it's personal. I know you're not usually shy about sharing anything, but you still have a right to your privacy."

"Sure, baby, but I don't want to keep anything secret from you." *And after this date, I won't be,* I added in the privacy of my mind. "What's your question?"

"Ash told me how the Moon Goddess came to you five in a dream and said you'd all share a mate. How did you feel about that? The sharing part, I mean."

Oh. Is that all? I rolled his eyes.

"Ash and I were only thirteen," I told her. "We didn't fully understand it, other than we wouldn't have to live apart from each other."

"Were you living together by then?"

"No. Jay and Ash went to live with Mase after Uncle Jay and Aunt Denise died. Everyone thought that would be best because the Black and Barlow households were in chaos, and Mase was so sad and lonely after Willow died."

Stopping at a red light, I looked over at her and saw her bottom lip wobbling, and Granite growled at me for upsetting her.

Life is upsetting, Gran, I said with a sigh. *I don't like seeing her sad, either, but the truth is the truth. You can't change it, and hiding it from her wouldn't make her any happier.*

He disagreed with a grunt, but otherwise stayed silent.

"It didn't matter who our official guardians were, though," I went on, "because we were together all the time, anyway. The dream came the night Mom and Dad declared themselves as chosen mates. Then they, Mama, and Papa asked the Moon Goddess to bless the five packs combining into one."

Goosebumps popped up all over my skin as I remembered what happened next. It was an epic, once-in-a-lifetime experience. I sent Posy my memory through our mate link and heard her gasp.

"Truly amazing," she breathed. "Were you together when you had the dream?"

"Yes. Cole and I had a sleepover at Mase's house. We all woke up at the same time the next morning, which, as you know, is not usual for us. Ash cried. I mean, we all woke up in tears, but Ash was so relieved, he sobbed."

I snickered as I remembered how Mase had picked Ash up and held him while he cried. Even at thirteen, Ash was as big as Mase, who was already a giant himself at sixteen.

"Why was he relieved?"

"His second set of parents died in the sickness about eight months before that," I explained. "He was so worried we'd separate when we found our mates. To him, sharing one meant he could stay with his brothers forever."

"What about you?"

"I was happy for that reason, too," I had no trouble admitting, "and also because the Moon Goddess promised us a perfect mate, and she delivered. We got you, precious girl."

"Did the Goddess talk to your wolves?" she ignored my compliments to ask.

"Yeah. It was weird, like Granite was standing next to me. All our wolves were ecstatic, but Quartz was a little iffy about the sharing part." So she didn't get the wrong idea, I hurried to add, "But only because he thought five mates would be overwhelming."

"What about your brothers?" Posy asked. "You were happy and Ash was relieved, but how did Mason, Cole, and Jayden feel about the sharing part?"

"Since Mase and Cole were older, Papa and Dad had already given them The Talk, so they understood more than the rest of us. Mase was satisfied and content that the Goddess had arranged a major part of our future, although he shared Quartz's worry because the rest of us were a little wild. Don't be fooled by Jay's guitar-playing, book-reading nerd front," I scoffed. "He went as hard as the rest of us in the raising of hell. Fortunately for *you*, we've settled down a bit."

I smirked when she raised one eyebrow and gave me a disbelieving look.

But, "What about Cole?" was all she asked.

"He was a little anxious about how sharing would work. Would we get jealous or even come to resent each other? Mase said that, if it was the Goddess' plan, it would work out, then made us all swear by the moon such a thing wouldn't happen. That was all he needed to hear."

"And Jayden?"

I waited until I pulled into a parking spot and cut the engine before I turned to her.

"I won't lie to you, but I want you to promise to hear the whole answer before you react, okay?" I gave her a serious look.

"I promise," she said.

Still, I hesitated as trepidation glimmered in her eyes.

"Remember, we didn't know *you* were our mate. She was some faceless figure in our future, so don't take it personally," I delayed, then decided to just say it. "He was happy we'd all stay together, but disappointed about sharing. Can you guess why?"

Her eyes never left mine as she shook her head.

"You can't?" I raised one eyebrow. "Really?"

"Because of Quartz?"

"That was some of it. Jay should be the one telling you this, but I know him. He *never* will, so I'm telling you to help you understand him a little better," I admitted, then sighed. "He was afraid the rest of us would overshadow him and he'd end up being crowded out."

She reacted exactly as I thought she would. Her eyes widened and her mouth fell open in a little o, making me chuckle.

"Think about it, cutie. Mase and Cole are ultra-dominant, powerful alphas with charisma to match. In a room full of people, everyone looks at them first. Anyone but the king would feel lesser next to them."

"They can both be scary," she said, which I guessed was how she interpreted alpha charisma.

"Which one do you think is scarier?"

"Mason." She didn't even hesitate.

"How so?" Now my curiosity was piqued. "I always thought Cole was scary because of his hot temper. You know, that jerk tried to knock my teeth out while we were at Peri's making your cards? All because I made a simple comment."

"Did *you* knock *his* teeth out?" She tilted her head to the right and blinked up at me.

How does she always *know?* I wondered.

Mate smart. Mate understands us, Granite said with a proud smile. *Remember what I said, Wy. Never bet against mate.*

Hush, wolf.

"You *did*, didn't you? Fifth star, you shouldn't hurt your brothers."

"It was him or me, and I only knocked out one tooth!" I protested. "He needs to learn to control his temper!"

"And maybe *you* need to learn when he's done playing and wants you to lay off." She wagged her index finger in my face. "You have to admit, you push a lot."

Leaning down, I caught her finger between my lips and gently bit it before releasing it.

"Part of my sparkling personality, Posy." I grinned at her tomato-red face. "Needless to say, we all knew our mate wouldn't neglect or forget about *me*. I'm always going to make myself known, even if the attention I get is negative."

"You bad boy," she teased me with a giggle, which made *me* giggle.

"Do you think *I'm* scary? Or Ash or Jay?"

"I think you all can be very scary when you want to be, although I think Ash deliberately downplays that side of himself to appear harmless." She shivered. "Ha! I doubt *he* was worried about his mate neglecting him. He's too big to miss."

"So is his personality. Jay, though, always felt like he wasn't very interesting. Ash and I told him lots of times that Mase was *way* more boring. I mean, Mase was always working or studying, but Jay came up with the best ideas for what trouble we could get into next. Now, I ask you, which one is more boring?"

"Wyatt!" she gasped and whacked me on the bicep with the back of her little hand. "Not one of you is boring! And don't mock Mason. He had to take on a big responsibility—"

"Sorry, Posy. I was only teasing." I decided she didn't need to know we actually *had* said that to both Jay and Mase's faces. "I respect Mase immensely, but now I need to know. Why do you think he's scarier than Cole?"

"Because he's always so tightly controlled and hides everything he's thinking and feeling behind that blank face. It makes you think he's safe right up until he's not."

"You have a point," I agreed with a nod.

We walked into the gallery and I watched her face, entertained by the bright curiosity in her eyes.

"So all of these pieces are for sale?" she asked.

"Yep! Let me know if you see something you'd like."

"But how do I know how much they are?" She turned to me with a frown on her pretty, plump lips.

"Baby, cutie, Posy, my love, you do not worry about the price. If you see one you like, I will get it for you," I said while fighting the urge to show her the painting I'd done especially for her and Lark.

After ten minutes of looking around, she squeaked and dragged me over to a painting.

"Look! It's your wolves! Sid, Quartz, Topaz, and Garnet," she pointed at each one, "and there's Granite hiding behind Sid! That's crazy! How did some artist know their coat patterns so exactly?"

She bounced up and down on her toes and clasped her hands under her chin, and I had to bite back a grin.

Who going to win this bet? I teased Gran.

Just wait for it.

Hey, no cheating and giving her or Lark a clue, I warned him.

I not need to, he taunted.

"Can I have it? Please, please, please?" she begged.

"Oh, I'm so sorry, baby. Look. The sign says sold."

Now who cheating? Gran snorted.

27

I thought Posy was going to fall to the floor, her shoulders dropped so far, and I couldn't take it. I opened my mouth to confess when she squealed and threw her arms around my waist.

"Wyatt! *You* painted it! Those are *your* initials!" She squeezed me hard, probably as hard as she could, and I grinned. "You're teasing me about it being sold, aren't you?"

"Yes and no. It *is* sold - to you. It's a gift for you and Lark."

"Thank you, thank you, thank you! I love it! It's so beautiful and perfect!" Suddenly, she gasped, wiggled away from me, and started scanning the rest of the wall. "Oh! Does that mean you have other paintings for sale here, too?"

Laughing, I told her to look for herself, and she quickly found my other pieces and made a fuss over each one.

"Big secret reveal number one," I murmured, blushing a bit at her compliments. "My brothers don't know I sell my art."

"What? Why?"

I shrugged, which I knew wasn't an answer, but how could I tell her I was afraid they'd mock or tease me for it? I was the *worst* at teasing others - and the easiest to be hurt by it.

"If you can't take it, don't dish it. Otherwise toughen your heart up because it's going to take a lot of hits," Mom warned me a thousand times, but I didn't listen - and I paid for it.

"Really, Wyatt, one day, you'll have art in a museum," she said as we left, her painting packaged and held firmly under my arm. "You should be proud of yourself, not hiding it from the guys."

"What if they—" I hesitated to say the truth, then went with, "What if they think it's dumb?"

"How often do you make fun of Jayden for playing the guitar or reading?"

Damn! Granite giggled. *Mate not pull punches!*

"I know, but—"

"Wyatt, they are your *brothers*. You tease them and tease them hard, so it's only fair if they tease you back. However, I think they will be too impressed with your amazing skill to say anything but compliments."

Hmm. Maybe she doesn't know us as well as I thought she did, I mused.

Dumb Wy. Gran closed his eyes and shook his head slowly. *I'm telling you. Never. Bet. Against. Mate!*

"I'll think about telling them," I hedged.

"Well, *I'm* telling them I got this painting at the gallery, and when they realize it's one of yours, boom, there's your opening to explain and surprise them with your success." She patted my shoulder. "You're welcome, fifth star."

28

Snorting, I tucked her and the painting into my car, then climbed in on the other side.

"I was going to take you to a nice restaurant, but now I'm wondering if you've had enough culture and want to swing by McD's for your chicken nuggies?" I reached over and caressed her cheek with my hand. "I'm fine with either, so you pick."

"It won't ruin your date if I pick the nuggies? Because I haven't had them in a really long time."

"Posy, I would fly you to Paris for a single macaron if you wanted. Nuggies it is."

She giggled and we chatted a little more as I drove us to a nearby McDonald's. No way were we eating in my precious Jag and making her smell like fries, so we went into the restaurant, and Posy enjoyed her nuggies while I downed a couple of double quarter-pounders with bacon and cheese.

After dinner, we walked out to the Jag holding hands and killed some time admiring the sunset that turned the clouds pink and purple.

"It looks like a painting, doesn't it?" she said happily. "Perfect for our art date!"

"Speaking of, this evening's entertainment is a painting class."

"A painting class?" She stared up at me with a puzzled frown. "But you obviously know how to paint already."

"You don't, and won't it be fun to learn?" I had a moment of doubt. Maybe this was a bad idea.

"As long as you're with me, yes." She perked up and smiled. "And you can help me so mine doesn't turn out too bad, right?"

"How could anything you make turn out bad?" I tapped her on the nose. "I just hope the instructor picked an interesting subject and not something dull like a fish or an apple."

"It doesn't matter, does it? It's just to learn and have fun."

"You're right." Starting the car, I looked over at her with a grin. "So let's go learn and have fun. Even if I have to paint a freaking fish."

#

I had to paint a freaking fish.

As soon as the instructor showed us the design, I groaned and Posy buried her face in the back of my shoulder to muffle her giggles.

At least it was white and orange koi on a blue background, which I felt I could do something with. And, hallelujah, the instructor gave us a choice rather than forced us all to use the same supplies. I immediately set Posy up with acrylics and gathered watercolor supplies for me.

"I'll teach you watercolors later if you want, but acrylics are easier to start learning with," I explained as I made sure her smock covered her pretty dress.

"Okay. That's fine," she said vaguely and didn't look at me, all of her attention on the instructor, and I shook my head in amusement.

She's going to follow the directions step-by-step, I thought to myself with a little smile.

She did, too, and I allowed myself to focus on my painting after I saw she was lost in her own creative space. By mutual agreement, both of us kept our eyes on our own work until we were finished.

"I'm happy with it," Posy said and turned her painting for me to see. "You can tell it's a fish, which was my main goal."

"Good job!" I complimented her. "I like the thicker strokes to create texture and the way you added gray for depth. Did you enjoy the process of creating it?"

"I did! It makes you focus. I can see how it's good stress-relief, although it would break my heart every time I messed up and had to start over. Can I see yours now?"

"Sure, but first, sign your work. You can sign your whole name, your first name, use a symbol or a nickname. Whatever you want."

"I'll copy you and use my initials," she said as she carefully used a fine brush to paint PAE in the lower left corner. "Done! Now yours."

I was a little anxious that she'd compare hers to mine and be upset, but she surprised me again.

"Oh, my! That is gorgeous, Wyatt! I love it! Can I hang it up somewhere in the house? Or do you want to sell it?"

"Baby, how could I sell our first couple paintings? We're going to hang these side by side in my office so when I'm doing the ruddy paperwork, I can look up and restore my soul."

Her dimples broke out, and I wondered which part of that made her so happy.

We did the group photo thing, then the instructor pulled me aside. I quickly told her I was married and flashed my ring in her face, and she gave me a startled look before asking if I'd be interested in selling my work at a gallery. Relieved that's all she wanted, I told her I already did, and she laughed and said she should have known that because my talent was obvious.

Her words made me feel like a million bucks. It was one thing for my mate and family to praise my work, but a complete stranger, a professional artist at that, was different. She had no reason to lie or coddle my feelings, and she knew what was good and what wasn't.

After the paint was dry enough to transport, I carried a painting in each hand as we left the studio and nudged Posy in the opposite direction when she would have gone toward the Jag.

"We're not getting in the car?" she asked, trying to take her painting from my hand, but I held it away from her.

"Nope. I have one more place to show you."

"It's dark," she murmured and bit her bottom lip.

"I know, baby, but I'm here. Even carrying two paintings I can protect you, and I will. We're only going a block and the sidewalk is well lit. Trust me, Posy."

"I do. I just don't like the dark, or being outside when it's dark."

"We'll be inside soon, I promise."

And we were. We walked into the brightly lit lobby of an apartment building and I led her to the elevator. Once we got on, I asked her to press the ten button and she did.

"Wyatt, where are we going?"

"Big secret reveal number two," I said, staring into her eyes. "My art studio."

"What?!" she screeched, and her eyes grew huge. "Why is it secret? And why don't you have it at the house instead of wherever we are?"

"You know why it's secret," I mumbled as the elevator came to a stop and we got out. "The same reason I keep the gallery a secret. Only Mase knows I rent this place, but not what for."

I led her to apartment 1020, the last one on the left side of the hallway, and set the paintings against the wall so I could take my keys out of my pocket.

"Why does only Mason know?"

"He takes care of our personal finances, as well as the pack's," I explained as I unlocked the door. "He immediately saw the rent coming out and my deposits from the gallery going in and asked me about it. I told him I'd tell him when I was ready."

I snorted, remembering *that* conversation. Mase's accusations had hurt. I still couldn't believe he thought I was setting up some clandestine love nest for a side piece until we found our mate. I'd made a promise to myself that I'd wait, just like my brothers had, and I did. What kind of man did he think I was to suggest that?

Opening the door, I ushered her inside and flicked on the lights. After setting the paintings against the bare wall, I turned to Posy to see her reaction. Her big eyes darted all around, even though there wasn't much to see other than my easels and storage racks in front of the floor-to-ceiling windows in the living room.

31

"This is a great space for a studio," she said, "but I don't understand why you waste money renting it when there's plenty of room at our house. The whole basement—"

"Yeah, I know, but so far, my sales have more than paid for this apartment. If I moved my studio to our house, my brothers would find out about the gallery. They'd see my works in progress and they'd also see—"

I stopped talking and looked everywhere but at her.

"What?" she asked. "They'd also see *what?*"

"Me," I whispered and stared at my shoes.

Two little sandals came into my line of vision and met the tips of my Oliver Cabells.

"I understand you feel vulnerable. You're scared your brothers - who you love so much - will laugh at you. The *real* you. The heart and soul of you that you put into every piece you create."

She laid her small fingers under my chin and pushed it up until I met her eyes.

"Wyatt, your brothers *see* you. They see *you*. They know as well as I do how fragile your heart is, and they love you far too much to ever hurt you like that. Could you please give them a chance to prove it? If I'm wrong, I'll never push you out of your comfort zone again."

"And if you're right?" I asked in a rough voice.

"Then you go all in." Her blue eyes were dead serious and she wasn't smiling. "You go the whole hog. You give up this place, set up a studio at our house, and proudly let everyone know your work is for sale at the gallery."

I gulped. I didn't know if I could make good on either end of that bargain. Was I courageous enough?

Her hands moved to stroke my cheekbones with her thumbs.

"And I will always stand at your side, regardless of what you decide."

"Posy," I whispered and dropped my forehead to hers. "I love you so very much."

"I love you, too, my fifth star." She sniffed, then pulled back a bit. "Okay, enough deep talk and drama or I'll start crying. Will you show me around your secret studio?"

Taking a deep breath, I nodded and gave her a tour. I'd hired a human cleaning crew to fix the place up yesterday. I really only used the living room area and the bathroom, but Posy didn't need to see the fine layer of dust on everything.

I'd snuck over here this morning to drop off my overnight bag and her change of clothes as well as set up a pillow fort for later tonight. When I took her into the bedroom, I flicked on the fairy lights, and my cutie gasped, then flung herself on me.

"Oh, Wyatt! I love it!"

"It's just a mattress and some blankets and pillows." I rolled my eyes.

"It's an adorable little nest for us," she disagreed.

Slipping off her sandals, she fell to her knees and began to crawl forward, and I was instantly as hard as a rock watching that sweet ass sway from side to side. Giggling, she fell on her back amid the pillows and stretched her arms over her head, causing the hem of her dress to rise and expose her silky smooth thighs.

Cursing under my breath, I reached down and adjusted myself.

She wiggled around a bit to get comfortable, which made her dress rise enough that I could see the crotch of her blue panties, and I knew right away they were something Ash had bought and she'd be wearing a matching bra because that's what he taught her to do. It would fit her perfectly and, as soon as I undid the clasp, her full breasts would spill into my hands and fill them up—

Don't come, don't come, don't come, I chanted to myself as I tried to imagine something much less arousing.

"Are you going to join me?" she asked.

Without my brothers here, I planned to test the waters a bit.

I had zero interest in degrading her, and I would cut out the tongue of anyone who called her a whore or a slut. While I might try tying her hands up sometime, that was as far as my interest in bondage went, and I had *no* interest in anything sadistic. I just wanted to dominate her.

Here goes, I thought with equal parts excitement and nervousness.

"Let's play a game." I smirked and took a step back, then crooked my finger at her. "Come here. Crawl to me like a good girl, but don't say a word."

Pink flared on her cheeks and her blue eyes glittered with excitement. She rose to her knees and did as I asked, her hips sashaying and her eyes locked on mine.

"That's it. Keep your eyes on me," I crooned. When she reached the edge of the mattress, I spoke in a little sterner tone. "Now untie my shoes."

She looked up at me with uncertainty.

Am I allowed to look at them to do that? she linked me.

Yes, baby. And if something hurts or you get uncomfortable at any time, just tell me to stop. I get no pleasure from hurting you or making you uncomfortable.

Okay, my fifth star, she agreed eagerly and untied my shoes. *Should I answer you if you ask me a question?*

33

No, baby. That's part of the game. You can link me anything at any time, though.

I understand.

"Now stand on your knees," I commanded her while I kicked off my sneakers, "unbutton my shorts, and slide them down. Just my shorts. Not my boxer briefs."

She obeyed instantly and it was so hard not to tell her to take me into her mouth as she knelt in front of me, but I knew she wasn't there yet. Ash had shared their conversation with us, and we knew we had to let her decide when - or if - she was ever ready to suck us off.

"Good girl," I praised her once my shorts were at my ankles.

I kicked them off, then stripped out of my shirt and threw it on the floor.

"Now stand up," I told her, and the top of her head was under my chin before I could blink.

Are you still okay following my orders? I checked in with her.

Yes. It's kind of fun not knowing what you're going to make me do next, but it will *end up with us, um, you know, right?*

She's had us or our wolves in every orifice and she still can't say sex? I asked Gran and shook my head with a little smirk. *Hell, she can't even say mate half the time!*

I know, Granite crowed. *I love our pure, perfect mate!*

Yes, cutie, I linked Posy. *Now back to work.*

Yes, sir!

I groaned, my eyes rolling back, and my dick nearly exploded out of my boxers to get to her sweet pussy.

Or her hands, I admitted to myself. *Or her mouth. Or between her titties. I'm not fussy.*

That reminded me of something, though, and I linked my brothers an idea while it was fresh in my mind.

Goddess, Wy! Cole snarled. *You know I'm going last and you sent me* **that**? *Thanks for the boner, jackass!*

I can make it worse and send you the live feed of what we're doing now, I offered.

He cursed me out and slammed the link closed while Ash and Jay giggled.

And you smell like vanilla to her? Mase chuckled. *Boy, I've never met anyone less vanilla than you.*

Thank you, I murmured. *Now excuse me while I enjoy our girl's strip tease before I mate her brains out.*

Shut the hell up, Wyatt! all three of them growled in unison, then closed the link with a bang as I chuckled to myself.

"Turn around," I told Posy.

Once her back was facing me, I gathered all her hair in one hand, being gentle because Ash told us her scalp was really sensitive, and draped it over her shoulder. Then I eased her zipper down, letting the sides of her dress fall open and reveal more and more of her skin and the band of blue lace with its tricky little clasp.

"Stand still."

I took her shoulders in my hands and made sure she was turned how I wanted, then took her place on the mound of pillows. She waited patiently as I got comfortable and slipped my hands behind my head.

"Very slowly, fold your shoulders in so your dress slides down your arms."

She was smart, our girl. She figured out quickly that I wanted her to strip for me, and her eyes beamed with confidence now that she knew where I was going with this.

Good to know. She's fine with a little adventure, but wants to be solid on the details.

"Now take your arms out of your sleeves and let your dress fall on the floor."

As I ogled her body, I gave myself a pat on the back for being right about the bra.

"Reach behind your back and undo your bra, but don't take it off."

Her arms went behind her back for a second and the fabric covering her glorious tits loosened. My balls, on the other hand, tightened and I knew I was going to come, which amazed me as neither her hand nor mine was jerking me off.

Not that it matters, I thought with a shrug. *I'll be hard again in a minute and can come inside her all night long.*

"Take it off and toss it across the room," I instructed in a hoarse tone, seconds from blasting off.

As soon as her nipples were visible, I gripped the pillow under my head, squeezed my eyes closed, and came with a harsh groan.

Wyatt? Are you—

"Don't move, little girl," I gritted out.

When my head stopped spinning, I opened my eyes and drank in the exotic sight before me. I could never get enough of Posy's perfect titties. The gentle slopes rising from her chest. The round, heavy bottoms that fit perfectly in my hand. Her perfect nipples beaded up and hard like little pebbles...

"Hook your thumbs in the sides of your panties," I growled, "and slowly slide them down your legs. Stop when you get to your ankles."

She wiggled her hips a bit as she did and her tits dangled, plump and inviting, as she bent at the waist.

"Now stand up and kick them off. Yes, that's a very good girl. You're my good girl, aren't you, cutie?"

I licked my lips as my eyes dropped to her pussy and saw her juices trickling down her thighs. She was as turned on as I was, thank the Goddess.

"Put your hands on your hips and rub them up your sides. Yes, just like that. Play with your tits. Hold them in your palms and stroke your thumbs over your nipples. Hmm. Yeah. Just like that. Does it feel good, little girl?"

She moaned and sawed her legs together, and my dick sprang up, stiff and ready again.

Damn! I need to speed this up if I want to come inside her this time!

"Now get on your knees and come here. Crawl up my body until I tell you to stop."

When her knees were parallel to mine, I told her to take off my boxers. Her hands were so gentle as she eased them down, and my dick flew up and knocked against her tit, which made her giggle. I rolled my eyes as I lifted my hips so she could pull the boxers past my ass.

"Oh, my little girl thinks that's funny?" I asked in a dark, stern tone, hoping that wasn't pushing her too far.

You're still okay, right, cutie? I checked.

Mm-hmm, but Wyatt, please hurry, she moaned. *It aches so bad. Please make it better!*

I will, baby. Hang on just a little longer.

Yes, sir, she teased in a whisper, then whined a little and ground her pussy against my thigh.

I was trying so hard not to use terms I thought would trigger her. There was no way I would ever ask her to call me daddy, not after what her stepfather did to her, but she voluntarily called me sir twice now, and that would work just fine for me.

"You laughed at sir's dick, little girl. Now you have to take it as hard as I want to give it to you."

She whimpered, and I smirked.

Sitting up, I reached for the wedge pillow I'd propped up behind the curtain. Placing it in the center of the bedding, I positioned Posy's hips in front of it, then guided her down until her sweet ass was high in the air and her torso lay on the wedge with her head down near the mattress.

Okay, cutie, I'm going to mate you now. All good?

Please, sir! She rubbed her legs together to try and ease the ache. *Please hurry!*

36

Spreading her knees with mine, I fixed my eyes on her glistening wet pussy. I badly wanted to eat her out, but I needed to come. Like, *now.*

I lined up and slammed my hips forward, drilling balls-deep in one thrust. Her tight pussy locked down on me and her walls pulsed, and I cursed Ash for teaching her that. It made me come every time, and I didn't want to yet.

"Stop that, little girl." I gave her a light smack on her ass cheek, and she jolted slightly. "Let sir do all the work."

Posy? Was it too much to slap your bum? I asked, knowing she hated profanity, even something as minor as 'ass.'

Wyyyyaaaatt, she moaned, and I knew she was on the edge of climaxing, too.

We need to remember to buy a wedge for our bed at home, I told Gran with a smirk.

Yes! Now make mate come! he snarled. *Give her pleasure!*

I rolled my eyes, but had him to thank for distracting me enough to hold back my orgasm.

I didn't bother with any slow build up since neither of us needed it. My hands gripped the back of her thighs and shoved her ass cheeks up as my dick slid in and out of her in a hard, fast rhythm.

"Take sir like a good girl. That's right. Oh, yeah, little girl. Take sir's thick, hard dick in your tight, wet pussy."

Posy's moans turned into throatier, louder noises and then screams, and I gave up keeping count after she came for the sixth time, too focused on making sure my dirty talk didn't include anything triggering and keeping myself from coming. Fortunately, the first exercise helped with the second until I couldn't take it any longer and my balls felt like they were going to explode.

"Little girl," I panted, "when sir tells you, you clamp that tight pussy down on sir's meat. Clamp down good and tight so sir can come hard inside his little girl."

Three more thrusts was all I could manage.

"Now, little girl! Suck sir's dick with your pussy. Harder. Harder, little girl! Oh, yeah. Just like that." I spilled inside her, my whole body going taut and still. "Good girl. What a good little girl, squeezing sir's wood like a vice."

She cried out and shuddered through her own pleasure one more time, and I pulled out of her with a little wet 'pop.'

"Posy, cutie, my love, the game's over. Are you okay?" I ran my hands up and down her back, my fingers lightly tracing over the lines of scars.

"I'm dead," she panted. "You gave me so many orgasms, I died."

37

"It sure didn't sound like you're dead," I chuckled. "I think the whole building heard you."

"I'm so sorry! I didn't mean to embarrass you," she said instantly, making me want to throat-punch myself. "I was too noisy and—"

"Shh, baby. I was teasing. I love it. I love all your noises. They make me so hard, especially that moan you make when my tongue is tickling your clit."

"My *what?*"

A big grin spread across my face. Grabbing her wet thighs, I pushed her ass high up on the wedge again.

"This," I murmured before I dove in face first and began to eat her out from behind.

"Wyatt!" she screeched.

As I sucked hard on her clit, she gave me that moan I loved, and my dick didn't disappoint. In seconds, I was hard enough to plow her again, and I smirked as my tongue tasted my semen inside her pussy.

I'm going to mate you again and again tonight, cutie, I linked her. *I'm going to shoot you so full of pup-making juice, you'll taste it if you burp.*

Ew, Wyatt! That's disgusting!

And I never would have thought that a man could giggle, come, and eat his wife out all at the same time.

#

Posy

It was late morning before I woke up in a nest of pillows and blankets.

"I have something for you, cutie."

Rolling onto my side, I saw Wyatt sitting cross-legged next to me and holding out a white envelope. My heart skipped a beat because I knew what was in it.

I held the blanket to my chest as I sat up. If Wyatt saw my girls, I knew we wouldn't get out of bed for another hour.

"Thank you." I took the envelope from him with a smile. "You guys don't have to keep apologizing. I understand why you reacted as you did and already forgave you because you regretted it."

"It's okay to say sorry more than once for the same sin." He shrugged. "We want you to understand that we're sincere. And we know that riding herd on five idiots can be a daunting task. Let us make it up to you."

I reached up and cupped his jaw in my palm.

"I love you, Wyatt."

"I love you, too, cutie. Now please open my card, and then we'll get breakfast. Well, maybe brunch by now. Shoot! I wanted to take you somewhere special for lunch. If we eat brunch, you won't be hungry enough to—"

"I'm fine waiting for lunch at the special place," I hushed him. "We need to shower and clean up and pack our paintings in your car, anyway. It'll be lunch time before all of that, won't it?"

"Pretty close. I do need to take you to one more place, though, before lunch, so we'd better get this show on the road."

I frowned when he said he *needed* , not *wanted,* to take me somewhere, and curiosity bit at me. Knowing he wouldn't tell me even if I begged, I told myself I'd find out soon enough and opened the envelope.

The beautiful painted pansy on the cover made my eyes sting with tears, and the words he wrote inside made those tears fall.

"My fifth star," I read his signature, then looked up at him. "You are precious and perfect to me, too, Wyatt."

I threw myself at him, and we hugged for a long time until he stood up with me in his arms and carried me into the bathroom.

"Get a shower, sweet girl," he told me. "I need to run out to the car and grab your bag from your date with Mase. It has your toothbrush and toiletries in it. I'll be right back. Oh, and I left a bag of clothes for you in the bedroom."

"Thank you."

I kissed his cheek and he kissed mine, then I shooed him out of the bathroom before he got any ideas. I was going to need a nap this afternoon, especially if my next date was with Ash or Cole. Wyatt had worn me out, and both of those boys would do the same.

Maybe it will be my sweet dragon, I thought with a yawn as I turned on the shower and waited for the water to heat up. *I know he'd like nothing more than to curl up together with a good book or movie and would probably fall asleep before I did.*

When we were finally ready to leave, it was eleven o'clock, and Wyatt said my next date would just have to wait if we weren't done eating lunch by one. I told him that wasn't very nice, but he said he would make it up to his brother, although he wouldn't tell me which one.

"Give me a clue," I begged as we headed down the highway in his speedy car. "And tell me if I guess right."

"No."

"Wyatt!"

"No."

"Come on!"

"No." He looked at me over the tops of his mirrored sunglasses. "No means no, cutie."

I crossed my arms over my chest and popped out my bottom lip.

"There's no use pouting about it." He shrugged and turned off onto a side road that seemed like a private driveway. "I'm not going to give in. I'm not Ash or Cole to fall for your poochy lip."

He brought the car to a stop, but I was too busy giving him puppy dog eyes to look where we were.

"And I'm not Mase or Jay to give in to your big doe eyes, either." He booped my nose with his index finger. "Sorry, cutie. I'm immune to your charms."

Oh, really? Lark purred.

Challenge accepted, we said together and shared a smile.

She whispered an idea and I nodded.

Unbuckling my seat belt, I leaned across the console and stretched up so my lips were at his ear.

"Are you sure there's no way I can convince you?" I breathed, then blew a little air on his mate mark.

Seeing his skin shiver with goosebumps, I knew I was on the right track, so I kissed each star individually, then sucked lightly right over the moon. When I scraped my teeth against it, he started babbling like a brook.

"Jay, okay! Jay's picking you up after lunch! He's taking you—"

"Uh, uh, uh! I didn't ask all that," I murmured, then quickly blew a raspberry on his mate mark.

"Posy!" he roared, and I giggled as I threw open my door and jumped out of his precious car.

As he untangled himself from his seat belt and opened his door, I looked around in surprise. We were at a small graveyard surrounded by a black metal fence. The green grass was neatly cut around the memorials and a young willow tree stood guard over the dead at the front gate.

"Mase did this for us the year he became alpha," Wyatt explained as he joined me and linked our fingers together. "Come on. I have someone I want you to meet."

As we walked past the tombstones, I read their names with interest and compassion.

Willow Diane Price
Kelly Aroha Barlow
Jay Liam and Denise Olivia Carson
Gabriel Fetu and Kristy Ann Mitchell

Finally, Wyatt stopped in front of a shiny black stone that read, *Shawn Adam Black*.

Oh, my heart.

"Six years and it hurts as much now as it did the day he died," he whispered, staring down at his dad's tombstone. "If I could have traded myself for him, I would have without hesitation. If the Moon Goddess appeared to me here and now and said, 'Your father can live again if you give me your life,' I'd lay it down in a second."

Oh, my heart.

"Anyway, I have a confession to make," he went on before I could do more than wrap my arms around his waist. "Mase said you'd be cool about it, but I want you to know that I understand if you're not."

"Big secret reveal number three?" I asked, squeezing him.

"Yeah. Last one, too." He squeezed me back. "So, the thing is, I get overwhelmed sometimes and, um, disappear, I guess you could say. I disappear deep into my mind and leave Gran in charge. I don't even know I'm doing it until it's over. Sometimes it lasts for an hour or two, sometimes a whole day. The first time it happened, it lasted for six days before Gran, my brothers, and their wolves helped me come back to myself."

"Has it happened since we met?" I pulled back a bit to look into his face.

"Yeah. A couple or three times," he admitted, "but never for longer than a few hours. Ash calls it going wolfy. Anyway, I've set up some visits with Dr. York to work on fixing myself, but you need to know in case it happens and you're the only one around. I don't want it to scare you."

"Why would I be scared? I know Granite."

"You don't know Granite *unsupervised*," he corrected. "Every time you've ever been around him, either in my body or his, I was there, too. When I go wolfy, it's all him."

"Is he violent? What exactly are you warning me about? He's Lark's mate. He wouldn't hurt me or her."

"Sometimes he can be violent, and it's true that he wouldn't hurt you or Lark. Still, he's not a very mature wolf, as you know, and he makes bad decisions and has no common sense. He's an alpha wolf, with or without me present, and can shift, even if I go wolfy in my own body. Things can get a little hairy, no pun intended, until I ... come back."

I was quiet as I thought about everything he said, then I asked Lark what she knew about this, which was little to nothing, although she said she'd talk to her wolves and see what they had to say.

"Wyatt," I said at last, "the next time this happens, I want to know and observe so I can understand better, okay?"

41

"Okay." He nodded. "So you're not freaking out. I'm not sure what to do because you're not freaking out. I half-expected I'd need to chase you down and give you a sedative."

"Silly boy." I stepped out of his arms and frowned up at him. "Now, let's talk about the real issue. What makes you get overwhelmed?"

"Well, remember you were talking about how, um, how easy it was to hurt my heart yesterday?" His cheeks flushed pink, and I thought it was cute that he was embarrassed to talk about this part of himself. "Yeah. So things like that cause it to happen. Anyway, I'll be learning healthier ways to cope during my sessions with Dr. York, so hopefully, going wolfy will soon be a thing of the past."

"When's the first time it happened, Wyatt?" I could make a guess, based on where we were, but I wanted to be sure.

"When my dad—" his voice cut out, and I nodded, sad that I was right, but not surprised.

Looping one arm around my shoulders, he pulled me close again and kissed my forehead, his lips lingering for a long time as wet drops fell from his cheeks onto mine.

Oh, my poor, darling boy. How full of pain you are.

We going to help him, Lark murmured. *Granite say we already are.*

"And you have no more secrets to reveal now, right?" I asked Wyatt.

"That was all of them. And you're still here. You didn't leave screaming." His grin suddenly turned naughty. "Then again, I know for a fact that you only scream when you're coming."

"Wyatt Black!" I hissed and slapped his chest. "That is private talk for the bedroom!"

"Look around, cutie! There's no one. We're in the middle of a field surrounded by forests. Speaking of which," he waggled his eyebrows at me, "how about you get naked again? We have enough time for me to do something I've been wanting to do for a long while."

"What are you talking about?" My eyes nearly burst out of their sockets in disbelief. "You did it almost all night last night! What do you—"

"What are *you* talking about?" He gave me an innocent look, but I saw the mischief sparkling in his silver-shot blue eyes. "I only want you to shift and let me play with Lark for a bit."

"Grr! You better start running, Wyatt Shawn Black!" I huffed. "When I let her out, I'm going to tell her to bite you on the bum!"

"Huh. And here I thought Ash was the only one with a bum kink."

"AAARRGGHH!"

42

Wyatt's Letter:

Dear Posy,

I'm sorry for ruining your moment in the sun. I was afraid for you, and that made me lose my temper when I should have been lifting you as high as you wanted to fly.

I hate myself for hurting you. You are the most perfect and precious person in my life, and I love you. Please forgive me.

Your fifth star

3: The Alpha Library

Jayden

I woke up around seven, reached for Posy, and frowned when my arms didn't find her hidden among the covers or being smothered by Wyatt or Cole.

Oh. Yeah. Right. I frowned, but then remembered that today was my date and smiled.

More cheerful now, I rolled out of bed and headed for the bathroom, but was careful not to wake up Cole. He'd been a real bear lately, and I knew it was because he missed our girl. We all did, but he had the longest wait of us all, so it was understandable that his short temper was even shorter than usual.

Let the grump sleep, muttered my own grump.

I bit back a grin, not wanting to deal with Quartz's short temper this morning, either. As far as I was concerned, he had only himself to blame, just like my brothers.

After breakfast, Mase and I went to the alpha offices while Cole headed off to supervise fighter practice.

Ash had already left to check out a colony to see if it might work for Konstantin, the young dragon we'd rescued from the human prison. Poppy said he was half druk, a Bhutanese thunder dragon, and gave it fifty-fifty odds they'd accept the kid. Angelo, his apprentices, and Beatrix *were* going to take him, but King Julian called last night and needed a representative over at Midnight Run as soon as possible, so they went there instead and Mase, Ash, and Cole Rock-Paper-Scissored who would go to the colony.

No one here wanted to see Konstantin go, but what did a pack of werewolves know about raising a dragon? We didn't even know how to feed him properly, and it wasn't working for him to stay at the pack house, so we sublet Tristan's old apartment until his lease ran out. We told him that he was always welcome at Five Fangs, but my brothers and I felt he should be with his own kind. So, despite Posy's tears, we shopped around and found a colony whose matriarch said she'd meet him and decide, and today was that day.

As for Mase and me, we had a slow morning, which was a rare but welcome change, and cleared out all the outstanding paperwork. I went into his office to see what he had left to do and found him leaning back in his chair with his hands folded behind his head.

"Feels good, doesn't it?" He grinned. "I know it won't last, but let's enjoy it until the in box fills up again."

"Even our calendars are clear the rest of the day." I grinned back and crossed my arms over my chest as I leaned against the door jamb. "Ten bucks says we have about half an hour before something demands our attention."

"Nah, man. Give it ten min—"

Boys, Papa and I need to talk with you, Dad linked us. *We finally got that dire wolf to crack.*

We shared a chuckle before Mase linked back and told them to come over to the alpha offices.

"I'll do it," I offered.

"Thanks, but I got it. You have your date today, and whatever they found out might lead to tracking down their lair."

"You don't want to deal with Papa if you don't have to," I said gently.

"I won't forgive him, and I can't forget, but I want to move on and I can't do that with this burden in my heart."

Going over to him, I laid a hand on his shoulder and squeezed, then told him I'd make some fresh coffee while he relocated to the conference room.

Of course, I'd no sooner popped the pod in the maker than Sara linked us and said she and her sisters had found out something important concerning Landry's curse.

I'm on it, I linked my brothers, then told her to come to the offices whenever they were ready.

We're on our way. Landry needs to be there, too. He's still on sick leave, right? she asked. *So he should be free?*

He is. I'll contact him. I did, then linked Mase. *Sorry, brother, but you'll have to use the little conference room. I need the big one.*

I explained what Sara wanted, and he grunted.

Okay. Just make sure you get coffee going, please.

You got it, I told him.

When Dad and Papa came through the front doors, I directed them to where Mase was set up. Four of our five witches arrived within a few minutes of each other, then Oak showed up and I opened the bathroom door for him to run in and shift. We always kept a bunch of clothes in our linen closet for just such a reason, and Landry came out dressed in light gray joggers and a white t-shirt. Seeing his bare feet, I made a note to replenish our supply of slides.

We all settled around the long table in comfy rolly chairs, and I gestured for Sara to begin.

"So Landry, I'll keep it simple. We did some bibbidi-bobbidi-boo and discovered Nia Hashimoto was not your true mate."

Silence.

Neither Landry nor I reacted to her candid statement for several seconds as we processed what she'd said.

"Sara," Ariel chastised her quietly, "you could have been more gentle."

"Pull off the band-aid quickly, I always say."

"Um. What?" Landry broke out of his shock before me.

"The curse she used on you - Warm Hands, Cold Heart - came with a few bells and whistles," Maria took over explaining. "One tricked you into believing she was your mate."

"We reviewed your memory as well as alphas Ash and Wyatt," Ariel went on. "If you had touched her, that part of the spell work would have dissipated immediately, so she was running a risky game there. Also, you wouldn't have felt the mate sparks, and that would have been a dead giveaway something was fishy."

"Can you remember if you picked up a special scent that day?" Poppy asked. "Something that smelled so good, it was all you could focus on? All you could think about?"

"No," Landry mumbled with a frown. "I don't know. Maybe, but I can't— I can't remember."

"What about your wolf?" Sara asked. "Did he act crazy excited that day?"

"No, I don't think so, but I can't—"

"Remember?" the witches said in unison.

"That's part of it," Poppy said with a nod. "Mental fog during and after."

"Why?" Landry's face twisted with hurt and confusion, and his eyes welled up. "Why did she do that to me?"

"Only she can answer that," I murmured, only a little sorry that we'd killed Nia Hashimoto so quickly.

Well, it wasn't really quick, now was it? Quartz smirked, and I hushed him.

"Thank you for taking your time to look into this." Landry scrubbed his hands over his face, then stood. "I can't understand why it had to happen to me, but it's a relief to know that bitch wasn't my real mate."

His eyes suddenly brightened and he swiveled his head to look at me. I raised my eyebrows in question, and he grinned broadly.

"That means my Goddess-given mate is still out there somewhere!" he crowed. "Doesn't it?"

"It sure does, buddy." I pounded him on his shoulder. "Now you just need to find her."

"About that." Ariel raised one finger. "Another little bonus with the curse was that no other female could touch you or love you. We believe that may have interfered with you finding your mate."

"Now, you should have no problem sensing her," Maria summed up.

"So I could have been around her while I was cursed and not know it?"

"That's right. So if there's any girl in the pack who's turned eighteen since January, you may want to go say howdy and take a surreptitious sniff," Poppy teased him.

"Wait a minute!" Landry jumped to his feet. "Oak has been going wild all day today. Do you think that might mean—"

"Your mate is somewhere in the pack right now," Sara said simply. "That's why we knew we had to tell you today. We're still trying to find the dark witch—"

Landry didn't stay to hear anything more. Shifting on the spot, he shredded his - *our* - joggers and t-shirt into ribbons and lit out of the conference room.

"Good thing we installed a doggy door," I chuckled as I heard the flap slap open, then shut.

"As I was saying," Sara continued, "we're still trying to find the dark witch who crafted and cast that spell. That kind of karma-tempting work had to cost a pretty penny, and Nia was only a senior in high school without a job. We are very curious to learn how Nia paid her and with what."

I shivered a bit. I didn't know a lot about magic, but I knew enough about dark witches to know their services had price tags beyond the realm of dollars and cents. What had Nia gotten into? And why was she so determined to destroy Landry, who never did her any harm?

I assured the witches we'd support and fund their efforts one-hundred percent, then chatted with them about how their new shop was coming along. They liked the location next to Roger's Diner, which was only about half a mile from the Busted Knuckle, so they'd get a lot of shifter notice. Plus, as Poppy said, word of mouth spread fast among those who needed or wanted what the witches stocked and sold. Needless to say, all of them were looking forward to their new enterprise.

Finally, they bustled off to their individual destinations, and I went to join Mase only to find that Dad and Papa had also left. We talked for a bit about what they found and who to send to track down the dire wolves' lair and clean it out.

You can guess which wolf spoke up right away about wanting to be a part of that.

Then Cole came back from fighter practice with the White Pelt female we'd rescued with Konstantin and the other prisoners.

Mase and I looked at him in surprise, then greeted her and nodded at her polite reply.

"Flicker is very restless. Do you mind if I walk around outside?" She tilted her head at us and her hazel eyes showed how antsy her wolf was. "It might help calm her, as she is more used to that in the summer. We're only cooped up indoors during the winter."

We agreed, and Cole asked her to stay within calling distance in case we needed her. She nodded, then left and we heard the front door open, then close seconds later.

"Why did you bring her here?" I asked.

"She came to fighter practice." Cole shrugged. "She's not that great, but she's strong and hardworking. She said her alpha doesn't let the females train even if they want to. Anyway, I want to try to call him again. This is getting ridiculous. I can't understand why he's stalling to get her home."

"Well, there's no way that she's a problem for the pack," Mase snorted. "She's a lot like our girl."

"True." Cole and I both nodded.

So far as any of us had observed, Grace Turnbull was a curvy, sweet, shy, cute young lady. At nineteen, she was loving life here at Five Fangs, which was a far cry from White Pelt, a very primitive pack in the back of beyond in northern Canada that couldn't even offer reliable cell or internet service.

According to Grace, Alpha Rimsky had an office, which was little more than a trapper's shack, on the pack border near a human town. He kept a landline with an answering machine - not even voicemail! - that he checked once a day in the warmer months and maybe once a week otherwise. Cole had left three messages so far and had only received one call back, during which Alpha Rimsky explained that the pack was deep into preparations for winter as it would begin snowing in about a month, and he couldn't spare anyone to fetch her, nor could he fund a plane ticket until the summer pelts were sold.

Whatever *that* meant.

While some wolves thrived in such survivalist circumstances, Grace didn't want to go home. She was fascinated by even the smallest luxuries, such as television and indoor plumbing, and wanted to go to 'real' school, something she couldn't do at White Pelt. The den mother at our pack house said the poor kid didn't even know how to use the microwave.

A big problem for me was that White Pelt didn't have doctors of their own, let alone a clinic. If it didn't kill you, they reasoned, you'd recover eventually. I could understand that for those who had their wolves, but it was a harsh philosophy when it came to pups.

"I'd be fine keeping her here," I admitted with a shrug as I saw her outside our window.

She'd stopped walking around and simply stood there with her nose tilted up and her eyes closed.

"Cole, get a hold of her alpha soonest, even if you have to send a message by freaking sled dog or tie a note around a snow goose's leg," Mase muttered, making us chuckle. "Posy liked her when they met, and that's a good enough recommendation for me. If Alpha Rimsky's okay with her joining our pack - and Ash and Wyatt are, too - so am I."

And then the issue suddenly became moot in the best possible way.

Alphas, Landry linked us out of the blue, *Oak keeps saying to go back there. Is someone at your offices?*

We looked at each other, then turned as one to stare out the window at Grace. Her whole attention was fixed on the forest, her hazel eyes unwavering even as her body began to tremble.

Yes, we linked him, and left him hanging even as he pestered us to say who.

Grinning, we crowded around the window to watch the show and didn't have a long wait before Oak burst out of the treeline and skidded to a halt a few feet in front of the girl, who grinned and held out a fist for Oak to smell.

Landry, on the other hand, was panicking, and his fear plucked the gamma bond like I did my guitar strings.

What do I do? he shouted. *Alphas, what do I do?! She's so pretty! She's going to reject me. A beautiful girl like her won't want me!*

Calm down, Landry, Mase said on a soft laugh. *She'll love you. Stop panicking.*

Let her say hi to Oak, then come shift in the bathroom again, I suggested.

Unless, Cole snickered, *you want to give your mate a preview of what she'll be seeing later.*

Not funny, alpha! he snarled. *What if this is another curse? I don't think I can survive that again. What—*

Do you smell something irresistible? Mase intervened.

Yes. Honeysuckle. I want to bathe in it.

Is Oak excited beyond belief? Cole asked.

Obviously.

Get close enough that he can touch her. Do you feel mate sparks? I threw in my two cents.

We watched as Oak cautiously crept up to her and let her cup his snout in her hands as she stared into his eyes. Tears coursed down her cheeks and Oak shivered, his fur sticking up like he'd been rubbed backwards with a balloon.

Yes, he confirmed what we all knew.

Congratulations, dude, I grinned. *You found your true mate.*

#

Standing on the sidewalk in front of the hibachi restaurant, I looked up North Broad Street and then down it.

No sign of Wyatt or our girl.

With a sigh, I glanced at my watch. One thirty-seven.

Where is he? Quartz snarled.

Calm down, I told him. *Anger is clouding your mind. Something probably held him up.*

He's deliberately late and you know it! He wouldn't dare do this if it were Mase or Cole standing here waiting, but he knows you'll *let him get away with it!*

Leaning one shoulder against the wall, I closed my eyes and rubbed my forehead with one hand. Ever since Posy put him in his place at the training center, Quartz had been in a rage. Not at our girl, of course, but at himself - and that made it twice as hard to calm him down and keep him calm.

Yes, *Lark* was his mate, but Posy was to him what her wolf was to us: A pure and platonic love that had its own strong and vital bond. Doubly so since Posy had marked us as hers. None of us would survive losing Lark just as none of our wolves would survive losing Posy.

And knowing he'd hurt Posy cut Quartz as deeply as it did us to realize we'd been hurting Lark when we thought we were helping her.

Needless to say, I'd had a headache for the past two days.

Maybe he's teasing us, I told him with patience that was fraying fast. *He'd tease Ash like this, too.*

Yeah, but not for nearly forty minutes! He wouldn't push it more than ten or fifteen because he knows Ash would pound him into the ground. You, on the other hand, won't say a word. Don't you understand that only encourages him?

Quartz—

And why won't he link with you? Gran's been a riot of giggles all morning. I can't get a clear answer out of him for anything, but Wyatt should at least be answering you! What if there was an emergency? He's irresponsible—

Don't be mean. You're assuming a lot—

Jay! Wyatt linked me out of the blue. *Sorry, man! I lost track of time. We're almost there, I swear. Wait for us, okay?*

Okay, was all I linked back.

Minutes later, a familiar black Jag raced up the street and skidded into a parking stop, and Wyatt jumped out. Hustling around to Posy's side, he opened her door and scooped her up in his arms, then ran toward me with her clinging to him like a koala and giggling so hard that her cheeks were red.

50

"Dude, I am *so* sorry!" He thudded to a stop right in front of me and looked me in the eyes. "I took her to meet Dad, then she shifted to let me play with Lark for a bit. I didn't realize it was so late until we got in the car again."

"So you didn't eat yet?" I looked at Posy. She was the one who couldn't afford to miss meals, not Wyatt.

"Missed breakfast, too," Wyatt muttered as he put Posy down. "Damn, I screwed this up. Cutie, you must be starved. Jay, take her in and get her something to eat."

As soon as Wyatt set her on her feet, our girl wrapped her arms around my waist and squeezed me, and I hugged her back. Nuzzling my face in her neck, I took a huge inhale of her delicious scent and let it soothe both me and Quartz.

"But *you* wanted to experience the hibachi with her," I murmured to Wyatt.

"Naw, it's good, man. I'll take her another time." He patted my shoulder. "I've already taken too much from your date."

You heard him, Quartz rumbled instead of snarled, calmer now that our mate was here. *Take her into the restaurant and send him home.*

I looked in Wyatt's eyes and saw only happiness and peace in those silvery blue depths. He'd told us he was planning to tell Posy about going wolfy and when and why it first happened; he obviously did and it was like a burden had been lifted from his heart.

Don't do it, Quartz warned me. *He needs to grow up, and cosseting him won't help that happen.*

It's not cosseting, I argued. *It's compromising, something that would benefit you to learn. He explained and apologized, and now he's willing to give up something that was important to him to make it up to us. What more do you want?*

Quartz snorted and rolled his eyes, but stayed silent.

"You can't re-do a first time," I told Wyatt. "Come on. We can all eat together."

"Thank you, Jayden, for being patient and kind," Posy whispered in my ear, her small hands sliding up and down my back. "I missed you, my dragon."

"I missed you, too, sweetness."

Two days without her was two days too long.

Next time we do this, I linked Wyatt, *we need to put a free day or group date in between or something. It's torture to be separated from her for so long like this. I pity Cole for having to wait two more days before he sees her again.*

Agreed. He nodded. *Jay, really, man, I am sorry we were late. I should have waited to play with Lark until later—*

No, dude, I disagreed, *she needed that.*

Yeah, but I should have planned it better so it didn't lap into your time.

You told her everything? I changed the topic.

Everything.

The way he said it made me give him a sharp look as we walked into the restaurant.

What are you hiding, Wy? I asked gently.

I'm working up the courage to tell you, so don't pressure me. I'll tell you soon. I promised Posy I would.

Alarm widened my eyes.

I remembered the first time he went wolfy. It scared all of us to look into his eyes and see nothing of *him* in them. Several times before he came back, Granite almost got them killed - and realizing that Wyatt *wanted* him to broke my heart.

So, yeah, I *did* cosset him after that. No one else I loved was going to die. Not on my watch, and certainly not by his own hand - which is why it panicked me to learn he had a secret so big, he was nervous about sharing it with us.

You're safe, right? I demanded now. *You're not doing anything dangerous or harming yourself, are you?*

He smiled and met my eyes as our waitress led us to a table.

It's all good, Jay, I swear. Thanks for worrying about me, though.

His gratitude was new and mature, but didn't convince me, and I linked my other brothers to see who could keep an eye on him the rest of the day.

Mase went with Papa, Dad, and some of the pack warriors to track that dire wolf lair, Cole answered, *and Mom and Mama wanted to go shopping for the new pup. Since the paperwork's caught up and the calendar's clear, I volunteered to watch Wesley and the heathens. Might as well send him my way. I'm* almost *sure I can handle babysitting him and the little dudes.*

I snorted in amusement, making Posy and Wyatt look at me questioningly.

"Cole's stuck babysitting Wesley and the heathens and is being overwhelmed," I lied without blinking an eye. "Wyatt, you can lend a hand after lunch, can't you?"

"Sure, but where's Peri or Wayne and Arch? Why can't any of them babysit?"

"Peri and Ty are back-to-school shopping in the city. As for Arch and Wayne, who knows? Like Posy said, Mom and Dad kind of let them do their own thing most of the time."

"They're with Reau," Posy chimed in. "They were going to work on the secret fort today. He was really excited about it."

"Secret fort?" I smiled. "It's a walled garden."

"Reau sees it as something else," she giggled. "I'm glad Arch and Wayne like him so much. It makes me happy to know he has friends who are good to and for him."

The next trouble trio, Wyatt muttered in the link. *Goddess only knows what chaos will ensue in school this year. I just hope they keep our girl out of their mischief.*

I nodded in agreement.

"Now that Peri's mated, I can see this babysitting thing getting to be an issue," Wyatt griped.

"Don't you like spending time with your little brothers?" Posy asked with a frown.

"Of course I do! We all do. They're a lot of fun, and we miss out on a lot with them, but as alphas, we're swamped most of the time," Wyatt explained.

"Today is a rare exception, but even that had a bunch of interruptions," I added. "For the most part, Wade is at training or running through the woods with his buddies. They all got their wolves in the past couple of months, and he pretty much takes care of himself like Arch and Wayne."

"And the heathens just need to be kept busy or they get into trouble," Wyatt said. "They like building blocks and race cars and sports, which is right up our alley, but we just don't have the time to give them. That was another reason we were happy you said you wanted to wait for pups. We need a couple of years to organize a few things, then we'll have more time to dedicate to a family."

Posy's cheeks flushed pink when he started talking about pups and a family, and I smiled to myself.

"Wesley's the one I worry about," Wyatt continued, and I silently agreed. "I hope Mom and Dad are done after this last pup. Don't get me wrong. I love the little guys so much, but Wesley often gets overlooked because the heathens take a lot of energy and attention. He takes it in stride and is chill about it, but we try to do special things with just him once in a while."

"Hopefully, this next one won't be so high maintenance," I sighed as I thought about how much energy it took to keep up with William and Winnie - and I was only nineteen! I didn't know how Mom and Dad, both in their late thirties, did it.

"Does Dad help out?" Posy asked.

"Oh, yeah," I said. "He's great with them, but his time isn't always his own, either. He runs a full-time business *and* helps us out with the pack. He takes the older three with him to the garage a lot and sometimes Wesley, but Wesley's not as interested in cars as the rest of them, and the heathens are too young. So when Dad's busy and Mom needs to do something or go somewhere she can't take them, she needs a sitter."

"And Peri was the built-in, go-to sitter? Poor Peri! No wonder she wants to wait a few years for her own pups!"

"That, and Ty's obsessed with making sure he can provide for a family," I said. "He wants to have a nice nest egg in his savings before they have their first one."

"I can relate to that since I never had any money, either. You get a little paranoid about it." She bit her lip as she stared at the table. "I tried to give them some to get what they needed for their house, but they wouldn't let me, and Mason told me they wouldn't accept any from him, either. I understand, but I wish they didn't have to struggle just starting out."

"Mase is going to go more aggressive with Ty's investment portfolio." I patted her thigh reassuringly. "He'll make sure they won't have to worry about money soon enough."

"Hopefully, he'll get as lucky as he did with us!" Wyatt chirped.

"Hopefully," Posy and I said together, then giggled at each other.

"Wait a minute." Wyatt held up his hand. "I thought Cole was pow-wowing with the White Pelt alpha today."

"He did. Grace is staying, and her alpha has nothing to say about it."

"What?" Wyatt asked right as Posy asked, "Why?"

"Something amazing happened this morning." I was so excited to share the news, I did a very Ash-esque wiggle in my seat. "First, guess what the witches found out?"

"What?" Posy's eyes widened with interest.

"Nia wasn't really Landry's mate!" I chuckled as both of their jaws dropped. "Part of the curse she cast, or had cast on him, included faking they were mates."

"That's a major bit of spell work," Wyatt whistled.

"It is. The witches want to track down the dark witch and have Gelo deal with her after they ask a few questions." I was almost vibrating with excitement to tell them the best part. "Anyway, Grace was with us while Cole tried to call Alpha Rimsky *again*. Oak sensed something was up and came barrelling back to the alpha offices and—"

"Don't tell me she's—" Wyatt understood it before our girl did.

"Yes! She's his *real* mate!" I squealed, unable to hold it in any longer.

"She is?!" Posy gasped with wide, happy eyes. "Oh, that's wonderful! I really liked her, even though I only met her once."

"It's amazing how the Goddess' hand works," I said as I shook my head. "If Grace hadn't been captured by those humans, if Poppy had never escaped and found Five Fangs, and if we didn't raid that prison and bring Grace to our pack, then she and Landry *never* would have found each other. They would have lived their whole lives without their Goddess-given mates."

"A true miracle," Wyatt agreed with a big grin.

"I bet Landry was so happy!" Posy bounced in her seat and clapped her hands. "That just leaves Nick, Reuben, and Adam!"

"Little matchmaker," I teased her.

"I just want everyone to be as happy as we are." She gave me a smile so sweet, it stole my breath. "Where will they live? I think I remember one of you saying Landry lived with his older sister?"

"As with the betas, we gift our gammas with an available property of their choice when they find their mates," I explained. "It's the least we can do for those who do so much for us."

"I'm so proud of you guys! You're the best alphas in the world. You care about your betas and gammas as if they were family."

"They are," Wyatt and I said at the same time, even shrugging in unison, which made her giggle.

After that, we focused on enjoying lunch with our mate. Even though it was a result of Wyatt's poor time management, I wouldn't have wanted to miss this with them.

Watching Posy's face was more entertaining than any show the chef could have put on. The onion volcano made her gasp and clap, and she caught the shrimp when the chef flicked it to her, just as Wyatt predicted she would. As for Wyatt, he sparkled with cheerfulness. Not the unhealthy, fake kind, either, when he made jokes to distract himself from whatever was bothering him and everyone else from noticing.

And I was happy for him. Maybe he *was* telling the truth when he said it was all good, although I wondered how he kept Granite from spilling the beans. That wolf was lousy at keeping secrets.

Finally, we left the restaurant, and Wyatt asked us to wait while he fetched her toiletry bag from his car.

"What are we doing for our date, my dragon?" Posy asked as she hugged my arm and smiled up at me. "Do I need a change of clothes? Wyatt picked this dress for me to wear."

"It's a surprise, and you look perfect, sweetness," I murmured, leaning down and kissing her forehead.

"Thank you." Her pink cheeks made me chuckle.

Still so pure and innocent.

And she always will be, Quartz agreed.

55

Wyatt trotted back with her little bag and handed it to me, then pecked her cheek.

"Time for you to bid us farewell, brother," I told him with a fist bump.

Bid us farewell? Quartz snorted. *You're such an old man.*

Oh, shoosh. You're such a curmudgeon.

You should be grateful that I'm mature and intelligent enough to know what a curmudgeon is. You'd be explaining for an hour if I were Sid or Gran or Topaz.

And I had to snicker at that.

#

As soon as she stepped into the alpha library, her jaw dropped and her eyes grew wider and wider. She spun around, trying to take in everything at once, and I giggled.

"We're here until tomorrow, sweetness," I reminded her. "You have plenty of time to look around, and you can come back whenever you want to. No one will bother you, either. Only Ty and I come here."

"It's amazing," she breathed. "Like out of *Beauty and the Beast*!"

"Well, what's that expression? Marry the Beast and get the library?" I teased and grabbed her around the waist with a little growl. "You have five beasts, so the least you should get is five libraries."

"How are they organized?" she asked as she snuggled against me.

"Poorly at the moment, I'm afraid," I admitted. "When Mase ordered this place built, he asked if I'd be interested in being in charge of it, and I said yes, of course. I enlisted Ty to help, as I originally planned to make him the librarian here."

"You did?" she squeaked with surprise.

"Yep. Even designed the top floor as a beautiful apartment for him, but then Ev Breckenridge was killed and Ash needed a beta and Ty was next up. He's happier, anyway. As much as he likes it here and likes to read and research, he would have been bored after a while."

"So you still need a librarian?" She tilted her head as her eyes went far away, and I wondered what she was thinking. "What about Grace? She'll want a job, and she told Mason she wanted to go to school because she didn't have that opportunity at White Pelt."

"Hmm. Maybe. I don't know if she'd be interested." I frowned as I thought about it. "And I don't know if Landry would like living in an apartment, even if it is luxurious. I pulled out all the stops when I designed it because I wanted Ty to have everything he never did."

"You guys really love him a lot, don't you?" She pressed kisses all over my chest, and I wished I wasn't wearing a shirt.

"Yep. He's our kid brother, too." Almost bursting with excitement, I grabbed her hand. "Come on! I want to show you around!"

Giggling, she took my hand in both of hers and told me to lead the way, so I did. We spent three hours wandering around the bottom floor, and I showed her how each of our original packs had a room packed full of books, maps, paintings, journals, ledgers, loose documents, and so much more. Dark Woods' collection was the sparsest by far, as the hunters had burned a lot of buildings, including the alpha office, but Ash, Wyatt, and I had spent several summers scouring the territory and salvaging everything we could.

"Eventually, Ty and I want to organize the research books by topic on the second floor. It's dead stupid having to go from room to room and search for books on dire wolves rather than having them all located in one area."

"Makes sense," she agreed. "Is there any fiction, or is it all research?"

"Ty and I started our own collection of our favorite novels and books. Let's go up to the second floor and I'll show you."

"Can I see the apartment on the third floor, too? I'd like to see how you designed it. I'm sure it's incredible."

"Of course you can!" I beamed down at her, proud that she was interested in what I created. "Let's do that first."

Ash and I set up our bed for the night on the second floor, and I wanted to save that until after dinner, which I'd set back an hour because we'd had lunch so late.

So I took her on a tour of the apartment, my heart swelling with each exclamation of amazement. I'd spent months making it as appealing as possible. There were floor-to-ceiling windows, two full bathrooms with rainfall showers and spa tubs, three spacious bedrooms, a kitchen equipped with every labor-saving device known to man, and balconies off the living room, kitchen, and master bedroom.

I'd also included a stargazing area on the roof with Edison lights strung everywhere and comfy outdoor furniture. I refrained from showing her that, though, because Ash wanted to stargaze with her tomorrow night and I didn't want to steal his thunder.

By the time she was finished exploring the third floor, it was dinner time, and Ty linked me right on cue.

Alpha, it's ready.

I rolled my eyes.

I wonder how long it will take to call us brothers-in-law again, I muttered to myself.

If he were still pissed, he wouldn't have agreed to help Peri set up your feast, Quartz muttered back.

True.

As we started to walk down the spiral staircase to the first floor, a delicious variety of smells wafted to our noses. Thank the Goddess that the human city our pack bordered was diverse enough to include several ethnic restaurants.

"Jayden?" she murmured, coming to a stop three steps from the bottom. "Is someone else here?"

"Ty and Peri helped me out and dropped dinner off. Want to take a taste tour around the world with me?"

She gaped at me, then bounced around so much, I had to catch her so she didn't fall down the last few stairs. Chuckling, I swung her up in my arms like a bride and carried her to the Five Fangs room, which was mostly empty as we hadn't accumulated very much as a pack yet.

Ty and Peri had done a fine job. Ash and I had stashed some blankets and a pile of pillows in the closet, and they'd spread them around like we were on a picnic indoors. Posy stared up at me with star-struck eyes, and I smiled as I sat her down.

I'd stuck with water, which Ash said was too bland and boring and wanted me to try some different wines and mixed drinks. Posy preferred water, though, well, besides Pepsi, and she wasn't getting any caffeine this late in the evening. Been there, done that, been awake half the night with a hyper little bunny.

You weren't complaining at the time, even if it cost you a three-hour nap the next afternoon, Quartz smirked, and I grinned at the memory.

"What is all this?" Posy asked. "I don't recognize any of it specifically, although I can tell this is some kind of salad and this is a soup."

Getting focused, I served each course and explained what it was and where it was from. We munched our way through Greek salad, French onion soup, gyoza dumplings, taquitos, gyros, and baklava for dessert. None of it really went together, but Posy was so very interested to learn, and she enjoyed it all, although she said the taquitos were a bit spicy for her. That only reinforced the fact that she had little to no spice tolerance, which we'd discovered the first time we ate Chinese.

From years of eating bread and scraps, Quartz growled, and I hushed him before she heard or picked up on his anger.

Finally, she declared herself stuffed and I finished off the baklava. I was never going to refuse my favorite dessert!

"Are we sleeping here?" she asked. When I nodded, she lifted her arms and made grabby hands. "Can you carry me? Or have I gotten too fat? I think I gained ten pounds tonight."

"You are not too fat. You are beautiful. And I am strong enough to carry you even if you gain a hundred pounds, sweetness."

She giggled and tucked her arms around my neck as I picked her up and stood.

"Although we'll ride the elevator this time," I groaned, then made a show of almost dropping her.

"Oh! See, I *am* too heavy," she fretted.

"I'm teasing, baby," I assured her with a tender peck to her lips.

We kissed our way through the brief elevator ride to the second floor and all the way to the little nook Ash and I created. He was a terrific idea man, and I was happy and grateful he'd helped me, especially when Posy saw it.

Ash had the right idea with the flowers. They made her smile and her eyes glow, and she gasped to see the lace-layered bed with lilac and white pillows, billowy sheer curtains draped with more flowers and vines, and fairy lights everywhere. She blushed when her gaze fell on the rose petals on the Persian rug leading up to the bed, and I didn't know why.

I set her on the edge of the bed and her eyes widened when she saw my guitar leaning against the wall.

"Are you going to sing and play for me?" She clasped her hands under her chin in that way that made my heart flutter. "Oh, Jayden, this is so special and romantic! I could die from how happy I am!"

Damn. Now I have to tell Ash he was right.

"Don't talk about dying," I murmured as I kissed her delicious lips. "Not for another hundred years or so, anyway."

Leaving her giggling, I got up and reached for my guitar, then settled on the bed with her.

"What are you going to sing?" she asked, sitting cross-legged next to me.

"Something good, I hope," I smiled, then warned her, "I'm still learning this one, so I might make some mistakes."

"I won't notice if you do," she replied with a gentle smile, "and I'm sure you'll do wonderful as always."

So I strummed a few notes to warm up, then launched into the introduction, took a deep breath, and started singing "You" by Dan+Shay.

My eyes were on my fingers, making sure I didn't screw up too much, which disappointed me because I wanted to see her face when she heard the lyrics. Quartz decided to help me out, though, and showed me her misty eyes and how her soft mouth drooped into a little o that fed my soul, and I sent him my thanks.

59

He just grunted, proving he *was* a curmudgeon.

"That was so lovely," Posy whispered when I finished. Leaning around my guitar, she kissed my cheek, then my jaw, then my lips. "You always pick the sweetest songs to sing for me."

Her affection filled my stomach with butterflies, and I had to swallow hard before I could talk again.

"Sweet songs for my sweetness. This next song is from our parents' generation, but I like playing it on the guitar. The lyrics are bittersweet, but melodic."

Bittersweet, but melodic? I cringed as I realized what I said. *What must she think of me?*

"What does melodic mean?"

"Nice, pleasant music."

"Ooh! Then I'm excited to hear it!"

Smiling at her enthusiasm, I settled the guitar better in my lap and picked up with the first chords, skipping the whistling, which was the only part of the song I wasn't a huge fan of - *and* my whistling sucked.

So I launched into "Patience" by Guns N' Roses while looking into her eyes as they glowed with tender tears. I had to sing the chorus with a grin, which kind of ruined the mood of the song, but she didn't mind. I couldn't get my voice as high and rough as Axl Rose's at the end, but I put all my passion into my playing and the adoring expression on her face was all I needed.

"Beautiful, Jayden!" she whispered and clapped her little hands excitedly.

Grinning widely, I leaned over and kissed her until we both had to breathe.

"I love you, sweetness," I murmured against her lips. "More than any of these songs can possibly describe."

"I know that, Jayden, and I love you, too." Then she surprised me and added, "You're so handsome and sexy playing that guitar and singing."

Losing her confidence, she covered her red face and giggled.

Oh, this girl, I moaned. *She really is my whole world. My whole heart. All my happiness.*

"One more song?" she said as she peeked at me through her fingers. "Please, my dragon?"

I'd already planned one more, but I twisted my lips and wrinkled up my face as if I wasn't sure, wanting to tease her a bit.

"Pretty please?" she pouted, those plump, pink lips driving me to distraction.

"Okay, but you'll need to give me something in return." I waggled my eyebrows at her, and her pink cheeks flushed bright red again, making me chuckle. "So this song is really old. My dad used to sing it to my mom, and it was old even then. The lyrics are simple, but powerful. I hope you like it."

My voice was good, but nowhere near as smooth and deep as The King's. Still, I put my heart into "Can't Help Falling in Love with You." I could almost hear my dad as I strummed the final notes and remembered how my mom would look at him all gooey-eyed before she dragged him somewhere private and I wouldn't see them for a while.

Just like Posy's looking at you now, Quartz chortled. *Good thing you're old enough now to understand.*

Smirking, I settled my guitar back on its stand, then eased my mate onto her back and laid on top of her.

"Are you breathing, sweetness?" I asked as I kissed her mate mark.

"No." She sank her fingers in my hair and massaged my scalp. "You stole my breath away."

"You do that to me all the time."

Then my mouth sang a song of love to hers, my lips and tongue caressing every inch of hers.

"You're so smooth and soft," I murmured after I got all her clothes off and ran my hands all over her. "Your skin is like silk. I'm almost ashamed to touch it with my rough, calloused fingers."

"It feels amazing," she moaned. "I love it."

"I want to give you pleasure. I want to kiss you all over," I whispered as I kissed my way from her throat to her gorgeous breasts. "I always feel so good when I'm with you, and now I want to make you feel good, too."

"I won't complain," she teased.

I chuckled lightly before I sucked one of her nipples deep into my mouth and made her moan again.

Hundreds of kisses and quiet gasps later, we were both needy and ready, and I eased inside her slowly, an inch at a time, savoring every second and sucking her throat, her shoulders, her collarbones.

Wanting to be as close to her as possible, I wrapped my arms around her head and neck, keeping most of my weight on my elbows, then moved my hips ever so slowly and rocked my tip in and out of her.

"*Jaaaayden.*"

Every time she drew my name out on that long, low moan, my belly pulled painfully tight with desire. It was one of the reasons I loved going slow and gentle with her, seducing and teasing her until she was begging and panting. I got as much enjoyment out of it as she did, and I was convinced my brothers were morons for not trying it.

"Feels so good, baby," I crooned as I sank in a little deeper. "Sweet, tight, virgin girl. All ours. Our precious girl."

"More," she whispered. "Please, Jayden. I want all of you, my dragon."

What could I do but oblige? I gave in and stopped torturing us both, sinking my whole length so deep inside her, my balls bounced against her ass.

That made her moan and she wrapped her quivering thighs around my hips and began to ride me as I rode her. My eyes rolled back in my head at the pure pleasure of her tight, wet walls clinging to me and tugging on my shaft as if she could suck me even deeper into her perfect self.

I couldn't go as long as Mase. That bastard had the stamina of a bull, damn him. I gave it my best try, though, and she climaxed several times before I came with a low, hoarse groan, the relief so heady and intense that I saw stars.

"You were amazing, sweetness," I whispered as I pulled out of her and rolled us onto our sides so we could cuddle. "You always are."

"Really? Me? No, you're the one who's amazing." She shivered in my arms as the last of her orgasm chased through her.

"We can agree that we're each other's amazing, I guess," I chuckled. "I can't believe we were so lucky to find you."

"I was more lucky that you found me."

"And now you're ours forever." I hugged her closer. "And we're yours. For all the rest of our days. That's a comforting and lovely fact, isn't it?"

"Yes, it is."

I felt her smile against my throat and her body relaxed against mine. She was on the edge of falling to sleep, and I realized I was, too.

"Good night, sweetness. I love you."

"Good night, my dragon. I love you, too."

I kissed her temple and covered us up with the blanket, and she snuggled into me even more, draping her leg over my hip and pressing her chest tightly against mine as she wrapped her arms around my neck.

And I drifted off to sleep, my world safe in my arms and my heart full of happiness.

Jayden's Letter:

"You are the finest, loveliest, tenderest, and most beautiful person I have ever known—and even that is an understatement." - F. Scott Fitzgerald

Posy,

Every love story is beautiful, but ours will always be my favorite!

I love you so much!

Your dragon,
Jayden

4: Daddy's Little Girl

Quartz

Jayden woke up around four in the morning to go to the bathroom, which awakened me, too. He very rarely got up in the middle of the night, but I always woke up when he did.

For once, I was glad about it.

I had something I needed to do.

When he fell back into bed, he disturbed Posy, who went to use the bathroom next, and I figured eating dinner so late must have thrown their systems' schedules off. While she was gone, I asked Jayden if I could have permission to take control.

Now? Why? What's going on? he asked on a yawn.

I need to punish Lark for keeping a serious secret from her mates.

That got him awake.

You can't spank her, Q, he said with a thread of panic in his voice. *You know that, right?*

Sadly, yes, I admitted with a dramatic sigh to tease him.

Of course, he took me seriously as he always did.

Don't trigger her. You heard what Garnet said. She was so scared—

Chill, Jayden. I wasn't going to spank her, but she needs to learn not to keep secrets from her mates.

None of you are any better. You kept Wyatt's secret about going wolfy from her just like we did with Posy.

Only because he promised he'd tell her himself when he was ready, I argued, *and made Gran swear by the moon to keep his mouth shut until then.*

Well, how are you planning to punish her? he asked, worried.

Daddy's going to make his naughty little girl beg to come.

His dick jerked in reaction to my words, and I snickered in amusement.

Should I take her from behind? Or up against the wall? I taunted him. *Or on her back with her legs up in the air—*

Stop! he snapped, his dick hardening into steel.

What? I chuckled, liking this game. *Just yesterday, you imagined eating her out while Wyatt was titty f—*

Permission granted! he snarled. *And good luck getting inside her before you come with this raging boner!*

Who said I wanted to come inside her? I snickered as I took control.

Posy came back from the bathroom a minute later, yawning widely as she crawled into bed and snuggled up to me.

"Little one, can Lark come out to see me while you sleep?" I asked.

"Oh, hey, Quartz," she mumbled, her eyes already closed. "Yeah, sure. Have fun."

"I intend to," I answered with a dark chuckle.

A few seconds after Posy drifted off, her eyes popped open, glowing silver now. Lark raised her face to stare at me, and I wanted to coo at her shy smile, but controlled myself.

"You've been naughty, little girl," I said in a stern tone.

"Me?" She blinked innocently at me.

"You kept an important secret from your mates."

Her next words were so quiet, I never would have heard them if I wasn't a wolf.

"I scared."

"Have your wolves ever hurt you?" I demanded.

"No, Daddy."

"Have our boys?"

"No, Daddy."

"Have I?"

"No, Daddy."

I grabbed her hands and held them above her head as I rolled on top of her and completely covered her body with mine.

"And do you honestly believe that I would *ever* allow anyone to hurt you?"

The last part came out in a thunderous growl that rattled the room as I thought of anyone giving her so much as a scratch. She shivered under me as her silver eyes filled with tears, and my heart cracked.

"No, Daddy," she sniffed.

"No more being too afraid to speak to us," I commanded. "I know you were silenced for a long time, but now you're free, and you're going to use that freedom, not avoid or ignore it. Do you understand me?"

She nodded, which made me scowl.

"I didn't *hear* you, little girl."

"Yes, Daddy!"

"I think you need some practice using your mouth," I muttered.

Releasing her hands, I got on my knees, straddled her waist, and smirked as her wide eyes fixed on my straining dick.

"Since this is the first time you've been naughty, I'll only punish you a little. Isn't that nice of Daddy?"

65

"Yes, Daddy. Thank you."

I directed her to lay her arms along her sides, and she complied immediately, earning my praise. Walking on my knees up her body, I came to a stop with her shoulders wedged tight between my thighs, then laid my balls on her collar bones and poked her chin with my tip.

Soft little mewls slipped from that mouth I was about to pound into, which made me even harder. Suddenly, she wiggled around with a frown on her beautiful face, and I worried I was pushing her too hard too fast.

Are you okay, Lark? I asked immediately. *Remember, you can say stop at any time, and you can link me if your mouth is occupied.*

Which it was about to be.

"I okay, Daddy," she said, and I let out a breath of relief.

She knew that if she'd called me Quartz, verbally *or* through the link, this would have ended in a heartbeat. By calling me Daddy, she was letting me know she wanted to continue, and I was so glad Garnet had the idea to set that ground rule between the three of us.

As for the pups, they weren't interested in this kind of play, although Garnet and I privately shared the belief that Sid might enjoy a "mommy," if Lark ever wanted that role.

"Plenty of time to explore that in our future," Garnet had said, and I'd agreed.

"But it hurts, Daddy," Lark whined now. "Make it stop!"

I knew exactly what she meant, but wanted to hear her say it.

You're teaching her bad things, Jayden muttered.

I'm going to teach her a lot more, I smirked. *And you have no room to talk with Wyatt's filthy mouth in Posy's ear every night.*

He doesn't make her say those things, though.

Nor will he ever, I snorted. *Your little mate will be innocent for the rest of her life. Now be quiet while I corrupt mine.*

He huffed, but ceased his yammering.

"What hurts, little girl?" I demanded.

"My pussy, Daddy. My pussy hurts," she pouted, her bottom lip popping out. "Fix it, Daddy!"

"Oh, little girl," I breathed, "you do *not* give Daddy orders."

Bracing one hand on the wall, I reached down with the other, grabbed my dick, and rubbed it all over her face in hard strokes, wanting my scent everywhere on her and, eventually, *in* her. When I brushed the head teasingly against her lips, her little pink tongue darted out and frantically tried to lick it, and I quickly moved it out of her reach.

"Uh-uh-uh. Not yet," I purred.

She whimpered and a line of drool trickled from the left corner of her lips, and I smirked down at her.

As pre-cum leaked from my tip, I laid my stiff dick on her face and swiped the fluid onto my forefinger. Tilting her head a bit, I massaged it into her mate mark like lotion, and she moaned, her throat vibrating against my fingertip.

"Look at you with my dick on your face, drooling and panting for your daddy. You want me in your mouth, don't you, little girl?"

"Yes, Daddy! Please!" she begged.

I adjusted her pillow to angle her head better, then slid both hands behind her head to cradle her skull in my palms.

"Open wide for Daddy."

She did, and I wasted no time cramming my dick in. She blinked, and I paused, giving her time to get used to it and link me if she wanted to stop. Then I felt her tongue swirling around and exploring as her lips gently suctioned onto me, tugging me deeper. I was halfway in already, so I was content to let her draw me down as far as she wanted.

I kept my pace slow, easing in and out of her soft, warm lips ever so gently.

"Suck Daddy. Suck Daddy like a lollipop," I rasped, my eyes rolling as she did. "Harder, little girl. Yes, just like that."

Smiling a little, I moved my hands to the wall so I wouldn't be tempted to grab a fistful of her hair. We all knew she and Posy both hated to have it pulled. In my excitement, I moved faster and dove deeper until I went too far for her comfort.

She choked, and her body stiffened under mine.

Quartz, I scared!

I pulled out right away. Sitting my ass down on her stomach, I kept my weight on my thighs and cupped her hands in my face.

Dammit, Quartz! Jayden thundered. *Be careful! That was too much too soon!*

And I had to admit he was right.

Cove had warned me that humans needed to train their gag reflex for going deep during oral sex; I'd just forgotten in my need to come.

Yes, I'd talked to Cove about sex. I was curious how two human males mated. After I explained I just wanted to educate myself, Emerson gave his wolf free rein to answer anything I asked, and Cove had no qualms showing me a few positions the beta and Angelo had tried. While it didn't arouse me to see two dudes go at it, I took note of some things to try with Lark.

Humans were inferior to wolves in every way except their amazingly flexible body, and I planned to take full advantage of that during mating.

I'm sorry, Lark. That was my bad.

I sorry, too, she whispered, then tears suddenly sparkled in her eyes. *I trying to be brave.*

Oh, sweet little love, you are *brave!* I leaned over and dotted her face with tiny kisses. *And you don't need to try anything you don't want to, and especially not because you think we expect it.*

It not bother me with Sid. She tilted her head at me, her face full of confusion. *Why I panic with you?*

With him, you were on top and in charge, and he didn't go in as far as I did. I kissed the shell of her ear, and she shivered. *Lark, I need to come, then I'll give you what you want. Okay?*

I hadn't been able to stop my dick from humping her sternum, and now I was ready to explode.

"Okay, Daddy," she murmured with a little smile.

Pleased she still wanted to play, I growled in her ear, which made goosebumps pop up on her skin.

"Watch," I ordered her as I sat up. "Watch Daddy come all over his little girl's titties."

With her wide eyes fixed on me, I wrapped one hand around my dick and stroked it three times, and long ropes of semen shot between her breasts.

If stupid Wyatt hadn't called dibs on fucking them first, I'd be all over that right now, I griped.

Well, he did, Jayden snorted, *and your semen isn't enough lube, anyway. And watch your language, Mr. Vulgar.*

You didn't bring any lube, Mr. Prude? I pouted.

No, Q, I did not bring any lube. I was only interested in having vaginal sex tonight, and she's never needed any for that.

He had a point there. Our girl's pussy was a lube factory when she was aroused.

Speaking of arousal, my dick popped right back as I looked at my seed glistening on her breasts. I smeared it on her hard nipples, which I gently pinched between my thumbs and forefingers and tugged a little.

"Daddy," she moaned and squirmed beneath me.

Her arm moved from where it was wedged between my leg and her side. I felt her hand heading south and knew what she wanted to do. Quickly looping my feet over her hands, I locked her wrists down with my ankles, careful to keep my weight off of her.

"Don't you dare touch yourself, little girl!"

Are you okay to play some more, little mate? I checked in with her, wanting to be sure before I went any further.

"Yes, Daddy," she whispered.

"Daddy wants to take you with his brothers someday soon. Would you like that? All five of us coming on you and in you at once? Daddy in your pussy, Daddy Garnet in your ass, Sid and Gran in your hands and Topaz in your mouth?"

"Yes, please, Daddy!"

Chuckling, I leaned down and kissed her hard, tongue and all, before unhooking my ankles from her wrists and sliding down her body. As I knelt between her thighs, my dick finished hardening at the sight of her spread legs.

"I hope you like being on your back. That's where naughty little girls belong. Under their daddies, begging to come."

Sliding my hands up the back of her thighs, I raised and bent her knees, then pushed them together before setting her feet flat on my chest. After I guided myself to her entrance, I pushed just the tip in before grabbing her wrists and holding them fast to the bed. Leaning forward, I pushed my weight against her feet and rammed into her - and I was damn lucky not to come right then.

Holy shit! I owe Cove big for this!

Grunting at the intense pleasure of the position, I took her pussy with a passion, and the noises she made were sweeter to my ears than any song Jayden ever sang.

"Please, Daddy!" she cried out at last. "I need to come!"

"Are you sorry?" I panted. "Is Daddy's naughty little girl sorry for what she did?"

"Yes!" she sobbed. "I no keep secrets again. I promise, Daddy!"

Smirking, I released her wrists, grabbed her knees, and wrapped her legs around my waist, still hammering into her. Once her ankles were locked at the small of my back, I gripped her ass with one hand and rubbed the other lightly over her mound. Opening her folds with my thumb and middle finger, I tickled her little pearl with my forefinger - and she fell apart.

"Daddy, Daddy, Daddy!" she chanted as she came.

Her walls pulsing around my dick took me over the edge at the same time. My hips stilled, and I came deep inside her, where I stayed until her words dissolved into a breathless moan.

Finally pulling out, I leaned down and dropped kisses everywhere on her red, tear-streaked face.

You'd better cuddle her after that, Quartz! Jayden grumbled sleepily.

As if I wasn't going to. I rolled my eyes.

69

Flipping us over, I bundled my mate up on my chest and tucked her face into my throat right at my mate mark. Her hot puffs of breath made me shiver, and I kissed the deep scars on her shoulder.

"Shh. You're okay," I murmured. "You did so well. Daddy's very proud of his little girl."

Go back to sleep, I linked my human. *I know how to care for my mate. Worry about what you're going to do with yours in the morning.*

Morning's almost here, he mumbled on a yawn. *And I'm going to ask my mate if I can play with your mate. I'd like to get to know Lark better, too.*

Of course you would. My mate is as perfect as yours, after all.

On a soft snort of amusement, my boy drifted back to sleep, and I stroked Lark's hair until she stopped shaking and her breathing evened out.

"Quartz?" she whispered.

"Hmm?"

"I love you."

I inhaled deeply, but that wasn't the only reason my chest swelled.

How? I asked, shaking my head. *How can one tiny she-wolf turn me - **me!** - into a pile of mush?*

"I love you, too, Lark. You are my life."

"And you mine."

"Get some sleep, my dear little mate."

"Stay with me?" she mumbled, already more than half asleep.

"Always."

"Promise?"

"Promise. You're stuck with me until I draw my last breath and return to the Goddess."

A tiny snore was her only response, and I chuckled before I, too, allowed sleep to claim me.

#

The next day, after a lazy morning, Posy asked Jayden if he would take her to the park. She wanted to feed the ducks. Don't ask me why; those things were terrorists with feathers. Lark, on the other hand, wanted to chase them, and that was more my idea of fun.

So Jayden picked up some sandwiches and whatnot and drove us to the park, where they spread out the old blanket he kept in his SUV for such things. They chatted and ate, and Posy did indeed feed those little bastards a handful of birdseed Jayden bought her for a quarter at one of those dispensers that the park people installed around the river last year. Apparently, people had been feeding the ducks too many

70

things they shouldn't eat, and some well-meaning animal activists advocated for cracked corn and birdseed in dispensers.

Me, I figured it was survival of the fittest. If a duck was dumb enough to eat bread and not forage, let it fall over dead. Those winged rats weren't good for anything but a quick snack, anyway.

Posy, however, thought they were adorable, especially the wood ducks with their colorful feathers and little curls at the backs of their heads, so I kept my thoughts to myself and stayed out of it as Jayden gave her quarter after quarter until we were surrounded by the little sons of bitches.

By then, Lark was busting a gut to chase them, and it didn't take long for Posy to give in and shift in the public bathroom.

Good thing the park is nearly empty at noon on a Monday, Jayden chuckled. *Our girl looks enough like a young dog, but I didn't bring a leash or collar for her.*

Did you bring her toy? I asked Jayden as my girl pranced toward us.

Of course. I'll get it out after she has fun with the ducks.

Yeah. Let her eat as many of the nasty quacks as she wants to.

You're afraid of ducks? Jayden laughed. *Oh, my Goddess. How did I never know this?*

I am not afraid of ducks! I roared. *I am not afraid of **anything**! I am an alpha wolf! I have ripped out more throats than anyone in our pack save Dad and Papa! I fear only one thing in this universe, and it is not some pathetic, ill-natured waterfowl!*

I'm only joking. I know you're disgusted by them, not scared of them. He grinned broadly as Lark cannon-balled into his legs and he leaned down to pet her. *But now I'm curious. What is the one thing that does scare you?*

I snorted and remained silent. That was none of his business.

Thankfully, he got the hint and let me be as he cuddled and petted Lark and played with her. When she grew tired of chasing the ducks, he brought out the dog toy I'd got for her at the pet store and she happily bounced around, barking at him.

He tossed it, and I huffed out a chuckle as she caught it with a *grr!* and sank her tiny teeth in the stuffed animal, then whipped her head around to "kill" it. Jayden, too, laughed at her cute antics and grabbed the toy's tail to play tug with her.

As they tussled, I thought back to our first run with her. Jayden had said that it was dangerous to give a brutal bastard like me a mate to love. I'd agreed with him then and doubly so now.

Why?

Because I would do anything for my mate.

Anything.

71

To make and keep my mate safe, I'd betray everyone who called me brother or friend.

I'd go to Hell and slaughter every demon.

I'd set Heaven on fire and watch the angels burn.

I'd do *anything*, go to *any* lengths, for her.

For my dear little mate.

For a fifty-pound ball of fuzz currently gnawing on a rainbow llama-corn dog toy.

So, yeah, dangerous didn't begin to cover it.

And if something happened to her, the monster I'd become should be *everyone's* greatest fear.

Not just mine.

Quartz's Letter:

DEAR POSY,
I'M SORRY I LOST
MY TEMPER AND HURT
YOUR FEELINGS.

I LOVE YOU AND LARK
MORE THAN ANYTHING.

I COULD TELL YOU THIS
IN PERSON, BUT THEY
MADE ME WRITE A
~~FUCKING~~ LETTER. QUARTZ

5: Adventure Time!

Ash

Today was my date with our girl, and I was so excited, I felt like my soul was going to fly right out of my body!

Me, too, Ashy!

Sid leapt around in my head like a freaking leprechaun, feeding off my energy, and I had only myself to blame.

I'd always struggled with getting a little too hyper and doing dumb things, and Sid often got in trouble right along with me.

Fortunately, Aunt Denise saw what was happening early on and helped me put some strategies in place, and that benefited my wolf, too. It was hard to learn how to create lists, avoid procrastinating, manage my time, and keep distractions to a minimum, but I found my day went so much better if I had a firm schedule, dealt with things as they cropped up, set alarms on my phone, and kept my office clean and free of toys and stuff.

Thank the Goddess, Sid bought into it. Lists, timers, mindfulness routines - he loved it all and was always eager to help me stay on track.

Just like now.

Are we where we're supposed to be? he chirped.

I pulled out my wallet and extracted the index card I was using for today. I'd tried keeping lists on my phone before, but I inevitably started playing a game or went down a rabbit hole on the internet and didn't follow the list, anyway. A piece of paper worked best for me.

"Okay, it's noon now," I told him. "We pick Posy up in an hour, so I set an alarm on my phone for 12:45."

Then what?

"Bup-ba-baah!" I tried to imitate a trumpet. "She picks our first adventure!"

Yes! Can we play with Lark sometime, too?

"Of course!"

Sid was hopping around in my head and yipping as Mase strolled in my office and looked at the cards spread out on my desk. Jay and I had printed all the choices out on card stock, cut them apart, and glued them on the backs of playing cards. After we discarded the extra cards, they fit right back in the deck box.

"You sure about a 'choose your own adventure' date?" Mase asked. "There's no schedule, and loads of opportunities for you to get distracted."

"I can do it," I assured him. "Besides, a schedule doesn't matter, does it? The whole point is to be spontaneous. The only thing I need to be on time for is the riding lesson tomorrow morning. I already got the guest house key so we can show up whenever and won't trouble Angel Bel Aire."

"All right. Good job." He nodded and smiled. "Set an alarm for 5:30 tonight, though, so you remember to feed her dinner."

"Dude! Good idea! I already have one set for 7:30 a.m. tomorrow so we're not late for our riding lesson at 8."

As I took out my phone and added another alarm, Mase checked out the cards.

"Looks like you and Jay came up with a good variety, but how are you going to keep the restaurant cards separate from the activities cards?" he asked.

"Ooh! Jay had a great idea to keep them sorted!" I explained and showed him. "All the heart cards are restaurants for tonight, the spades are 'restful' activities, the diamonds are high-energy activities, and the clubs are middle of the road."

"Perfect. Very creative. I'm sure you two will have a great time."

"Thanks, Mase."

He nodded and left after making sure I was tracking when to pick up our girl, and I grinned as I pocketed my phone.

I love my brothers, I thought happily as I put the cards back in the box. *Even though we get mad at each other, we always have each others' backs.*

You should tell them every once in a while, Sid told me. *You hardly ever do. None of you do, unless something bad happens. 'I love you' is for good and happy times, too, right?*

Right, buddy. We don't, but we should. So I opened the alpha link and chirped, *I love you, my dudes! You're the best brothers in the whole world!*

I love you, too, brother, Jay linked back immediately like he almost always did.

Wuv oo, too, brudder, Wyatt sing-sang in a baby voice a second later.

Love you, Cole grunted and sent me an image of him flipping Emerson during practice, and I laughed at the beta's disgruntled face.

A thud came from across the hall, and Mase stuck his head around my office door a moment later.

"Is everything okay?"

"Yep!" I grinned at him. "Just happy. I love you, man. I don't say it enough."

With a smile, he came over and laid his hand on the top of my head, but knew better than to noogie me. Last time he did, I was ten and Aunt Denise had to cut a huge mat out of my curls. Going to school the next day was *not* fun, and I'd come home with bloody fists and a sour mood.

"Love you, too, Ash. Okay, I need to head out now. Tristan's on his way over to man the office since you're leaving soon, too."

"Where are you going?" I asked, unaware there was something pending.

"Matthew linked me a minute ago and said old man Oberon's raising a fuss about something killing his goats and he can't smell what it is. Matthew was going to deal with it, but I need some fresh air, so I told him I'd take care of it."

"Oberon West? He lives out near the Bel Aire farm." I frowned. "Let me know what you find out since Posy and I will be there tonight and tomorrow morning."

"Of course. Don't want anything dangerous in our girl's vicinity."

"Yeah, that, too." I shrugged and grinned. "I meant, I'd be around if you needed help killing it. Be careful. Oberon's so old, dude couldn't smell his own outhouse anymore, so it could be anything."

He chuckled, then told me to worry more about keeping our girl safe. We did our bro hug and he left - just in time for Jay to link me.

I'm taking our mate to the park. We're going to grab some subs for lunch, then Lark wants to chase the ducks.

Sounds good, dude. See you soon!

Shooting my arms up into the air, I did a happy wiggle, but then stood up fast when my chair creaked.

"Stupid thing. It's not even six months old!" I grouched.

Then again, I had to admit that my chairs never lasted very long. They just couldn't take my weight squirming around on them when I got excited.

You need an iron chair like on that show, Sid said, his eyes wide and earnest. *You know, that big chair the king sits on.*

It's called a throne, I told him.

Yeah, but don't get it made of swords. One, it would be cold and, two, you'd poke your butt.

Giggling at him, I decided we'd head out for lunch, too. I made sure I had my keys and my phone, then ducked my head to walk out of my office.

The cards, Ashy! Sid bellowed before I got three steps.

"Right!"

Spinning, I rushed back to my office, forgot to duck, and slammed my head into the wall above the door.

"Owie!" I screeched as I staggered back a step.

You have done that forty-seven times since we built the alpha offices, Sid stated ever so matter-of-factly, ignoring the little birds flying around my head and the way I was trying to uncross my eyes. *You so dumb, Ashy! Just let Wyatt fix the door already!*

"Sid," I groaned. "Pretty sure I'm concussed. Can you heal me first and lecture later?"

He rolled his eyes, but jolted me with healing.

"Thanks, buddy," I muttered and ran back into my office, swiped the deck of cards off my desk, and raced back out. In my excitement and hurry, I forgot to duck again.

"Ow, ow, owie!"

Make that forty-eight.

#

I found Jay asleep under a tree by the nature trail with Lark curled up next to him on our old picnic blanket. She was lying on her stuffed toy, but a tennis ball was by her snout, and my eyes lit up.

Does she like to play ball?! I asked Sid, working hard to restrain myself from waking the little pup.

Sure. Who doesn't like a ball? Except the party pooper. Sid dropped his voice to mimic Quartz's deep, rough one. *'I'm an alpha wolf. I don't play with dog toys. Growl, growl.'*

Watch it, pup, Quartz rumbled in a sleepy voice.

I grinned, and Sid tittered.

Q in a good mood, Ashy! Sid yipped, and I agreed with a grin.

Seeing as Jay and Lark were both asleep, I spun on my heel, ran back to my SUV, and grabbed the bag I'd packed for her. A couple of people shot me weird looks as I raced past them, but I was used to that. My height always attracted attention. It was like a car wreck: None of anyone else's business, but everyone wanted to stare.

And I *was* moving pretty fast, outstripping joggers and even one guy who was sprinting. As I drew level with him, he gave me a startled look.

"Hey." I jerked my chin up in acknowledgement.

"Duuude!" he gasped as sweat poured down his face and his chest heaved. "How are ... you not ... dying?"

Well, I'm a werewolf, I thought to myself, but, "Super intense cardio training," I told him instead.

Maybe with mate in bed, Sid snickered, and I giggled.

When we got back, Jay was still asleep, but Lark was awake. She had crept out from under Jay's arm and now pushed the ball with her front feet, her upper body bent low to the ground and her tail up and wagging.

"Hi, my little doll!" I said as I slid to a halt a few feet from her. "I'm so happy to see you!"

Hello, she said in a timid voice and hunched up a bit. *Posy still sleeping.*

That's okay. I like being with you, I assured her, and she perked up again.

"You want to play, little doll?" Dropping the bag I'd fetched, I grabbed the ball and held it up. "You want me to throw it for you?"

She nodded, and her silvery eyes were lively as they fixed on the tennis ball.

Yes, please!

Not too far, Ashy, Sid warned me. *My darling's legs are little.*

All of her is little, buddy, I chuckled.

I tossed the ball about twenty feet away and Lark took off after it, her back feet digging into the grass before she launched herself forward, and I squealed at her cuteness.

"Wha? Was wrong?" Jay slurred, sitting up in a hurry and blinking blearily.

"Dude! How late did you keep our girl up?" I noogied his head, messing his hair up even more than it already was.

"Woke up too early, then had trouble falling back to sleep," he mumbled and swatted my hand away. "Didn't help that my wolf was feeling frisky."

"Getting laid is worth a little lost sleep, isn't it, Q?"

Damn right, Quartz smirked. *Makes me feel downright mellow. Appreciate it while it lasts, Jayden. I'm sure something will piss me off and restore my usual bad humor soon enough.*

"Yeah, yeah," Jayden yawned and stretched his arms out.

I laughed at their banter and hunkered down as Lark brought the ball back to me.

"Can I hold you, little doll?"

She woofed at me and dropped the ball to smile at me, and I smiled back. Scooping her up in my arms, I turned her on her back and held her like a baby.

"You're so stinking cute! You know that?" I cooed at her and touched my nose to hers.

Her little pink tongue darted out and licked my nostril, which tickled and made me laugh.

"Well, I can see you two are set and don't need me third-wheeling." Jay got to his feet. "Want me to leave the blanket?"

"Sure, dude, or you can stay and finish your nap. It doesn't bother us, does it, little doll?" I rubbed my cheek against her soft fur. "We like spending time with our brothers, too."

"Thanks, man, but I gotta get going. Mase wants me to join him down at Oberon's in case he needs Quartz. He thinks it might be a couple of bears."

78

"You think it's Marlon? The shifter you rescued from the prison? I thought he went up into the national park." I frowned and tore my eyes away from Lark's to look at Jay. "Why would he come down from the mountains in high summer?"

"Naw, dude. A *real* bear or two. Mase and Garnet would recognize Marlon's scent if it were him, but neither of them sense any kind of shifter."

"Well, happy hunting. We're going to stay here and play." I turned my gaze back to Lark. "Is that okay with you, little doll?"

Yes, yes, yes! she yelped cheerfully, which made Sid bounce around with glee.

If Jay stayed, I could let Sid out to play with her, which would be awesome, but he got to do that all the time. It was *my* turn to hang out with her, and I was going to enjoy every second of it.

"You brought an outfit for Posy to wear after she shifts, right?" Jay asked. "And the deck of cards?"

"I brought *such* a pretty outfit for Posy to wear, and Sid made sure I had the cards." I shifted Lark to lay her head in the center of my chest so I could cuddle her. "I got alarms set on my phone, and I checked in with Angel Bel Aire to make sure everything was set for tonight and tomorrow."

"Great. Then I'll leave you to it. Have fun." He came closer and dropped a kiss on the top of Lark's fuzzy head. "Love you both."

"I love you, too, dude!" I grinned, my heart ready to burst.

"I *meant* Posy and Lark," he chortled, "but yeah. You, too, brother."

He punched my bicep lightly, then took off.

"And now there's just you and me, pretty little doll," I crooned. "We are going to have so much fun!"

Yes, yes, yes! she chirped, and her tail wagged against my stomach, tickling me and making me giggle again.

I am so happy, Ashy! Sid yodeled. *It's a happy day!*

Yeah, it is, buddy. It really is.

\#

Posy

Ash and Lark played for a good two hours before she flopped onto her side and fell asleep, much to his amusement.

He carried her, the picnic blanket, and a cloth bag to the park's family bathroom and left me to shift. I did and found that he'd brought me a darling little outfit of a blue and white striped shirt, a pair of white overall shorts, and my favorite pink slip-on sandals.

Wyatt called them the Pepto Bismol Shoes, but I loved them. Not only were they cute, they were comfy.

And, cherry on top, Ash was wearing a matching outfit! The only difference was, that instead of overalls, he had on white shorts. Even his slides were "Pepto" pink, and I jumped up and down with a squeal when I realized we were twinning.

He combed my hair and did it up in half-braids, which looked super cute, then took a bunch of selfies of us as we did goofy poses around the park.

"And now, princess, it's time for you to choose your own adventure!" he chirped.

Explaining how our date was going to work, he pulled out a box of playing cards, and I was *so* excited to see what Lady Luck had in store for us!

The first card I pulled out was for skateboarding. I was a little nervous when we got there and I saw so many concrete shapes. All I could foresee was a dozen scrapes and bruises. Ash came prepared, though. The back of his SUV was packed with every supply imaginable.

He dug out a cloth bag that held a purple helmet and matching knee and elbow pads. My skateboard, he was proud to show me, had beautiful flowers all over the bottom including several pansies, and I knew he'd had it custom made for me.

"We don't have to stay forever at any of these places," he said. "We can go whenever you get tired or bored."

"Is skateboarding something you really like to do? And I don't mind learning something new. It looks like a lot of fun, although I probably won't be any good at it."

"Cupcake, you are going to kill it! All you really need to have is good balance. And, yes, I like skateboarding. Any sports really. In high school, Wyatt and I were co-captains of the football team, and I was the quarterback. I was also the captain of the basketball team while he was the captain of the wrestling team."

"Make sense," I laughed. "You both are so active and athletic, it's no surprise."

He got me into the safety gear, gave me a few quick pointers, and held my hand as I stepped on the skateboard. He was right about the balance. Once I got the hang of it, it wasn't that hard to stay on. I figured out how to make it go, too, and he praised me to no end.

"All right," I told him after about half an hour, "now let me see you do some tricks. I can tell you're busting to, and I assume that's what all these funny concrete shapes are about."

He laughed and said they were. Then he amazed me with some of the things he could do, zooming down one steep bowl and going out the other side, catching the rim with one hand and keeping the board on his feet to come back down. He really was the most

80

athletic guy I ever met. He wasn't even breathing hard when he came back to me with a huge grin on his face.

We spent another half an hour there as he did a few more tricks, then we decided it was time to try something else. This time, I drew the arcade card. I had no idea what an arcade was, and he jumped out of his shoes in his excitement to show me.

No, he *actually* did, his slides flying across the grass, and Lark and I cracked up as he ran after them.

I enjoyed the arcade a lot. Not the video games so much, although I didn't do too badly at the original Super Mario Bros. I liked skee ball, and the air hockey table quickly became my favorite. I even managed to score a couple times against him! Both times my puck slammed into his goal, his fists shot up to the sky and he shouted, "Yes!" Then he picked me up and spun me around.

"Ash! I scored against you!" I giggled. "Why are *you* celebrating?"

"Because you're doing great! And it makes me happier to see you successful than myself."

"Aww!" My eyes teared up and I threw my arms around him, making his broad chest rumble with laughter.

We could have easily stayed there the rest of the day, blowing through his cash, but I'd tried all the games I wanted to and was curious to see what other adventures he'd thought of.

The next card I drew was go-karts, and after he explained to me what they were, I reminded him that I didn't know how to drive.

"Oh, yeah! Wyatt and I are dying to teach you!" His eyes gleamed brighter than they had all day. "I mean, you don't really need to learn how since there are so many others willing to drive you at any time, but it's a good skill to have in case of an emergency or to just make you feel independent. And it's fun!"

So we agreed to put go-karts back in the deck box for now, and I pulled out mini golf.

"I've actually done this one!" I grinned up at him. "Once, when I was small, Mom took me and my brothers to the Chicken Hut for Aiden's birthday. The final hole was an enormous rooster who went 'Cock-a-doodle-doo!' if you scored a hole-in-one. I remember James did, and I laughed so hard, I fell over."

"You were probably adorable! I bet the club was bigger than you!" Ash teased and I glared up at him, which made him giggle. "Well, we don't have a course in our territory, but there are a couple in the human city. We're not too far away from one that has a theme of outer space. The last hole is a rocket ship that blasts off if you get a hole-in-one."

I told him it sounded perfect, and we headed there next. The course was set up inside a small park that also had a playground and sand pit, picnic tables and pavilions, and a walking trail.

"Ooh! Can we go on the swings afterwards?" I asked as we walked past the playground.

"Anything you want, my darling cupcake."

Ash paid at a little hut shaped like a space rock, and the clerk handed us two golf clubs, two balls, a score card, and a stubby pencil. The club looked like a child's toy in Ash's enormous hands, making me giggle.

The boy really was a giant. He actually got on his knees to try the first hole, which featured a green alien with a ray gun, but still managed to score a hole in one.

I pouted a little. It had taken me three shots.

"Don't be sad, baby. You played one time in your life, and that was years ago, right?" He patted me on top of my head. "You'll get there, cupcake."

"Waffle!" I whined and swatted his hand away. "You'll mess up my hair!"

Before he could reply, I heard someone scream, "Luna!" and turned in time to be engulfed in Thoreau's bear hug.

Archer, Wayne, and Spring trotted after him. Archer juggled three clubs, three balls, and the scorecard while Wayne had the pencil behind his ear and his hands in his pockets.

"Careful, Reau," Ash told him right as Archer grumbled, "I told you not to run, Reau."

Ignoring them both, Thoreau and I hugged each other, smashing our cheeks together as we grinned at them.

"What are you guys doing here?" Ash asked as he fist-bumped the other two boys, then patted Spring's back.

"Just hanging out," Wayne said with a shrug.

I waited until Thoreau set me on my feet before asking the trio if they wanted to join us. The course was empty except for a couple of groups far ahead of us, and no one was waiting in line to come after us, so it wasn't like they would be cutting ahead or holding anyone up.

The three boys' eyes clouded up as they linked each other, and I took the opportunity to greet Spring. Standing in front of him, his nose was nearly level with my chest.

"Hello, Spring," I murmured. "How are things working out?"

Lovely to see you, luna, and perfect. I could not have asked for a better second chance. Reau is so easy to love, although he needs a lot of protecting! He finds trouble everywhere he goes!

I bet he does! I laughed. *Especially with these two pranksters at his side. How's it going with the other wolves?*

I'm getting along splendidly with Firth and Ocean, which is good because all Reau wants to do is be with Archer and Wayne.

Spring smiled up at me and wagged his tail, and I grinned as I scratched under his chin.

Can I ask you a personal question? You don't have to answer if you don't want to, I said.

What is it, luna?

Why did you accept Reau as your human?

Spring tilted his head and his amber eyes glimmered with some emotion I couldn't name.

It's true that there is no one else who can understand our pain, but it was more than that. I could not bear to know that such a cute, innocent pup had suffered so much pain and sorrow in his short years. Something in my heart told me to protect him and love him, and I have never regretted listening to my heart.

My bottom lip wobbling, I wrapped my arms around his neck and buried my face in his ruff.

"You're a good wolf, Spring," I murmured.

"He's *my* good wolf, luna." Thoreau gently put his hands on my shoulders and moved me so he could take my place. "*My* wolfie."

Yes, yes. All yours, you jealous boy, Spring told him in a gentle tone and nuzzled Thoreau's cheek.

"Sure, we'll join you," Wayne said as Thoreau giggled.

"We are on a *date*, dude." Ash rolled his eyes and cuffed Wayne's shoulder.

"She asked us!"

"You should have been smart and said no, little bro."

"I wouldn't have asked if I didn't want them to join us," I told Ash and rolled my eyes. "It's fine."

"*You* may be fine with it," Ash grumbled, and I elbowed him hard in the ribs. He grunted and rubbed his sore side with one hand. "Owie! Your elbows are as sharp as razor blades!"

"Hush, you giant waffle!" I hissed.

Thoreau burst out into loud giggles, then pointed at Ash and yelled "Giant waffle!"

"Calm down," Wayne murmured as he put his arm around Thoreau's shoulders. "You're getting too loud and excited."

"Sorry, Way-Way," Thoreau mumbled and hid his face in Wayne's chest.

"You're all right. Ready to play golf with Ash and Posy?"

"Yes, please!" Thoreau chirped, looking up with an angelic smile and sparkling eyes.

I think Wayne just melted into a puddle, Ash linked me with a smirk.

Who wouldn't? I giggled. *I mean, look at that face!*

We had a great time together, and I was interested in studying the younger boys' relationship. It was obvious to me that they cared deeply for each other, and I was fairly certain it wasn't as brothers. I only wanted them to be happy, though, and they clearly found their happiness in each other.

We were approaching the seventeenth hole when a chipmunk scampered over and stopped in the green. It stared right at us, twitching its whiskers, and Thoreau giggled and clapped his hands.

"Chippy!"

He tried to creep up to it, probably wanting to pet it. Naturally, it took off, and Thoreau ran after it.

"Don't run, Reau!" Archer shouted with a frown. "You're going to trip—"

And of course Thoreau, who was moving at his usual top speed, tripped at that moment and went down hard. Throwing his hands out in front of him, he tore his palms and knees up on the rough concrete walkway and cried out in pain.

We sprinted over to him, and Wayne helped him sit up as Spring sniffed all over him for further injuries than what we could see. One of Thoreau's thumbs went right in his mouth as big, fat tears rolled down his cheeks. He cried silently, not even whimpering, and I pressed my lips together tightly as I crouched next to him.

His 'mommy daddy' taught him to keep his pain quiet. Just like my stepfather did with me.

A memory flashed through my mind of Alpha Briggs snarling, "Shut up and stop sniveling!" as I laid in a pile of broken bones at his feet and bled on the floor.

I began to shake, and Ash's arms suddenly came around me, swaddling me in his sweet scent. My other mates prodded the mate link, sensing my upset through our bonds, and I quickly assured them I was alright, just disturbed for a moment by a bad memory.

I've got you, Ash whispered in the link. *Whatever you've remembered, it can't hurt you anymore.*

"Can you heal him, luna?" Wayne asked as he held Thoreau and petted his curls.

I blinked and came back to myself, feeling selfish for giving in to dark thoughts when Thoreau was in pain.

"I haven't tried to heal anyone before. I would love to, but I don't know what I'm doing."

"You healed Landry by laying your hands on him," Ash said. "Try that again. I'm pretty sure that will do the trick."

Nodding, I laid a trembling hand on Thoreau's arm. I felt gentle warmth gather around my fingertips where I pressed them to his skin, and his scrapes began to close.

"Good job, baby," Ash whispered in my ear.

Wayne whispered soothing things to his friend until I was done, then Spring licked away the blood. Leaning back into Ash's arms, I gave Thoreau a small smile.

"There. All better."

Archer stood over us with his arms crossed and a scowl on his face, although I couldn't tell if it was from anger or upset.

"How many times have we told you not to run?" he snapped, which only caused tears to fall from Thoreau's eyes again. "If you listened, you wouldn't get hurt so often!"

"Dude," Wayne grumbled. "Chill!"

He got to his feet, then leaned down, picked Thoreau up, and held him like a baby. Still sucking his thumb, Thoreau wrapped his free arm and both legs around Wayne and clung to him.

"Shh, you're okay, Reau. It's just a couple of scrapes," Wayne whispered. "I know it hurt, but luna healed it all up. You're fine now."

Thoreau dug his face more into Wayne's neck and drew in a shuddery breath.

"Chi-Chi is mad at me," he said around his thumb.

"Chi-Chi?" Ash murmured. "Does he mean *you*, Arch?"

"Yeah. He's made up these little nicknames for us." Archer scrubbed the back of his neck with one hand and pink scored across his cheekbones. "I said no to Archie, so that's what he came up with instead."

"And what's your nickname for him?" Ash smirked, and I knew he wasn't going to leave the boy alone about this.

"Don't worry about it," Archer growled, his face looking very much like Cole's when he was getting *angry* angry.

Leave it, Ash, I told him.

Aw, baby, you take all my fun away!

"You should let him know you're not mad at him," I told Archer with a small smile and nodded toward where Wayne was walking around with Thoreau.

"But I am." Archer's brows came down. "He should listen. He's such a—"

"Don't say something in a temper that you'll regret and have to make up for later," I interrupted him.

Oh, he is so much like Cole!

"Yeah, that's how you end up in the doghouse, pup. Trust me on that. I'm trying to work my way of it as we speak," Ash laughed, and

I went to elbow him again, but he caught me and slung me up and over his shoulder. "Besides, it ain't that deep, Arch."

"And he's more upset that you're mad at him than that he got hurt," I called out from where I hung down Ash's back.

I heard Archer take a deep breath and let it out slowly, and Spring snickered as the boy walked over to his friends.

Put me down so I can see! I ordered Ash.

Chuckling, he positioned me to sit on his arm with my legs dangling on either side of his hip.

I want to hold you, cupcake, so this will have to do.

"Fair enough," I said as I watched Archer lay one hand on Thoreau's back and the other on his head.

"Hey, Reau, calm down," Archer murmured. "I'm not mad at you, okay?"

"Yes, you are! I heard you tell luna you were!"

"Yes, I *was* mad, but I'm not anymore, and I was wrong to get mad in the first place." When Thoreau remained silent, Archer sighed and held out his arms. "Wayne, let me have him."

Wayne frowned, but let Archer take Thoreau from him. Thoreau had looked small in Wayne's arms; he looked positively tiny in Archer's. Archer and Wayne were growing taller by the day, and it was clear that Archer was going to share his brother Cole's bearish build.

"Listen, Ash is right. This wasn't anything to get mad about." Archer laid his cheek on top of Thoreau's soft curls and closed his eyes. "It's just, when you get hurt, it hurts me. That's why I tell you not to do things like run around where there are so many things to trip over. I'm trying to keep you safe. Now stop crying, okay, curls?"

"Okay," Thoreau hiccuped. "I am sorry, Chi-Chi. I will listen better."

"Good boy." Archer dropped a kiss on the top of Thoreau's head, and Ash, Spring, and I *aww*ed together in the link.

"*Curls*," Ash snickered. "He called him *curls*!"

"Mmm. I could call you curls, but I like waffle better." I kissed his cheek to distract him, which worked, but at my expense.

"You going to eat your waffle later, baby?" he rumbled and touched his nose to mine. "Because I'm planning to devour every little bit of my cupcake tonight."

"That's disgusting, Ash!" Wayne's whole face twisted in a grimace. "Link that shit instead of saying it out loud."

"Language!" Archer grumbled, laying a hand over Thoreau's ear and keeping the other pressed against his chest. "No profanity around innocent ears!"

"Yes, *Dad*," Wayne sneered. "Goddess, you're being a bitch today, Arch."

"Again with the language!" Archer said impatiently. "Didn't I *just* say—"

"All right, all right! I take it back!" Wayne held up his hands with a grin. "You're not being a bitch today, anyway. You're being a *Cole.*"

And Wayne is so much like Wyatt, I thought with a giggle, watching as Archer's face turned red and his eyes spat fire at Wayne's teasing.

"I like cupcakes *and* waffles," came a little voice from Archer's chest. "Why is that disgusting, Chi-Chi?"

As the rest of us - even Spring - fell over laughing, Archer explained that Wayne was just teasing and ended up promising the boy that they'd go to Roger's later and he could order as many cupcakes and waffles as he wanted.

#

After a delicious dinner of fish and chips, Ash drove us out in the country.

"You haven't had a chance to meet Spero Bel Aire," he said as we bumped along a gravel driveway, "but he owns that pet store you took our wolves to, and his family owns this horse farm. His daughter, Angel, breeds and trains horses for trail riding."

"Maybe we can visit some of the horses! I've never had a chance to pet one, but they're gorgeous!"

"They're larger than they look," he warned me. "You won't get scared?"

"Not if you're with me." I gave him a dimpled smile *and* puppy dog eyes. "Please?"

"We're going horseback riding tomorrow morning," he admitted. "Lesson first, then a trail ride."

"Yes!" I bounced up and down in my seat. "Thank you, thank you! I'm so happy!"

He chuckled as he brought the vehicle to a stop in front of a breathtaking little house straight out of a fairy tale.

"Oh, my word!" I breathed. "I feel like Snow White finding the house of the seven dwarves or something!"

"It is special, isn't it? I was lucky that there was a last-minute cancellation. Otherwise, we'd be at an airBnB or hotel right now. This is the Bel Aire's peak season, and this guest house is usually booked solid a year in advance."

"Well, I'm glad they gave it to you."

"I *paid* to rent it, Posy," he said in a dry tone. "Out of the nose, too, but it's worth every dollar. Let's check out the inside."

He got out of the SUV, came over, and opened my door.

"Can I carry you?" he asked as he held out his arms with a grin.

He asked that every time he opened my door, and I gave him a nod and a smile. I liked being carried by my boys.

"Have you been here before?" I asked him as he walked us up the stone path to the front door.

"No. Mom and Dad came once on a getaway weekend. He recommended it and now I know why. It's a perfect place to bring your love."

He leaned down and kissed me gently, and I sighed into his mouth.

The cottage was absolutely darling, and I could see why it cost a pretty penny to stay here. We toured around the place and ended up, predictably enough, in the master bedroom.

"Want to get a shower with me?" Ash asked while wiggling his eyebrows. "We can get dirty while we get clean."

I blushed, but nodded. I wasn't going to pass up *that* offer. I hadn't showered with any of them yet and, after the show Mason and Cole gave me the other day, I was excited to try it.

So we helped each other undress, with kisses and tickles slowing us down a little, then Ash carried me into the bathroom and sat me on the counter as he got the shower running.

I took the opportunity to survey his amazing body. The muscles in his back flexed and rippled as he moved, and my breath turned sharp and shallow.

Greedily, my eyes roamed his muscular arms, his narrow waist, tight bum and those long, long, *long* legs.

He turned around, and my gaze instantly went *down there*.

"Whatcha looking at, Posy?"

I closed my eyes and blushed, even though I'd done a lot more with *that* than just stare at it.

"Still so innocent?" he chuckled softly. "Quartz is right. We could mate you in every possible position, and you'd still be our innocent cupcake."

Now my face burned like fire.

He came closer, took my hands, and laid my palms on his hard chest. My eyes flew open to meet his dark brown ones.

"You can touch me as much as you want at any time you want." His voice grew gravelly. "I am yours. Utterly and completely."

Since he invited me, I stroked my fingers over every inch of his chest and abs, smiling as he shivered. My hands smoothed over his shoulders, then down his arms. Linking my fingers with his, I pulled him down and kissed him.

"Posy," he murmured against my lips. "I want to love you. Can I?"

"If you don't," I breathed, "I may never forgive you. I want you so much, Ash!"

Chuckling, he kissed my cheek and worked his way down my neck.

"You're our luna." Kiss. "Our mate." Kiss. "Our Posy." Kiss. "Our princess." Kiss. "And I love you."

By then, his mouth was at my breasts, and he took my left nipple in his warm mouth. I arched against him with a moan, his busy tongue exciting me *and* him, if the rumble deep in his throat was anything to go by.

I sank my hands in his curls, careful not to tangle them, and tugged gently. He growled in response, then skimmed his fingers down my spine, leaving a trail of delicate sparks behind. His big hands slid under my bum and lifted me off the counter, then his fingertips tickled my core, sending shudders through my whole body. With a nearly soundless whine, I clung to his shoulders and sawed my thighs together.

"No, no, no, princess," he purred. "Let me."

Holding me against his chest with one arm, he sank a long finger deep inside me. I gasped when his thumb found the right spot and tormented me. When he slipped another finger inside me, a shock wave rippled down my spine, and I shattered into a million pieces with a harsh cry.

"So responsive," he murmured. "You ready, baby?"

I met his dark eyes, which sparked with the same need that burned like a bonfire inside me.

"Yes! Hurry!"

Huffing out a soft laugh, he walked us into the shower. The hot water felt divine, but his hard body felt better. Sliding his hands in my armpits, he lifted me straight up, and I squeaked in surprise.

"So high off the ground," I muttered, throwing my arms around his neck.

"Better hold on tight then, princess," he demanded in a hoarse voice. "Wrap your legs around me, too."

I did, and he slid me down his slick torso, my core riding the ridges of his abs, and I gasped as he sat me on his thick, hard penis.

"Sex in the shower. Wyatt would be disappointed in me for not saying something about getting you wet. I better step up my game."

My face flushed red at both his words and the memory of the sinful things Wyatt liked to whisper in my ear while he was taking me.

"I love your breasts and tight vagina and hot mouth, but I am *obsessed* with your sweet ass." His hands kneaded my bottom as he thrusted in and out of me.

Wyatt's favorite naughty words were pussy and titties, but Ash's words lit me on fire just as much. It must have excited him, too, because he picked up the pace.

His sleek muscles scraped my taut nipples as he bounced me up and down on his hard length, and a loud moan escaped my throat as I overdosed on pleasure. Gripping his wet shoulders, I squeaked when I discovered that arching my back made my nub grind into him.

"Feel good, princess?" he asked.

"Ash!" I cried out, pleasure jolting through me like lightning.

"Yeah, baby. Scream my name as I make you come."

Now *that* was much more Wyatt-like.

Everything inside me tightened, and bright light burst behind my eyelids. He pumped into me a few more times, then dropped his face into my neck with a hoarse groan.

Wave after wave of electric shocks pulsed through my whole body as our chests heaved against each other. When our breathing calmed down, he slowly lowered me back to my feet and kept his hands on me until I had my balance.

Plunking my forehead on his upper abs, I shuddered against him, still trying to catch my breath. As he murmured soft and soothing words of love and caring, he curled one arm around my head and held it to his chest and wrapped the other over my shoulders.

"I love you, Posy," he whispered at last and kissed the top of my head. "So, so much."

"I love you, too."

Washing each other was fun and intense at the same time. His hands were *everywhere* and teased more than helped. Of course, he could probably make the same complaint. By the time we got out and dried off, the moon had risen.

Ash slipped on a pair of boxer briefs, then slid a camisole nightie over my head and tugged the hem down past my hips. Of course, he stopped and squeezed my bum along the way, which made my thighs clench, and I wondered if another round might be in my future before he fell asleep.

"It's dark enough that we can stargaze now," he told me.

"Is that why there are windows in the ceiling above the bed?"

"Yeah." He swept me up in his arms and carried me into the bedroom. "Let's see if we can find Orion."

"Orion?"

"That's about the only constellation I know," he said in a huge yawn.

It was way past my poor boy's bedtime, so I wouldn't be surprised if he knocked out as soon as his head hit the pillow.

"I can walk, Ash," I said. He didn't need to be carrying me when he was sleepy and tired.

"*You can*? Guess I did something wrong," he teased me with a grin, and I buried my hot face in his neck, making him laugh. "Don't worry. If I don't fix that by morning, Cole for sure will tomorrow night. He misses you so much."

"I miss him, too." I admitted as he dropped me on the bed and climbed in next to me. "While it's hard to be away from the others, I liked getting to be with each of you individually."

"Yeah, it feels weird without my brothers here, but every moment with you is precious."

"*You're* precious," I murmured and kissed along his collar bones. As his skin shivered under my lips, I added, "My handsome waffle."

"Handsome *giant* waffle," he corrected. Grabbing my hand, he pressed it to his groin. "Did you forget how giant it is already?!"

Feeling him harden and swell under my fingers, I stroked him the way he liked and hid my smile as he groaned.

"Hmm. Maybe you should remind me," I murmured.

Smirking, he yanked up the hem of my nightie, flipped me to lie flat on my back, opened my knees, and buried his face between my thighs.

"Ash," I whimpered as his lips suctioned onto me.

What? he linked. *I did promise to eat my cupcake all up tonight, didn't I?*

"Ash!" I squirmed as he slipped two fingers into my wet heat while his tongue licked my nub.

Then I'll roll us over and you can ride your handsome giant waffle like a horse. It'll be good practice for tomorrow.

"ASH!"

"Wow! That was fast!" He raised his glistening face to grin at me. "Did it excite you *that much* to think of being my little cowgirl?"

Still panting, I buried my red face in my hands and heard him chuckle as he leapt off the bed. I didn't care much for him leaving me shuddering and alone, but he was back in a few seconds, so I let it go.

Plopping down, he grabbed me and rolled onto his back so I straddled his hips, then plunked something down on my head. Curious, I finally dropped my hands from my face and reached up to find a pretty cowboy hat. It even had pink roses embroidered on it.

"Now that you're properly equipped," he smirked, "saddle up, cowgirl, and ride me till I pass out."

Giggling, I set the hat back on my head and did *exactly* what he wanted.

#

The next morning, I couldn't believe the size of the horse Angel Bel Aire brought out for Ash to ride.

Granted, my boy was a giant, as he proved again and again last night, so I guess his horse needed to be a giant, too. The top of Ash's head was about a foot above the horse's blond mane, while my eyes were on level with its nostrils. I was a little intimidated by it at first, but it was such a gentle creature that I soon warmed up to it and petted its soft, velvety nose.

"His name is Henry," Angel said. "He's a Belgian draft horse."

"What a draft horse?" I asked her.

"The kind that's used for jobs such as pulling wagons and carts or plows on farms. This guy is a great trail horse, though, because he has a gentle temperament and can't be spooked."

She then went on to explain that most horses did not react well to shifters of any kind, and wolves especially set them off.

"Luckily, Henry doesn't care what you are," she laughed. "He likes everyone."

"Good thing, and good thing he's so big," Ash said, petting Henry's face. "I wouldn't want to hurt him because I'm so heavy."

"How much *do* you weigh, alpha?"

"About 325."

My eyebrows shot up. All of my mates were unnecessarily tall compared to me, but I didn't realize they weighed three times as much as me, too.

"That's not a problem for Henry," Angel assured him.

"Will his big boots fit in those holder things?" I giggled. "What size *do* you wear, anyway?"

"Seventeen," he shrugged.

"What size shoes do I wear?" I tilted my head as I stared up at him. He did most of my shopping for me now, and Peri and Queen Lilah had helped me when we went the first time.

"Sixes, cupcake. Tiny little princess feet," he smirked.

"They're called stirrups, luna, and yes, they will," Angel told me. "Now, are you ready to meet *your* horse?"

"Yes, yes, yes!" Clasping my hands under my chin, I tried to keep myself from jumping up and down.

"I think every little kid dreams of riding a horse at some point," Ash said. "I've never been on one, though. I assume you haven't, either?"

"Nope, and I'm happy we're sharing a first!"

Then Angel came out of the barn leading an adorable light brown horse with a pale mane and tail and a white stripe down its face.

"Is that a *pony*?" Ash giggled.

"This is Edgar." Angel walked him over to me, and I saw he was only as tall as I was. "He's a Haflinger, which is a horse, not a pony. He's an old guy, but still game for a nice ride."

As I marveled at his cuteness, Edgar very gently laid his chin on my shoulder, and I stroked the thick tuft of blond hair that fell down the center of his face. Brushing it to the side, I stared into his big, gentle eyes and I knew I could trust this horse.

"He looks like he's wearing a wig," Ash chuckled.

"He's darling!" I grinned and laid my cheek against Edgar's.

"I think he's halfway in love with you already, luna," Angel joked. "Edgar has always been a ladies' man, so it's no surprise."

"Now, listen here, Edgar," Ash pretended to frown, "this little lady is taken."

As if he could understand Ash's words, Edgar lifted his head and stared at him, then made a funny sound with his lips, and I giggled.

Angel went back into the barn and brought out her horse, who she said was named George. He was pale gray with white spots all over and a white mane and tail. He looked like something out of a fairy tale, and I didn't think the name George suited him at all. It should have been something much more elegant.

Angel showed us how to get onto the horses, and I managed to half-pull, half-swing myself into the saddle. Ash and Angel got my boots settled into the stirrups, which Angel adjusted to fit my short legs, and I grabbed the knob thing at the front of my saddle to make sure I didn't fall off.

After we were all mounted, Angel showed us how to hold the reins and what to do with them, and reviewed the verbal commands the horses knew. She also explained how to use our knees to nudge them into motion.

This was the part I had been dreading. I was scared that, when I told the horse to go, it would take off and I wouldn't be able to stop it.

After meeting Edgar, though, I knew that wouldn't happen. For one thing, he was very calm. For another, he seemed content to follow George.

"Edgar and George are a bonded pair," Angel told me when I commented on Edgar following after George. "They've been together nearly all of their lives."

"Aww. That's so sweet. What about Henry?"

"He's a more recent addition to the farm. The other horses get along well with him, so that's good, but he hasn't made any super special friends yet."

"Don't worry, Henry." Ash reached up and scratched his horse behind the ears. "I'm sure you'll find a buddy soon."

Angel gave us a few more directions and tips, corrected our posture a bit, and cautioned us not to lean forward if we went downhill. Then we were off on a short trail ride.

"If you enjoy this," Ash said as we swayed from side to side on the horses' backs, "we can do it again. None of my brothers have ever been on a horse, either."

"Sure! And it's not surprising they haven't if most horses don't tolerate shifters."

"That's our specialty here at Bel Air farms," Angel said. "We find and train horses that shifters can use and enjoy. We get buyers from all around the world because there aren't many who do that."

"Most shifters aren't interested in horses," Ash snorted.

"Well, they should be," I said. "Not only are they beautiful, they're gentle, nice creatures and fun to pet."

"Well, *these* horses are gentle and nice," Ash chuckled.

"Yes," Angel said, "they're trained for trail rides. You don't want an excited, aggressive, or easily spooked horse on a trail ride. Especially not with novice riders."

What is a novice? I asked Ash through the link.

Beginner, he said simply.

As we rode along a path through the woods, I decided I *would* like to do this again with all of my mates. I began to plan a group date when I stopped and wondered if it was a good idea. Just seeing Ash on horseback was enough to make me drool, but all five of them in cowboy hats and boots? Plus seeing them on horses?

I wasn't sure if my heart could take it.

Worry more about you pussy taking it, Lark snickered.

Lark! I hissed in horror as fire tore along my cheeks.

What? You know you all end up naked somewhere before halfway through ride. Good news is, you get another kind of ride.

Stop! I scolded her, although I could hardly deny it, nor was I opposed to the idea.

Just make sure they find shady spot. I no want to heal sunburned butt!

Shush, you bad wolfie!

But that only made her snicker harder.

DEAR POSY,

I AM SO SORRY, PRINCESS! I NEVER MEANT TO CALL YOU STUPID OR STOMP ON YOUR FEELINGS LIKE A JERK OR EMBARRASS YOU IN FRONT OF THE OTHERS. I'M ASHAMED OF MYSELF.

ON THE OTHER HAND, YOU REMINDED US ALL THAT YOU ARE ONE BADASS BITCH, LUNA! AND I COULDN'T HAVE BEEN PROUDER OF YOU! I LOVE YOU MORE AND MORE EACH DAY, CUPCAKE.

IF YOU CAN'T FORGIVE ME, I UNDERSTAND. I SAID A HORRIBLE THING. BUT PLEASE, BABY, PLEASE CONTINUE TO BE PATIENT WITH ME. SOMEDAY, I'LL MAKE YOU PROUD OF ME, TOO.

♥ ASH

6: *Wildflower Prince*

Cole

As I walked into our house shortly before noon, I smelled the rich aroma of freshly baked chocolate chip-cookies, heard the unmistakable sounds of Ash banging Posy in our bedroom, and knew I'd never be able to hold myself back until we got to the cabin.

Who was I kidding? I wasn't even going to last the hour until his date was up.

Dude, I linked him in desperation, *can I at least watch?*

Come join us!

I know there's still time left on your date, I grimaced, *but I can't wait any longer.*

Get up here, bro. I've been dying to take her ass for days now.

Smirking at that, I grew harder the closer I got to our bedroom and could hear her moans and whimpers. When I opened the door, my balls nearly exploded at the sight in front of me.

They lay on their sides facing me, and Ash held her leg up with one hand and had his other arm across her neck to squeeze her opposite shoulder, just like the very first time he mated her. Her tits shook with each of his slow, deliberate thrusts, and I dug my fingernails into my palms to keep from coming.

"Get the lube, dude," Ash rasped.

Yanking the drawer open, I snagged it and hurled it on the bed next to him, then ripped off my clothes and darted over to them. I dropped down in front of Posy and devoured her parted lips, swept my tongue inside her mouth and swallowed her gasp.

Goddess, I missed you, honey! I linked her as I relearned her taste and texture.

Cole, she moaned and ran her hands up and down my abs. *I missed you, too. So much!*

As I kissed her, I slipped my fingers into her dripping pussy to tease her little pearl. I blinked when my fingertips accidentally brushed Ash's dick while he slid in and out of her, but he didn't seem bothered by it, so neither was I.

A few seconds later, our girl pulled her mouth away from mine, tipped her head back against his chest, and came with a harsh cry.

"Ash! Cole!"

Good time to switch, Ash grinned, not breaking his rhythm.

I feel like I'm interrupting your time with her. I mean, did you even come yet?

You're not, and I want to come in her ass this time. He giggled. *If you don't stop touching my dick, though, I'm going to come here and now.*

Just to mess with him, because that's why little brothers existed, I drew my hand from Posy's slick folds, reached down, and fondled his balls. He came immediately, gasping in surprise, then pulled out of her and fell back on the bed with a groan.

With a grin, I sank my aching dick into our girl without missing a stroke in the slow rhythm he'd set - and Ash's whining in the link was the only thing that kept me from coming the second I entered her tight, wet sheath.

You douche! he howled as he draped Posy's leg over my hip and sat up. *I said I wanted to come in her ass!*

I grabbed the back of her knee and pulled her quivering thigh around my waist, then rolled on top of her.

Your stupid dick will be standing back up by the time you have her stretched and you know it, I smirked as I rocked in and out of her. *Thanks for getting her so wet for me, by the way.*

Just remember that's my cum you're dipping in, dude, he smirked back.

Like we all haven't done that *before,* I said, rolling my eyes at him.

Picking up the pace of my thrusts, I dug my face in Posy's throat and sucked on her mate mark, which made her writhe and whimper under me. Unable to go slow any longer, I levered myself up, planted a hand on either side of our girl's head, and hammered into her, savoring the feel of her tight pussy.

I'm surprised you're still going, Ash chuckled as he picked up the lube. *After three days without her, I didn't make it three minutes the first time I mated her last night.*

Learn from the master, little boy, I rumbled.

Little *boy? Ask Posy how 'little' I am, you shaved bear.*

"I love you, Cole," she breathed, unaware of our bantering. "My strong pine tree."

"Love you, too, honey," I panted. "You are my everything."

You need to work on your cardio, you sappy pine tree, Ash snickered.

And you need to work on your stamina, you floppy waffle.

Both Topaz and Sid giggled at us, and a tiny smile tugged up the corners of my lips, too.

Duuuude! Ash whined after three or four minutes. *You have to share, bro!*

I sighed, but I knew I owed the idiot, so I slowed my pace again, rolled us over so I was on my back, and folded Posy's legs to put her bent knees in my armpits. She started to sit up, probably thinking I wanted her to ride me, and I quickly wrapped an arm around the back of her neck and pulled her down on my chest.

"Baby, can you do something for me?"

"What?" she whimpered.

"Reach behind you and spread your cheeks for Ash."

As she did, I held her shoulders to make sure she could support her weight in that position.

How's the view, brother? I asked Ash as he knelt behind her.

Awesome, my dude!

Posy shivered as he began to prep her, and I looked over her shoulder to see him frowning.

Everything okay? I asked them both.

Yes, she whined.

I'm getting a butt plug, Ash muttered. *She's as tense as the first time again!*

You can work up to that conversation, I told him as I closed my eyes and concentrated on plowing our girl at a smooth, steady tempo until he was inside her. *Take your time. I'll keep her distracted and happy.*

Oh, the sacrifice.

Yeah, I'm noble like that, I grinned as he rolled his eyes.

I checked in with Posy to see if she was able to balance herself. When she nodded, I released her shoulders and moved my hands to her breasts to torment her nipples with little twists and tugs. Her breathing picked up again, and she moaned low in her throat as Ash scissored her open.

"Princess, I'm going to enter you now," Ash murmured softly. "Are you good with that?"

"Yes!"

I ground the heels of my hands into her tits as he gently pushed into her back hole, and she gasped before biting her bottom lip, her cheeks rosy red and her eyes squeezed shut.

I linked Ash the image and we grinned at each other.

Thank the Goddess he *was* a giant. He could straddle my legs and Posy's feet and still be at the right height on his knees to pound her ass, which he did with gusto. With her arms occupied, her nipples rubbed up and down my chest, which I liked, but I was worried. This was a different position than when we made 'sandwiches,' and her body was still so thin and fragile. I didn't want to accidentally hurt her while trying to pleasure her.

Before I could link Ash about it, he linked me.

Dude, she'd come if you rubbed her clit a little.

I want her to come with me, and I need just a minute more.

Me, too. Wait for me, and we can all three come together.

"Honey, I'm so close. Ash is, too," I warned her.

"Please," she panted. "Ash, Cole, please!"

Knowing what she wanted, what she *needed*, both of us moved a hand toward her pussy. Ash's beat mine there, though, and he was making *damn* sure his fingers brushed my dick as he furiously rubbed her little pearl.

Bastard.

"Ash! Cole!"

Posy's pussy clamped around my dick, Ash groaned and stilled as he spilled in her ass, and I gave in, too. Clenching her tits roughly, I arched my hips and came hard enough to make my head spin.

#

After another round in the shower, this time just the two of us, I left Posy to dress at her request and went to the kitchen, where I found Ash putting hamburger buns on three plates.

"I see you found the mountain of burgers Jay grilled last night," I chuckled. "Dude was stress cooking or something."

"I guess so!" He opened a pack of cheese slices and began arranging them on the buns. "Where is he, anyway? And the others? Are they coming for lunch? I only put eight burgers in to warm."

"Wyatt's meeting with the border patrol captains, and Mase and Jay found what was causing the ruckus down at Oberon's."

"Was it a pair of bears?"

"Nope." I shook my head. "It was Kon."

"Kon? As in Konstantin Russo? The half thunder dragon? But I dropped him off at the colony!"

"Yes, him! How many other dudes named Kon do you know?" I grumped. "Anyway, he ran away. He said the other dragons were bullying him for being a half breed. Also, the matriarch told him he would have to mate with her to prove he was worthy of a Goddess-given mate. "

"Damn, dude! I would have run away, too." Ash looked at me with stunned eyes. "He's just a kid. Can you imagine hearing your luna tell you that at— How old did Gelo say his age equaled out to? Fifteen?"

"Seventeen," I corrected Ash.

As a half dragon, Konstantin aged slower than humans, but faster than dragons. Angelo figured it was about one year for every two. So while he'd been *alive* 35 years, Konstantin was only a teenager mentally and emotionally. Because of his years lived, we'd decided to put him in the pack house instead of the orphanage, and now I wondered if that was a mistake. Still, he'd be 36 - or 18 - next spring, so I guess it didn't matter all that much in the long run.

"So he ran back here and camped out in the woods?" Ash asked.

"Pretty much. He got hungry enough yesterday to pick off a couple of Oberon's goats, or we never would have found out. Or at least not for a while." I smiled and shook my head. "He's an honorable kid, I have to say. He offered to work off the cost of the goats before Mase or Jay could even bring that up."

"I don't want to be the one to tell Posy he's been hiding in the woods and living off goats," Ash muttered as he reached for a tomato to slice up for our girl's burger.

"You think *I* want to tell her?" I raised my eyebrows at him.

"Tell me what?" asked our girl as she swept into the kitchen wearing a pretty red dress.

Speak of the luna and she shall appear.

Dodging the towel wrapped around her head, I scooped her against my chest, burying my face in her throat to inhale my favorite smell in the whole world while I squeezed her tight. We'd been apart for far too many days, and two brief sessions of mating barely calmed me down.

I couldn't say how long I stood there holding her, but the rumbling of her stomach persuaded me to put her down, and even then I held her on my lap as we ate our cheeseburgers.

"What were you two talking about?" she asked after she daintily piled tomato slices on hers, much to my disgust.

"Guess what, cupcake?" Ash chirped.

"What?"

"Kon's back!"

"Yay!" She grinned, but it quickly turned into a puzzled frown. "Wait. What about the colony?"

"It didn't work out so well," Ash hedged.

"What happened?" she demanded.

Ash shrugged, then looked at me.

"The matriarch was a jerk," I summed up, "and the other dragons were mean to him because he isn't a pure dragon."

She gasped and covered her mouth with her hands.

"He's fine. He's with Mase and Jay right now," I assured her.

Pulling her hands down, I nudged her plate closer to her, encouraging her to finish eating. She picked up her burger again, but narrowed her eyes at us.

Ash and I both knew what was coming and sighed in unison.

"Well, I hope you know he's staying with us forever now. I gave you a chance to find him a home - against my gut instinct, might I add - and it didn't work. We may not be dragons, but we have witches to help us know how to care for him."

100

"Where will he live? The pack house isn't the right place, nor is the O," Ash pointed out before I could. "And him living alone in Tristan's apartment isn't ideal, either."

"*And* we have another problem," I said, "Mase and Jay got him to open up a little more last night. Seems he's having trouble controlling his dragon side."

"What's going on with his dragon side?" Ash wanted to know.

"Does he have a completely independent dragon spirit like we do with our wolves?" Posy asked.

"Yes," I answered our mate first. "His dragon's name is Chime Karma, and he needs to consume magic. Not a lot or very often, but some. To keep it simple, he's starving, which makes it hard for Kon to control him."

As we talked more about it, I cleared away our lunch remains while Ash unwrapped Posy's hair from the towel and started to brush it out. Her eyes were far away, and I didn't think it was all from the pleasure of having him comb her hair. As she thought, she tapped her chin with her forefinger, which was the cutest thing ever and always made my heart flip when she did it.

"Does it matter if it's dark or light magic?" She finally focused her pretty blue eyes on me.

"According to him, no. Why?"

"Is he still with Mason and Jayden?"

"Yes," was all I said, not wanting to tell her they couldn't convince him to leave the little stick shelter he built out in the woods.

"I think I have a solution. Do you mind if we take a few minutes and deal with this before we leave for our date? Or are we on a time schedule?"

"No, honey, it's fine. We don't need to be anywhere by a certain time. Besides, I have all the patience in the world for you."

Yeah, now that you're not sexually deprived, Ash smirked.

Sure, now that you've had her pussy, Topaz said at the same time.

Shut up, I growled at them both, making them giggle.

"Cole, you link Mason and Jayden to bring Kon here. Ash, you link the witches and see which of them is free to join us."

"Which witch. Aye-aye, captain." Ash fake-saluted her.

"And who are *you* going to link, little luna?" I asked.

"Angelo. I need to ask him a few questions."

#

Posy

It didn't take long for Mason and Jayden to arrive with Konstantin in tow.

101

My mates squashed me between them in a hug and showered my face with kisses, making me giggle, then I made them put me down so I could greet our guest.

"Hi, Kon! Welcome back!" I waved and smiled at him. "Do you think I could meet your dragon? Please, Kon? I will be super respectful, I promise. Pretty please?"

"You are always that, Luna Posy," he laughed, "and yes. He would like to meet all of you, too. He'd *need* to, anyway, before he'd accept you as his keepers."

"Keepers?"

"That's how dragons view their leaders as they're the ones who keep them in check."

"Do you want us as your keepers?" I asked him. "Or do you want us to try and find you another colony? We're happy so long as you're happy. We'd love for you to stay with us, but we want to do what's best for you."

"Then I'd like to stay, luna." He scratched the back of his neck and looked at the ground, then whispered, "If I'm not too much trouble."

Oh. My heart.

Smiling sadly, I held my arms out in invitation, and he hesitated only a second before he leaned down and hugged me gently.

"I'm surprised the alphas aren't growling at me," he murmured in my ear as he awkwardly patted my back.

"They see you as a pup. Don't try this next year, though."

Leaning back, I studied his face and winced at the deep well of sadness in his eyes.

Wasn't it enough that his colony was wiped out by the sickness and he'd had to survive as best he could for the past six years? Did he have to be captured and imprisoned by maniac humans, too? *And* be rejected by the dragons at the new colony?

Strength is what we gain from the madness we survive, Lark murmured.

That's pretty deep, wolfie.

I not make it up. It something Coal, Ranger's wolf, told me.

I need to get that printed on a t-shirt, I muttered. *It could be our pack motto.*

"So you want to meet Chime Karma right now?" Konstantin asked as he dropped his arms and stepped back.

"Yes, yes, yes!" I bounced up and down on my toes.

"You won't be scared, right?" He raised one eyebrow. "He *is* a thunder dragon."

"No. Amazed, maybe, but not scared. I promise."

102

Cole hooked an arm around my waist and pulled me into his side when Konstantin's eyes turned white as his dragon ascended.

"That's not creepy or anything," Jayden muttered, and Ash giggled.

Then the most amazing creature stood before us unlike anything I'd ever seen or imagined. He didn't look like what I thought a dragon would - a lizardish thing with huge flapping wings and spikes. Instead, Chime Karma looked like a twelve-foot-long snake with four legs and clawed feet. His triangular head had a thick mane of fur that ran down his back and ended in a bushy tail, and long tufts of hair grew like mustaches on either side of his snout. He was all white - as white as lightning - except for his golden antlers and black nose, and I had never seen anything more breathtaking in my life.

"I am Chime Karma," a deep voice rumbled.

"Hello," Mason said formally. "I am Mason Price, one of the alphas of Five Fangs, and this is our luna, Posy Everleigh."

Cole, Jayden, and Ash also introduced themselves, then Chime Karma nodded his head.

"As with you and your wolves, what my boy knows, I know," he said, "but thank you for officially introducing yourselves."

"Oh, you're so handsome! I wish I had a better vocabulary because handsome doesn't do you justice," I whispered, clasping my hands under my chin. "My heart's beating so fast just looking at you!"

"Hey, now," Cole said in my ear.

Mason growled, and Ash and Jayden both frowned. I rolled my eyes at them, then grinned.

"Oh, come on, Mr. Jellies, I don't mean it that way and you all know it. Tell me that you can look at Chime Karma and not be amazed at his beauty."

"Thank you," the dragon chuckled, a tiny boom at the end of each word, and I wondered how he would sound if he ever lost his temper.

Deafening, Lark said with big eyes. *Like being in thundercloud itself during a big storm!*

"Luna, alphas, Kon and I are happy to join your pack if you will permit this." Chime Karma nodded his head, making his fluffy mane stir like tall grass in the wind. "However, we have one concern that my boy has already voiced."

"Yes, we are aware of your dietary needs," Cole said, "and our luna has a suggestion."

Right then, a tiny, light green car came flying up the driveway a little too fast and swerved a bit before sliding untidily into a spot in the parking lot.

"Oh, my Goddess," Cole said from the side of his mouth, "Matthew did it. He bought Maria a car."

"Have mercy," Jayden murmured. "A Fiat, too."

"She'll have it wrecked in a week," Ash added. "Do birds heal as well and fast as wolves?"

"Angelo's going to kill him." Mason shook his head and raised his eyebrows.

I giggled as I watched Maria tumble out of the car. She had leaves and flowers tangled in her messy hair and no shoes on. Her eyes shimmering with excitement, she skipped up to us only to trip over nothing. Fortunately, Ash snagged her with one long arm before she could land in a sprawl at the dragon's clawed front feet, and she smiled her thanks up at him.

"Hi! I'm Maria!" she told Chime Karma. "I'm an air witch and mated to Beta Matthew Rose. My coven is building a shop just outside of pack territory. Would you be interested in a job as either our guardian or our magic clean-up and disposal unit or both?"

The dragon grinned, his sharp white teeth on display.

"Maria, I am all ears."

As they began to hash out details and terms, Cole squeezed me in a tight hug and grinned.

"Great idea, honey. Our girl is so smart."

"I think it's more about common sense," I disagreed with a blush.

"Common sense isn't so common, you know," he laughed. "Practicality is an excellent trait for a luna to have and, thankfully, you have loads of it."

A tiny smile flitted across my lips as I hid my face in the center of his chest. I didn't think I'd ever get used to being complimented.

"You're so cute when you're acting shy," he whispered as he kissed the top of my head. "Now, my love, how about we say goodbye to everyone and start our date?"

"Oh, yes!" I raised my head to grin up at him. "I'm so excited to spend one-on-one time with you."

"Me, too, baby, and I think you're going to love where we're going."

"Then what are we waiting for?" I jumped up and down in his arms. "Let's go!"

#

Cole's SUV swayed from side to side a little alarmingly, but we were creeping along the dirt road at such a slow speed that I knew he was fully in control of the vehicle.

"Almost there, honey," he told me. "Just around this next corner."

Curious about why we'd driven so high into the mountains, I eagerly leaned forward and watched to see what secret was about to be revealed.

And I wasn't disappointed when we turned that corner and I saw an amazing log and stone cabin perched on the edge of a lake. The dark brown metal roof gleamed in the sun and inviting chairs awaited us on the deck built over the water.

"Oh, Cole, it's incredible!" I covered my mouth with my hands, then dropped them to ask, "Is it yours?"

"Jay's grandpa had it built for his grandma. We spent every summer of our childhood here with all the families. The parents still bring the younger ones up after school lets out, then again over spring break."

He paused and drew in a deep breath before letting it out slowly, his whole body seeming to loosen up the closer we got to the cabin.

"Mase and I haven't been here for a couple of years, though," he said in a soft, quiet voice. "It's like coming home again."

"Then I'm glad you're here, and that you brought me along. Let's sneak up here - all six of us - sometime, even if it's only for a long weekend or overnight."

"Yeah, I'm sure Mase misses it just as much as I do. Maybe during the winter, huh? It's so pretty up here with the snow on the trees. Plus, the lake freezes over and we can go ice skating."

As he rambled, I heard his words, and one part of my brain was even *listening* to them, but mostly I was too busy absorbing this side of Cole. I never realized how tense he was most of the time until I saw him like this, and I loved that he was relaxing.

After he parked, he got out and was at my door before I got my seat belt unbuckled. Then he lifted me up by my waist and set me on my feet. Holding my hand, he led me up a flagstone path to a pair of French doors.

"Welcome to Pippi's Place," he said as he threw them open and waved me inside.

"Was that Jayden's grandma's name?"

"Yep. And we've always called it that. Or just the cabin. Goddess, I can remember coming through that door and smelling all kinds of cakes and cookies baking in the oven. Pippi was always feeding us homemade goodies. She used to say that feeding boys was like filling a silo; neither were ever full."

I didn't know what a silo was, so some of the expression was lost on me, but I got the gist of it and smiled to know yet more facts about my mates.

He took me on a quick tour of the massive living room with its stone fireplace and arching ceiling. We went into the kitchen, which was outfitted with black cabinets and a big old stove that looked straight out of *Little House on the Prairie*, but he assured me it was a modern gas stove.

"We replaced all the appliances and updated the electricity and plumbing," he said. "We tried to keep Pippi's style as much as possible, and Wyatt insisted this was the right stove. I have to say, it really does make the kitchen come together, doesn't it?"

"He has a great eye," I agreed. "It's the artist in him."

When we got upstairs, Cole had me stick my head in the guest rooms. They weren't huge, but each was done up in a different theme, which I thought was cute. Then he led me into the master bedroom, and it looked just the way I expected it to: An enormous bed the size of ours at home, two big windows showcasing the mountain scenery, a stone fireplace, comfy chairs, and another set of French doors leading out onto a balcony.

"It's so pretty! I love it." I whirled around to tell him and he caught me in his arms.

Picking me up, he tossed me onto the bed and I bounced before he followed me down.

"It *is* pretty," he agreed as he laid next to me. "I'm glad you like it. The cabin is one of my favorite places to be."

"And this is one of *my* favorite places to be," I teased him as I wrapped my arms around his neck and pulled him down on top of me.

He laughed and hugged me, then propped himself up on one elbow.

"I have something for you. Wait here."

My heart rate picked up, knowing it was probably his sorry card. I felt bad for a moment. I didn't need them to keep apologizing, but I *did* like seeing the cards they'd created and reading their special words.

"Here, honey."

Cole held out a white envelope. Sitting up, I propped a few of the dozen pillows behind me - probably Wyatt's doing; that boy *loved* pillows - and accepted his card.

Once I got it out of the envelope, my jaw fell.

"Oh, my! This is so pretty!" Then I opened it, and my jaw fell further. "And your handwriting is beautiful! This is cursive, right? Emerson said he'd teach me and Ty how to do it, and I hope he remembers. I want to know how to write like this."

"I can teach you," he murmured. "Mase can write in cursive, too, but forget Jay, Ash, and Wyatt. They can't read it or write it. My class was the last one to be taught penmanship in elementary school."

"The school stopped teaching it? I wonder why."

"I don't know. I guess the powers-that-be thought it wasn't necessary in this digital age." He shrugged, then his eyes widened. "Uh-oh. I just realized that you probably can't read this."

"Will you read it for me?"

I gave him my best puppy dog eyes, the ones that always made Mason and Jayden give me whatever I was asking for. I even added what Wyatt called my poochy lip, and that *always* got Ash and Cole to give in.

Sure enough, he took the card I held out in a heartbeat, and I bit back a giggle.

With red scorching his cheeks, he cleared his throat, then began to read.

"Dear Posy,

Once when I was in elementary school, I lost my temper and hurt someone very badly. My parents punished me, as did my own conscience, but neither affected me as much as something Uncle Jay said. 'Anger clouds the mind and doesn't solve anything,' he told me. 'It builds nothing and can destroy everything.'

I didn't learn my lesson, did I?

Honey, I am so sorry I lost my temper and hurt you. I destroyed your moment of triumph when I should have been celebrating it.

Please don't give up on me. I'll do better. I'll be better. I'll become the mate you deserve.

You are everything to us. Our mate, our love, our beautiful and strong luna. I respect, love, and care for you with all of my heart.

I am forever yours,

Cole"

As soon as he finished, I threw myself in his arms, blinking back tears.

"Thank you, Cole," I said. "Not only for making a beautiful card, but for taking time to write such a lovely letter."

"Listen, honey, I may get mad, I may act stupid, I may do or say things in a temper that I don't really mean, but I am *never* going to want to live this life without you," he murmured, his fern-green eyes bright and glimmering. "The Moon Goddess may have chosen us all to be mates, but even if we were humans, my brothers and I would have found you and chosen you. I truly believe that."

Tears stung my eyes again as my heart ached in the best possible way.

"I didn't know," I whispered, shaking my head. "I could have never even guessed."

"What, baby? What didn't you know?" He cupped my face in his palms.

"That I could feel this way."

"And how is that, honey?" he asked as he swiped tears from my cheeks with the pads of his thumbs.

"Not broken."

Smiling through my tears, I hugged him tightly as hope and wonder filled my heart. A few more years of love like this from my mates, and maybe I'd feel like I was never broken in the first place.

"That's good, Posy. I'm glad we're healing you as much as you're healing us." He leaned down and placed a gentle kiss on my cheek. "Now, how about I show you around a bit? There's a beautiful meadow where we can pick wildflowers or climb trees, or we can swim in the lake and go to the meadow in the morning. Whichever you prefer."

"Ooh! The meadow now, then swimming." I shifted positions to look into his eyes again. "Maybe we can swim under the stars tonight!"

"Didn't you stargaze with Ash last night?" When pink colored my cheeks, he smirked. "I take it you saw another kind of stars. I'll show you those, too, but you really should see the stars in the sky tonight. With us so high in the mountains, they look close enough that you could reach out and pluck one from the black velvet sky."

"I can't wait, pine tree," I whispered and pecked his lips, then worked up my courage to add, "To see *both* kinds of stars."

"Me, either, honey," he chuckled. "Me, either."

#

Cole and I lay together on an old quilt in the wildflower meadow about a mile from the cabin. It was such a beautiful early evening, one of those summer days that just seemed to last forever, and you wanted it to because it was so perfect. The birds trilling nearby, the light perfume of the flowers combining with Cole's pine scent, a giant sycamore shading us from the summer sun...

For one crystal moment in time, *everything* was perfect, including the man I was snuggled up with.

"Cole? Can I ask you something?"

"Anything, honey."

"I don't want to hurt you." I bit my bottom lip as his hand stilled on my back for a second before it started petting me again.

"Well, then it's either about my mom or what I wrote inside your card. I can't think of anything else you'd be worried about asking me."

"I *would* like you to tell me about your mom sometime," I admitted. "I'd like to know a little about the woman who gave birth to one of the men I love. Only when you're ready, though."

"So it's about the other thing, huh? I should have guessed you'd want to know."

"You don't have to tell me," I hurried to say. "It obviously still bothers you a lot, and I thought talking about it might help, that's all."

"Mason and Willow were in fifth grade," he didn't hesitate to start the story, "I was in fourth, Jay in third, Tweedledee and Tweedledum in second, and Peri in first."

"Wow. All the fam in one school building at the same time!" I teased. "Well, I guess it made it easier when one of the parents had to come in to sort out trouble."

"Yeah, it did," he snorted. "Anyway, one day, the fifth graders were leaving the playground as we fourth graders were coming out. I saw Mase standing in front of Willow as he stared down a group of five human boys. Of course, I *had* to get involved."

"Of course," I said dryly.

"They were teasing Willow about being a tomboy and saying she should exchange her boobs for balls and got more vulgar from there. Even as a kid, Mase was never the kind to get into a fight unless he had to, but these boys had pushed him to his limit. As for me, I was the opposite. Always a little too quick to throw hands. Even though we didn't have our wolves yet, our training had made us much stronger than those damn humans, and we had them on the ground in seconds despite it being two against five."

"I'm not surprised." I shrugged and lifted my head to stare up at him. "It sounds like the reaction I'd expect out of you both, but why didn't you stop once you had them down?"

"One of the idiots wouldn't stop running his mouth. I had *way* less control of my temper back then than I do now." He wouldn't meet my eyes as he spoke, and I felt his shame in our mate bond. "He was in a coma for three days. Thank the Goddess he woke up and recovered without any permanent damage or even scars. I never felt so disgusted with myself. He was just a stupid human kid who made a bad decision. Nothing that should have almost cost him his life."

"What was Willow like?" I asked after a moment, steering the conversation in a different direction. "*Was* she a tomboy? Was she like Mason, or the exact opposite? That is, if you're okay to talk about her."

"Such a considerate, polite baby," he teased with a lazy smile and finally looked at me. "Yeah, I guess you could call her a tomboy. She was always hanging out with us and doing whatever we were doing. Fishing, climbing trees, hiking, messing with cars in the garage.

She was brave and strong and dependable, and she feared absolutely nothing on this earth."

"So a female version of Mason?" I confirmed with a small smile.

"A *louder* version, anyway," Cole chuckled. "Even before Royal started to hound him so hard, Mase was the type of kid who kept everything inside. Willow, on the other hand, kept nothing to herself."

"So Papa wasn't always so hard on Mason?"

"No, that only started after the sickness had devastated the five packs and the parents decided to join them into one. Papa thought Mase had to be perfect because he was going to be first alpha."

"Mama told me that Mason is more like her than Papa." I raised one eyebrow. "Do you think that's true?"

"*Very* true. Mama is the ultimate mom. When we eventually have pups, Mase is going to be the ultimate dad. Don't you see the way he fathers all of us now?" Cole chuckled.

I grinned, nodding in agreement. Mason *was* going to be the ultimate dad.

"My mom, on the other hand—"

"No, Cole," I cut him off. "Only when you're ready."

"Sweet, sweet girl," he crooned and cradled my face in his palms, then pecked my lips. "Always so careful of others' feelings. I'm happy to tell you about her. I miss her, of course, and I think about her nearly every day, but I can talk about her now. I can talk about all of them now."

He laughed suddenly, and his eyes crinkled up at the corners.

"What?" I pouted.

"Nothing." He shook his head, still grinning. "Just imagining how she would have reacted when she met you for the first time."

"Would she have liked me?"

"To be honest, she probably would have intimidated the hell out of you. She would have grilled you about everything from your cooking knowledge to your bank balance to make sure you were good enough for her boys. Ha ha ha! But I know you would have seen the love and kindness hidden under her spiky exterior."

"Spiky exterior?"

"Dad used to call her fire and ice. One minute she was angry and ignoring him over something, and the next she was dragging him off to the bedroom. One thing about Kelly Barlow, whether she was mad or happy, she let you know it. Dad used to say that, because half of her came from Alaska and the other half came from New Zealand, extremes were in her blood. At least you never had to wonder where you stood with her; she'd tell you."

"So you're saying she was grouchy like you?"

"*I'm* grouchy?" He widened his eyes comically and put a hand over his heart.

"You grouch around a lot; you have to admit that."

"I guess I do," he confessed and kissed the tip of my nose.

"You know," I said slowly, "everybody warns me about your temper, but I've never seen you really lose it. I'm starting to think it's a lot like Quartz. Everybody warns me how violent he is, but I haven't seen any of that. Well, except for that incident with the king when he first met the queen, and Quartz calmed down as soon as I petted him."

Cole tilted his head back and laughed long and loud, and I didn't know why.

"Oh, baby," he chuckled finally, "we control it around you. That's the truth of it. You haven't seen either of us cut loose because we've made sure you haven't."

"Aha!" I sat up and jabbed my finger into his chest. "You *can* control it! You just choose not to unless you're around me!"

"Pretty much." He grabbed my finger and the rest of my hand, then pulled me down on top of his chest. "It does help that you're like a tranquilizer for us. Just your voice or your scent or your touch is enough to calm us right down."

I rolled my eyes, but folded my arms on his chest as I laid on top of him and listened as he continued talking.

"My mom was the first in the family to die of the sickness, then Willow a week later. Two weeks after that, Alpha Jay Carson died, and Luna Denise lived two days without him. Yeah, she had the sickness, but we all knew the truth. She couldn't live without her mate. That's when Ash and Jayden went to live with the Prices. The four of us clung to each other in our grief and weathered the storm as best we could as the adults around us fell apart."

"And Wyatt?" I asked in a quiet voice, already knowing part of the answer.

"He tried to help everybody. Even though he was only twelve, he took charge of Peri, who was only a year younger than him, and Archer, who wasn't quite nine. Wy was a rock for them *and* us and did everything he could to help. He really is kinder and more sensitive than most people give him credit for, you know."

I *did* know that about my fifth star, but it was nice to hear Cole acknowledge it. Too often, I feared people only saw the troublemaker and not the troubled heart.

"I mean, he can be selfish and an absolute douche at times—"

"Cole," I warned him with The Look.

"He kept our spirits up and held us together," he hurried to correct himself. "Then a month later—"

He took a deep, deep breath and let it out slowly, and I already knew what he was going to say. All of my boys had loved Wyatt's dad so much, and his death had scarred them deeply.

"And then a month later, Alpha Shawn Black died, and it was like the world stopped for all of us. I wish you could have met him, Posy. I love my dad. He is one of the greatest men I've ever known, but Shawn Black was in his own league of greatness. I know people often over-exaggerate the virtues of the deceased, but when it comes to Alpha Shawn, it's no exaggeration. He truly was an exceptional person."

"Wyatt told me a little when he took me to his father's grave on our date. He explained about going wolfy when his dad died."

"It was so scary, Posy. He went right off the deep end. I was afraid he would do something to hurt himself." He paused, then whispered, "Or worse. Knowing he was suicidal pulled me out of my grief *real* fast. Mom was gone, but Wyatt was still alive, and he needed our help if we were going to keep him that way. Gave me a purpose. A reason to—"

"Get up and keep going," I interrupted.

"Exactly. Listen, baby, don't ask Mase about Willow. Or Wyatt about his dad. And definitely not Jay about either of his parents. If they open up on their own, that's one thing, but asking them when they're not prepared for it, well, that wouldn't be good. Mase will shut down, Jay will break down, and Wyatt will go wolfy."

"I haven't pried, and I won't," I assured him. "I just listen when they want to talk. Mason told me a little about Willow when I asked about his tattoo, and Ash told me about his parents and Jayden's the day we looked through photo albums. Ash seemed fine to talk about it."

I raised my eyebrows and tilted my head to let him know that was a question.

"Ash is, yeah. Talking actually helped him grieve. Sometimes, he would go to the cemetery and talk to their tombstones if no one else would - or could - listen to him."

"Wyatt said Mason had all their graves relocated to that little cemetery in the woods."

"Um-hmm. He gave orders for that the day after he became alpha." Cole snorted. "Man, Papa was so hot at him for wasting his time on what he saw as something trivial when there was so much 'important' work to be done, but my dad stepped in and shut him down. Dad told him it would help all of us to move on, and Papa reluctantly agreed and let it go."

"Maybe he didn't want his daughter's grave moved?" I suggested, trying so hard to give Royal Price the benefit of the doubt.

"Maybe. Look, I know you've only seen and heard the worst about Papa, but the truth is, he never recovered from Willow's death.

Mama, either. Dad and Mom think a pup would help them move on, but Mase and I don't agree. A pup doesn't 'fix' things, and I think Papa is wise enough to know that."

I nodded my agreement. A pup should be a celebration of love and commitment between mates, not a band-aid over deeper issues.

"Anyway," Cole went on, "he's done a lot for each of us, for our families and packs, for Tyler after ... what happened to his parents, for the Breckenridge twins after Ev died. He's not evil at heart. None of that excuses how he treated Mase, of course, but I thought you should know he's not all bad."

"He *did* apologize to me and Mason, and he talked with Mason about earning his forgiveness," I reluctantly conceded.

"He's going to be the grandfather of our pups, so you'll have to build some kind of relationship with him." Cole shrugged. "I mean, I'm mad at him, too, but I recognize that he'll be a part of family events for as long as he's alive, and he's only thirty-nine."

"Oh, the same way you're trying *so hard* to build a relationship with my brothers?" I raised my eyebrows, and he had the grace to blush.

"Touché, little mate."

"Two what?"

"It means you made a good point. It comes from the sport of fencing. You say it to acknowledge that your opponent scored a hit."

"Fencing? I know what a fence is. How is it involved in a sport?"

Chuckling, Cole wrapped me up in his big arms and gave me a bear hug.

"It's sword-fighting. I don't know why it's called fencing. We'll look it up online later. But yes, I need to work on building some kind of relationship with your brothers, too."

"Jayden has never said anything about his parents." Reaching up, I tugged Cole's scrunchy out and let his long, black hair fall around his face and down past his shoulders. "Not even mentioned them in a passing comment."

"It's a very deep wound for him. He lost both at once and so suddenly. No one could ever get him to talk about them, not the surviving parents or even the therapists that King Magnus sent around to packs after the sickness was eradicated. While Ash found comfort in talking about them, Jay sealed everything up inside himself."

"Not healthy," I murmured, worried about my dragon now.

"We're aware, but what can we do? Alpha command him to talk? One day, he'll open the lid on the memories, or someone will do it for him. All hell will probably break loose, but in the end, I think it would be like draining poison from a wound, you know?"

"When were you able to talk about your mom without breaking down?" I asked gently.

"Hmm. I guess about two years ago. Arch was having a tough time and we had a talk. That was the first time I could, without crying, say Mom and mean her and not Evie. It was like I knew Arch needed me, so I *had* to get up and go on, you know? Just like I did with Wyatt."

"I couldn't even think about Mom for nearly a year after she died," I admitted. "Alpha Briggs was growing crueler and crueler each day, so I was in survival mode, and thinking about her only made everything hurt worse."

"Was she—" He cut himself off and sighed. "I just told you not to ask the others and here I am asking you, but if you ever want to talk about her, I'm always ready to listen."

"I never doubted she loved me. She loved James and Aiden, too, but I was her baby and now I know that I was all she had left of her true mate." Tears pooled at the corner of my eyes, and I stuffed my face in his throat and clung to him. "She protected me all the time. Looking back now, I can see how often she stood between me and Alpha Briggs. He was so mean to her, and she was so sad. So very sad. And now I know why."

"I cannot imagine having to live with the person who killed my mate," Cole growled, and I felt his temper rising through our bond. "To have to cook for him and eat with him and *sleep* with him—"

With each word, he squeezed me tighter and clenched his jaw harder.

"Calm down." I smoothed my hands up and down his arms. "Cole, calm down. That's never going to happen to us."

"Damned right it won't! My brothers and I will shred anyone who tries to take you from us!"

"Shh, my pine tree. I'm here. Shh."

It took several minutes before he relaxed against me and his fists unclenched from the back of my dress.

"Sorry, honey," he whispered. "I wanted you to feel safe enough to talk about your mom, and I ruined it with my temper."

"You didn't ruin anything." I kissed his cheek. "And I feel safe with you. I know you will never, ever hurt me and that you got angry because you're outraged."

He held me close for another moment, then eased back to look in my eyes.

"You said that now you're able to see how she was protecting you. You didn't know at the time that he was hurting her?"

"No. Not until Jayden read the letter she left with the photo album." I bit my bottom lip for a second, then asked, "Was I a bad daughter not to notice?"

"No, Posy. You were just a child. And I bet she hid as much from you as she could. She probably became an expert at that. You didn't know he was hurting your brothers, either, did you?"

"At the time, no, but I was in a haze of pain most days after Mom died. Then my brothers moved out when Aiden turned eighteen, and I hardly saw them after that. I *do* remember some of what James said that day at Green River, and I started to have suspicions once I was able to think more clearly, but I wasn't completely sure until Aiden showed us his back right before my luna ceremony."

"Hmm. I wonder if Lark knows more?" He kissed my forehead. "I bet she became an expert in protecting you, too."

"She has always protected me. Someday, I'll ask her, but not today. Today, I think we've talked enough about deep topics." Scrambling to my feet, I slipped my feet back into my sandals, then leaned down and held out my hands to help him up. "Let's pick wildflowers!"

"What are you going to do with them?" He paused to stretch his arms over his head and yawn. "Take them back to the cabin and put them in a glass of water? That's what Grandma Pippi used to do. She always had glasses of flowers sitting all over the place."

"Maybe that, too, but you'll see," I said with a secret smile.

He finally put his hands in mine and let me pull him to his feet. Well, he pulled himself to his feet and let me *think* I helped.

Soon we'd each gathered an armful of poppies, daisies, Queen Anne's lace, chicory, and a half dozen other flowers I couldn't name and returned to the quilt. I sorted them out, then began to trim the ends.

"So that's why you asked me to bring scissors," Cole chuckled as he laid down with his hands under his head and watched me.

Nodding, I concentrated on arranging the flowers how I wanted them, then wove them together in a long strand. Once I had a nice length, I joined it to make a circle and held it up for his approval.

"Very pretty. A flower wreath. Are you going to hang it on the front door?"

"It's a flower *crown*!" I corrected, then I stood on my knees, set it on his head, and squealed at how adorable he looked. "See? A crown for my prince!"

As he rolled his eyes, I reached into my mini backpack, took out my phone, and snapped a picture of him.

"Posy! Don't you dare send that to anyone!"

"I won't," I said, blinking at him as I hid my phone behind my back.

"Ha! Don't give me those innocent eyes! You'll show my brothers the first chance you get!"

He tackled me to the quilt, and I giggled and looped my arms around his neck as he laid on me. I stared up into his fern-green eyes, admiring how his darker skin tone set them off so beautifully. The flower crown made them pop even more, and my heart fluttered in my chest at how handsome he was.

"I love you, honey. More than I ever knew it was possible to love someone."

"And I love you, too. So very much." Giggling, I added, "My wildflower prince."

With a pretend growl, he lowered his head and kissed the giggles right out of me.

Cole's Letter:

Dear Posy,

Once when I was in elementary school, I lost my temper and hurt someone very badly. My parents punished me, as did my own conscience, but neither affected me as much as something Uncle Jay said. "Anger clouds the mind and doesn't solve anything," he told me. "It builds nothing and can destroy everything."

I didn't learn my lesson, did I?

Honey, I am so sorry I lost my temper and hurt you. I destroyed your moment of triumph when I should have been celebrating it.

Please don't give up on me. I'll do better. I'll be better. I'll become the mate you deserve.

You are everything to us. Our mate, our love, our beautiful and strong luna. I respect, love, and care for you with all of my heart.

I am forever yours,

Cole

7: County Fair

Posy

For the first time, I balked at the outfit Ash picked out for me.

He'd already done my hair with the top and sides in a fussy braid that went into big, bouncy curls down my back and even helped me with some simple makeup - just mascara and clear lip gloss - but when it came time to put on the clothes he wanted, I shook my head and backed away.

He himself was dressed in a pink t-shirt printed with a black rose, black shorts with a black belt, and black loafers with pink laces, and I didn't know why he couldn't have picked something like that for *me*. I usually trusted his dress sense without question, but this time, I put my foot down.

"Come on, princess! You'll look so cute in it!"

I bit my lip. It *was* cute, but it had teeny tiny straps that would leave my upper arms, shoulders, and some of my back visible. While the sandals were super adorable, the dress was not going to happen.

"Ash, if she doesn't want to wear something, don't make her," Mason rumbled as he stepped out of the boys' massive closet. "She *can* pick out her own clothes, you know."

I looked at what he was wearing - khaki shorts with a brown leather belt, a white t-shirt, and white sneakers - and was tempted to just go as I was in Cole's oversized t-shirt that went to my knees.

"But she *likes* me to do it, don't you, cupcake?" Ash argued.

"Usually." I twisted my fingers together and stared at the floor.

"Let me see this outfit." Mason walked over to the bed where Ash had laid it out. In half a second, he whirled on his brother and slapped him upside the head. "You idiot! Why do you *think* she wouldn't like this dress thing?"

Then he came over to me, untangled my fingers, and lifted my chin with one hand.

"Baby, your scars show how strong you are," he murmured, "but it's your decision to show them to the world or not."

I nodded, and he sighed when I stayed silent. Pulling me into his arms, he held me tight against him, and I closed my eyes and laid my ear against his chest. I loved listening to my mates' heartbeats. It was something that never failed to soothe me.

"Shit, Posy," Ash began.

"Language!" Cole grumbled as he, too, came out of the boys' closet.

Opening my eyes, I saw he was dressed similarly to Mason, only his shorts were navy blue and his shirt was light gray.

"Sorry, Posy," Ash mumbled. "I didn't think about that."

Still squeezed against Mason, I looked at Ash's sad face.

"It's okay," I told him. "It's a very pretty dress."

"It's a romper, in case you go on rides." He showed me that what I thought was a knee-length skirt was really two pant legs. "Gingham is perfect for a county fair. I forgot about your scars. I don't really notice them anymore. They're just a part of you. Part of what makes Posy *Posy*."

I swallowed hard, loving him for saying that.

"We can fix this easily enough." Cole grabbed Ash's arm and towed him toward my closet. "Just find her a thin shirt to wear under it or something lightweight to wear over it."

"Ah!" Ash brightened up. "You're right!"

He raced into my closet as Cole rolled his eyes.

Looking up at Mason, I found his gray eyes staring down at me.

"Do you really not notice the scars anymore?" I asked him quietly.

He picked me up, and I was suddenly squished between two huge bodies. His face pressed into my neck on one side and while Cole's dove in on the other.

"We'll always know they're there, little flower." Mason murmured, his lips brushing my skin with every word. "We can't forget them because we hate how you got them. We're sickened to know someone caused you so much pain."

Cole interrupted with a growl, his chest rumbling against my spine, and goosebumps rose all over my skin and made me shiver in their arms.

"If the Moon Goddess blessed you and washed them all away, would it change anything?" Mason continued. "I mean, I'm sure you'd feel more confident without the scars, but would it change who you are? Would it wipe away the memories of what you've gone through?"

I sighed, knowing he was right.

"I wish we *could* wash them away," Cole muttered. He slipped his fingers under the hem of my t-shirt and slid them between my back and his stomach to find the place on my spine where Alpha Briggs had branded me with his initials. "This one especially because you are *not* his. You never were."

At the same time, Mason traced the moon on my mate mark with his tongue, and I shivered again, drowning in their touch and smell and love.

"Your scars tell your story," Mason raised his head to murmur, "and we love stories, don't we, brothers?"

"Yes, we do," Cole said.

119

Ash joined us and added, "Especially stories with a heroine who goes through hell and emerges as a badass bitch."

Rolling my eyes, I buried my pink cheeks in Mason's chest.

"Be proud of them, not ashamed." Sparks tingled down my arms as Cole slid the neck of my t-shirt down and kissed the deepest crater on my shoulder. "You are a decorated warrior. A seasoned soldier. No one else has survived the kind of battles you have unless it's Reau. In our eyes, these scars are the marks of valor."

"What's valor?" I whispered into Mason's shirt.

"Courage in the face of danger, honey. You *earned* these medals. They are marks of victory."

"Like I told you before, you survived and he's in the ground," Ash said. "You still don't get it, do you? That big, terrifying man who hurt you over and over? *You* defeated him. *You!* Posy Anne Everleigh. You went ten rounds with the devil and won. Every one of those scars is you giving him the middle finger, baby!"

At first, I froze when he began to describe Alpha Briggs, but then I heard his words. Hugging Mason's waist, I let the humor flood through me and shake my shoulders as I silently giggled.

Only Ash would say it like that! The middle finger.

You think it funnier if you knew what middle finger means, Lark smirked.

Probably, I agreed, my smile growing into a grin against Mason's shirt.

The bedroom door flew open and banged against the wall.

"Is she upset?" Jayden asked right as Wyatt said, "I thought you were getting her dressed, not making her cry!"

"You hurt her feelings, Ash!" Cole snapped.

He stepped away from me, and I heard the sound of him slapping Ash upside the head.

"I did not!" Ash protested. "It was you two making her feel self-conscious about her scars! *I* was cheering her up!"

"Posy?" Jayden whispered in my ear. "Please don't cry."

I turned my face and opened my eyes, letting him see my huge grin, and every line of his body relaxed. He gave me a questioning look, and I linked him what Ash had said about the middle finger and Lark's comment.

He chuckled and stepped back.

"She's fine. She's giggling because Lark reminded her that she doesn't know what the middle finger means," he announced to his brothers.

"Jayden!" I whined and stepped away from Mason's warm bulk.

"What?" he whined back. "You didn't say it was a secret."

120

He grabbed me by the waist and whirled me around before passing me to Wyatt, who studied my face for a second, then leaned down and whispered in my ear exactly what the middle finger meant.

"Don't you *dare* say that word, though, you understand me?" he said sternly. "If you do, Sir will be unhappy with his little girl."

For some reason, his words and tone made my belly tight and my lady parts damp. Swallowing hard, I widened my eyes and nodded.

"Okay, fifth star." I bit my lip, wondering if I should ask, then decided to go for it. "Um, Wyatt?"

"Yes, cutie?"

"What does *that* word mean? Lark won't tell me," I pouted.

Five groans rattled the room before he promised to explain after we came back from the fair.

"Why wait?" I tilted my head as I stared up at him. "Can't you just tell me now?"

"No, cutie." His lips tugged into a dark smirk and his blue eyes glittered. "We'll have so much more fun *showing* you."

#

The fair was amazing!

The boys explained that we came in the late afternoon because the crowds would pick up the later it got. I was so grateful for them to think of that. I was slowly getting better about being around others, but strangers still made me uncomfortable, and a lot of them could make me panic.

"I want to take you on the Ferris wheel!" Ash crowed after we paid and walked through the gates.

He pointed to the ride towering over the rest of the fair, and my heart rate sped up just looking at it.

"Um," I tried to tell him I didn't want to go on that ride, but Wyatt jumped in first.

"Aw, I wanted to do that! All right, then. I'll take her on the roller coaster."

"Um."

"Then *I'm* taking her on the swings," Ash countered.

"Um."

"Then *I'm* taking her on the salt and pepper shakers," Wyatt smirked.

"Um."

"Then *I'm*—"

"Shut up, you two!" Cole roared. "Stop interrupting her! She doesn't want to go on those types of rides! She doesn't like heights!"

"Oh," Ash and Wyatt said in unison, then Ash added, "I forgot."

"How could you forget?" Mason rolled his eyes. "*You're* the one who discovered it, remember?"

"Oh, yeah!" His eyes lit up. "She didn't like sitting on my shoulders! No way would she enjoy those kinds of rides."

"Let's stop talking about her like she's not here," Jayden suggested, giving me a secret wink, "and *ask* her what she wants to do."

"Well," I said, smiling up at all of them, "I saw a sign for a scavenger hunt. That's something we can do together all through the fair. I want to see the animals, and Peri said there are games that you can play and win prizes."

"Sounds perfect!" Cole hugged me and kissed my cheek.

"But what about rides?" Wyatt pouted.

"There has to be *something* that doesn't go high in the air," I reasoned, "and I want to watch you all go on some, especially those funny little cars. I saw them on the TV advertisement for the fair. What are they called? They crash into each other."

"Bumper cars," Jayden, Cole, and Ash said in sync.

"Yes!" Wyatt threw his arms up in the air. "I am the king of bumper cars!"

"You wish you were, pup." Mason caught him in a headlock and gave him a noogie.

"Mase!" he whined and tried to twist away from him.

Chuckling, Mason ground his knuckles in harder.

"What are we waiting for?" Ash bounced up and down on his toes. "Let's grab a scavenger hunt board and get started!"

So we did.

#

Wyatt

The guy running the scavenger hunt booth gave us a laminated sheet of paper and a dry erase marker. As we found the printed pictures, we were supposed to check them off and then bring the completed board back for a free snow cone.

"What keeps people from cheating?" I asked the guy, seeing all kinds of flaws with this system.

"Even if they do, it's for one free snow cone." He shrugged and didn't look too concerned. "Most people just do it for fun and half don't even bother to claim the prize."

I frowned. What was the point of that? If you were going to go on a scavenger hunt, you had to complete it. And if there was a prize, why wouldn't you claim it?

Humans make no sense whatsoever, Granite said.

Agreed.

We took Posy to the animals first, hoping they didn't react too badly to so many shifters in one group. I knew our girl would want to pet them, which wouldn't go well if they were panicking at the wolves surrounding them. Fortunately, most were either too young or too used to crowds to care. We petted baby chicks, pygmy goats, and even cute little piglets, and Posy got to hold a giant Flemish rabbit named Peder - not Peter, his young owner was quick to clarify. I could definitely see us getting a rabbit hutch sometime in our future because she was in love with the fluffy things.

I eat bunnies in future? Granite asked with excited eyes.

Don't you dare, I warned him. *Don't even think about it.*

"I should have worn my bunny ears," our girl lamented as she handed Peder back.

"It's a good thing you didn't." Putting my hands on her hips, I pulled her back against my chest and kissed the side of her neck. "I'm already having trouble keeping my hands off of you."

My dick twitched against her back, and I knew she felt it when she let out a quiet moan.

"Come on, cutie," I whispered in her ear. "Let's slip away and you can show me which panties you're wearing."

She hummed and melted into me.

I grinned as I skimmed my fingers up her ribs and if we weren't in public, I would cup her titties and tug her nips before I untied these straps and let her dress thing drop around her ankles—

Wyatt! Mase growled. *Control yourself.*

Or at least close the link, dude, Ash snorted. *We're all hard as rocks now, thank you very much.*

Welcome, I smirked. *I can't help it. I love her little body so much!*

We all do, Wy, Jay said calmly, *but we're in public and we are not mating her in a port-a-potty at the county fair with hundreds of humans around.*

I'm fine with all of that but the port-a-potty, I admitted. *Surely there's somewhere more sanitary nearby—*

Wyatt! they all bellowed and I rolled my eyes.

"Can we go on that?" Posy said suddenly, pointing at the teacups. "The little seats look so cute!"

Mase explained what it was and how the ride worked, and we decided Ash should be one of us to go on it with her. Since the cups didn't have a roof, his height wasn't a problem like it was on the tilt-a-whirl. Then we Rock-Paper-Scissored to see who else would go on, and I smiled smugly when I won.

So Ash and I seated Posy between us in a teacup and put our strength to work to make the cup spin as fast as we could. Mase, Cole, and Jay crammed into the cup right next to us, although they spent most of the ride watching her animated face rather than trying to make their cup spin. She giggled and giggled until tears leaked from her eyes and down her red cheeks, and Mase linked us to stop before she got dizzy and vomited.

She's fine, I assured him in a deadpan. *Mr. Worrywart.*

And she was, too. She got off the ride laughing so hard, she held her stomach, which made Mase fear she was about to puke, and it took her several minutes to convince him she was fine.

After that, we got on the carousel. As we all predicted she would, she selected the rabbit, and we settled for animals around her. Ash chose a black horse, I climbed on a tiger, Cole appropriately sat on a bear, Jay picked a white goat, and Mase took the giant seahorse.

She liked the carousel so much, we rode it three times. She didn't have a chance at catching the brass rings, so we all made a point to collect as many of them as we could. In the end, we handed her nearly two dozen iron rings and two brass ones.

After we explained what they meant, she gave the brass ones to some little kids in line, then made us throw the iron ones at the lion target next to the carousel. If you got the ring in the lion's mouth, he roared. When Ash hit it the first time, the noise startled Posy, but then she clapped and jumped up and down and praised him for his "skills."

Needless to say, none of us competitive bastards missed the lion's mouth after that.

We skipped the haunted mansion and went into the magic maze. She wasn't too keen on that until I held one of her hands and Jay the other. Strangely, the rolling checkerboard floor made her dizzy, but the tilt-a-whirl and teacups didn't.

As we walked by the obstacle course, Posy came to a dead halt, bringing Ash and Mase to a stop, too, since they held her hands.

"What's that?" she asked.

We explained how you had to dodge swinging sandbags while running across a balance beam, climb a cargo net, and cross a suspension bridge without falling into the water below before sliding down a long drop into an air pillow.

"The goal is to do it quickly," Mase added. "They keep a scoreboard and the fastest time at the end of the fair wins a prize."

"Well, then, you *have* to do it." Her pretty blue eyes twinkled up at us. "Although I think you'll all finish right around the same time since you're so fast and athletic."

"Oh, really?" I raised an eyebrow. "Hundred bucks says I'm the fastest."

"Hundred bucks says you fall in the moat," Jay challenged with a smile.

"Hundred bucks says you don't even finish," I shot back.

"Let's speed this up, boys," Cole smirked. "Whoever's fastest gets a hundred from each of us and everyone who falls in the water owes the others a hundred."

"It doesn't have to be a bet," Posy said hesitantly and started to twine her fingers together, a signal we all recognized as her getting nervous.

"Oh, baby, you know we can't *not* compete," Mase told her with a broad grin. "The betting just adds another layer of fun. It's all good. I promise."

"If you're sure. I don't want anyone to get hurt because of a stupid bet."

"We'll keep an eye on them, luna," came a voice from our left, and we whirled to see Emerson and Angelo standing a few feet away.

"Em! Gelo!" Posy smiled and launched herself at Emerson for a hug. "Are you going to run the obstacle course, too?"

"Hell, yeah!" Angelo grinned.

"Now we got a contest!" I rubbed my hands together, also grinning.

"You leave your baby at home, Em?" Ash asked with wide eyes.

"Are you joking? Keep that kid away from something as colorful and busy as the fair?" Emerson rolled his eyes. "He's here with his besties. They've been here every night this week. You'd think they'd get bored of it."

"I don't see that happening," Cole smirked. "Not for Reau, anyway, and Arch and Wayne make their own amusement when they're bored."

"Maybe we'll run into them!" Posy chirped, finally releasing Emerson.

"Most likely," he agreed. "Poppy and Leo were job-hunting all day and came home disappointed. Gelo and I decided to tag along with the boys to give them some alone time."

"Hopefully, we won't go home to clothes strewn all over the living room again," Angelo muttered. "It may be the best stress relief, but that was not easy to explain to Reau."

"Yeah, we can only say they're doing laundry so many times," Emerson laughed. "Last time, he said they needed to buy more clothes so they don't have to run the washer so often."

We all chuckled except Posy, who had a thoughtful look on her face.

"Cutie?"

"Why are they job-hunting?" she asked. "I thought Poppy would work at the witches' shop?"

125

"She will when it's up and running," Angelo said, "but that's months away. They want to move into their own place soon. We've both told them they can stay as long as they want, but Leo's feeling the drive to provide for his mate."

"It's not because Kon moved in, is it?" she asked next.

I wondered the same thing. It probably wasn't easy to live with Thoreau and his issues as it was; a wary teen dragon shifter might have been the tipping point.

Em offered, Granite pointed out with a shrug, *and it his home. Leo and Poppy guests just like Kon.*

I didn't bother to argue with him and just gave him a small hum.

"Not at all. They both treat Kon like a little brother, just like they do Reau."

"Good," Jay said. "We figured it would be like that. Still, we should try to find Leo something to do. I can't imagine going from being a busy alpha to jobless."

"I have an idea!" Posy piped up. "It wouldn't be right away, though. We'd have to find something for in the meantime, but I think he'd make an excellent principal or assistant principal at our school!"

We all kind of froze for a few moments as we thought about that, then Mase and Jay started nodding.

"I can see that," Angelo and Ash said at the same time.

"Me, too," Cole said. "He could keep anyone in line, knows how to organize, has experience with reports and paperwork, and can be counted on to run a tight ship."

"Like running a pack," Posy agreed with a nod and small smile.

Damn, our girl smart, Wy, Granite murmured.

I know she is, wolf.

"Now go run this obstacle course!" She grinned brilliantly. "I'm getting hungry and want my dinner soon!"

She put her hands on my shoulders and tugged like she did when she wanted us to bend down to her level. When I did, she kissed my lips gently.

"I love you, my fifth star," she said as she stepped back. "Good luck."

Grinning, I waited for her to kiss each of my brothers and wish them good luck, too. Then we lined up to run the obstacle course, having determined we'd go in age order, followed by Emerson with Angelo going last.

Fortunately, none of us fell into the water. Our order of finishing was Ash first, Mase second, me third, Jay fourth, Cole fifth, Emerson sixth, and Angelo seventh. Our times were all within a minute of each other except for Angelo, who was two minutes slower than Ash. Couldn't really tease him, though; for someone who was basically human, he'd had an impressive showing. Few non-shifters could have kept up with alpha and beta wolves.

"What's next?" Cole asked our girl. "Dinner?"

"Yes, please!"

"Papa! Mama!" a familiar voice screamed. "Maamaaa!"

We all grinned as we saw Thoreau racing toward us with Archer and Wayne hot on his heels. Even from here, I could hear Archer's angry voice fussing at him to stop running while Wayne just ran after him with a wide smile.

Archer is so much like Cole. I shook my head. *Little dude needs to chill and enjoy.*

Wayne a lot like you, too, Granite said.

I know, wolf.

I loved all of our younger brothers, but Archer and Wayne had a special place in my heart. They might be magnets for mischief, but they were fun as hell to hang out with, liked all the things I did, and were just good kids.

Thoreau's yelling drew a lot of attention our way, and several people around us began to murmur and laugh when he threw himself into Emerson's arms while screaming, "Mama!"

"Chill, Reau," Angelo laughed as Emerson caught the kid and hugged him. "Is something wrong?"

"No, Papa! 'M just happy! 'M a happy boy, Mama!"

Goddess, his big, innocent eyes just drew you in and ate you up with their cuteness!

"Listen, Reau," Emerson muttered, "call me Bubba in public."

"You're not my mama anymore?" Thoreau's bottom lip quivered, and Emerson sighed.

"Of course I am, but hu— People don't understand a boy calling a grown man Mama, okay?" Emerson patted Thoreau's head before releasing him from the hug. "Why do *I* have to be mama, anyway?"

"Because Papa said so." Thoreau shrugged and lost interest in the conversation as he attacked Posy in a hug.

"Oh, did he?" Emerson narrowed his eyes at Angelo, who looked like a deer in the headlights before giving him a big cheesy grin.

Emerson stalked closer and wrapped his huge hand around Angelo's throat. Leaning down so they were eye to eye, he raised one eyebrow.

"We'll continue this discussion later tonight, *little mate.*"

"Is that so, *orsacchiotto* (teddy bear)?" Angelo smirked.

"Yes," Emerson growled, then smashed his mouth on Angelo's.

"Hey, stop that! There are little ears and eyes present!" Archer snapped.

Turning, I saw he had his hands pressed over Thoreau's ears and Wayne had his hands covering the boy's eyes.

"Don't worry, Chi-Chi," Thoreau giggled. "I see *lots* of love between Mama and Papa at home!"

"We're going to go eat now," Posy said. "Do you all want to join us?"

What's with her and inviting others into our dates? Ash grumbled in the link.

She has a heart that can hold the whole world, Jay replied.

We nodded in agreement and just accepted that these five were going to crash the rest of our date.

At least we're taking her home alone, I smirked.

Thank the Goddess for that! my brothers echoed each other.

#

Posy

Having the others join us made everything that much more fun, although I wasn't sure my mates were okay with me inviting them along. We were on a date, after all, and I kind of thought that meant it was supposed to be just us.

They not care, Lark assured me, *as long as you happy. That all they want.*

Smiling, I held Cole's hand as Thoreau claimed the other and let them lead me to the food area. There were so many choices and the boys made sure I understood all of my options before asking me what I wanted.

After a moment of thought, I went with a corn dog, since I'd never had one, onion rings, and a cherry slushie. Wayne and Thoreau told me the best part of fair food was the desserts, and I was looking forward to that.

We had just sat down at a couple of tables when I saw two familiar faces approaching the picnic area.

"Landry!" I stood up and waved my hand high in the air. "Grace! Come join us!"

"Hey, luna!" Landry set a tray of food down on the empty end of the table, then turned to Grace and took the two drinks from her and put them down, too. "Alphas. Beta. Boys."

Grace smiled at me shyly, then blushed as Landry put his arm around her waist and dropped a kiss on top of her head. We all greeted the two of them, then Landry helped Grace sit next to me and he sat next to her. He arranged her food and drink in front of her just like Mason and Jay had done for me, and I bit back a smile.

"Reau, where's Spring?" Landry asked as he demolished a chili cheese dog.

"Oh, yeah!" My eyes widened. "I just realized he's not with you!"

"Aw, we tried bringing him the first night," Thoreau said. "He hated it! It was too busy and he couldn't go on any rides, anyway."

"And Reau gave him too much junk food and he got sick," Wayne snickered.

"He's off on a run with Bay tonight," Emerson added, and I remembered Bay was Crew's wolf.

"Good that they're reconnecting. I'm sure the beta wolves have missed him," Landry commented.

Grace and I chatted quietly as our boys talked a little business, and she told me about their new house and how much she was enjoying all the new experiences here at Five Fangs. I told her about my series of dates and how I was also experiencing a lot of firsts. She was interested in the flea market, so I told her she should ask Landry to take her on Saturday.

"Do you think he would?" she whispered, her pretty dark eyes anxious and her shoulders hunching a little. "I don't have any money and I don't want him to think I'm greedy."

I remembered when I felt the same way - before I found out my mates were richer than kings. Then I checked myself; I *still* felt that way from time to time, but not as much as before.

"Grace, I'm sure he would. And don't worry about money. He gets a good paycheck as our gamma. Do you want a little job, though, so you feel more independent?"

"Yes, luna. I don't know what I'd be good at, but I would like that."

"Like what, angel?" Landry looked at her with interest, having caught the end of our conversation. "Whatever you'd like, you'll have. I'll make sure of it."

"A job," she murmured, her eyes shining with so much love as she looked at him.

"Angel, I *told* you. *I'm* your job. I even warned you that it was hard work to take care of me, but you said you were up for the challenge," he teased her.

"I am. I just think I should contribute some money—"

"You do not worry about that, angel. What's mine is yours. I've waited all my life to share everything with you. If you want a job, that's fine. I'll help you find whatever work you want to do, but please remember that money is the *least* of what I want to share with you."

129

"Aww!" Ash, Emerson, Wayne, Jayden, and I cooed at the couple.

Grace blushed bright red, and Landry grinned.

"Now ice cream!" Thoreau shrieked, oblivious to the moment. "Luna, big sissy Grace, you come with me to get ice cream!"

Or maybe he not so oblivious, Lark mused. *I think he get jealous when the attention not on him.*

I giggled and shared that thought with Grace, who also giggled.

"Don't go far," Archer told him. "Just to the ice cream truck and back."

"Do you have your wallet?" Wayne asked as Thoreau stood up and jogged over to us.

"Yes, Chi-Chi. Yes, Way-Way. I am proud to buy ice cream for luna and big sissy."

"Oh, you don't have to—" Grace and I said at the same time, then looked at each other and giggled again.

"I *will*," Thoreau insisted, then leaned down to whisper to us. "You're 'posed to say thank you. 'S good manners."

"Thank you, Reau," I said politely.

"Yes, thank you very much," Grace added.

He grinned and held out his hands to us. We took them and climbed out of our seats, then he led us back to the food trucks to look for one selling ice cream.

"There!" Since his hands were occupied holding ours, he nodded his head. "That says ice cream, right, luna? Big sissy?"

"Yes," we chorused, then looked behind his back to smile at each other.

He's so sweet, Grace linked me.

He is. The sweetest.

He's not— Um, I mean, he's ... special, isn't he?

He is, I confirmed. *He's a precious baby and he always will be.*

She understood what I was saying. No matter how old Thoreau became, he was never going to age. He would be child-like forever, and I doubted he'd ever be able to live independently.

Wayne and Arch take care of that, Lark said with a knowing wink. *They will never leave that boy alone.*

I hope not.

Just as with Peri and Tyler, I wouldn't jinx anything by saying it out loud, but I'd be shocked if the three of them weren't mates. There was too much love and chemistry there for it to be otherwise.

"What kind of ice cream do you want, luna? Big sissy?"

I blinked and realized we were standing at the counter, behind which a bored-looking teen human waited with an impatient scowl.

"You going to order something, toothpick?" he sneered, taking me aback, then looked at Grace. "Not you, though, fatty. A lard ass like you needs to buy a treadmill, not ice cream."

My jaw dropped, and I couldn't respond to save my life. Why was he being so rude to us? My hands started to shake, and Grace sucked in a sharp breath before hunching in on herself.

"What did you say?" Thoreau narrowed his eyes at the human.

"*I said*, Little Miss Starve Myself better order three scoops, but Tubby here needs to walk off fifty pounds instead of stuff her face with more food."

I hated any kind of cruelty, especially bullying. Grace was on the edge of tears and I was getting angry. Before I could stand up for us, though, Thoreau beat me to it.

"You better stop being mean to luna and big sissy!" Thoreau shouted. "You just give them ice cream. Right now!"

"First, Anorexia and Chubs walk up to my window, and now a retard." The human propped himself up on his elbows on the counter and raised an eyebrow. "Listen, freaks. The circus isn't in town until next week."

"Better say sorry, meany, or I'll get my mama!"

While I was ready to walk away, Thoreau was getting more and more upset. He paced around, his hands clenched into fists, and his whole face turned red with frustration and irritation.

"Come on, Reau," I said quietly and laid a shaking hand on his shoulder. "Let's go somewhere else."

"No, luna!" He shrugged off my hand, his face screwed up in a scowl that would have made me coo at his cuteness in other circumstances. "He is a bad boy!"

Then he turned and shouted into the crowd.

"Mama! Mama! Bad boy hurt luna and big sissy's feelings! Bad boy called me a retard!"

A dozen heads swiveled in our directions, making me lower my eyes in embarrassment and awkwardness, and Grace grabbed my hand and squeezed it. I squeezed back as I felt her anxiety rattling through the pack bond, and knew that Emerson would be lucky to get here before her mate or mine.

Somehow, he did, though.

"What happened, Reau?" he growled, his eyes narrowed on the human, who clearly thought he was safe in his food truck.

"Dude, just take your monkeys back to the circus. Fatso here doesn't need to eat for a week or two, and I've heard too much sugar is bad for retards—"

And that was all he got out before Emerson's huge hand wrapped around his throat. My beta dragged the ice cream boy out of the serving window and threw him on the ground at our feet.

"Your mouth just talked you into a whole world of hurt," Emerson hissed in the boy's ear, and his grin was nothing I ever wanted directed at me.

The human stared up at him with wide, shocked eyes, and I couldn't blame him. Emerson in a temper was one of the scariest things I'd ever seen - and that included seeing *my mates* lose their tempers.

As the human started to scramble away, Emerson leapt forward, grabbed the boy by his ankle, and dragged him off.

By then, my mates, Angelo, Landry, Archer, and Wayne had joined us and Thoreau was telling them what happened a little *too* accurately for agitated, overly protective mates.

Fortunately, Emerson was already out of sight, the shocked, muttering crowd having parted for him like the Red Sea, or my mates would have gotten into an argument with Archer and Wayne over who got to beat the human up.

Don't kill him, Em, I linked him.

Even though I got no response, I knew he'd obey.

No matter how much he didn't want to.

#

Jayden

"Leave you alone for a minute and you'll find trouble." I shook my head as I hugged our girl. "All the more reason for you never to leave our side."

She giggled as she hugged me back, knowing I was teasing. Nothing that happened was her fault. Neither was it Grace's or Thoreau's. It was the stupid human's who thought he had the right to disrespect others for his own twisted entertainment.

"All right, we're staking our claim," Wayne said with a huge grin. "Arch, give me a boost."

Also grinning, Archer linked his fingers to make a cradle, Wayne stuck his foot in it, and Archer lifted him up. Giggling, Wayne climbed into the ice cream truck's open serving window, then spun around and bowed to us.

"Good evening! What kind of ice cream would you like?"

"Get out of there, Way-Way!" Thoreau's eyes grew big and a little scared. "You'll get in trouble!"

"We'll pay for it." Archer shrugged. "It's okay, curls. I promise."

132

Once he saw none of us complaining or voicing our disapproval, Thoreau relaxed and his eyes grew brighter as he watched Wayne caper around like a monkey inside the ice cream truck.

Soon we each held a cone or cup and Wayne jumped out of the truck as Archer held his ice cream cone for him. Mase made sure to leave enough cash to cover our costs - and probably more besides - then turned the Open sign to Closed and shut the serving window.

By then, Emerson had joined us and Angelo silently handed him a cup of chocolate chip cookie dough, which Emerson took with a grunt.

We sat down at the picnic tables again to enjoy our treat, and I was half thinking it was soon time to go home. It was getting dark, and Posy did not like the dark. Plus, the crowd was starting to pick up, and she didn't like too many strangers around her, either.

And I wanted to love her in our bed.

We all do, Quartz grouched. *The boys and I want our mate tonight, Jayden.*

Okay. I'll talk to my brothers, I promised him.

"Angel, what's wrong with your ice cream?" Landry's sudden question caught my attention.

"Nothing. It's good. Thanks."

"You only ate one bite," he argued. "I know you love strawberry ice cream, so what's up?"

"I just don't want any more." Her bottom lip trembled, and I had my suspicions.

"Why are you lying to me?" Now his eyes narrowed, and I debated whether to intervene or let him crash his own plane.

"I'm sorry." Grace covered her red face with both hands. "I swear, I'm trying to lose weight. I've been working out, running, and going to fighter practice. I watch every single thing I put in my mouth, but I've only lost five pounds since I've been here!"

I traded wide-eyed looks with the others. None of us knew what to say to reassure or comfort the girl, but we all knew there was only one person whose words would make any difference, anyway.

"I'll do better," she continued in a whisper. "I promise I will, Landry. I stopped eating lunch. Maybe I can skip breakfast, too. I don't want to embarrass you any more."

"Fix this," I heard Posy hiss at Landry, who was staring at Grace with wide, bewildered eyes.

"Why would you think I'm embarrassed by you?" Landry asked as he stood up and towered over her.

"I know I'm unattractive. Like that boy said, I'm fat—"

"Shut up, angel," Landry said through gritted teeth. "We're going home, where I'm going to show you again and again just how attractive I find your gorgeous body."

He pulled her to her feet, then bent, put his shoulder in her stomach, and stood up with his sweetly rounded mate dangling down his back in utter shock. He clamped one arm over the back of her thighs and the other behind her knees.

Posy grinned and waved at Grace's upside down face as Landry started to walk off, and the rest of us chuckled.

"Wait, Gamma Lan, big sissy! Your ice cream!" Thoreau yelled and held up their paper cups.

"I got a much better dessert to eat at home," Landry growled without stopping, and he carried Grace off into the night.

"What's better than ice cream?" Thoreau cocked his head in confusion.

Cole and I burst out laughing, Mase and Angelo rolled their eyes, Emerson snorted, and Ash, Wayne and Wyatt fell on the ground giggling. Posy just looked as confused as Thoreau, which was even more amusing.

I mean, how many times has one of us eaten her out and she still doesn't get it? I linked my brothers, making them chuckle harder.

Archer was the only one who answered Thoreau.

"Funnel cake, Reau," he muttered and pressed the boy's face into his chest while glaring at the rest of us. "He means funnel cake."

"Funnel cake?" Thoreau and Posy said in unison. "What's that?"

"Finish your ice cream and we'll get one," I sobered up enough to answer.

Can we please go home soon? Quartz rumbled. *There are too many people, and I want to eat my better dessert at home, too.*

You're right, Q, I smirked. *We'll leave after funnel cake and have an even more delicious dessert at home.*

#

Lark

"We need to give that pretty little mouth something more to do than scream," Quartz taunted, his breath hot in my ear. "Which of my brothers do you want to suck off first? Hmm, little girl? Daddy Garnet's thick tip alone would fill up your whole mouth. You want to taste him, little girl?"

I shuddered and moaned. His words were as arousing as his fingers in my dripping pussy.

When we got home from the fair, it didn't take long for us to race to our bedroom and strip down. Thankfully, our humans were willing to let us ascend, and my mates were all over me before the last pieces of clothing hit the floor.

"Or maybe you want to gag on Sid first," Quartz continued to tease me with both his words and his hand. "Would you like that, little girl? Would you like Sid's long dick thrusting down your throat?"

"Quartz!" I cried as my vagina throbbed, wanting to be stuffed full by one of my mates.

"No, it can't be me. I have other plans. You know what? I think our baby has a need that Daddy Garnet can fill the best."

"My pleasure," Garnet purred.

Is that okay with you, my love? Quartz linked me. *I've warned him and he knows to be more gentle than I was the other day.*

Yes, I moaned to both him and Garnet, too excited and needy to think of a longer reply.

"On all fours, little girl," Quartz commanded, and I quickly did as he asked.

Raising my head, I watched with wide eyes as Garnet walked on his knees across the mattress and came to a stop right in front of my face, his penis rigid and hard as steel.

"Get ready, little girl," he rumbled.

Meanwhile, Quartz stopped fingering me and moved away, and I whimpered for a second until I felt him kneeling behind me. One hand held my hip and the other guided his tip to my entrance. He rubbed it up and down on my outer lips a few times, coating himself in the juices that ran down my thighs, then fitted himself just inside me.

"Open your mouth," he demanded.

I raised my eyes to Garnet's and saw his gaze riveted to my face. His hand was around his thick length, stroking it, and a few drops of liquid glistened on the head. I licked my lips, hoping I could do this right and satisfy him without panicking.

"Open. Your. Mouth."

A spike of desire went through me at Quartz's hard tone, and I did as he said. Garnet palmed the back of my head with his free hand and guided his wet tip between my lips. A groan sounded from deep in his chest, and he pushed in just a bit as his hand moved to the nape of my neck.

Are you fine, Lark? he asked, worry thick in his voice.

Yes, Daddy. You taste so good!

"Move her hair. Show me," Quartz commanded, and Garnet gathered up my hair into a ponytail that he held with one hand. "That's good, little girl. Now take more of Daddy Garnet into your mouth. The deeper you take him, the deeper I'll go in your tight pussy."

Then he drew his hips back just enough that it felt like I was going to lose him, and a little whine left me. Greedy for the pleasure I knew was coming, I sucked Garnet deeper into my mouth.

Quartz linked me again to make sure I was okay, and I was so gone in the pleasure that all I could do was moan a yes.

Reaching around my hips, Quartz anchored his hands on my inner thighs, then slammed his whole length into me in one heavy thrust. The force of it pushed Garnet deeper into my mouth, making me gag a little as he hit the back of my throat.

Lark? they both linked me.

Good, I reassured them. *I good. More please, daddies.*

Slowly, Quartz withdrew until he was almost completely out of me and Garnet pulled out of my mouth until only his tip was inside my lips. In concert, they thrust back in, Garnet going no deeper or harder than what he'd already done.

"Good girl," Quartz murmured. "Such a good girl for your daddies."

The smell of them, the heat from their big bodies, and Q's words all combined to make me lose my mind, and I came hard.

"Oh, no. Tsk tsk tsk." Quartz bent over so his chest was flush against my back. "You came without Daddy's permission. What a naughty little girl. Jayden said no spanking, but I think we can come up with a suitable punishment. What do you think, Topaz?"

"Granite and I are going to suck your titties, dearest, and you're going to jack Sid off."

Topaz's voice ran over my bare back like a caress, and goosebumps flared all over me.

Is that okay, Lark? he asked.

Yes! Please, Paz!

Grinning, he and Granite laid down on either side of me and their mouths latched on my breasts in a heartbeat. Quartz and Garnet thrust in sync again and again, and the tension began to rebuild in my core. Hard shudders shook me as my mates worked my body, and I didn't know how they expected me *not* to come with so much pleasure shooting through me at every end.

A second later, Sid joined us, kneeling next to Garnet, and tugged at the hand I had knotted in the sheets. I wasn't sure I could balance on one hand with Quartz slamming into me from behind and Garnet from the front, but Topaz and Granite put their free hands on my shoulders and steadied me. They held my weight easily as they nipped at my breasts, and I knew I'd find little love bites everywhere later, the naughty boys.

Sid carefully took my hand and guided my fingers where he wanted them.

"Stroke me," he whispered. "Please, my darling. Will you stroke me?"

I moved my hand up and down his firm shaft as he grunted in satisfaction, and I grinned, proud of myself for pleasuring him.

Relying on Topaz and Granite to hold me up, I sucked Garnet harder and pumped Sid faster. Then, all of a sudden, Quartz stopped thrusting and pulled out of me completely. At the same time, Granite's mouth left my breasts, and I whined loudly. I didn't realize they had only stopped to readjust positions. I thought they'd finished and left me wanting as part of my 'punishment'.

They soon proved just how wrong I was.

Topaz moved to kneel on Garnet's other side while Granite shifted to lay fully under me. He lined his dick up with my pussy, then hammered into me. At the same time, Topaz took my free hand and guided it to his dick, and I knew he wanted me to pump him like I was Sid. Gladly, I obliged.

An enormous penis in either hand, one in my mouth, and the other in my pussy - and I came again, whimpering and shivering. Granite growled as I fluttered my walls around him, and I tightened my hold on Topaz and Sid while sucking Garnet further down my throat. All four of them groaned, but none of them came with me, making me pout a little.

"Again, little girl?" Quartz clucked his tongue again. "We've been too lenient with you. Daddy's going to punish you hard this time."

Half excited, half nervous, I wondered what he had planned. Then warm liquid slid between my cheeks and wet fingers rubbed and prodded my bum hole, and I quivered in anticipation.

Slowly and gently, he eased a finger into my bum hole and took his time working up to two. All the while, I sucked Garnet, stroked Sid and Topaz, and moaned as Granite hit the right spot again and again.

My breathing picked up as the tension wound tighter and tighter in my belly. Granite realized what was happening and reached down to rub my little pleasure button.

"Come for us, my love."

I screamed around Garnet's dick as the orgasm hit me. Juice gushed from my pussy and dripped down my thighs onto Granite's, and he laughed as he sucked on my mate mark.

"Such a good girl," Garnet murmured as he slid in and out of my mouth. "Daddy is proud of you."

I beamed at his praise, but my attention quickly went to what Quartz was doing when his fingers scissored my bum hole open and his thick tip pressed in.

Garnet grabbed my face between his hands and Granite tugged and twisted my nipples, both distracting me as Quartz carefully pushed until he was balls deep inside my bum.

"That's right, little girl," Quartz growled. "Take your daddies and your mates. Take us all like a good girl."

He began to move in sync with Garnet and Granite, and Topaz and Sid covered my hands with their own to guide my speed. My mind spiraled into mush. I was on such a sensory overload that I was ready to crawl out of my skin.

Please! Please let me come! I beg them through the link, even though we all knew Quartz would make the decision.

All of their movements grew more frantic, and they rode me hard and fast until they each shot their load at the same time: Garnet in my mouth, Sid and Topaz in my hands, Granite in my pussy, and Quartz in my bum.

Daddy? I pleaded, desperate for release as tears streamed down my cheeks. *Daddy, please?*

Still deep inside me, Quartz laid his sweaty chest against my back and wrapped one hand around my throat, squeezing enough that I could feel it, but not enough to hurt or make me panic. His other hand reached around my hip, found my pleasure button, and tickled it mercilessly.

"Come, little girl," Quartz rasped in my ear. "Come hard with Daddy Garnet in your mouth, Daddy Q in your ass, and Granite in your tight little pussy."

And I did.

So intensely, in fact, I lost consciousness for a few minutes.

When I returned to my senses, I found myself smushed in a pile of heavy bodies, all five of them trying to cuddle me at once. I was sticky *everywhere* and wanted a shower, but my body was boneless with satisfaction, and I didn't want to move.

Like, ever again.

Topaz and Sid had other ideas, however, and dragged themselves out of bed for some reason.

I didn't like that and whimpered, wanting all my mates with me.

"Shh, sweetheart," Garnet whispered in my ear as Granite stroked my hair and Quartz lay draped over my back, still panting a little. "They just went to get the bathroom ready. You're going to take a shower with them. They'll get you all cleaned up, sweetheart."

"But we're going to get you dirty again first," Topaz chuckled as he untangled me from three other sets of sweaty limbs and lifted me into his arms.

I hummed as butterflies of anticipation filled my tummy. Laying my head on his chest, I said, "I love you. I love you all."

"We love you, too," they chorused, and I heard Sid call out, "I love you, my darling," from the bathroom.

"Thank you, my loves. Thank you for loving me."

"It's we who should be thanking you, little mate," Quartz murmured as he stood up and cupped my face in his hands. "Thank you for caring about us, for sharing us, for making each one of us feel special and loved. You are our perfect mate and our perfect luna."

"And you my perfect alphas. I the happiest she-wolf in the world."

"Then we're doing our job right." He gave me a happy grin, not one of his sarcastic or dangerous ones, which was a rare gift indeed. "Thank you for trusting us and our boys. We will work hard to keep you happy all of your days."

"Me, too, Daddy." I kissed his nose and he blinked in surprise, which made me giggle. "I work hard to keep you happy, too, my sweet and precious alpha mates."

8: *Made for Me*

Grace

"You've been skipping lunch?" Landry growled the second he set me on my feet.

I stared up at him with wide, anxious eyes. This was the first time I was encountering his anger, and I was unsure how to handle it, especially since it was directed at me.

He hadn't said a word after leaving the others at the fair. In silence, he carried me to his car, buckled me in, and drove us home. Then he scooped me up in his arms and carried me inside and all the way up the stairs to our bedroom.

He wasn't even breathing hard.

The romantic side of me wondered if he was carrying me so much to prove I wasn't too heavy. The practical side of me, however, reminded me that werewolves were immensely strong, and the higher the rank, the stronger the shifter. Landry was third in command of one of the most powerful packs in the kingdom. Even if I weighed three hundred pounds, he'd still be able to carry me with ease.

Since we met three days ago, I'd discovered a few important things about my mate. One, he was stubborn. Once his mind was set, it was almost impossible to change it. Two, he was incredibly gentle. Not just with how he treated me, but also in his interactions with others, which was rare to find in a shifter of his standing. In my experience, the more powerful the wolf, the more brutal the man. Then again, I was learning fast that my former pack, White Pelt, wasn't anything like my new one.

The third thing I learned was that Landry was a talker. The boy's mouth. Never. Stopped. Moving. Even at night, I heard him murmuring in his sleep as he spooned me. Just this morning, when I woke him up for breakfast, he was mumbling something about gingerbread houses, which made me giggle.

And I loved that about him. After being around people who were too exhausted just surviving in the wilderness to make conversation, he was a breath of fresh air. His deep, velvety voice was a joy to my ears, and I happily listened to my little chatterbox all day long.

That's why his silence tonight was so unnerving. I didn't like it anymore than I liked the anger in his blue-green eyes.

I had far too much experience with angry males who treated females like we were only good for cooking, cleaning, and producing pups. However, while nineteen years' worth of experience made me cautious, I knew Landry would never raise his hand to me or treat me that way. I trusted him completely with my heart, mind, and soul.

Now, if only I could trust him with my body, too, I thought miserably.

So far, we kissed and cuddled and shared the same bed every night in our new house, but only to sleep. I knew most new shifter couples finished up the whole mating process within twenty-four hours, but I asked him to wait a bit so we could get to know each other better first. He innocently agreed, wanting to please me, but never guessed it was an excuse to hide how scared I was.

What would I do if he rejected me after seeing what was under my clothes?

Despite the late July heat, I was careful to keep covered up. Landry, on the other hand, roamed around in his shorts most of the time. He knew what that did to me, and his smug grins when he caught me staring at his honed body brought a heavy blush to my cheeks. That made him chuckle and drop kisses all over my face, but I was still too shy to tease him back.

"Answer me, Grace!" he demanded suddenly, bringing my attention to the here and now.

His voice was a little louder and sharper than normal, and I jumped.

"Aw, baby, I'm so sorry!" He cupped my face in his big palms and kissed my forehead. "I never meant to scare you. I'm just upset and it came out in my tone. I *would* like you to answer me, though."

I hesitated. I didn't want him to be mad at me anymore, but I didn't want him to know how ashamed I was of my chubby body, especially when his was so fine. He really was the hottest guy I'd ever laid eyes on, and I wasn't any kind of hot unless it was a hot mess.

He Gracie's mate, Flicker whispered, trying to encourage me. *He love Gracie. All of Gracie. Even muffin handles.*

Muffin top or love handles, I corrected her absently.

Same same. She rolled her eyes at me. *Trust mate, Gracie. Flick trust Oak. He good wolf. Landry good man, too.*

I know he is, Flick.

"Yes, I've been skipping lunch," I whispered at last.

"Okay. Let me clarify so I know I'm not misunderstanding. Every morning, you pack a big, healthy lunch for me to take to work, but you yourself eat nothing?"

His intense blue-green eyes bore into me, and I swallowed hard.

"I eat an apple or a cup of yogurt," I admitted. "I get too hungry if I don't."

141

"You are a werewolf, Grace, and an active one," he said with a heavy scowl. "You've been coming to fighter practice every day, and I get that you're probably going for the exercise, although I'm worried you'll get hurt because you're not experienced and the pack warriors can get rowdy and violent at times. There are other ways to get exercise, but we'll talk about that later because I want to focus on the current issue, which is that you need more fuel than an apple and some yogurt. And *no way* are you skipping breakfast! Don't even think about it."

There was a lot to unpack in his rant, and I dropped my eyes as I processed through it. He was right about needing more fuel; shifters' natural metabolism burned through more calories than humans, and hungry wolves were not safe wolves.

He was also right about the fighters getting out of hand sometimes. It happened just yesterday when two young hotheads lost their tempers and ripped into each other. Landry had slung me over his shoulder and ran me out to his truck, where he locked me in until he and the other gammas shut the fight down just in time for Alpha Wyatt to arrive. Even after the alpha dragged the two idiots away by their ears, Landry insisted on driving me home instead of letting me get my last half-hour of practice in.

"Grace, take off your clothes."

His softly spoken words made my eyes fly up to meet his, and I gulped when I saw he was dead serious. Shaking my head, I blushed and played with my fingers. With a sigh, he dropped a kiss on one cheek, then the other, then pecked my lips.

"Take off your clothes, angel. Please? Only your shorts and shirt. I'll take mine off, too. Can you trust me just a little?"

Get it over with, I told myself. *You shouldn't have let it go this long. You're too attached to him now. If he rejects you, you're going to die.*

Taking a deep breath, I slipped off my shoes, then unbuttoned my shorts and skinned them down my legs. Closing my eyes, I fingered the hem of my shirt and bit my bottom lip. The sound of clothing rustling made me open my eyes, and I saw that he'd already stripped down to his boxer briefs.

I knew he meant to encourage me, but seeing *all that* on display made me feel even worse about what I had to offer. The boy looked like he'd been carved from ice. The heavy slabs of his pecs, the solid squares cut into his stomach, and those deep vertical lines that curved around his hip bones and disappeared into his waistband...

"Your shirt, too," he said in a rough rasp, and I blushed because he caught me devouring him with my eyes.

Biting my lips hard, I started to pull my shirt up. Apparently, I wasn't going fast enough because his hands soon whipped the fabric over my head. His eyes raked up and down my body as I stood before him in my bra and panties, and his hands clenched into white-knuckled fists.

Is he really that angry? Or is it disgust at what he's finally seeing? I thought and wanted to crawl in a hole and die.

The longer he looked, the redder his high cheekbones became, and his Adam's apple bobbed as he swallowed hard.

"Grace," he breathed. "By the moon, you really *are* perfect."

That was when I understood he hadn't been mad at all. He was as nervous as I was and trying not to show it. That made me feel *a lot* better.

He slowly walked around me, then stepped closer until his chest just barely brushed my back. Keeping his hands at his sides, he leaned down and kissed my shoulder, then moved his lips to my neck, and I couldn't hold back the little sounds slipping out of my mouth. He chuckled and his warm breath slid over my skin like a caress, stoking the fire burning in my lower belly.

He finally put his hands on me, holding my waist as he pressed his hips into my back. Something long and hard poked my spine, and I blushed *again* when I realized what it was.

Knowing he was aroused, the intoxicating smell of him, the heat coming off his rock-hard body, the sparks dancing everywhere his skin touched mine... Well, let's just say I was lucky my knees didn't give out.

"You feel that, angel?" He brushed his lips against my jaw, and my eyes rolled back in my head. "Does that feel like I find you unattractive? Does that feel like I think your body is anything other than absolutely perfect?"

"My squishy belly and thick thighs make *that* happen?" I asked with disbelief.

"*Any* part of your luscious body makes that happen." His voice dropped an octave, making goosebumps pop up all over my skin. "And you have no idea what I want to do to your pretty thighs and what's between them."

His penis twitched against my back, and my belly twisted in a tight, hot tangle. Goddess, I wanted this man! But did he *really* want me, or was he making do with what he'd been stuck with?

"That's just the mate bond," I sniffed, tears pooling in my eyes. "You would never even look at me if it weren't for the moon magic binding us."

"Not true." Grabbing my chin in one hand, he tilted my head and kissed me with so much tenderness that my heart melted. "Remember the first time we met?"

I blinked at the change of topic, but nodded.

Peri and her mate, Beta Tyler, had taken me out to dinner two days before Luna Posy freed Landry from his curse. We'd just picked up our menus at Roger's when all of the gammas but Rio walked in. Gammas Nick and Adam grabbed another table and shoved it next to ours so they could join us, and my eyes were immediately drawn to Landry.

Something stirred inside me as I stared at him, which I knew now was the mate bond trying to break through the curse. At the time, I only knew he made me uncomfortable in a rub-my-thighs-together kind of way.

He gave me one long look, then avoided my eyes for the rest of the night, and I was convinced he found me so unappealing, I wasn't worth a second glance.

"I saw your delicious body, beautiful face, and sparkling eyes, and I wondered why I couldn't have been blessed with *you* as my mate." He paused to kiss my throat. "The curse shut down those thoughts pretty quick and didn't let me feel anything for you other than disdain, but you can ask the alphas, Beta Ty, or any of my gamma brothers. They'll tell you I've always preferred girls like you."

"You've been with other girls?" My heart sank down to my toes. "But you told me you were a virgin, too."

"I am. I've saved every single first for my mate. But I wasn't *dead*," he snickered. "I still *looked*, angel, but that's all I did. I swear on the moon."

"And you 'looked' at fat girls?" I raised a skeptical eyebrow.

"*Beautiful* girls," he corrected. "Big, beautiful girls with curves in all the right places."

His hands ran up and down my sides, and I felt a flash of shame for the little rolls he was touching, but he didn't seem to even notice them, and the shame evaporated as his mouth made a meal of mine.

And the mate sparks helped, too.

"I love you, Grace," he murmured when he ended the kiss. "I love your quiet voice and your sweet nature. I love your kindness and your compassion. I love your work ethic and your personal integrity. But this body of yours? I love it so much that I get angry when I hear you say bad things about it."

He cupped my breasts and squeezed them gently through my bra, and I moaned.

"Every part of you is perfect for me, angel. Your little noises are perfect. They drive me wild. And your breasts! Goddess, they're so big! I love how heavy they are! I'm rock hard just holding them while you still have your bra on!" he chirped.

I giggled. I could feel *exactly* how excited he was with his penis digging into my back.

"Can I hold them naked? Can I feel them with nothing between us?" he prattled on. "Can I undo this... What is it called? A buckle? A hook? This thing here."

He pulled at my bra clasp, and I nodded. He didn't waste any time undoing it, then slid the straps down my arms and pulled the fabric away. His hands took the place of my bra, and my breasts filled his calloused palms to overflowing.

"Landry," I moaned and tipped my head back against his chest.

"I'm finally touching Grace's beautiful breasts," he purred.

Humming, he lifted my girls and squashed them together, his hands kneading them a little roughly, and my nipples hardened in response. Ever so gently, he rolled them between his thumbs and forefingers.

"Mmm. I can't wait to take them in my mouth," he breathed in my ear, raising goosebumps all over my skin. Then he sighed. "Much as I could do just this all night, I want to tell you about the rest of your perfect body."

His hands left my breasts to skim down my stomach, and I squirmed against him in embarrassment.

"I'm sorry," I whispered. "I wanted to lose more weight before—"

"Stop that," he scolded as he tickled my jiggly-ness and made me giggle. "Your 'squishy' belly is perfect. I love it. I'm going to bite a big mouthful of it later."

Before I could do more than squeak at that comment, his hands went around to my butt and gripped my round cheeks.

"This is also perfect. I'm going to gnaw on it later, too."

Pleasure spiked through me at both his words and his touch, especially when one hand cupped me between my legs.

"Landry!" I squealed.

"Goddess, I want you, angel!" he hissed, rubbing his fingers against my panties. "I want your perfect body so bad, I'm going to come in my boxers! Do you— Do you feel *anything* like that for me?"

His voice cracked when he asked that, and my heart cracked with it. Our first day together, he'd told me about the girl who'd cursed him into believing she was his mate just so she could reject him. I could see for myself how badly that damaged him and knew his self-esteem was as low as mine. Despite his hot body, handsome face, and pretty eyes, he struggled to believe I wanted him just like I couldn't believe he wanted my pudgy body, plain face, and boring brown eyes.

Gracie and Landry both feel same way and not know it, Flicker giggled. *Both so unsure and both so in love.*

"Yes, Lan," I breathed and half-turned to stare up at him over my shoulder. "I'm on fire for you."

"You are? You're not just making the best of this and settling for me?"

I hated seeing the aching vulnerability on my mate's face, and I despised the one who put it there.

Turning all the way around, I took his face between my palms, leaned up, and kissed him on the lips.

"You are my Goddess-given mate, Landry," I told him sternly. "I love you and want to be your mate in every way possible."

"Do you know what you're saying? You want me to mark and mate you?"

"You won't change your mind after, right?" Anxiety made my heart flutter. "You're so handsome and I'm—"

"Perfect!" he interrupted with a fierce scowl as his hands squeezed my hips. "You're perfect, angel!"

"I was *going* to say I'm worried that you'll be disappointed."

"I won't be disappointed. How could I be? Like you said, the Goddess herself made us for each other, and I could ask you the same things. I've already been rejected once in my life. Even if it wasn't real, it sure *felt* real. I don't think— No, I *know* I wouldn't survive if you threw me away." He suddenly stopped and sucked in a sharp breath. "Oh, my Goddess! Is that why you asked to wait? You've been deciding whether or not to keep me?"

The anguish in his tear-filled eyes was something I never wanted to see again.

My poor boy. I am going to love all the hurt out of you, even if it takes me the rest of my life.

"No, Landry. Quite the opposite. I am so in love with you, it doesn't seem real. I love your deep voice and how you talk all the time. I love your pretty eyes and handsome face. And this *body*."

I took a deep breath, trembling from how badly I wanted to kiss and touch every inch of him, and he stood there, dumbfounded and silent, as I looked him up and down.

"This body is killing me! My heart feels like it's going to explode just from looking at you. You know it, too, don't you, you little booger?" I teased him. "Every time you strutted around the house in your shorts, you knew what it was doing to me to see all this tanned skin and hard muscles on display."

"I hoped it would help woo you," he admitted, then ducked his head and stared hard at the ground. "So why *did* you ask to wait before we mated? I've been so scared that it was because you find me lacking. Nia said— Nia said I was worthless."

Flicker stirred and wanted out to go find that witch and kill her slowly and painfully. Fighting my own desire to do the same, I had to remind both of us that the girl was already dead. With a disgruntled harrumph, Flicker flopped down and scowled until Oak began to talk quietly to her.

"Lacking? Worthless?" I put my fingers under his chin and lifted his face. "She was a fool. I don't know why she singled you out to bully and torment, but she couldn't have been further from the truth. You are a hardworking gamma, a wonderful brother to your sister, and an amazing friend to the other gammas. Everyone, including me, respects and likes you, Landry. You're adorable, gentle, charming, kind, and absolutely precious to me. You're my sweetheart."

His eyes widened at every word, and even the tips of his ears burned pink when I finished.

"Really?" he mumbled.

"Really," I assured him. "The only reason I wanted to wait was to give you time to be sure *you* wanted to keep *me*. What if you're embarrassed later, having to introduce your fat mate to your friends and family?"

"Call yourself fat like it's a bad thing one more time!" he snarled. "You won't like the consequences."

His eyes flashing, he bent down a little, wrapped his thick arms around my thicker thighs, and lifted me up. Startled, I latched onto his shoulders as he carried me to the bed.

"You are an angel - *my* angel - and you are perfect. I love every squishy inch of you, and I'll say it over and over until you believe it."

He dropped me on the bed and his eyes fixed on my breasts as they bounced. Reluctantly tearing his eyes away from them, he crawled on top of me and buried his face in my neck so his mouth could explore, and I shivered and squirmed under him until he found the spot that made me shiver and squirm harder than any other.

"This is it, Grace," he breathed against my skin. "This is the spot and this is the moment. There's no going back after this."

"There was *never* any going back. Not after I caught a whiff of pineapples and saw your gorgeous wolf running toward me." I smiled and kissed his cheek. "Now, Landry King Benson, don't you think it's time to claim what belongs to you?"

"Past time, Grace Elizabeth Turnbull."

His eyes flared silver as Oak ascended, then his canines dropped and bit into my neck. I gasped at the sudden pain before pleasure flooded through my veins in a rush of heat. Then Oak licked away the blood and sealed the punctures, sending sparks skittering all over me.

When Landry lifted his head, his blue-green eyes went to the mark and he smirked.

"And now, my beautiful, perfect mate, I'm going to take your virginity and give you mine. We're going to share every first that mates can share, even if it takes all night long."

He reached down and ripped off his shorts, and my eyes bugged out at my first ever sight of a fully erect penis.

Are they all so big? Then I giggled at myself. *It's not like I'll ever find out. A gentle man he may be, but Landry would kill any man who flashed me his privates!*

"Don't be nervous, baby, but my balls are about to explode. I can see from your expression you don't know what I mean, and I'm not trying to be vulgar, but I'm going to come. I *need* to come, and I want it to be in your hands. Touch me, angel. Please?"

"Umm, okay, but I don't know what I'm doing," I murmured with a beet-red face. "Can you show me?"

"Of course. You're not going to have to do much, though," he chuckled. "Trust me on that."

Rolling us onto our sides so we faced each other, he took my hand and showed me how to stroke up and down his rock-hard length. Then he placed my other hand on his ball sack and guided me in fondling it.

"A little harder, angel. Oh, yeah. There you go. Perfect, just like you."

His eyes dropped to my breasts and, as if he couldn't resist any longer, his hands left mine to grab them. Little cries tore out of my throat as his lips latched onto one of my nipples and sucked it hard. Whimpering in need, I lost focus on touching him, and he groaned low in his throat.

No, no, no, angel! Don't stop, he linked me, his mouth busy with my breasts. *Please? I'm almost there, baby. Please, Grace!*

His hips jerked to prod me into stroking him again and, feeling empowered, I tightened my hold and rubbed him good and hard. Seconds later, his body went still and white goo squirted all over my belly.

"Grace!" he gasped against the swell of my breast.

Then he rolled away from me and leapt out of bed.

"Did I do something wrong?" I whimpered.

"No, baby. I'm going to clean up the mess real quick, then I'll take care of you. One second."

Before I could even process his words, he was back with a warm, wet washcloth. He wiped his semen off my hands and stomach, then tossed the cloth to the floor.

"And now it's your turn," he murmured with a wolfy grin as he climbed on top of me again.

"Landry?" By this point, my panties were soaked, and I rubbed my thighs together in desperation.

"I don't like the word pussy, so I'm going to call it your kitty, okay?" Not waiting for an answer, he laid his hand over my panties right where I ached. "I'm going to spread your legs and put my mouth on your kitty and taste every part of it. Then I'm going to use my fingers and imitate what *this*—" he rocked his semi-hard penis against my hip "—is going to do to your kitty when it's hard again so you're not surprised."

"*Landry!*"

"Don't worry. I'll get hard again fast, baby, I promise. It happens just by smelling your honeysuckle scent. Seeing you sprawled out under me like this is making it happen even faster. Then I can put it inside your kitty, but don't be afraid, angel. I'll go slowly and gently and do my best not to hurt you. Once Flicker takes away the soreness from your first time, I'm going to mate you and mate you and mate you until you're lying in a puddle of semen and can't remember any name but mine as you come and come and—"

"*LAN. DRY. BEN. SON!*"

I loved that my boy was a talker, but if he didn't shut up and take me soon, I was going to jump out of my skin!

"You got an objection, angel?" he smirked as his hands pulled my panties off.

"Yeah," I whimpered, arching off the bed.

"You do? What is it?"

"You haven't started yet."

A dark chuckle was all the warning I had before his hands opened my knees and he dove in face-first.

#

Landry

I was drunk on my girl.

On the taste of her, the smell of her, the sight of her. On the throaty moans that slipped from her plump lips as I ate her little kitty all up.

Goddess, that little kitty! So wet and hot and responsive. My tongue barely touched her jewel and she was panting and squirming under me, which brought a pleased grin to my lips.

"Landry? What's happening?"

The thread of panic in her voice didn't please me, though. I knew she was a virgin, but that right there let me know she'd never so much as touched herself, which was more than I could claim. As many times as I'd jacked off in the shower the past couple of years, I should be blind.

Or rubbed raw.

You're coming, baby, I explained in the link, since my mouth was otherwise occupied. *It's going to feel so good. Just relax, angel, and let go. I love you. I love you, my beautiful, perfect mate.*

Wrapping my lips around her rigid jewel, I sucked lightly, and she fell apart with a soft cry. I licked her up and down and plunged my tongue into her soft, wet heat to help her ride it out.

I myself was hard again and aching to sink balls-deep into her, but I needed to make sure she was ready first. As she shuddered through her very first orgasm, I kissed the insides of her thighs and let my fingers carefully explore her precious kitty, all while murmuring how much I loved her and needed her.

When I eased my index finger inside her, she instantly clamped down on it and her whole body tensed.

"Landry?"

"Shh, it's okay, angel. I can stop if you want me to. Does it hurt?"

"No, it doesn't, and don't stop. I just got scared for a second."

Well, that broke my heart.

"Oh, baby, don't be scared."

Leaving my finger inside her, I scooted up to lie next to her and kissed her cheek, her chin, her nose, her lips. Kissed her lips again.

"I know new experiences can be scary, but I'm figuring this out with you, okay? I'm worried I'm going to hurt you or disappoint you—"

She put her hand over my mouth, and I kissed her palm.

"Just give me a second to get used to it," she asked and dropped her hand.

"Take all the time you need, angel."

"But isn't it difficult for you?" Her beautiful face scrunched up with worry. "I don't want to hurt you, sweetheart."

"Baby, the worst that will happen is I'll come in the sheets like I did on your squishy belly." I kissed the tip of her nose. "Then I'll get hard again and we can continue or stop as you want to."

She nodded. Then, with her big brown eyes fixed on mine, she slowly pulsed her walls around my finger.

"Goddess, Grace," I hissed and dug my face into her neck.

To distract myself from the need to start stroking in and out of her, I kissed her mate mark, then sucked it lightly, making her moan and squirm against me.

"I— I feel like I should move," she whispered at last. "Or like I want *you* to move."

"Can I try something?" I asked against her skin.

When she said yes, I laid open-mouth kisses from her throat to her breasts and circled one nipple with my tongue while I slowly moved my finger in and out of her. She gasped and her hands slid into my hair to hold my head in place, and I was happy to begin learning what she liked.

As I suckled her, I risked a second finger and was rewarded by her low, long moan.

Angel, you feel so good, I linked her since my mouth was once more occupied. *I love your hard nipples and soft, wet little kitty so much, baby.*

"Landry!" she panted. "More, Landry! Please, sweetheart, I need— I need *something*!"

While sucking hard on her nipple, I smushed my face into her big, soft breast, nearly suffocated myself, and pulled back just enough to get a little air through my nose.

Perfect. So freaking perfect!

Stroking her kitty a little faster, I spread my fingers a bit to stretch her, wanting her to experience only minimal pain when I entered her.

That was the thing I was dreading the most.

I'd talked to Rio first, but Emmeline hadn't been a virgin when they met. Knowing Peri for sure was, I went to Beta Tyler next, and he told me about the conversation he'd had with the alphas the night before his birthday. According to him, Alpha Jayden had gone first with the luna and taken her in one hard thrust. Like ripping off a band-aid, he'd thought to get the pain over with all at once, but it had taken her several minutes to recover enough for him to continue.

Tyler, horrified by that idea, said he'd taken Peri in a series of small nudges over several minutes. That was almost worse, though, he admitted, because it had hurt her for longer.

I wasn't close enough to any of the other betas to ask them something so personal, and none of my gamma brothers had ever taken a girl's virginity, so I was stuck. I didn't want to hurt my angel *at all*, but there didn't seem to be a way not to.

Distract her, Oak murmured. *Distract her at that moment.*

151

Distract her? I swallowed hard. I'd be distracted enough myself at 'that' moment, trying to make sure I was doing everything right!

Rub little kitty. Enter her as she comes.

How did my wolf have better advice than the alpha and beta? I didn't know, but I was going to take it!

As my angel whimpered and arched her hips into my hand, I moved my thumb to slide up and down her jewel.

"Landry?"

"Shh. You're okay, baby," I murmured as I quickly knelt between her thick thighs, my thumb and fingers working faster now as she spiraled higher. "I'm going to make you feel good again."

With my free hand, I grabbed myself and looked down to line up with her, wanting to be ready for 'that' moment, and the sight made me harder than I'd ever been in my life. Her legs spread wide. My fingers inside her little kitty. Her wet folds. My thumb teasing her jewel.

"Goddess, Grace!" I growled. "You're gorgeous like this!"

My eyes flicked up to see her breasts shaking and her hands twisting into the sheets, and I knew I couldn't hold back much longer. Pulling my fingers out of her, I slid them to her jewel and rubbed it faster than I'd intended, but she seemed to love it. She tilted her head back and chanted my name, and I felt on top of the world to know I was giving her so much pleasure.

The second she came, I guided my dripping tip to her kitty and pushed forward a little.

"Angel, does that hurt?" I murmured and kept my hips still despite the drive to rock deeper into her.

"No," she moaned and lifted her arms, her hands motioning me down. "Lay on me. I want to feel all of you."

"As you wish, my love." Grinning, I did as she asked, but kept most of my weight on my elbows as I hovered above her.

She didn't like that, though, and looped her arms around my neck to pull me right down on top of all her softness. Not expecting her to do that, I had no time to stop my hips from following the rest of my body, and I sank deeper into her.

A little panicked, I lifted my head and sealed my open mouth over hers in time to swallow her little cry of pain.

Why did you do that, angel? I fussed as our tongues dueled. *I wanted to make it as painless as possible for you!*

I'm fine, Landry, but I again feel the need to move. Or for you to move.

Give it a second to make sure you're okay.
What happened to 'As you wish, my love'?

Feisty girl, I chuckled. *Have Flicker ease the soreness, and I will.*

Once I was sure she wasn't in any pain, I pressed my hips deeper into the cradle between her thighs, and my eyes rolled back in my head at how good it felt to have her tight, wet kitty surround me.

She pulled her mouth away from mine with a wet pop, then speared her fingers in my hair to angle my head to the side.

"What are you doing, baby?" Shivering with need, I slowly arched my hips back, then forward again, making us both moan.

"I'm going to mark you, Landry," she rasped. "You are mine forever."

"Grace, baby, angel, thank you. I love you. I love you. I love you."

She kissed along my throat as I pushed in and out of her, keeping my pace slow and gentle like I'd promised her I would.

Well, I did until she found that special spot and sank her canines in. Then my brain went on vacation and my body took control, the jolt of moon magic from my perfect mate tipping me right over the edge. I smooshed her magnificent breasts together and buried my face between them, slightly ashamed of myself for pounding into her like I was.

"Yes!" she cried out. "Yes! Oh, Goddess, yes!"

Sound like mate love it, Oak chuckled. *Be proud, not 'shamed.*

Grinning like an idiot, I kept my face hidden in my new happy place and let the passion take me.

#

Grace

Two hours and countless orgasms later, Landry's sweaty, sticky body finally collapsed next to mine.

"Love you, sweetheart," I said for the hundredth time and let my heavy eyelids close, as exhausted as I was satiated. "Love you with all my heart."

"I love you, too, Grace." He nuzzled his face into my throat near my brand-new mate mark. "I love you, angel. I love you, my beautiful mate. I love you so much..."

And I fell asleep with my sweet mate's voice leading me to dreamland.

9: Twenty Questions

Posy

"You peed, right, baby?" Mason asked as he handed me up into Ash's SUV.

"Yep! I should be good for a couple of hours at least," I assured him.

Grinning, he leaned in, pulled the seat belt around me, and buckled it in place before giving me a long, lingering kiss.

"Come on, Mase! Move!" Wyatt whined as he climbed in on my other side. "I won the right to sit next to my cutie!"

He shoved Mason's shoulder, and Mason rolled his eyes.

"Yeah, yeah. I'm moving, you little butt." Mason winked at me before withdrawing from the vehicle and closing my door.

Wyatt happily leaned over and kissed my cheek, then gathered my hand in his much bigger one.

"You ready to go, Posy?" he asked with a bright smile as the others piled into the SUV.

"Yep! I'm excited to be there for the royal coronation, but also to see my friends again!" I squeezed his hand in my excitement, and he chuckled.

I was trying hard to not think about King Julian looking for my father's family. I didn't want to get my hopes up if he found nothing.

We had just reached the end of the driveway when my phone rang.

There weren't that many people who called me, only people outside our pack, so I didn't carry it in my pocket. I had to dig around in my purse to find it, then saw Aiden's name and quickly accepted the call.

My brothers called me at least once a week just to chat and check in on me, and I really appreciated it. They caught me up on their lives and their mates, and I enjoyed hearing how the twins were settling in at Green River and taming my brothers into little puppies.

Not that James or Aiden admitted that last part, but it was easy to tell by the stories they told and the way they talked when all four of them were on the call.

I was especially glad to hear from Aiden right now. James had called me a few days ago to inform me that Aiden was on suicide watch. I'd wanted to go right to Green River, but James convinced me not to, saying Keeley and the pack's new therapist were working with him. He also pointed out that Aiden would be ashamed for me to know that he was so 'weak' - Aiden's word - and that could affect his recovery.

I understood and reluctantly agreed. While some might have thought that having a mate would instantly cure mental and emotional trauma, I knew it didn't. There was no quick or easy cure, not even the love of a mate. That love, however, *did* help you see that life was worth living and made you want to find and use coping methods.

So instead of hightailing it to Aiden's rescue, I hired Poppy to go down there and conduct an absolution ceremony. She'd done it for Leo when he couldn't get over that bad business with the demon and what it had made him do at Tall Pines. In essence, she washed the guilt and shame away and left it up to him to decide if he wanted to move on or pick that burden up and carry it again.

Leo chose to move on, and I was hoping Aiden had, too.

"Hello," I said as I put the phone on speaker in case my mates wanted to join the conversation.

"Hey, baby sister." He sounded happy, which made me smile in relief. "Are you safe and well?"

"Of course I am. We're on our way to the queen's coronation," I told him.

"Sounds fun. Glad I'm not going. Don't want to hobnob in a monkey suit again anytime soon," he laughed. "Still coming to the Swift reunion next weekend?"

"Yep! My mates are taking me on vacation after we leave the royal pack, then we'll head over to Crystal Caverns."

"Oh? Where are you going? Are they taking you to Bora Bora?"

"Um, no, I don't think so. I need a passport for that and I don't have one. I wish they'd tell me, though," I pouted and shot a look at Wyatt, who sat next to me.

"It's a surprise, cutie," he smirked. "We're not going to tell you."

"I'm shocked she hasn't wormed it out of you yet," Aiden snorted. "Usually, she crooks her little finger and you cave in a heartbeat."

"Just like I imagine you do with Keeley," Wyatt retorted.

"You'd imagine correctly," my brother chuckled. "These mates, man. They have us whipped."

"It's the same for us, you know," I said. "We'd do anything for you boys, too."

"I know, Posy," he said. "Well, enjoy the coronation and we'll see you guys next weekend."

We all chorused a variety of goodbyes, then I put my phone away with a happy smile, glad my brother was healing.

Strength is what we gain from the madness we survive, I repeated what Lark quoted the other day. *I really am going to see about getting that printed on t-shirts.*

Or tattoo over one of you scars, Lark suggested.

A tattoo? I cringed. *I don't think so.*

"What are you thinking so hard about, honey?" Cole reached up from the back seat and massaged the back of my neck. "I can practically hear the gears turning in your head."

"Lark suggested tattooing over my scars, and I told her to forget it." I shivered.

"I thought you liked tattoos." Mason turned around from the front seat and frowned at me.

"I like *your* tattoos. They're super sexy!" I giggled as his cheekbones blazed red.

"Thank you," he said through his bashfulness. "Tattooing over scars can be difficult, especially depending on how damaged the skin is. I wouldn't recommend it even if you wanted to do that."

"I don't. I'm scared of needles, and I've had enough pain to last a lifetime." I waved a hand to dismiss the idea.

The boys all shifted and a few spikes of anger flared in the mate bond, and I winced. I needed to be more careful with my words.

"Let's pass the time on the long ride with Twenty Questions," I suggested.

"All right, cutie," Wyatt agreed. "You start. Ask us something."

"I told you that I was afraid of needles, and you know I'm afraid of the dark. What are you each afraid of?"

"Nothing," Cole, Mason, and Wyatt said at the same time.

"Going bald," Ash said with a shiver of dread. "I couldn't live without my curls. I hope I never lose them."

"Vampires," Jay admitted. "Blood-suckers freak me out. And Wyatt, you know you're scared of small, closed spaces. You freaked out when we went through that long tunnel under a mountain in Pennsylvania."

"I do *not* have claustrophobia!" Wyatt snarled. "I just hate feeling like I'm trapped."

"That feeling is called claustrophobia, baby brother," Mason chuckled.

"Whatever." Wyatt crossed his arms over his chest and slumped back in his seat. "You and Cole are afraid of things, too. You're just too proud to admit it!"

"You don't have to answer if you don't want to," I jumped in to soothe ruffled feathers. I shouldn't have asked a question that would threaten their egos. "It's not easy to admit fears."

"I used to be afraid of lightning when I was a kid. Just lightning, not thunder." Cole shook his head. "I was afraid I'd get hit by it and blow up."

"When I was little, like toddler age, I was afraid to poop," Mason said with a tiny smile. "Mama said I kept telling her it would hurt and my insides would come out with the poop."

We all laughed pretty hard at that, and I reminded myself to have Mama and Mom show me some baby pictures of my mates.

"Can I ask the next question?" Ash lifted one hand off the steering wheel and held it up.

"Sure!" I said.

"How many pups do you want when we're ready?"

"Ah. Oh." My eyes grew wide. "Hmm. Well, Lark and I think at least two of each gender is the perfect number. That way everyone has a brother and a sister."

"Aww! What a cute sentiment!" he squealed. "I like that idea. Sid wants a dozen, by the way."

"A dozen?" I choked. "Sid, my heart, I'm sorry, but that is not going to happen."

We will see, he purred back, and I rolled my eyes.

"What about the rest of you?" I asked them. "And please don't say a dozen."

"Six," Mason said without hesitation.

"Six." I blinked, trying to picture six miniatures of my mates running around.

"Yep, but some of them will be girls who look just like you and have your sweet personality."

"You can't *order* that to happen," I giggled. "We'll get what the Goddess gives us."

"True," Cole chimed in, "but I *do* hope we have at least one little girl to wrap us around her fingers."

"And lots of sons to protect their precious sister," Wyatt added. "Six sounds like a great number to me, too."

Well, at least that's half of what Sid suggested, I tried to look on the bright side. *Still ... six! That's six pregnancies and six labors!*

Unless you have twins or trippies, Lark pointed out.

For the love of the moon, don't mention that to them! I snickered. *They'll take bets on how many pups each one can put in my belly at one time!*

That made her laugh huskily and the wolves wanted to know why. While they pestered her to answer them, I asked Jayden if he had a preference for how many or genders.

"Sweetness, as long as they're healthy, I'll be happy." He sent me a wave of love that warmed me down to my toes, and I sent him one back. "And I'll be happy with however many pups you want to give us."

"I wonder how the moon magic will work for us with children?" Mason asked as he stared out the side window. "Will they biologically belong to one of us or all of us?"

"Oh! I hadn't thought of that!" My eyes widened. "What is like for other alphas who share a mate?"

"They're all blood brothers," Ash pointed out. "We're the only ones we know of who aren't. It's an unusual situation."

"We'll find out when we have our first pup," Wyatt said and squeezed my hand. "Either way, all of us will love them equally, and that's what matters."

"Exactly," Cole and Jayden said at the same time.

"That's true," Ash piped up. "Right, Mase?"

"Hmm? Oh, yeah. Of course. I was just curious who they'd look like, that's all. Hopefully, the boys will take after Jay."

The rest of our eyes swiveled to Jayden, whose ears turned red.

"Um, what?" he gulped.

"Oh, come on, brother." Mason turned around to grin at him. "You have to know you're the most handsome out of us."

"I beg to differ," Wyatt squawked, then seemed to change his mind. "Well, at least my hair is the best. They should get my hair."

"You each are equally handsome," I told them with a frown. "Don't compare yourselves. Have you ever heard me compare any of you to each other?"

"No, but you should," Ash smirked, his eyes catching mine in the rear-view mirror. "We all know your giant waffle has the biggest, thickest d—"

Mason slapped the back of Ash's head.

"Warranted, Mase," Cole growled, "but not while he's driving."

"Dude, we could run head-on into a rig at ninety miles an hour and still survive." Ash rolled his eyes. "Werewolves, remember?"

"Let's not put it to the test," Jayden grumbled. "Posy, ask the next question before someone else says something dumb."

"Um." I racked my brain for a good question, then clapped my hands when one came to me. "What's the craziest thing you've ever done?"

Ash and Jayden broke into giggles, and Mason snorted.

"Are you really asking *Wyatt* that?" Cole chuckled. "He wouldn't know where to start!"

"It's a question for *all* of you," I corrected and held onto Wyatt's hand so he couldn't reach back and smack Cole.

"In my defense," my fifth star growled, "I don't go looking for crazy. It finds me all by itself."

"And I don't do crazy things period," Mason said and turned around to face forward again.

"Not once? Not one time *ever*?" I asked.

"Nope. Not unless you consider it crazy to stay up all night studying, then chug three energy drinks and two cups of coffee to stay awake through the exam the next day."

"Dude, your whole body was vibrating," Cole laughed.

"But it worked!"

"It's a miracle your heart didn't explode."

"What about you, Cole?" I asked.

"Hmm. Okay. One time, Jay dared me to jump from the roof at Dad's house into the pool and I did. Broke my leg in three places. Thank the Goddess I'd gotten Topaz a couple of weeks before and he healed me so I didn't even have a bruise, let alone need a cast."

"Unlike Wyatt, who had so many broken bones growing up, he should be glowing from all the x-rays," Jayden teased.

"What about you, then, my dragon?" I hurried to ask before Wyatt got grumpy, but I should have known better. They were never *not* going to tease each other to the brink of a fight.

"I invited this little blond-haired kid to join me and my cousin, Ash, in a game of kickball at recess when we were five," he snickered. "Haven't been able to ditch Wyatt since."

"Hey!"

This time, I wasn't fast enough. Wyatt slipped his hand out of mine, lunged over the seat, and smacked the side of Jayden's head.

"Aw, come on, Wyatt! That was funny," Ash giggled.

"The craziest thing Jay and Wyatt have ever done was to play tennis at midnight," Cole said.

"How is that crazy?" I asked as all my mates began to laugh.

"Well, it was so dark, we couldn't see the ball, so we soaked it in gasoline and lit it on fire," Wyatt explained.

"It got out of hand pretty quick," Jayden added with a chortle, "because our rackets caught on fire after a few hits."

"Oh, my goodness!" I covered my mouth with my hands. "And which of you caught yourself on fire?"

"How did you know?" Mason chuckled. "Wyatt, of course. Singed all the hair off his left forearm. Thankfully, Jay had the good sense to douse him with a bottle of water and *not* the can of gas."

"Yeah, that would have lit up the night!" Ash giggled.

"Well, I'm glad you both were all right." I glared at Wyatt. "Why do your stunts always end in an injury?"

"Just lucky that way, I guess." He shrugged with a smirk.

Shaking my head, I asked Ash for his answer.

"All right. Two years ago, Jay brought home these realistic, whole-head masks. His was a pigeon, mine was a horse, and Wyatt's was a rooster. We dressed up in our good suits, went into the human city, and stood on a corner in the shopping district with them on. Wyatt carried an old-fashioned cane umbrella, Jay had a cup of coffee, and I bought a newspaper. People had the weirdest reactions to us!"

He laughed so hard, he snorted, and that made the rest of us laugh, too. Jayden linked me to the memory, and I giggled like mad to see them lounging against a brick building with those silly masks on.

"Mason, you ask the next question," I said, wiping a tear from my eye as I hiccuped.

"Okay. What's your worst pet peeve?"

"What's that?"

"Something little that irritates or annoys you or makes you roll your eyes in frustration."

"Oh! Um, I guess doing the dishes." I thought about it for a second, then added, "Although I'll do them if I *have* to. It's not a problem; I just don't like it."

"Same, cutie," Wyatt chimed in. "I also don't like slow drivers. Ash?"

"When one of you miscreants leaves clothes all over the closet. I mean, it's organized for a reason, my dudes! What about you, Jay?"

"Ah, I don't know if I should say it."

"Come on," Wyatt yammered. "We said ours."

"Sorry, Ash, but when you're dysregulated, you tap your fingers on any solid surface nearby. Loudly. Repeatedly. Forcefully. You left four divots on my desk last week, for the love of the Goddess!"

"Huh. I never realized." Ash turned his attention to his driving as he put on the signal and merged into the passing lane. "I'll try to notice next time. Cole?"

"Idiot drivers and people who chew gum loudly. Mase?"

"Being late and when you guys interrupt Posy while she's trying to talk. Little flower, go ahead and ask another question."

"Well, I've been wondering what your favorite foods are. Like for a meal, not snacks or whatever."

"Steak," Cole said.

"Bacon cheeseburger" was Mason's answer.

"General Tso's chicken," Jayden said.

"Meat lovers' pizza!" Ash shouted.

"Barbecue. Any kind. Especially ribs," Wyatt told me. "And yours is chicken tenders, right?"

"Yep! Especially from Roger's diner. I could eat them every day!" I smiled. "Okay, Cole, it's your turn to ask something."

"Let's see." He tapped his chin with his index finger. "What's something I don't already know about all of you? Okay, what's your current phone wallpaper?"

Mason said it was a photo of all of us from my luna ceremony, Jayden had a picture of me holding Peder the rabbit at the county fair, Ash used a selfie of us in our twinnie outfits at the park, and Wyatt's was the photo he took the day I dressed up and we went to register for school.

"And you, Cole?" I asked.

Instead of answering, he handed me his phone so I could see a picture of me by the pool. Wearing the blue and white bikini Peri bought for me, I was asleep on one of the loungers with my mouth slightly open.

"Cole, that's a horrible picture of me!" My jaw dropped open. "Why would you use that?"

"But you look so innocent and sweet," he murmured as he leaned up and pecked my neck behind my ear. "I love watching you sleep."

Blushing, I handed him his phone back.

"Posy? What's yours?" Wyatt asked, then paused. "Um, wait. I mean, do you know how to set your wallpaper?"

"Yes, Emerson showed me. And I change it all the time. Currently, it's a picture of Cole wearing the flower crown I made for him on our date."

"Let me see!" Wyatt demanded and held out his hand.

"What? No!" Cole howled. "Posy, that was just between us!"

I giggled and linked the boys the image instead of unearthing my phone again.

"Aww!" Ash cooed. "You're so cute!"

"I told you." I turned to smile at Cole over my shoulder. "My wildflower prince."

"Hush, Posy." His face burned red and his bottom lip pouted out, which made me giggle.

"Wildflower prince, huh?" Wyatt opened his mouth to add something probably mean, but Cole beat him to the punch.

Literally.

"Ow!" Wyatt howled.

Leaning over as far as I could with the seat belt around me, I kissed his cheek and rubbed his head where Cole hit him.

161

"What's your favorite ice cream flavor?" I asked to settle them down.

Mason's was mint chocolate chip, Cole's rocky road, Jayden's birthday cake, Ash's butter pecan, and Wyatt's black raspberry.

"Mine's cookies and cream," I told them. "I never tried it before Wayne took over the ice cream truck at the fair, but it was yummy-yummy!"

"Cutie, you're too adorable for words," Wyatt crooned and raised my hand to kiss the back of my knuckles.

And so the miles flew by as we asked questions and teased each other, with only an occasional smack upside the head to interrupt our giggles.

10: The Everleighs

King Julian Hemming

I raised my hand to knock on the guest house door, then paused when I heard ... nothing. With the five alphas, silence was a rarity, and I worried that something had happened.

Have luna now, Onyx reminded me. *Mate makes difference. Mate tames and calms.*

She surely does, I agreed with a smile, thinking of my own queen.

I knocked and waited until Wyatt pulled open the door. Seeing me, he raised one finger to his lips and I nodded, then he led me into the living room.

Ash was walking around the room while holding a sleeping Posy, one arm under her bum to support her weight while the other hand rubbed up and down her back. Her head lolled against his shoulder, her tiny fists gripped his t-shirt, and her legs hung on either side of his waist. Every once in a while she sniffled in her sleep, and Ash bounced her gently and hushed her until she quieted again.

Even from here, I could see the red tip of her nose and the wet streaks running down her cheeks. Although I didn't like knowing something had upset her, I was pleased to see that those cheeks were no longer sunken in. Her skin was also a little tan, now that she was no longer sun-deprived, and the dark circles under her eyes were gone, as were the tense creases along the sides of her mouth.

Lilah will be so happy to see that her friend is doing well.

Link mate picture now, Onyx demanded. *Nyx share with Kestrel. Nyx's pretty little wolf happy. Jul make mate happy, too.*

I rolled my eyes, but did as he asked so he didn't keep pestering me about it.

"What's wrong?" I whispered. "Did something happen during the trip?"

"She's afraid to meet her father's family," Wyatt whispered back, "and had a little breakdown. Ash just got her to sleep when you knocked."

"Thinks they won't like her," Jay added as he walked into the room. "That they'll hate her because of what her stepfather did."

"Well, you can assure her that isn't the case," I told them all.

"Ash, tuck her in bed, then we'll talk," Jay murmured.

With a nod, Ash slowly walked out of the room with his precious bundle and disappeared from sight.

"Where are Mase and Cole?" I asked.

"Unpacking our suits and dealing with Posy's gown," Wyatt said with a shrug.

"It got a little wrinkled on the way," Jay explained. "They're trying to figure out how to iron it or whatever."

"We googled it," Cole said as he and Mase joined us. "We steamed it in the bathroom and hung it up. It should be fine for tomorrow."

"Good to see you guys again," I said.

We all did our bro-hug handshake, then took seats around the room. Cole, Mase, and I each took an armchair while Jay and Wyatt plopped on either end of the couch facing us.

"So how is she really?" I met Mase's eyes. "Other than the anxiety about meeting her family?"

"Better. Stronger."

"I can see she's gained some weight," I asked without asking.

"Yeah. About ten pounds so far. Doc at the clinic wants to see her gain at least fifteen more, but a slow gain is best. We haven't been pushing her to eat, just tempting her with new food experiences."

"And Roger's chicken tenders," Ash chimed in as he entered the room and wedged in between Wyatt and Jay on the couch. "She's obsessed with them."

Wyatt scowled and shoved Ash's shoulder.

"What?" Ash shoved him back.

"Dude! There's a whole other chair and loveseat over there!" Wyatt whined. "You can't sit here. You're too big—"

"That's what Posy said, too," he smirked, and Cole chuckled as Mase and Jay rolled their eyes.

"And you always accuse *me* of being crude." Wyatt narrowed his eyes and whapped Ash across the chest with the back of his hand.

"Crude?" Ash squawked. "Honest, you mean!"

"Enough," Mase snapped. "King Julian, what did you find out about the Everleighs?"

His no-nonsense tone helped me rein in my amusement at the guys' playful banter.

"Let me start at the beginning," I said and settled back in my chair. "My dad was so upset with himself for being fooled that he took the lead in the investigation. He discovered that everything Posy's mom wrote in that letter was true. Her name was Naomi, if you didn't know, and she was the only daughter of William Swift, the former alpha of Crystal Caverns. Dad talked to William, who confirmed that Naomi's agreement with Kendall Briggs included the stipulation that if either ever found their mate, they'd go their separate ways in peace."

"So *she* did become his chosen mate willingly." Cole frowned as he stared into space. "I'd wondered if he'd forced her in some way."

"No, as far as William knew, it was a mutual agreement. He didn't like it, but what could he do? Naomi was twenty-nine and had given up on finding her Goddess-given mate." I shrugged. "Anyway, Dad dug deeper and found several complaints against Briggs that were swept under the rug. That led him to discover that one of the royal office staffers was Briggs' brother and was keeping the dirt from sticking to him, so to speak."

"Bastard," Ash muttered. "I hope you have him in your cells."

"I do. You can visit him later if you'd like," I smirked, then got back on track. "Naomi and Logan Everleigh were living here at the royal pack when Briggs caught up to them. He killed Logan, faked Naomi's death, and dragged her and their two sons back to Green River. Posy was born seven months later, and you know the rest."

"Bastard," Ash repeated. "I wish you had *him* in your cells. Garnet and Quartz killed him too quickly, you ask me."

His brothers grumbled their agreement, and I nodded, understanding the feeling.

"On a brighter note," I held up my index finger and smiled, "the surviving Everleighs are all very excited to meet her."

"That's great!" Ash crowed.

"Yeah." I rubbed my hand over the back of my neck.

"What *aren't* you saying?" Jay, of course, noticed.

"Just as Posy has a right to her secrets, so do her family members." I took a deep breath, held it for a second, then let it all out in a rush. "That being said, I am going to tell you something before you meet them, and you five can decide what to do with the information."

"Is there something wrong?" Wyatt tilted his head to one side and tried to read my face.

"Her oldest cousin, Ethan, is struggling with his wolf. He's worried he'll scare her off, especially if Maple ascends in her presence."

"What's going on with his wolf?" Mase asked.

"Well, Ethan is twenty-three and hasn't found his mate yet. Every year, Maple grows more and more despondent. Right now, he's in a deep depression and sleeps most of the time. When he is awake, he's sullen and silent." I paused, then carefully added, "Except for when he's not."

"And when he's not?" Cole raised one eyebrow.

"Well, so far he hasn't killed anyone, and Ethan's been able to get him back under control every time."

"That's way better than my track record with Quartz," Jay muttered.

"Which is why I haven't had to order his wolf put down yet. Still, it's not pretty. He goes on a rampage and attacks anyone who gets in his way."

"Has the dude been actively looking for his mate, or just hoping she'll magically appear?" Wyatt crossed his arms over his chest and frowned.

"Of course he's been looking. He was at Five Fangs about four years ago. Royal and Nathan were still alphas. Anyway, he's getting ready to make another circuit of the kingdom before he heads off to Europe. He'd like to meet Posy first, but understands if that won't be possible."

"You're underestimating our girl," Ash said with a smirk. "She deals with Quartz on the daily. She's got this."

"I hope so," I sighed. "Her family wants this to be a positive experience for her."

"It will be," Jay assured me. "Hundred bucks says she'll see the sadness and pain in his wolf, not the savagery and temper."

"Agreed," said Ash and Cole at the same time.

"Did you tell them anything about her life at Green River?" Wyatt wanted to know.

"All I told them was that you five were her mates, that she grew up thinking Briggs was her father, and that Naomi Swift Everleigh died in the sickness." I glanced down at my clasped hands before looking back up at the boys. "I only know what you told me and what she shared with Lilah, so I couldn't have told them much even if I wanted to. It's Posy's business and her decision if she wants to share her past, but they're not dumb people. They guessed that her life wasn't good just from knowing what Briggs did to her mom."

I didn't need to say more. Their eyes fogged over as they conferred, and I left the matter in their hands. They'd know what was best for their girl.

We talked for about half an hour. They caught me up on what had happened with their gamma, and I offered any help they needed in catching the witch. Then I shared what my investigators found at the prison Jay and Angelo had raided, and they let me know the half-dragon, Konstantin, was going to stay in the pack for the foreseeable future.

"Posy put her foot down, did she?" I snickered.

"Of course she did," Cole grunted. "Ariel called it. She's a sucker for the underdog."

"And that's not a bad thing," Jay said.

"Not at all," I agreed.

Just then, Lilah's anxiety twanged through our mate bond. As I linked her words of love and encouragement, I wondered if I should go home and get one of my minions to show the alphas where the Everleighs lived. A quiet voice, however, interrupted my thoughts before I could.

"Hello, King Julian."

I turned to smile at the tiny luna who stood in the doorway and twisted her fingers together, but she held her shoulders back with her chin up. Her posture alone said she'd healed a great deal since I met her, and I couldn't help but smile at her progress.

"Hi, Luna Posy. It's a pleasure to see you again." I got to my feet and held out my hand.

She swallowed hard and came toward me, but ignored my hand and hugged me.

"I'm allowed to do this, right?" she whispered as I very carefully wrapped my arms around her tiny self.

"Of course. Hug me any time. Well, maybe not in the middle of Lilah's coronation," I teased her.

Blushing, she cleared her throat and took a step back. I immediately dropped my arms and also stepped back. Mase half stood and looped his arm around her waist and pulled her to him.

"I thought you'd sleep longer, baby," he murmured as he sat her on his lap.

"Did you find my father's family?" she ignored him to ask me, her eyes wide and hopeful.

"I did. Well, my dad did. He wanted to make up for the wrong of believing Alpha Briggs. He wants to apologize to you when you meet at the coronation."

"I don't need an apology, but I understand why he may want to give one," she murmured with a smile.

What a great mate and luna my friends had found! After being so badly broken, she still had the strength to comfort others and the capacity to forgive. In her shoes, I didn't know if I could have been so brave.

"If you'd like to meet the Everleighs, I'll take you there now," I told her in a gentle tone, mindful of her earlier tears and the alphas' overly protective natures.

"Really?" Her face lit up. "Yes, please! How many are there?"

"You have a grandma named Alberta. Her son, Lincoln, is your father's twin, and he and his wife, Aye, have three surviving children. They very much want to meet you."

"*Surviving* children?"

"A daughter, Elise, passed away in the sickness. So did your grandpa. His name was Arthur. They're good people." I hesitated, then decided to tell her. "Alberta said none of them ever believed that your father could hurt your mother. She said they loved each other deeply."

"Um." She shrank back against Mase's chest and played with her fingers. Her voice came out as an agonized whisper as she asked, "Do they hate me because of what happened?"

167

"No, Posy. No. They're happy to get a little piece of Logan back. You're the last connection they have to him, and they miss him very much."

Her eyes widened, and I got the sense that she hadn't looked at it that way before.

"I'd like to meet them today," she said at last and slid off Mase's lap to stand up. "Thank you for doing this. I know your time is precious, especially with the coronation tomorrow, and I appreciate that you came yourself instead of sending someone else."

"It was my pleasure to see you again and my privilege to bring you happy news." I got to my feet as the alphas also stood. They instantly surrounded her, and I hid my grin. "I'll show you the way to Alberta's house, but then I *do* have to go. Lilah is nervous about tomorrow and, between the hairdresser and the tailor, she's ready to run away. I don't want to have to chase her down again."

"*Again?*" Cole smirked.

As Posy giggled and the other boys snickered, Wyatt nudged me in the ribs with his elbow.

"Hmm. I wonder what you could do to relieve her stress? Well, it may be *hard*, but I'm sure you'll come *up* with something."

I rolled my eyes and didn't dignify his comment with a response. It wasn't like he had to emphasize the words; we all knew *exactly* how I planned to soothe my mate.

"Ooh, I know! Cuddle her! That always calms me down."

Posy not know, Onyx chuckled. *So innocent.*

Wyatt, Ash and Jay giggled into their hands, Mase kissed the top of her head, and Cole gave her a soft smile.

"Ash, come help me with my hair real quick so we can go." She grabbed his hand and tugged him along. "We'll only be a minute, King Julian."

"Take your time. A few minutes here or there won't make a difference."

"Thank you."

"Good thing we already planned your outfit," I heard Ash's deep voice rumble as they left the room and disappeared down the hallway.

Raising an eyebrow in amusement, I looked at the other alphas and grinned.

"He does her hair and picks out her clothes?"

"He's her personal stylist," Wyatt replied with a shrug. "Have to admit, he's great at it."

"He's been learning more complicated hairstyles, too, by watching YouTube videos," Jay added.

"And scrolling through Pinterest," Cole said.

I didn't know what Pinterest was and I didn't ask. Just from Cole's grin and tone, I could tell there was a story behind his comment, most likely one in which someone got teased and a fight ensued.

Onyx rolled his eyes in agreement, but stayed silent otherwise.

I knew he was longing to hang out with Quartz, and I told him he could go on a run with his buddy tonight after Lilah fell asleep. That pleased him and he grinned, which I still wasn't used to. It was a far cry from the sulky, miserable wolf he'd been just a few months ago. Now, there were times when he was so happy, it made me giddy.

The miracle of a mate, I thought with a soft smile and thanked the Goddess for her blessing.

11: You're My Grandma?

Mason

We followed the king to a well-kept house with pale yellow siding and white trim. There were two vehicles in the driveway, so we pulled up along the curb behind King Julian's truck.

"Posy, do you want one of us to go in first?" I asked as I swiveled around to look at her.

"Um. Let me think about it for a second." She was twisting her fingers and gnawing her bottom lip, which were not good signs.

At least she's talking, Garnet murmured. *Silence would be the worst reaction.*

Nodding in agreement, I looked over at Jay.

"Go thank the king, please, and tell him we'll catch up later," I said. "I know he's dying to get back to the queen."

"Sure thing."

Jay jumped out after kissing our girl's hand, and I linked my brothers.

Any volunteers to ask her?

You, the three of them linked back, almost in sync.

Sighing heavily, I reached back and laid my hand on Posy's knee.

"Little flower, would you like one of us to tell them a bit about what your life was like at Green River?" I kept my tone as gentle as I could. "Or would you prefer to do it? Or do you want to keep it to yourself?"

"They're going to guess some of it, aren't they?" asked our clever girl. "The king told them what Alpha Briggs did to my real dad, right? So they're going to know things weren't great."

"Most likely," Cole agreed and ran one hand up and down her arm. "King Julian said the same thing."

"So they'll already pity me." She dropped her head and stared at her hands.

"You don't know that." Wyatt reached over, unbuckled her seat belt, and pulled her onto his lap. "And even if they do, so what? You know you don't need pity."

"That's right!" Ash wiggled around in the driver's seat to grin at her. "Badass bitches don't need no pity!"

She rolled her eyes, but a small smile appeared on her lips.

"Let's wait and see," she said. "I'll figure it out once I meet them."

170

By then, Jay was back. The king drove off with a brief honk, and we waved absently, our attention on our girl as Jay opened the door and scooped her off Wyatt's lap to set her feet on the sidewalk. We all hopped out and joined them, and Jay held her one hand while Ash claimed her other.

"There's something about one of your cousins," I said cautiously as I leaned down and kissed her head. "Do you want to know about it going in, or meet him first? To be fair, it might be ... unsettling, but you won't be in any danger."

Because we'll kill any who threaten you, we all heard Quartz snap.

"Easy, Q," Jay murmured. "There is no threat here, only family."

Family was the threat before, he disagreed, and Jay's eyes glimmered gold.

"Alpha Briggs was *never* her family," Jay said firmly.

"It's okay, Quartz," Posy murmured and took her hand out of Jay's to press it over his heart. "We know you're here if we need you, and we'll hope that we won't."

The wolf light disappeared completely from Jay's eyes, and we all took an easier breath.

"It's a cute house, isn't it?" Our girl smiled as she took in the pretty woodwork and wrap-around porch. "I bet they're nice people."

"They produced you, so yeah, they *have* to be," Ash laughed.

We waited for her to signal she was ready to go up the walk and knock on the door. Her eyes went far away for a moment, and we looked at each other, wondering what thoughts she'd gotten lost in, then she took a deep breath, lifted her chin, and led us up the walk.

Our strong luna, I linked my boys as my heart swelled with pride.

Stronger than all of us, Wyatt agreed.

She knocked on the door and only a second passed before it opened and revealed a man my father's age. Everything about him - from his posture to his expression - was soft and submissive, and I smelled his omega blood.

His gentle brown eyes went straight to Posy's face and filled with tears as he studied her.

"Hello." He stopped to clear his throat. "Welcome. I'm Lincoln Everleigh. Please come in."

He stepped back and held his arm out in invitation. Posy smiled at him, then stepped over the threshold, and we followed.

Duck, I reminded Ash as Cole and I both had to dip our heads to make it under the lintel.

Dude, he groaned. *Not a baby!*

171

Sid, how many times has he whacked his head on the doorway of his office alone? I smirked.

Up to fifty now, Sid snickered, and all of us had to fight back grins as Ash whined about us bullying him.

I'm fixing that door when we get back home, Wyatt grumbled. *I should have done it long ago.*

He was handy like that and enjoyed carpentry, something I had no skill with or knowledge of.

Thanks, Wy, I told him sincerely. *That's really nice of you. I'm sure you'll do a good job, and it will help our brother cut back on self-inflicted concussions.*

Wyatt didn't respond, but I felt a rush of warmth in the alpha bond and knew he was pleased I'd praised him.

Needy pup, I muttered to myself, and Garnet smirked.

We entered the living room in a pentagon around Posy, and our silent chuckles at Ash's pouty face cut off as we surveyed the occupants. Our instincts to protect were on high alert, but there was zero threat here. Only an elderly lady, an Asian woman who was maybe my mama's age, and two kids younger than Posy.

My brothers and I and our wolves all relaxed.

The elderly lady stepped toward us, her brown eyes flicking around to all our faces with a hint of confusion, and I knew she was wondering where Posy was. Since we surrounded her, she was hidden from view as much as her family was hidden from her sight, and I linked Wyatt and Jay to step aside so Posy could see.

"Hello. I'm Alberta Everleigh." The old lady's eyes filled with tears as they finally landed on Posy's face. "Logan Everleigh was my son."

Posy approached Alberta, who hesitantly held out her hand. As with the king, our girl ignored the outstretched hand and walked right into her grandma's arms and hugged her. Posy was so short, her head lay on Alberta's chest, and the old lady's tentative smile bloomed into a full one.

"You're my grandma?" Posy raised her head after a moment and stared up at Alberta.

"That's right." Tears streamed down her cheeks, her brown eyes bright with tenderness and love. "I'm so happy to meet you. So, so happy."

They hugged a little longer, then the man who let us in the house popped up at Alberta's elbow.

"Ma." He laid his hand on her shoulder. "Share, would you? We all want to meet her."

"Sorry, my boy. Posy, this is my son, Lincoln. He's your father's twin."

"Oh!" Posy stepped back and her eyes studied Lincoln's face. "You don't look like the photo I have of him."

"Fraternal twins often don't," he told her patiently, studying her as intensely as she was him.

That led to a discussion of what fraternal meant, which twin was born first - Logan - and how she'd managed to get a photo of her father.

Then Lincoln asked her for a hug, which she gave him with a beaming smile, and he told her to call him Uncle Link. After that, he introduced her to his wife, Aye, who was originally from Korea. Posy found that fascinating and asked a dozen questions until Aye promised to teach her as much as she wanted to know about Korean culture.

When Posy finally stopped grilling his wife, Lincoln took a deep breath and cupped his niece's face in his hands.

"Logan would have loved you so much," he said in a husky tone. "Same with Dad. I just wish—"

His voice cut out as he began to cry, and his mate put her arms around him and led him to a chair, where they sat together and he wept on her shoulder.

"If we knew you existed," Alberta picked up, "we would have fought tooth and nail to bring you here. To have you with us. I would have loved and spoiled and treasured you as much as my other grandchildren."

"*Spoiled?*" the younger boy piped up with a grin, obviously looking to lighten the mood. "We're not spoiled! You'll give her the wrong impression of us."

"Oh, you're a spoiled boy and you know it," Alberta grinned through her tears. "Posy, these are your cousins, Link and Aye's children. The cheeky boy is Evan, and Eden is his twin. They're seventeen."

"Hello!" Posy twisted her fingers together, clearly unsure of them.

"Nice to meet you, cousin!" Evan practically shouted before he caught her up in a bear hug and swung her around.

All of us growled as Posy's body went stiff, and the boy set her on her feet quickly, shooting nervous glances our way.

Idiot! Wyatt thundered.

He should have asked her first! Cole snarled.

Keep it together, I cautioned them.

If he triggers a panic attack, I'll—

We never got to hear what Ash would do because Posy giggled, the sound like silver bells on a cold, clear night, and that settled us right down.

173

"Don't piss off her mates, dumbass," hissed Eden before approaching Posy with a smile. "Hi, Posy. Forgive my twin. He's enthusiastic about everything, even waking up to go to school in the morning."

She shuddered, as if that were a fate worse than death, and Posy giggled again before hugging her.

"My oldest brother, Ethan, would like to meet you, too," Eden said, "but he's worried you'll be scared of him."

"Why would I be?" she asked.

"He looks dangerous." Eden shrugged. "Sometimes he even is when his wolf, Maple, gets upset. But he's a good guy, I promise."

Posy looked over her shoulder at us with wide eyes, and we all gave her reassuring smiles.

We're here, little flower, I murmured through the mate bond. *Nothing and no one will harm you.*

I know. She smiled, her dimples flashing us, then turned back to her cousin.

"I'd like to meet him. Is he here?"

Eden nodded and her eyes unfocused as she obviously linked her brother.

A few seconds later, a tall guy walked into the room. Smelling of gamma blood, his face was closed and cold, wolf light flickered in his eyes, and, if King Julian hadn't given us a heads-up, I would have deemed him too dangerous to even be in the same room as our girl.

He stopped about a foot inside the door and his gold-shot black eyes fixed on Posy's face.

"Hello." His wolf underscored his voice, turning it into a rumbly growl. "I'm Ethan Everleigh. I'm happy to meet you."

"Hi, Ethan." Posy held her hand up and curled her fingers at him in an adorable little wave.

"I remember your brothers." A bead of sweat ran down Ethan's cheek as his wolf glittered a little more in his eyes. "I have a very clear memory of playing tag with them in Grandma's backyard. It was a warm evening and the sun was starting to set. James was it, and Aiden and I were laughing as we ran away from him."

"Oh! Next time I talk to them, I'm going to ask if either of them remembers you!" Posy smiled, then looked around at her new family members. "In fact, I think they would love to meet you all. Even better, why don't you come to the Swift family reunion next weekend at Crystal Caverns?"

"That's very kind of you, Posy," Alberta murmured, "but I don't know that they'd be happy to see us. We met them once when Logan first found your mother, and she was her daddy's little girl. I can't imagine Alpha William would want us there after— After what happened."

"Nonsense." Posy's frown should have been all Alberta needed to see to know she'd be wasting her breath to continue arguing. "My father did nothing wrong. Why would they hate him or you?"

"He wasn't strong enough to protect his mate," Lincoln said with a bowed head. "They'll hate us for allowing Alpha Briggs to harm Naomi."

"No, they won't," Posy disagreed. "And if they do, I'll set them straight."

"The Swifts are all alphas, betas, or gammas while Ethan is the only one in the family with anything other than omega blood," Alberta tried again. "They are dominant and powerful. We are submissive and subservient. They'll look at us as lesser and blame us for—"

"I won't allow that to happen. And omega doesn't mean *lesser*. It means kinder, gentler, and nicer."

"But—"

Tired of this conversation, I decided it was time to step in.

"What Posy wants, she gets," I decreed in my unyielding 'end of argument' tone. "I'll call Alpha Liam and let him know to expect all of you."

Ethan was too busy trying to push his wolf back to care about whatever I was saying, but the rest nodded with wide, wary eyes, and the youngest cousin, Eden, actually trembled. The smell of fear filled the living room, and I felt a little bad about that, but I couldn't be soft with strangers like I was with Posy. I was first alpha of Five Fangs, after all.

Posy's family, Garnet murmured. *Not strangers.*

They are family, but still strangers, I corrected. *They are not part of our pack. I cannot trust them completely and relax my guard. Not with our little mate here and vulnerable. If they fear me, they won't try anything.*

Omegas wouldn't, anyway, he argued, *and they love her already.*

Better safe than sorry.

He frowned, but said no more about it.

"Visiting the Swifts might be a good idea for another reason, too," Jay chimed in. "I helped Alpha Liam with an issue a few months ago. One of our betas and his gamma died in the ... incident. Ethan, maybe you could find a place there as his gamma."

"Thank you for the thought," Ethan said with a nod, "but unless I find my mate, my wolf's going to get us killed. A job is the least of my worries right now."

175

"Hey, Ethan!" Posy moved to stand next to him and grabbed his hand in her excitement. "Maybe you'll find your mate at Crystal Caverns! Wouldn't that be amazing?"

She bounced on her toes as excitement lit up her face, and Ethan's tense expression softened as he stared at her. All at once, the glint of wolf light winked out of his dark eyes, and the Everleighs exchanged amazed glances. I looked at my brothers and we all nodded, understanding that this was probably the first time in years that his wolf wasn't fighting to ascend and rip the world to shreds until he found his mate.

You should talk to him, Ash told Jay in the alpha link.

And say what? Jay snapped. *Just because we share similar experiences doesn't mean that I know what to say to help or comfort him.*

You always *know what to say*, Cole retorted. *It's one of your best traits.*

Well, not this time. Other than to say, yeah, it sucks, what could *I say?*

Just remind him that there's light at the end of the tunnel, Wyatt suggested. *You can assure him that once he finds his mate, his wolf will settle and his life will be worth living.*

True as that is, Jay can't guarantee that Ethan will *find his mate*, I interjected. *Besides, that might rub it in that Jay found relief and Ethan, who's been suffering for four years longer, hasn't.*

Exactly, Jay sighed. *Posy's doing more good than I could right now, anyway.*

Seeing Ethan's peaceful eyes as she held his hand, we all had to agree.

Then Posy launched into introducing us, and we plastered on our polite faces so we made a good impression. The *last* thing we wanted to do was embarrass or disappoint her in front of her family.

#

Posy

"I'd like to show you something," Grandma whispered in my ear. "Will you come with me?"

Turning my head, I met her twinkling eyes and couldn't help but return her impish smile. With a nod, I took her wrinkled hand in mine.

"We'll be back in a bit," she said and led me out of the room.

Of course, my mates weren't satisfied with that and flooded the link with questions.

She wants to show me something. Stop fretting, I giggled. *I'm fine.*

176

"Your mates are lovely fellows," Grandma said as we walked through the kitchen and out the back door. "They have such big personalities, don't they? But I guess that comes with being alphas. So forceful and dominant, yet each is sweet and beautiful in his own way."

"That's true. They're my whole world. I love them very much." My heart warmed in my chest and I smiled. "They're my heroes, my cheerleaders, my comforters, and my counselors."

"That is as it should be, and I can tell you are the same to them."

"Oh, I don't know." I blushed and stared at my feet.

"*I* do," she chuckled with confidence.

Her hand tightened around mine as we stepped into the backyard, and she guided me toward a wooden frame with slats for a roof and a porch swing hanging in the center. There was also a glass-topped table and a pair of chairs with thick cushions.

I could see dozens and dozens of butterflies flitting around from shrub to shrub and flower to flower, and my jaw dropped in amazement.

"So many butterflies! It's a little paradise in your backyard!"

"Your grandfather built this pergola for me two years before he passed away. Since I sit out here quite a bit, my grandsons and granddaughter helped me create a butterfly garden around it."

"It's beautiful," I told her. "I'd sit out here a lot, too. When we go back in, I'll show you pictures of the balcony garden my mates created for me."

"As much as we love our mates, it's nice to have a sanctuary to go and think and relax in private." She led me to a twiggy little tree. "During the summer months, hardly a day goes by without a butterfly emerging from its chrysalis somewhere out here."

"Oh! Do you think I might see one hatch?" My eyes widened and I bounced a little on my toes.

"Let's hope so," she smiled. "It's called eclose, darling. Eggs hatch. Butterflies eclose from their chrysalis."

Dropping my hand, she moved some leaves aside to reveal three little sacks hanging from a branch. Together, we leaned in and examined them, our heads close together. One chrysalis was a solid, chalky green, so I figured it was not 'ripe' yet. One was nearly see-through, and I wondered if that meant it was close to eclosing. The last one, though, made me squeal when I saw a butterfly climbing out of it!

"Oh my goodness! I can't believe I'm seeing this!"

I clasped my hands under my chin and watched as the monarch's spindly black legs carefully felt around the remains of its chrysalis. Once it had a good grip, it paused as if it were taking a deep

177

breath. Its wings were folded and wrinkly looking, and its belly was huge! It looked more like a squashy beetle with orange and black flaps than a butterfly.

"It'll take about an hour for its wings to dry and then it will fly off to find a mate," Grandma explained.

"Incredible!" I couldn't take my eyes off the butterfly, too fascinated by the whole thing. "And to think they started out as little caterpillars!"

"Exactly. It is the butterfly everyone admires, but few consider the enormous process the caterpillar had to go through to transform into something so beautiful."

As I thought about her words, I realized she was talking about more than butterflies. I slowly turned to meet her eyes and saw a world of wisdom in their dark depths.

"I know your life with your stepfather couldn't have been a good one, and I am so sorry you suffered. It had to have been a nightmare for your mother, so I can only imagine how bad your childhood was."

"I'm fine—"

"I don't need to see the scars to know you have them, darling," she whispered, touching her forehead to mine. "Your caterpillar had a long, painful journey, and your chrysalis was a dark one, but just look at the beautiful, strong woman who emerged from it. You inspire this old woman, Posy Anne."

Tears welled up in my eyes, matching those in hers. She held out her arms, and I went into them with a soft sob.

This moment was something I didn't even dare to dream of, and I dreamed a lot of crazy things while I was locked in that dark room. Yet here I was, snuggled into my grandmother's warmth and breathing in her soft powdery scent as she dropped tiny kisses on my forehead.

"Oh, my little butterfly, I am so happy to know you." She squeezed me tighter. "You're the piece I never realized was missing from my heart. I love you, granddaughter."

Smiling widely, my heart sang with happiness as I said something I never thought I'd have the chance to say.

"I love you, too, Grandma."

12: Intervention

Posy

"*Black* suits?! I thought we were wearing blue!"

Wyatt was apparently unhappy about the clothes Ash had packed and was making sure everyone in the house knew it. I myself stayed out of it and carried on eating my Cheerios in the kitchen as I listened to them argue in the bedroom upstairs.

"Black is formal," Ash tried to tell him. "And it's what everyone's wearing. I asked Zayne and Zayden and they said they're wearing black. Alpha Ranger and the king are, too. Even Gisella is wearing a black tux. She told Luke he'd have to drug her or beat her to get her in a dress. So there!"

I bet he stuck his tongue out, I chuckled to myself.

"Stick your tongue out at me again and I'll cut it right out of your mouth!" Wyatt yowled. "Black is depressing! It's for funerals and shit, not a damn coronation!"

Language! I mouthed, mimicking Mason's stern tone in my head.

"Language!"

"Well, it's true! And you brought me a white dress shirt! Cole's is blue, yours is black. Hell, even *Mase* has a lavender one, and you brought me plain old white?"

"Jay's is, too."

"But his vest is pink!"

"Well, *you* insisted on wearing your white sneakers!" Ash retorted.

"What does that have to do with anything?"

"No other color of shirt would have worked!"

Any second now, Jayden's going to step in to play peacemaker, I thought as I ate another spoonful of cereal.

"Well, I'm not wearing it!" Wyatt yammered.

"Oh, yes, you are," Ash growled. "You don't have a choice. It's all I brought—"

"Wyatt, what's wrong with your black suit? I think it looks nice on you." Right on cue, my dragon interrupted them.

"It's not as sexy as Ash's," Wyatt admitted.

I could just picture his pout and had to bite my lips to keep from laughing out loud.

Now Ash is going to tease him, not realizing that Wyatt's serious, and Wyatt will tackle him.

"Come on, man! I can't help that I'm sexier *or* that your dress sense completely sucks!"

A loud thump came as two big bodies hit the floor, followed by the familiar noises of a scuffle.

Now Cole's trying to hold onto his temper and Jayden is falling over laughing, leaving Mason to break them up.

"That's enough! Jay, stop giggling and help me!"

A few grunts and what sounded like fabric ripping, and everything went quiet upstairs. I frowned, put my spoon down, and strained my ears. With these boys, when things got quiet, it was time for me to investigate or intervene.

"Shame on you!" Mason whisper-hissed. "Fighting over a suit when our mate is peacefully eating breakfast downstairs!"

"But he picked his best suit and my worst!" Wyatt whined. "He didn't even ask us for any input!"

"Dude, I *did!*" Ash insisted. "And you all agreed that I could pick out the accessories to go with our black suits."

"No, you didn't! I remember saying yes to you picking out the accessories for *our suits*. You never said the word black!"

Poor Ash. I put my palm over my face and shook my head. *I imagine he* did *tell his brothers he wanted the black suits, but only inside his head during one of his internal monologues. Then he forgot that he didn't actually say it out loud.*

ADHD problems, Lark snickered.

Shush, wolfie.

"Yes, I did!" Ash snarled. "It's how we came to the compromise that you'd wear a vest and tie so long as you could still wear sneakers!"

"I remember that, too, but you did *not* say black!"

"Did so!"

"Did not!"

"Did so!"

"Did not!"

"Did so!"

And Cole is going to lose his temper in 5, 4, 3, 2—

"*SHUT UP!* Goddess, you're both so annoying!"

Lark smirked, and I grinned. *So predictable, my mates.*

"But he *deliberately* brought along his sexiest suit and my worst—"

"Dude, I didn't! I swear! I didn't even know you hated your black suit. Look, the next time we go to a royal coronation, you can pick out the color."

"And how often do we do that, moron?"

Now Ash will apologize because he's just like Sid and can't stand for one of his brothers to be mad at him.

"Okay, any formal occasion when we want to coordinate," Ash adjusted his offer. "I didn't mean to upset you. I just wanted us to present a strong, united front and look good doing it. I'm sorry."

And Wyatt will accept his apology, but won't be able to let it go without a little snark.

"Sorry, too, for getting mad," Wyatt mumbled. "I'll wear the damn suit. Just, next time, bring my blue one. It makes my eyes pop and I look hot as f—"

"Language!" Cole and Mason both barked, and I giggled into my hand.

Right then, the doorbell rang, and I thought nothing of hopping off the barstool and heading to the entryway. I could smell who it was, and I was decently covered in Ash's ginormous t-shirt and a pair of soft shorts.

"Posy?" Mason called down from upstairs. "Don't you dare open that—"

"It's only Uncle Link," I called back over my shoulder before I turned the knob.

As soon as I opened the door, I knew something was wrong. My uncle's hands trembled as sweat trickled down his face, and the strong odor of fear and despair nearly knocked me over.

"What happened?" I asked with wide eyes.

"Maple's on a rampage. It's been two hours now and Ethan hasn't been able to regain control. I'm afraid the king will put him down this time. I know I have no right to ask this of you, but we all saw you tame him yesterday. Will you help him again?" Lincoln dropped to his knees. "Please save my son's wolf! I'm begging you! Please, Posy!"

Oh, my heart! Poor Maple! Poor Ethan and his family!

Raising my chin and ignoring my mates' frantic calls to wait for them, I helped Uncle Lincoln to his feet and propped him against the door, then hustled over to the hall closet and grabbed my flip flops.

By then, my mates had clamored down the stairs in various stages of undress and made a beeline for me.

"Posy? What are you thinking?" Jayden asked calmly.

"I'm thinking I'm going to go save my cousin's wolf," I answered just as calmly.

Slipping into my shoes, I rushed back to my uncle, grabbed his elbow, and tugged him outside.

"Take me to him," I said.

"No, take *all* of us to him," Mason commanded, reverting to what I called his 'business' voice and face: blank, emotionless, and intimidating as all get-out.

Next thing I knew, I was in Ash's SUV and Cole was buckling my seat belt. The boys were muttering and cursing under their breaths as we took off after Lincoln's car, but I tuned them out to hear what my wolf was saying.

Quartz going to be a problem, Lark cautioned me. *We both know it. We need a plan or going to be a tragedy.*

Do you have an idea? Because I'm fresh out, I admitted.

Maybe. How sure you can calm Maple?

Pretty darn, especially if I draw on the power of all six packs. I tilted my head as I tried to guess where she was going with this. *Why?*

Then I have idea.

I'm listening, I told her.

#

Quartz

No way in hell was I going to let my mate face down an out-of-control gamma wolf!

As we followed Lincoln Everleigh's car, I fought a losing battle against the ball of rage in my gut.

No, that wasn't true. I wasn't even fighting. I was fine with letting it consume me.

Calm down, Jayden advised me. *Control your temper; don't let your temper control you.*

I growled at him.

Quartz, Lark linked me. *You let us do this.*

No, I won't!

Yes, you will. I am luna of six packs. If anyone can help Maple, it me.

You are an amazing she-wolf, I said slowly, *and I will support you in everything you do, little mate.*

Thank y—

So long as you're safe, I continued. *And a runt going up against a gamma wolf ain't anything close to safe.*

I agree, but he not going to attack us. That not rage; that pain. Posy can calm him down just like yesterday.

Yesterday was different! Yesterday, he wasn't shifted and he wasn't angry and he hadn't been in absolute control for hours!

Please, Quartz. Please trust me.

I trust you with my life, I said with clenched teeth, *but not with yours. It's the most precious thing in the world to me, and you'd throw it away in an effort to save a waste of space mutt.*

He not a mutt, she barked indignantly, *or waste of space! He family! And we going to help him with or without you permission!*

Not if I alpha command you, you won't! I bellowed.

Lark sucked in a sharp breath as a flash of fear hit our mate bond, and Jayden face-palmed.

Shit.

I screwed up.

I screwed up real bad.

Worse than when I'd growled at Posy after she helped Gamma Landry.

How many times do I have to tell you? Jayden said with a heavy sigh. *Anger clouds the mind! You never learn, do you, Q?*

With a frustrated snarl, I counted to ten. Then I counted to ten again.

Lark, Posy, I apologize. I spoke in anger.

No response.

I'm sorry, I tried again. *I allowed my fear for your safety to trigger my temper, and I'm ashamed of myself for threatening to alpha command you. I swear by the moon that I will never do that. I am not the monster your stepfather was.*

At least, not to either of them. Only my enemies needed to know the monster I could be, never my little mate.

How sorry is you? Lark mumbled.

Extremely.

Prove it, she challenged. *Help with Maple.*

What do you have in mind?

With Jayden's permission, you use his body and guard us. If Maple attacks, you respond as you want. If he not attack, you stay a guard only.

You know if he attacks you, he's a dead wolf. I raised one eyebrow. *No discussion. No debate. No second chance.*

Yes.

You're that confident? I questioned.

Yes.

Then I agree to your terms and will abide by them.

Thank you, Q. I knew I could count on you, she purred with a toothy grin.

And a tiny spark of suspicion flared in my brain. Had she played me? Did she deliberately goad me into losing my temper, then use my regret to make me do what she wanted?

What does it matter if she did? Jayden snickered. *Besides, she would have talked you into it either way. A few sniffles and you would have caved.*

That's rich, coming from you, I snorted. *One crystal tear falls from Posy's beautiful eyes and you and your brothers whimper like pups and fall all over yourselves to make her happy again.*

Who knew we would be so happy to be so whipped? he chuckled.

Speak for yourself, I muttered. *I ain't whipped.*

You're putty in her paws, wolf, and you know it.

I am not.

Are, too.

Am not.

Are, too.

*I am an alpha wolf! I am **not** whipped!*

Jayden only laughed, and I settled into sullen silence as Ash slammed on the brakes and threw the SUV into park. We all got out, and I made Jayden hurry to Posy's side as Lincoln led us to a trail leading into the woods. We began running as loud howls filled our ears, and we reached a small clearing a minute later.

Maple sat in the center of it with his head tipped back and his muzzle pointed up, pouring his pain out to the sky. All around him, splintered trees, churned up grass, and destroyed undergrowth lay like the debris after a tornado.

At least he had the sense to get away from civilization. Otherwise, that debris would most likely have included blood and bones.

Permission? I asked Jayden.

Sure, but Quartz?

Yeah?

You are, too.

And that ignited my temper all over again.

#

Cole

After we found Maple, we told Lincoln to go back and wait by the cars, just in case things got ugly. He didn't like it, but left without arguing.

Once he was gone, Jay quickly caught us up on the agreement Lark and Quartz had reached, and we watched with building anxiety as Posy crept closer to Maple. Quartz-in-Jay's-body stayed a few feet behind her, holding to his promise not to interfere unless it looked like Maple was going to attack.

Having him so close to her helped ease our minds, as did the unmistakable grief and pain in Maple's anguished howls. However, we were still very uncomfortable with our mate putting herself in danger.

"She can do this," Ash murmured, sounding like he was convincing himself more than us. "She's strong and powerful."

"Damn right she is," Wyatt laughed.

Mase, Ash, and I swiveled our heads to stare at him. A smirk pulled up one side of his mouth and his eyes sparkled with amusement. He even had his hands in his pockets, he was so relaxed!

184

"What in the world, Wyatt?" I muttered. "Our mate is in danger and you're—"

"Chill, dude! Remember how she alpha-commanded *us* at the training center? And not just five alphas, two of whom are the most powerful in the kingdom, but also our betas, their mates, and several others. What makes you think she *can't* do this?"

I shuddered as I remembered how it felt to bear the weight of her power. The only thing that ever came close was kneeling under the king's.

"Oh, yeah, that's right!" Ash chirped. "She did! Dudes! She's got this!"

I glanced at Mase to see him rolling his eyes, which made me snicker before I returned my attention to our girl as she knelt next to Maple.

Ash is right, Topaz told me while we watched Maple's eyes fix on Posy. *Believe in mate.*

"Plus, Quartz will rip him to shreds if he even looks like he's going to try something," King Julian's voice came from behind us.

Speak of the devil and he shall appear, I thought.

My brothers and I turned to stare at him. Like us, he was half-dressed in a suit.

Unlike us, though, he has others to change into if that fancy one gets ruined, I griped.

"Don't you have a coronation to get ready for?" I asked with a raised eyebrow. "You didn't need to make a house call. We have things under control here."

"Naw, dude, *we* don't," Ash disagreed, shaking his head and making his curls bounce wildly. "Our badass bitch does!"

"I see that," the king said, amusement dancing in his eyes as he stared at the center of the clearing.

We spun around and saw Maple had laid down with his head in our mate's lap as she gently stroked his fur. His eyes closed and, seconds later, he gave in and let Ethan shift back.

"I don't like our girl holding a naked man," I grumbled, earning a grunt from my brothers.

I didn't know if Posy heard me or not, but she whipped off her t-shirt and draped it over Ethan's lower half. Fortunately, she was wearing a sports bra under it, or we would have growled even louder.

"Goddess have mercy," King Julian whispered.

His eyes took in the scars running down Posy's back, then the dark pink craters on her shoulders and upper arms, and a little rumble of power rolled around the clearing as he fought his anger.

"Those white lines on her back are from a silver knife," he growled, his eyes flaring green with wolf light, "but what did he use on her shoulders?"

"Mercury," Mase rumbled, Garnet heavy in his voice. "Liquid freaking mercury."

"And what's above her waistband? Right in the center of her back?"

"His initials," I spat. "Burned them into her with a silver brand dipped in mercury."

King Julian, who I knew had seen and inflicted much worse himself, growled deep in his throat as Onyx gleamed in his eyes.

"By all that's holy, I wish I'd had that bastard in my dungeon to torture for a few years. How could he do that to such a sweet, delicate creature?"

"He's in the ground and she's alive." Ash went over and laid a hand on the king's shoulder. "That's what matters."

Then we heard Posy say, "**Sleep, Maple. Sleep,**" in her Ultimate Luna Voice, and all of us yawned, our eyelids feeling heavy.

The king blinked and his lips parted, but he didn't yawn.

"Powerful, isn't it?" Wyatt smirked at him.

"That's... Is that what you feel when I roll out *my* power?"

"Close," Mase admitted. "Hers is incredible, but I can *almost* fight it, and I can move under it. Yours is absolute and holds me down like a lead blanket."

"She's getting better about pinpointing it, too," I told him. "The first time, at the training center, we *all* had to obey her. This time, we only yawned."

"Boys, you—" The king shook his head and frowned. "Don't let this knowledge spread too far outside your pack. If some power-hungry bastard ever caught wind of what she can do, he wouldn't hesitate to take her from you—"

Hearing his warning, Quartz let out a roar so furious and power-laden, branches fell and a few saplings toppled over.

Well, this just went to the next level.

#

Posy

"Maple?" I called in a soft voice as I slowly approached him. "Maple, sweetheart, can I hug you?"

The distressed wolf stopped howling and rolled his head to stare at me with bright gold eyes. When he raised his upper lip to show me his fangs, Quartz huffed a warning, and Maple instantly bared his neck.

186

Quartz, please. He won't hurt me, I linked him. *He didn't snarl or snap.*

I don't like this, little one.

I know, but it will be all over soon.

In one way or another, he agreed, and I sighed.

"Maple, I know you feel like giving up right now, but think of the reason why you've held on this long. What is it that's kept you from quitting up till now?"

He woofed a bit, both of us knowing I couldn't understand his words, but I understood his heart well enough.

"That's right. Your mate. She's out there waiting for you, longing for you to find her just as much as you do. If you quit, if you give up, if you stop fighting, she'll be left alone for the rest of her life. Are you that selfish? To do that to your innocent, lonely mate? She's been fighting to stay positive as she waits for you, too. Are you going to disrespect her that way?"

He grumbled again, a burr of anger in his noises now, and I didn't need to look to know Quartz had moved closer to us. I rolled my eyes, knowing I had to hurry this up before he took matters into his own hands - er, paws - and forgot all about the agreement we had.

"Of course not," I answered my own questions. "And you know what? I think you two are going to meet soon. I feel it in my heart. So don't be sad. Don't despair. Keep going. Keep trying. It will get better soon. I *know* it will. I know it in my bones, Maple."

And it was true. I really did have the feeling that his suffering was drawing to a close.

With a soul-deep sigh, Maple flopped down next to me and laid his head in my lap. I raised my hand slowly and made sure he was okay with it before I petted his soft ears.

"Do you think you can give Ethan control again, please?" I asked after a few minutes of comforting him. "Uncle Link is really worried about you both."

Maple nodded, and the hair on my arms stood up as moon power filled the air around us. Seconds later, Ethan lay in my arms. Blushing at his naked state, I kept my eyes on his face as I tugged off my shirt, glad I had on a sports bra, and draped it over his lower half.

I didn't like my scars being on full display under the bright summer sun, but who was here to see them beside Ethan and my mates, and my mates were already familiar with them.

Ethan's eyes fluttered open and I was pleased to see that, while Maple still glittered in them, it was only faintly now.

A good improvement. Nice job, luna, Lark complimented me.

Thank you, wolfie.

187

"I'm sorry," Ethan muttered. "I'm sorry you were drawn into this train wreck, Posy."

"I will always help my family," I assured him with a smile. "Can I try something to calm your wolf? I never did anything like this before, so I might mess up, and it might not be the best idea, but I think it will work."

"Go for it, little cousin. I'm grateful for any help, and it's not like he can get much worse."

Actually, he could, I thought to myself, but didn't say that because I wanted his agreement.

"You don't even want to know what I'm going to try?" I squeaked.

"I trust you. You've already been able to do more to help him today than I have in the past few years."

As I had after healing Gamma Landry, I reached deep into the six packs, then infused my next words with all that power in what the boys had started to call my Ultimate Luna Voice.

"Sleep, Maple. Sleep. Until you find your mate, sleep."

I didn't know if it was the right thing to do or not, but he couldn't go on a rampage - and no one would have a reason to put him down - if he was asleep.

Ethan yawned widely, his whole body relaxing in my arms, and the gold vanished entirely from his heavy-lidded eyes.

"Wow." He stared at me with wonder. "Thank you, cousin—"

Quartz's ferocious howl deafened us both and rattled the trees around us. I didn't know what had set him off, but I wasn't going to let him hurt an innocent wolf.

Flinging out the power I still held, I yelled, **"NO! DOWN!"**

#

Wyatt

Of course, Posy didn't know that Quartz was reacting to the king's warning. Most likely, she thought he was breaking their agreement, and she flung out power in a wild wave to hold him back.

"NO! DOWN!"

Her Ultimate Luna Voice was an invisible hand that slammed Quartz to the ground hard enough to knock the breath out of him. While he lay flat on his back, gasping and cursing, her power pushed my other brothers and me to our knees.

That didn't surprise us, but seeing the werewolf king stumble back a step definitely did.

"She shoved me!" King Julian gasped with wide eyes.

"She's awesome, right, dude?" Ash said with a broad grin. "I told you, our girl is a badass bitch!"

Then Posy dropped her power, and we could move again. Quartz didn't, though, so Mase and Ash went over to check on him while Cole and I ran to our girl.

"Q didn't break his word," I hurried to tell her. "The king said something that upset him. He wasn't going for Maple."

"Oh, no!" She lifted her face to stare up at me, her eyes filling with tears. "I made a mistake! Is he okay?"

"He's fine," Cole assured her, but the words went in one ear and out the other.

"Sorry, Ethan." She pushed at his shoulder and tried to shove him off her lap. "I need to check on Quartz!"

Ethan rolled away, winding the t-shirt around his waist as he went, and Cole helped him stand.

"Let me get you to your dad," Cole offered. "He's waiting at the cars. I'm sure he's going to be very happy to see you and know Maple is fine."

As they left, Posy ignored my efforts to get her on her feet and simply crawled over to Quartz, who still sprawled on the grass like a starfish.

Dramatic little bitch, ain't he? I smirked.

Always. Granite rolled his eyes.

"Q? Are you okay?" Posy asked frantically, her hands patting up and down his body. "Did I hurt you?"

"And to think I was worried *he'd* hurt *you.*" Quartz sat up and pulled her into a hug. "I think you could hold your own against nearly any wolf."

Letting out a sigh of relief, her shoulders relaxed and she dropped her forehead to his chest.

"I'm sorry!" Her words were muffled, but audible. "I shouldn't have doubted you'd keep your word."

"No, little one. You did exactly as the gammas trained you to do. I'm proud of you."

"Thank you." Posy lifted her head and smiled a big sunshine smile. "And thank you for working with me."

King Julian cleared his throat and glanced at his watch, and Posy jumped, clearly shocked to see him. Her smile fell and her eyes dimmed almost instantly, but I couldn't tell if it was because she knew he came to end Maple or if she was embarrassed for him to see her scars.

Since she tried to hide herself behind Quartz, I figured it was the scars.

"Good job, luna," the king praised her, and her face turned beet red.

"Thank you, your majesty."

"All right, boys," he said, looking at us, "seeing as I'm not needed here and I am elsewhere, I'll say so long for now and see you at the palace in about two hours."

"*Two hours?!* " Ash shrieked, freaking out. "Oh, my Goddess! I have to get Posy ready! Her hair alone is going to take almost half of that!"

He bent down, stuck his hands in her armpits, and lifted her up, then started to run toward his SUV with her held out in front of him like she was a baby with a stinky diaper.

"We better hurry after him." Mase waited for Quartz to yield control, then helped Jay stand up. "He won't hesitate to leave us here if fashion's on the line."

As we trotted back to the vehicles, we could hear our girl scolding Ash for being more concerned about her hair than his brother's well-being, and we traded smirks.

"At least it's not Wyatt getting into trouble this time," Mase teased. "Small miracle."

If I wasn't in my suit pants and him in his dress shirt, I would have tackled him, but I wasn't trying to get yelled at for having grass stains on us at the coronation.

Plus Ash really *was* going to leave us here if we didn't hustle.

That's why I settled for a quick punch on his bicep before I skipped away. I had my hair just how I wanted it and didn't need a noogie to mess it up.

Chuckling, King Julian shook his head.

"Your luna is a truly remarkable woman. Not only can she manage your wolves, she can knock you boys on your asses, keep you on your toes, and bring you to your knees."

"Damn right!" I said with a grin. "And we wouldn't have it any other way."

13: Coronation

Posy

The cathedral was a sea of beautiful dresses, elegant suits, glittering jewels, and heavy gold crowns.

Lots of crowns.

Jayden told me kings and queens from all over the world were present. The only king who didn't attend was the Australian one, whose flight was grounded because of wildfires. And then there were all the former kings and queens, who wore circlets, and the princes and princesses, who wore tiaras and smaller crowns...

"You stand tall today, sweetness," he murmured, "and don't be intimidated by a metal ring on someone's head."

"Yeah, the ones on your finger are worth more than half of some of their little kingdoms, anyway," Wyatt smirked.

My eyes flew wide. I knew my wedding rings were made from platinum and set with diamonds, but I didn't know they were worth that much! Now I was even more nervous to wear them all the time!

I didn't remember much of the actual ceremony, but it only took half an hour. A guy in big white hat and silver robes - Mason said he was a moon priest - said a lot of words that sounded like they came from some ancient time. I understood only about one word in every ten! Then the queen knelt on a silver velvet pillow, the priest placed the sparkling crown on her head, and King Julian helped her stand and face those of us in the audience.

"Long live the queen!" the priest called in a louder, deeper voice than he had been using.

It surprised me to hear it coming out of such a thin, elderly man, and I bit my lip to keep from giggling.

"Long live the queen!" we all chorused back.

The king took Queen Lilah's hand in his and escorted her down the white-carpeted aisle with Luke and Gisela following them. After a few moments, ushers began to dismiss us row by row. Since my mates and I were in the front on the queen's side, we were second to leave. The king's front row went first and Cole, who seated next to me, explained who was who as they exited their pew.

"That's Magnus. He's King Julian's father." He pointed to a man wearing a silver circlet on his graying black hair. "He wants to talk with you before we leave on Monday, so he may approach us at the reception. Just FYI."

I nodded and looked at the next person, who looked like an older version of Magnus.

"That's the king's grandfather, Alfred. He's Magnus' dad."

"Makes sense. They look a lot alike."

"They do. Plus, there's only eighteen years between them, so a lot of people think they're brothers, not father and son."

The next people I knew. Alpha Ranger Hemming of Tall Pines, the king's little brother, and his luna and mate, Junia, the queen's cousin and best friend. I gave them a little wave when they glanced over our way. Ranger smiled and Junia giggled and waved back.

"I hope we get to see them a bit at the reception," I told Cole. "The queen, too. I know she's the star of the show today, but I've missed her."

I'd already had the chance to visit a bit with Beatrix, Zayne and Zayden, who sat at the end of our pew, Zayne next to Wyatt and Beatrix squished between her handsome mates. I could see them at home any day, though. The queen and I texted and called each other a lot, but it wasn't the same as seeing each other in person.

"I know, and we will." Then he surprised me by adding, "The king and queen have invited us for tea tomorrow afternoon."

"Just us?" I smiled brightly with excitement. I could only imagine how much fun that would be! Still, it would be nerve-racking if I had to remember to stick out my pinkie and avoid spilling tea on my dress if a lot of other people were there.

"Just us. They're sending off all the foreign dignitaries in the morning, having brunch with their families before noon, then meeting us for tea around two. After that, they're leaving on a mini vacation."

"Oh!" I clapped my hands quietly. "Are they coming with *us*?"

"No, honey," he chuckled. "I don't know where they're going. You can ask them tomorrow, but the king may be keeping it a secret."

"Just like you are from me, you big meanies." I pooched out my bottom lip in a pout and blinked up at him.

He swiftly turned his head.

"Don't look. Don't look. Don't look," he muttered under his breath, making me giggle inside. Clearing his throat, he nodded toward the rest of the folks leaving the king's first row. "Those are his uncles and cousins. Not one woman in the Hemming family survived the sickness."

"Oh, that's so sad!"

"It didn't spare anyone, honey, royal family or not."

I nodded and opened my mouth to reply, but the dark-suited usher now stood next to me, since I was seated on the end of the pew, and smiled down at me.

"Luna, if you would, please?" He held out one white-gloved hand.

"Am I supposed to take your hand?" I asked as I leaned away from him into Cole.

"If you wish, luna. Do you need assistance to stand?"

"Um."

"No, she doesn't. Thank you," Cole said for me, then basically lifted me to my feet and guided me into the aisle.

I stumbled a tiny bit when I saw the sea of faces staring back at me, and Cole grabbed my elbow with worry flashing in his eyes. It had been much easier to walk to the front row an hour ago when no one else had been seated yet.

You are the luna of Five Fangs, I told myself sternly. *You will put your shoulders back and hold your head high and not shame your mates.*

Listening to myself, I linked my arm in Cole's elbow, tilted up my chin, and walked that long, long aisle with steady, measured steps. My poor mate had to pause every few steps to not get ahead of me, and I imagined Ash was bouncing on his toes with impatience behind us, but I was *not* going to stumble again.

Finally, I made it past the last row and let out a sigh of relief to see the open foyer.

"Now straight ahead to the receiving line." Ash leaned down to whisper from behind me. "Aren't you glad you didn't have to shake this many hands at your luna ceremony?"

"Yes," I nodded gratefully. "I need to thank Mom and Mama again for that."

He chuckled and dropped a kiss on the side of my neck, making my heart flutter, before stepping back so I could carry on.

"Posy!" Queen Lilah squealed as we reached the royal couple. "I'm so glad to see you! You look radiant in that color, and those pink pearls make your skin glow."

"Thank you, your majesty." My words were muffled as she hugged me tight against her, and I giggled. "I missed you, too. And if anyone looks glowing and radiant, it's you. And what an amazing gown!"

"It is, isn't it?" She released me from her arms and looked down at her gorgeous blue gown. "I told the tailors it had to be lightweight and comfortable, and it is! I could wear it all day. I shouldn't have bothered with a reception dress when this one would have been just fine to dance in. This crown, though. Ugh!"

She frowned as she put her hands up as if she were going to take it off.

"Uh uh uh, my darling." King Julian waggled his index finger back and forth. "You have to leave that on until the reception."

"I know," she grumbled, then leaned down to murmur in my ear. "It weighs a ton! I think some of my neck vertebrae herniated when that priest plunked it on my head!"

"He *hurt* you?" the king growled with Onyx underscoring his voice.

"I'm teasing, my love." She rolled her two-colored eyes, then winked at me with the blue one before turning toward her mate and kissing his cheek. "You can't hurt a moon priest even if he *did* hurt me."

"The hell I can't," he grumbled.

"Julian!" she scolded him.

"Good to see you again, your majesty." Knowing the line was backing up behind us, I decided to hurry this along.

Dropping a small curtsy in front of him like Emerson had taught me, I smiled as I remembered Thoreau practicing it, too. Even though Emerson told him he would bow as a male, Thoreau still curtsied with me. He said it was for moral support, and I gave him good boy pats *and* a good boy kiss while Emerson rolled his eyes.

"You as well, luna. The boys told you about tea tomorrow, right?" He took my hand in his and bowed over it.

"Yes. I am looking forward to it!" I grinned at him, and he pecked my knuckles, making me turn bright red.

Five throats clearing behind me made him smirk as he stood up and released my hand. Glancing over my shoulder, I saw my mates bow briefly, then they crowded around my back close enough for me to feel their body heat, their mate scents coating me like perfume.

"Congratulations, my queen," Mason said, his business face and voice out in full force as he spoke for the group. "May your reign be long and prosperous."

"Thank you, alphas." Queen Lilah's eyes twinkled with good humor as she slowly dipped her head in a very queen-like way. "I look forward to visiting with you all later."

"Your majesties," my other boys rumbled.

Then Ash's hand was in the crook of my arm, and the rest followed close behind as he tugged me along a little too fast. I frowned. Had it upset them that much for the king to kiss my hand?

My heels weren't very high, but I wasn't used to walking in them, and my ankle turned suddenly. I yipped at the tiny flash of pain, but mainly in surprise, and quickly righted myself.

"Posy!" Ash came to an instant halt and grabbed my shoulders. "Are you okay?"

"Boy, if you don't stop dragging me!" I griped with an unusual flash of temper.

As I scowled up at him, Cole slapped the back of his head, and he grimaced. Then Wyatt scooped me up in his arms before I could blink or finish telling Ash off.

"What were you thinking, Ash?" he scowled. "She turned her ankle!"

"Sorry! I forgot not to walk so fast with our shortcake! I just want to get outside. I'm suffocating in here, and I can't be still any longer."

Jayden came over and fixed my skirt, fluffing it over my knees, then nodded at Wyatt, who carried me through the front doors and down the stairs.

"I can walk, you know. Lark already took away the sting, and it didn't even hurt that much."

"Cutie, how many times do we have to tell you? We *like* to carry you. It makes the caveman in us happy, okay?"

"Okay, caveman," I giggled, which made him smile.

"Posy, I really am sorry." My waffle sounded so sad, and I couldn't stand it.

I held out my arms and made grabby hands at him. His face lit up, but before he could take me, Wyatt set off at a fast clip, his chest bouncing me up and down with silent chuckles.

"Two strikes, waffle!" he called over his shoulder as he started to run. "One for hurting her ankle and one for being too slow!"

"What happens when he gets three strikes?" I looped my arms around Wyatt's neck as he trotted along.

"Well, that's for you to decide, cutie." He dropped a kiss on my nose. "Punish him however you see fit."

Oh? Lark's ears lifted with interest. *Princess Bossy Pants come out to play?*

Lark! Quartz is ruining you!

I hate to tell you, but I like *being ruined,* she purred. *Specially by Daddy.*

Shush, wolfie!

#

The reception was so much fun! We feasted on things I'd never heard of and I tried champagne for the first time. The bubbly fizz tickled my nose, which made my mates chuckle. Although alcohol didn't have much effect on wolves or most shifters, some still enjoyed drinking it for the taste. I wasn't one of them. Champagne? Eh, you could keep it. I'd stick to Pepsi!

Even though I had *no* idea what I was doing, I danced with my mates, the king, the king's elegant grandfather, Ranger, Zayne, Zayden, and Luke. They were all patient as I figured out the steps and rhythm, although Luke cheated and put my shoes on top of his and just waddled us around the dance floor. Gisela snapped a ton of pictures of us while laughing at me, and I gave her a dark glare. It didn't even bother her! With a raised eyebrow, she said I looked like a concussed kitten and told me to stick to looking cute instead.

Pouting, I huffed at her, which made her laugh again, then the king's father asked me for a dance.

"Luna," he began as he guided me around the dance floor, "I want to formally apologize for what happened concerning your father. I allowed myself to be advised by someone who wasn't trustworthy. That individual has since been dealt with, but I hold myself ultimately accountable for Logan Everleigh's death."

"Kendall Briggs planned and committed the crime," I murmured, staring at his shoulder instead of meeting his eyes. "It wasn't your fault."

"Maybe not directly, but every wolf in my pack is my responsibility. I've made restitution to the Everleighs and would like you to consider what I may provide for you as well. I cannot change the past, as much as I would like to, but please tell me what compensation I can give you for your loss."

"Do you mean money?" I tilted my head and finally met his eyes, trying to work out all his long words. "I don't want or need money because there isn't enough in the world to replace the father I never knew. However, you can fund my school project for our pack and help build a legacy in his name. I want to open a secondary school so our members don't need to go to the human one."

"I would be more than happy to do so," he chuckled. "And, yes, compensation usually takes the form of money, but if a school is your wish, so be it. Whatever you ask, luna."

"Hmm. Then I ask that you form a committee to do some investigations so that things like this don't happen anymore. Same with creating a group of people to go around to packs in secret and make sure alphas are behaving and caring for their members the way they should."

I watched his face as I spoke, which is how I caught the glitter of *something* in his eyes. I didn't know what it was; I could only hope it wasn't his wolf stirring with anger.

"How did you know that?" he asked with a funny little smile.

"Know what?"

"Know that my son is changing a few laws and procedures concerning those issues? He's going to inform the rest of our family at brunch tomorrow, then hash out some details with your mates during tea. How did you know about it?"

"I didn't, but it's the intelligent thing to do." I shrugged, then gave him a cheeky grin. "So I guess you have one very intelligent son, sir."

He stared at me without blinking for several seconds, then a bright smile spread across his face and crinkled the corners of his hazel eyes into a web of wrinkles.

196

"And I think Five Fangs has a very wise luna," he chuckled.

The dance ended and Magnus handed me off to my mates where they still stood talking with Luke and Gisela. Wyatt immediately tucked me under his arm and squeezed me tight against him.

"Got the king's father wrapped around your finger, too, huh?" he teased, making me blush. "You even made the old fart smile and laugh. You got magic in you, cutie."

"Like I said, a miracle worker." Jayden leaned in and kissed my forehead. "Our precious girl. You have more power in your gentle, kind heart than anything you can draw out of the six packs."

My face really on fire now, I turned it into Wyatt's side and tried to burrow into him.

"Stop teasing her," Mason rumbled from my other side.

"I'm not teasing her. I'm *complimenting* her."

"With Posy, it's the same thing," Mason insisted.

"Ha ha ha, dude! If she turns any redder, she's going to put tomatoes to shame," Ash laughed. "Every time I think you can't get any cuter, you do. You're the cutest cupcake ever!"

"Now *you're* teasing her!" Mason squawked.

"Yeah, Ash. You're being a bad boy today," Cole snickered. "One more strike and Princess Bossy Pants gets to punish you."

"Oh, yes, please!" he chirped, which made me giggle as I dug further into Wyatt's chest. "I'm always up for being under Princess Bossy Pants!"

"Baby, are you up for being under me?" I heard Gisela ask, and my blush spread to my ears and down my neck to my chest.

"Yeah, we're, uh, just going to, um, go," Luke said awkwardly, "because I don't even want to know, and Ela sure as hell doesn't need *any* more ideas for the bedroom."

Turning my face a bit to peek at them, I saw him hustling Gisela away as she complained loudly, and all of us burst out laughing.

14: More Secrets, Lark?

Posy

The reception was scheduled to go until midnight, but I reached my limit at ten. The unending social interaction, too much rich food, a dozen or more turns around the dance floor, and I was ready to call it a night.

At my request, Ash walked me over to tell the queen good night, then we headed for the door.

"I'm such an old lady," I grinned up at Ash. "Ready for bed at ten on a Saturday night."

"Then I'm an old man," he joked. "I'm so ready to crash!"

"Make sense since we're only about half an hour away from your usual bedtime. Where are the others?"

He raised his hand and pointed to Mason, Cole, Wyatt, and Jayden, who were clustered around the king. All of them wore serious faces as they talked and I wondered what was happening, but didn't want to interrupt them.

Besides, I was falling asleep on my feet.

"I'll tell you about it later," Ash said as I snuggled under his arm. "Let's get you back to the guest house, okay?"

"Yeah." I covered my mouth as a yawn snuck up on me. "Sounds great, waffle."

After he linked them that we were leaving, Ash led me out of the reception hall and toward the car park. Mason said they'd get one of the pages to run them home later so that we could take Ash's SUV. I was so grateful for that, not feeling up to the four-mile walk to the guest house. The half-mile trek through the garden to *get* to the car park was more than enough.

Nuzzling my face into Ash's ribs, I smiled and took a big inhale of his scent - only to freeze as another scent wafted in with it. It was only for a second, and I couldn't place it, but I knew it from somewhere.

And it was *wrong*.

It shouldn't be here.

It belonged in a windowless room, not *here*.

Frozen in place, I clung to Ash, who dragged me along a step before he realized something was up and stopped walking.

"Princess? What is it?"

I shrugged as I tried to convince myself I was imagining it.

You're being ridiculous. Kendall Briggs is dead, and that isn't his scent anyway.

198

Still, something about this shifter's smell took me right back to that dark room.

Lark? Do you recognize it?

My wolf didn't answer. Didn't even stir.

Worried as well as scared now, I tilted my head and tried again.

Lark?

When I got no answer, I linked my other mates to see if one of their wolves held her attention, and was confused when they all said no.

"All right, Posy. What's going on?" Ash put his hands on my shoulders, then bent down to look in my eyes.

Lark? I called once more.

Still nothing.

I could sense her and knew she wasn't asleep, so what was going on?

How is she blocking me so completely? I'd never been able to put up such a solid wall between us. Then another thought, *How many times has she done it before? And why?*

"Ash, see if Lark will respond to Sid," I murmured. "She's blocking me for some reason."

"She's probably overwhelmed. Goddess knows I am! Been on my best behavior for hours now."

The disturbing scent wafted stronger for a second, and a chill went down my spine. Alarmed now, I shot my eyes around in search of a threat. There was nothing. Just the gravel pathway lined with flickering lamps and the dark silhouettes of hedges crouching in the distance.

My imagination. Has to be.

Still, I couldn't shake the feeling that someone or something was watching us, and my breathing picked up as my mouth dried to dust.

"No, it's more than that. Something's wrong, Ash. I can *feel* it."

"Okay, princess. Sid's talking to her now. Don't worry. We'll figure it out together."

Biting my lip, I nodded, glad to have him at my side, and waited for my wolf to explain what was going on.

#

Lark

He was here.

He found me.

Just as he promised he would if anyone ever found out what happened.

199

Moon Goddess, protect me.

Like my human had learned to do, I went still and silent, sinking deep into my mind and shutting out everyone and everything. Fear paralyzed me down to my bones and I didn't know what to do. Posy called me, my mates called me, their boys called me, and I could answer none of them.

But I didn't tell! I fretted. *Not even Posy knows!*

Something told me that he wouldn't care about the truth, though.

As my distress flared, others began tapping on the link - the betas and their wolves almost frantically - and shutting them out made my head pound as hard as my heart.

I no want to die. Not anymore. Not when I have so much to live for. What do I do? What do I do?!

Then a soft voice came from right in front of me. It filtered through the panic and wrapped around me like a hug.

I love you, Lark. I love you so much. Can you hear your Sid, darling?

H-h-h—

I am here, darling. What's wrong? Tell your Sid.

H-h-h—

Shh. Calm down, he cooed. *What upset you like this, hmm? Did someone scare you?*

He here! I finally managed to choke out.

Who's here?

He going to hurt me! I shook harder. *He going to hurt me, then he going to kill me!*

Never. No one will touch Sid's darling, my mate murmured in a quiet voice, as if he knew I would shatter at anything louder or harsher. *Tell me his name.*

I not know it!

Then show me, darling, he crooned. *Show me his face and he will trouble you no more.*

Unable to bear the burden alone any longer, I selfishly and weakly let the memory pour out of me, not knowing Sid would share it with the others.

15: Burnt Oil Man

~Two years ago~

Lark

I lay on the blood-stained floor of our dark room. The only light came from under the door, a thin sliver of silver.

I shuddered. I did not like silver.

Silver *hurt*.

My eyes stayed fixed on it, though, because footsteps approached - and that never resulted in anything good.

Thank the Goddess Posy sleeping, I thought. *My poor girl.*

Father beat her badly yesterday for asking a question, and I managed to heal the worst of the injuries before I gave out. Now she was trying to sleep off the rest of the wounds while I kept watch in her human body, too hurt and drained to shift into my own.

Mate will come soon and we leave Father. Survive two more years till mate find us.

I clung to that belief. It was all that kept my spirits up, and I used it to keep Posy's hope alive, too.

Sometimes, she and I imagined our mate. We weren't so concerned about his appearance, but we hoped that he would be kind and good-humored, that he wouldn't beat us too often and could overlook the scars. Those daydreams may have been simple and naive, but they gave us something to live for, a reason to keep getting up and going on.

A kind mate, Moon Goddess. That not asking too much, is it? A kind mate who might even one day come to love us.

My thoughts were cut short when, from the other side of the door, Alpha Kendall Briggs' low growl made my heart stutter in fear.

"I don't know why Calvin told you about her! He was only supposed to hire a supplier, not spill secrets!"

"That's a matter for you to take up with him," replied a man with a voice like rough cotton. "All I know is he thought you might need help administering the correct dosage due to her unique size."

I took a deep inhale of his scent, confirming he was a stranger, and I did not care for him already. It reminded me of the time Posy accidentally burned the oil in the skillet while frying chicken.

That was the day I discovered burns were hellaciously painful and a bitch to heal.

It not have been so bad if Father no dumped whole pan on her as punishment, I thought bitterly.

"If I find out you've said one word to anyone, especially to someone at the royal pack, you'll pay with your life," Father threatened the stranger.

"It would not be in my best interests to tell anyone. I'd lose my new customer, wouldn't I?" Burnt Oil Man sounded amused. "I'm only curious as to what sort of beast requires such ... special treatment."

"Beast?" Father laughed. "She's a runt. Weak and useless. Put on this earth to serve her betters without complaint. Stubborn thing that she is, she constantly needs to be reminded of this. That is where you and your "special treatment" come into play."

The door flew open before I was ready, and I quickly stood and put my back to a corner.

"SHIFT, RUNT," Father commanded the second he walked in the room, and I had no choice but to comply, no matter how exhausted or hurt I was.

Once I was back in my own fur, I wrestled out of Posy's worn t-shirt, shorts, and underthings.

One good thing about being so small, I thought. *I not trash her few clothes when I shift in them.*

In my mere four years of life, I'd learned to count victories and see silver linings anywhere I could.

Keeping the stranger in my peripheral vision, I fastened my gaze on the *real* monster in the room.

"She's just a pup," Burnt Oil Man mumbled.

Although I didn't take my eyes off Father, a flicker of hope sparked in my heart. Would this stranger help me?

And for a second, my silver eyes brightened at the thought.

"Pup or not, she's mine!" Father roared. "Mine to do with as I wish!"

"I wasn't making a judgment on your morals, only an observation on her size," Burnt Oil Man scoffed. "Because she's so small, you can use less and it will last longer."

As quick as it came, the spark of hope died.

His words made Father happy, though. With a wide grin, he stalked over to my corner and stopped three feet away, then held up a glass vial full of clear liquid.

"Runt! Do you know what this is?"

I knew better than to move, let alone speak. Curling my tail under my legs and lowering my head, I faked submission to avoid another beating.

"This is wolfsbane distilled into liquid." He smirked and shook the glass bottle in my face. "One tiny shot of it and you'll become a docile little lamb."

With a hard swallow, I tried - and failed - to calm myself. Aconite was not an enemy I could fight. All I could do was watch and wait for the moment I could make a run for it. I wasn't fast, but I was desperate enough to try to escape again. I couldn't let Father put me to sleep and leave Posy utterly defenseless against him.

"I've had it with your insolence," Father continued his tirade. "I'll leave you awake enough to heal Posy, but no more. I'll force you to watch everything I do to her and you'll be helpless to—"

"You'll have to dose her carefully," Burnt Oil Man interrupted. "Not enough and she'll only be drowsy. Too much, and she'll go to sleep forever. Unless that's what you want?"

"No, I don't want to kill her. I need her alive for another two years. After that, it won't matter. Posy won't need her wolf for what she'll be doing after she turns eighteen."

"She'll develop a resistance to the bane the longer you use it, so you'll need to slowly increase the dosage. Hmm. For her size, no more than a milliliter to start with, then increase it by five drop intervals as her tolerance builds."

"How long does it take to work once administered?" Father asked.

"Couple of minutes. Five at the most."

"All right. Let's do this."

The two men moved at the same time. Burnt Oil Man shuffled off to the side and leaned his shoulder against the wall while Father came toward me.

"Make it easy on yourself, Lark," he smirked. "Don't fight. You know I always win."

I shook with stress, but knew I had to take the chance. The door stood open behind him, and Burnt Oil Man was on the far side of the room now. If I could only make it past Father...

As he reached for me, I dodged and bolted, easily slipping between his legs. My heart bursting with hope, excitement and fear, I pushed myself to run as fast as I could and almost made it. My left front paw was actually on the threshold.

Then Father roared, "FREEZE!" in his alpha voice, and I hit an invisible brick wall. My whole body locked in place, and my momentum knocked me tail over ears. My head smacked hard into the door frame, and the room spun like crazy.

"Stupid female. You never learn," Father grumbled.

Stomping over, he grabbed my tail and dragged me back into the room. One heavy boot kicked me in the stomach, knocking all the air out of me and sending me flying. I fetched up against the wall near the stranger's feet and looked up at him in a daze. My vision was blurred from the pain and mild concussion, but I could make out piercing blue eyes and long, black, curly hair.

Then Father wrapped one hand tight around the back of my neck and pinned me to the floor.

"Give me the syringe," he demanded, and Burnt Oil Man sighed as he walked over to the black leather bag on the floor by the door.

Syringe? What a syringe? I asked myself in a panic. *What does it do? Does it hurt?*

"Here." The stranger held out something I couldn't see, but would come to know all too well in the future. "I'm not doing anything to her, though. My hands are clean in this."

"Oh, please. Your hands are dirtier than mine. And if you ever tell anyone about what happens in Green River, I will make sure the king knows *exactly* how dirty your hands are."

"What if she escapes? She'll never stay quiet about this."

"She won't escape," Father chuckled darkly.

"But if she does?" Burnt Oil Man crouched next to me. "Listen, runt. If you tell a soul that I was here, I promise I will hunt you down and kill you."

I cried and whined, but there was no mercy in either man.

Father parted the thick fur of my ruff, then something pinched my skin and made it tingle. In seconds, numbness circled the area and spread quickly until I couldn't feel my body anymore. Disoriented and scared, I whimpered as my vision narrowed into a tight circle. Then my heavy eyelids drooped all the way down.

Mate will come soon and we leave Father, I chanted my favorite mantra, the one that kept me sane. *Survive two more years till mate find us.*

"What about quicksilver?" I heard Father ask from far, far away. "Can you supply that, too?"

He kept talking, but the words turned to mush in my ears, and I jerked myself awake.

No! No leave Posy. Wake up! Must protect my girl and survive for mate!

I fought with all my might to force my eyes open, but it was no use. I couldn't fight the wolfsbane flowing through my veins. No wolf could.

No leave. Wake up. Must protect.

Froth bubbled out of my mouth as my brain slowed to a crawl. *Survive. Mate.*

My little brown body jerked once, twice, then went still. *No. Wake—*

And I was out.

16: On the Hunt

Ash

Watching Lark's memory was worse than being tortured myself. Tears poured down my face and pre-vomit bile filled my mouth. Swiping at my eyes, I swallowed hard to keep from hurling everywhere.

Finally, thank the Goddess, the home movie of horror ended.

Can you show me his face more clearly, darling? My wolf kept it together far better than I did as he continued to coax an identity from her. *If not, can you share his scent with me?*

I knew Sid very well. He might have sounded calm, but a tidal wave of rage surged inside him. Any second now, he was going to explode, then someone was going to die.

Which is no less than this son of a bitch deserves, I growled to myself, *but I am curious if I know the guy.*

Then Lark showed us a man's face and shared his scent - and I recognized him right away.

Ezra Ikhlassi.

He was one of very few shifters who had more moon magic than normal. His wolf had died in a freak accident only a year after he got him, and he went a little crazy and did some sketchy shit that was hushed up since he was just a kid. Ever since, the king kept him around the palace as a precaution. A 'keep your friends close and your enemies closer' sort of thing.

Huh! I grunted, not really surprised. *I always did get a bad feeling around that dude. Now it makes sense why I wanted to punch him in the face every time I saw him.*

And Wyatt joked that I only disliked him because his hair was sexier than mine!

As if, I scoffed.

Usually, I would have gone down the rabbit hole thinking about how he let his curls get stringy and frizzy while mine were *always* well kept, but for once, my brain decided to stay focused.

Hmm. Wonder if Gelo knows him?

Knowing all hell was about to break loose, I took a few seconds to decide who to contact first.

The king? I mean, the least we could do was let him know we were about to kill one of his wolves, right? Or Gelo, who hopefully has some insider intel on this soon-to-be-dead man?

As I dithered, Sid got sick of waiting and took over without warning, and my favorite black suit became $5,000 worth of fabric confetti.

He bolted, and I screamed at my brothers to get Posy and let the king know what was going on. There was no stopping Sid now, which was fine, but that left our mate all alone - and that was far from fine.

Cole and Wyatt are already on their way, Mase linked back. *I'm still with the king. He wants Ikhlassi alive to question. We need to know what he knows and if there were others working with Briggs.*

Good ol' Mase. He was always two steps ahead, thank the Goddess.

Cole will stay in human form and get our mate to safety, he continued. *Granite, too. He's ascendant, but he wants to be with Lark. You-know-who has already shifted, of course, and is on the hunt.*

Aww, man! Jay looked great in that pink vest! I groaned. *I suppose it's in ribbons now like my whole suit?*

It is. Good thing we took our conversation to the king's study before he shifted, Mase said with his usual deadpan humor. *Quartz and Sid, I know you heard us. King Julian wants him alive.*

Dead silence.

Hello? I sing-sang to both of them. *The king wants him alive.*

Then the king better stop us, Quartz grunted, *because nothing else will.*

Knowing that was true enough, I left it. If King Julian wanted Ikhlassi alive badly enough, he'd see it done.

I had other matters to attend to.

Did you know? I asked Posy cautiously, ninety percent certain she didn't solely based on the fact that she hadn't recognized his scent.

Know what?

Did you see anything Lark linked us? I frowned.

No. Tell me what's going on, Ash! Sid told me to wait here, then shifted and took off. It's dark and I'm scared and alone and—

*The boys are on their way, princess, but if anything happens, use your Ultimate Luna Voice and protect yourself at all costs. They should be there any second, but you are strong enough to make and keep yourself safe. You shoved **the king**, baby!*

Um, that was an accident. I didn't mean to.

Well, you did, I teased her with a grin, hoping to distract her.

The betas were lighting up the link with demands to know what was going on with their luna, and I asked Wyatt to give them the bare bones while I kept Posy calm.

Just keep talking to me until they get here, she requested with a tremor in her voice.

No problem. I like talking to our pretty girl.

What Lark showed you... Is someone in trouble? She's not hurt, is she?

No to both questions. She remembered how your stepfather got the wolfsbane, that's all. She showed us the supplier's face and shared his scent, and now the king, ah, wants a word with him. Since Sid knows the dude, he, um, volunteered to find him.

You're a terrible liar, waffle.

Hey, most of that was the truth! I said indignantly.

I get the feeling you left out some important details.

But baby—

We're here, Cole and Granite said together, then Wyatt added, *We got her, Ash. We're taking her to Mase and the king right now.*

Don't think this conversation is over, Ash, Posy scolded me. *And don't let Sid get into trouble. I know he's on the hunt, not just volunteering for escort duty.*

Can you blame him? Cole snapped. *He's the man who supplied Kendall Briggs with enough wolfsbane to almost kill Lark! I wish I had my hands around his throat right now!*

Keep it together, brother, Jay linked in, *so you can take care of our girl.*

He was silent for a moment, then Wyatt linked us an image of Cole hugging the life out of our mate, his face buried in her mate mark, and that made us smile despite our worry and anger.

As Sid ran fast and low with his nose to the ground, I linked Jay, knowing he was in the same situation I was. Our wolves weren't going to listen to us, never mind relinquish control any time soon, so we might as well have a little convo while we were along for the ride.

No better sedative, am I right? You should find a way to bottle Eau de Posy. How are you going to keep Q from killing Ikhlassi without her there to calm him down?

I'm not, he admitted. *If the king wants him alive, he'll figure it out or unleash Onyx to stop him. Doubt that latter one, though. The reception's still going on, so he can't be out of sight for too long before tongues start wagging, and I'm sure he wants to keep this under wraps until he finds out the size of the hornets' nest Lark just kicked over.*

True enough. He could send Gabbro or Pumice, though. Better yet, send both of them.

Other than his family, Quartz didn't let many others get close to him. Pretty much the only ones besides Onyx were Magnus' and Alfred's wolves. None of us knew why, but Mase thought it was because they were Onyx's father and grandfather, and Quartz loved Onyx like a brother. Whatever the reason, he had mad respect for both former kings and would listen to them.

Well, maybe.

Good idea, Jay said. *I'll link Mase to see if that's possible. Otherwise, we're going to need a necromancer to ask him anything because our wolves are going to straight up slaughter this prick.*

Facts, I smirked, then sobered up. *So, um, do we tell Posy the whole story? I don't know how Lark blocked her so completely for so long, but she has no clue what her wolf endured.*

I think, he said slowly, *that there were times when Posy was so knocked out, Lark didn't have to block her so much as just not tell her what happened while she was unconscious.*

So do we tell her? I repeated. *I mean, it was her wolf that went through it. Shouldn't she know about it? But I don't want her to suffer anymore. I don't want this to be a step back when she's doing so well.*

I hear you. He was silent for a moment. Finally, he said, *Link Angelo and ask him what, if anything, he knows about Ikhlassi while I link Dr. York and get his opinion.*

And what do you think?

I think that scenting Ikhlassi tonight forced Lark's hand to tell us, but she's still protecting Posy from the knowledge. I don't think we should interfere. At least not yet.

Okay, but dude! I have so many questions! For someone who'd been worried he'd fall asleep driving back to the guest house, I was wide awake now. *I mean, why and how did Ikhlassi get involved with Briggs?*

I thought that was obvious. He all but admitted he was paid to go there and supply the wolfsbane. How did you miss that? Dude, you are as dense as the rock Sid's named after.

So he wanted an insult battle, did he? Good because I was all in! I didn't know if he initiated it for himself or me, but I welcomed anything to relieve some of the stress and tension that was stirring me up.

But who was that Calvin guy Briggs mentioned and how did he know about Posy? I demanded. *And you need to wipe your mouth because you have some bullshit on your lips.*

I bet a hundred that Calvin is Briggs' brother. The one the king mentioned who's now a guest at Hotel Torture. And if I wanted to hear from an asshole, I would have farted.

No bet. So let me get this straight. Briggs wants wolfsbane and other banned things, so he contacts his brother in the royal pack to send him some and cover it up. The brother, possibly named Calvin, hooks him up with Ikhlassi, who shows up at Green River with the wolfsbane. And duuude! Your ass must be jealous of all the shit that comes out of your mouth.

I'm not a proctologist, brother, but I can spot an ass when I see one.

Looked in the mirror again, huh? I smirked.

He wasn't going to win this time! We were currently tied three to three, but I had this insult battle in the bag, baby!

Well, I did until my brain once more did something unexpected and got back on track.

You don't think there were others, do you, Jay? My heart rate picked up at the thought. *Others who hurt Lark without Posy knowing?*

I don't know, but we'll find out and kill any who did.

Damn right we will, I snarled.

Oh, and Ash?

Yeah?

Somewhere out there, a tree is working very hard to produce oxygen so that you can breathe. I think you should go and apologize to it for wasting its time.

I blinked at that one, processing it, and he took the opportunity to give me a big fake smile.

Aww, it's so cute when you try to keep up with me, little brother! I won, but here's an award for participation. It's the only trophy you're ever going to get in a war of the words.

How do you figure you won? My face twisted in confusion. *It's not over yet.*

You poor, naive puppy. It was over before it began. I just let you fire a few rounds to make you feel good about yourself.

Do you hear how stupid you sound? I rolled my eyes.

Of course I sound stupid! How else would you understand me?

Mase may have said you are the most handsome of us, I purred, *but let's put a bag over that personality, hmm? It's ugly as f—*

ENOUGH, YOU TWO! Cole bellowed in the alpha link.

Oopsy! Did we leave that open? I giggled.

You should be working on getting your wolves under control, not improving your roasts! he scolded us.

I don't know, Wyatt chuckled. *I quite liked the one about the bullshit on your lips.*

All of you naughty puppies have such deplorable language. Now Mase joined in on the scolding. *You should be ashamed of yourselves. Once you get in the habit of swearing, it's so hard to get out of. You have professional positions, and you can't be dropping the f-bomb when you're signing alliance treaties and negotiating million-dollar deals!*

You going to ground us, Papa Bear? Wyatt, as usual, pushed right back.

Wy, if I had a dollar for every time you shut up when it mattered, I'd give it back to you as a thank you.

Jay, Cole, and I dissolved into giggles at Wyatt's dropped jaw. It was so rare for Mase to participate in our verbal skirmishes, but when he did, *all* of our asses got burned.

I know I'm an acquired taste, Wyatt recovered quickly and sassed back. *If you don't like me, go acquire some taste.*

I have great taste, and I'm jealous of people who haven't met you. Ash, don't let Jay's brutal honesty inconvenience your ego. Jay, your name isn't Google, so stop acting like a know-it-all. And Cole—

Hey! What did I do?! I'm literally right next to you, innocently holding Lark!

Oh, I'm sorry. Did the middle of my sentence interrupt the beginning of yours? He paused and none of us dared to respond, not sure anymore if he *was* playing. His monotone deadpan gave nothing away. It never did. He could be seething and I wouldn't know. *Well? Is part two of your argument coming out any time soon, or is that it?*

Uh. Cole's mouth flapped a couple of times, but no other sounds came out.

That's what I thought. You and Wyatt take our mate back to the guest house. Ash, Jay, just to let you know, the king has Ikhlassi locked up in the dungeon. He's out of your wolves' reach, so make them understand that and get back to the guest house. I want you both there within the hour.

Yes, Papa Bear, I snickered, unable to help myself.

Is this how Wyatt felt all the time? What a glorious thrill! Pushing the iceman to the edge just to see if he'd crack!

Ash, Mase sighed, *you have your entire life to be a jerk. It's been a long day, so take the rest of the night off, okay?*

Dammit! Nothing shook him! He didn't even raise his voice!

Someday you will get him, Ashy, Sid giggled.

Oh, you're back! Yay!

But I didn't get to kill him, he pouted. *Meanie King Julian stole my prey!*

Well, look on the bright side, buddy. Now you're free to go home to our girl!

Yes, yes, yes! He hopped around like a psycho, and I was happy he was back to his normal self. *When you fall asleep, Ashy, can I take over and be with my darling?*

Sure, buddy. Once the adrenaline fades, I'll be out before you know it. Just make sure she wants to mate first. She's had a rough evening.

Mate? No, not tonight. Want to cuddle! Want to cuddle my tiny darling! Her little furry body is so small and soft and—

That's fine. You can cuddle her as much as you want.

Oh, I will, Ashy! I will!

17: Damage Control

King Julian

I waited until the alphas had their mate settled on Cole's lap before I sat down on the coffee table in front of them.

Studying Posy's face, I saw she was calm, but her eyes showed worry and a tiny bit of fear. All in all, it was a better reaction than I'd hoped for.

Start, Jul, Onyx demanded. *Ask questions so Nyx can return to mate.*

Yes, oh, mighty evil one. I rolled my eyes, then rolled them again when he preened, taking my sarcasm as a compliment.

"Posy, I need to ask Lark a couple of questions. It will be fast as I need to return to the reception before too many people notice my absence. We'll talk more tomorrow during tea, okay? For now, can Lark ascend, please?"

"On one condition." She held up her forefinger. "Don't spoil the queen's night with this. I don't want to be the one who messes up her big day."

My heart squeezed at her compassion and selflessness.

Posy always so careful with everyone's hearts, Onyx murmured. *Posy as sweet as Posy is strong.*

Yes. Yes, she is.

"That's easy enough. Right now, my father says she is busy telling Gisela, Beatrix and Ranger embarrassing stories about their mates as children." I grinned as Dad sent me a picture of Junia burying her bright red face in Ranger's shoulder as he laughed at something my queen said. "We have a few more minutes before she becomes suspicious."

"Very well, then." She looked at Wyatt on her left, then Mase on her right. "Boys, I'm really tired. I might fall asleep while Lark's ascendant. Before I do, I want you to know that I'm sorry for ruining the evening."

"Honey, you've ruined nothing," Cole reassured her and kissed her cheek. "These things happen."

"Look at it this way, cutie," Wyatt chimed in, "you're helping to catch a bad guy."

"Oh!" That made her perk up and she swiveled her head to look at me with wide eyes. "All right. Here's Lark. Goodbye and good night."

We all murmured our good nights as her blue eyes closed. When they blinked open again, they shone like moonlight.

"Hello, Lark. I'm so sorry you've experienced something traumatic this evening," I told her.

"No let him get me. Sid promised he no let him get me." Her body shook so hard, Cole had to tighten his arms around her so she didn't fall on the floor.

"No one will get you. I give you my word as alpha and king. He will never touch you, never even *see* you again if that is your wish." I laid my hand over my heart as I made my vow. "I need to know a couple of things tonight. First, were there any others who brought Kendall Briggs banned items?"

"Not that I know of. Not to alpha house. Father never let anyone into alpha house. Only that man I showed Sid."

"Other than Briggs, did anyone else ever hurt you? Can you remember if anyone from another pack came to hurt you? Or maybe someone who wasn't even a shifter?"

"Sometimes he made James and Aiden and Beta Roy."

I already knew all about that, so I waved it off.

"No one else?" When she shook her head, I went on. "You're sure? He kept you in the alpha house for six years and you never met, saw, or smelled *any* stranger there other than Ikhlassi?"

"Who?"

"The man you showed Sid."

"Burnt Oil Man." She twisted her fingers in her lap until Wyatt reached over and grabbed her hands to hold them.

Onyx snickered at the pseudonym, and I shushed him before she heard.

"Yes. His name is Ezra Ikhlassi."

"Only him. Father not like anyone in alpha house. No one allowed in."

Probably so they never caught on to what he was doing to her, I thought grimly.

"And in that memory you shared, you heard Briggs say the name Calvin, correct? You're sure it was Calvin? No doubts?"

"Yes, your majesty."

"Very well. Thank you." I gave her a gentle smile. "Why don't you rest? You are safe now. Your mates are here, and Quartz's legend alone is enough to scare away anyone with half a brain. I'll also send a troop of soldiers to guard the guest house."

"And Burnt Oil Man?"

"He's in my dungeon. The captain of the guards locked him in our most secure cell, and a squad of my best men will stand guard over him until I can interrogate him later."

She nodded, but bit her bottom lip hard enough to turn the skin white. She was surrounded by her mates, and still the poor girl trembled.

Glancing at the boys, I saw their eyes were glassy as they linked with each other, and Wyatt's smirk and Cole's angry scowl made me wonder if the missing brothers were up to something stupid. Mase closing his eyes and pinching the bridge of his nose confirmed they were.

Quickly, I linked the captain of the guards and let him know that Quartz and Sid were forbidden to enter the dungeon under any circumstances.

With respect, he responded slowly, *how do you expect us to stop them? Especially Quartz? If they won't listen to reason, am I authorized to use force?*

I don't want that many dead wolves for no reason, I grumbled. *If they won't be swayed, link me and do what you can until I can get there.*

Yes, sire.

"Wyatt, take her back to the guest house," Mase said quietly. "I don't think Ash and Jay are going to regain control on their own. Cole and I are going to have to go after them."

I knew neither of them wanted to leave their mate while she was vulnerable. I wouldn't, either.

"Wait. Let me see if Gabbro or Pumice will go instead," I offered.

"Thank you," Cole and Mase said in unison.

So I linked my dad and my grandfather, and Granddad immediately said he'd go. Pumice could get Quartz to calm down, then Quartz could make Sid listen. It was the best I could do other than going myself, which was impossible at the moment. I'd already been gone from the reception for too long.

Knowing I'd done all the damage control I could, I reached out and laid my hand on the side of Lark's face.

"It's going to be okay, little sister," I murmured. "You have your mates with you now. That was your goal, wasn't it? To survive until your mates found you and you could leave that place?"

"Yes, your majesty."

"Well, guess what?" I half-rose and kissed her forehead. "You achieved your goal. Congratulations. Now you can rest easy. You can sleep and let these big, bad wolves protect your girl *and* you for a while."

She blinked at me a few times, then gave me an impish smile, complete with dimples, and I grinned, proud of myself for getting her to smile when she'd been so distressed.

Good boy, Jul.

Thanks. I rolled my eyes at my sarcastic wolf as Mase swung Lark up in his arms and started for the door, his brothers trailing in his wake.

Gave little sister comfort. Onyx apparently thought I needed clarification on why I was being praised as a 'good boy.' *Helped alphas. Caught bad guy. Jul is good boy.*

Realizing he was sincere, I smiled a little as I, too, walked toward the door.

You know, Nyx, I'm really glad you're mellowing—

Now enough being softy! he interrupted me. *Go back to mate! Right now, Jul! Chop chop!*

"So much for becoming mellow," I muttered to myself.

My wolf tilted his head to the side as he asked, *What **is** mellow, Jul?*

Everything you're not.

His eyebrows scrunched up in a frown for a second as he thought about it, then he shrugged.

Kestrel love Nyx the way Nyx is. Nyx will be Nyx forever.

I huffed out a nearly silent laugh. Little did he know how much he'd already changed for his little wolf mate, but I wasn't going to be the one to tell him!

18: Bedtime Cuddles

Garnet

Once we were back at the guest house, Lark asked Mason and Cole if we wolves could have control of their bodies.

"If you okay with that." Looking nervous, she clasped her hands in front of her. "I like them to hold me."

"Anything you want, precious." Mason smiled softly, then handed me the reins as Cole did the same with Topaz.

Granite was already ascendant, and the three of us surrounded our girl in no time. The pups wanted to bury her in a puppy pile on the bed, but I grabbed her around the waist and pulled her away from them.

"We need to get out of these fancy clothes first," I explained, "and take off our shoes."

"Taking shoes off is easy!" Topaz crowed and plopped down on the floor. "Look, Lark! Just pull this little string, see? And then spread this part a little and ta da! Shoe off!"

He held it up with a look of triumph, then tossed it over his shoulder.

"Hey, be careful!" I scolded him. "The boys pay a lot for their shoes."

Topaz rolled his eyes, then attacked his other shoe.

"Just don't ask them to tie the laces," I grinned at Lark. "I tried to show them so many times—"

"But all the bunnies make me hungry!" Gran interrupted.

"What?" She tilted her head to the side. "Bunnies tie shoes?"

Tossing his other shoe, Topaz burst out into song:

> *Bunny ears, bunny ears*
> *Playing by a tree.*
> *Criss-crossed the tree*
> *Trying to catch me.*
> *Bunny ears, bunny ears*
> *Jumped into the hole,*
> *Popped out the other side*
> *Beautiful and bold.*

"I love it!" Lark clapped her hands. "Sing again, please!"

"No, don't," I told him with a frown. "At least, not until you learn to sing it on key."

"Key? Ash keys here somewhere." My innocent sweetheart craned her neck to look around. "Why he needs a key?"

"I meant Paz can't carry a tune in a bucket," I laughed.

"Hey! I can carry lots of things in a bucket!" Topaz jumped to his feet and scowled, and I covered my face with the palm of my hand. "I can carry rocks in a bucket and frogs, oh, and water! I'm sure I could carry a tune in a bucket!"

Wait for it...

"What's a tune, anyway, Garnet?"

Damn you, Quartz, for leaving me to deal with them alone! At least the baby isn't here.

Then I frowned, worried because he wasn't.

Just like River, Sid only had two settings: Happy, sweet boy and death-to-all killing machine. Unlike River, who could switch between the two at the drop of a hat, it took a lot to push Sid into the second setting. When he hit it, though, he became one scary bastard.

That didn't concern me so much. A scary bastard of an alpha wolf could take care of himself anywhere, no problem. What did concern me was the fact that he would return to his baby self once he calmed down.

And he was currently alone in a place where a curious, naive pup could find all sorts of trouble.

"Enough about buckets, bunnies, and keys," I grumbled, focusing on what I *could* control. "Let's just get changed."

"Lark, wait. We help you," Gran told her, and she nodded.

So the pups stripped out of their suits fairly quickly, although they both needed help with the buttons on their shirts and vests. Fortunately, this gave me the chance to stop Topaz before he destroyed his pants trying to get the zipper down.

I made them hang up their suits, showing them how everything went on the hangers, and gave in when they said they wanted to sleep in just their boxers. Neither Posy nor Lark minded anyway, so why should I bother getting them into pajamas or even t-shirts?

After I got them to brush their teeth, which was not a job for the faint of heart, the pups ran back to Lark, wanting to help her get ready for bed, too.

"Uh-oh! Lark's shoes! No strings." Gran looked at her little pumps and scratched the top of his head. "What now?"

"They slide, silly," Lark giggled and sat on the edge of the bed to show him, but he beat her to it.

Kneeling in front of her, he wrapped his hand around one calf and raised her leg a bit. Then, with a look of keen concentration, he carefully eased her shoe off her foot.

"I did it!" he yipped and gave her an adorable grin.

"Thank you!"Lark patted his head. "Wonderful! My feets is sore. Too much dancing."

216

I bit my lip to keep from chuckling at 'feets.'

Now that she was free to speak, her speech was improving all the time, not that it had ever been as basic as Gran's or as baby as Sid's when he regressed. Still, it was so cute when she mispronounced something or garbled up the grammar of a longer sentence.

"I'll rub them!" Both Topaz and Granite said at once, then glared at each other.

"She has two feet," I soothed them.

Back to happy faces, the pups each took a foot. Granite showed Topaz how to take off Lark's other shoe, and I snatched them up before the pups could toss them. Carrying them into the closet, I saw that Mason had their shoe boxes all lined up and ready to re-pack.

I don't know who Christian Louboutin is, but the boys sure like his shoes. Him and the Gucci.

It only took a moment to slip Lark's pumps into the little red bag, then I tucked them back in their box and put the lid on. Giving myself a pat on the back for a job well done, I walked back to the bedroom with a smile.

"What's this?" Topaz rumbled in an angry tone, and my eyes zeroed in on him.

Still kneeling in front of Lark, he scowled down at the foot in his hand.

"Oh. Um." Lark dropped her eyes to her lap and knotted her fingers together. "A scar. Sorry."

"How did you get it?" His fingers explored along her heel and he tried - and failed - to bend down enough to see it. Cole's body really was like a bear's, and he was simply too big for that to happen. "Gran, is there one on that foot, too?"

"Yeah. I feel it."

Simultaneously, they lifted her legs to inspect the bottoms of her feet, and it was a good thing Lark was sitting on the bed. The pups' sudden movement pushed her over and she flopped on her back in a cloud of pink. Her dress rode up, but we were too focused on examining these newfound scars to do more than give her silky thighs a quick glance of appreciation.

"Can't see them," Granite muttered. "Take off extra skin, my love."

"It's not skin!" I corrected him with an eye roll. "They're called pantyhose. And let me do it. You two will tear them. They're delicate."

"I can take them off myself," Lark giggled. "I know how!"

So we helped her stand again, and she captured our undivided attention as she shimmied them off, wiggling them down her hips.

"You should take off your dress, too," I suggested. "Don't want it to get wrinkled."

217

Nodding, Lark turned around for someone to unzip her dress, and I leapt forward before Topaz could butcher it.

"Yeah, that's your *only* reason," Topaz teased with a smirk, and I couldn't deny it.

"I might be a wolf," I murmured, "but I can still appreciate our mate's fine human body."

"Mighty fine," he agreed with sparkling eyes as we watched her dress fall to the floor.

And damn if she wasn't wearing my favorite little boy shorts with the lace that clung to her ass cheeks.

I had to stop and clear my throat before I offered to hang it up for her.

"Thank you, Garnet."

Topaz whimpered as she bent over in front of him to pick it up, and I smirked as he reached down and cupped himself.

Taking the frothy pink thing from her, I took it into the closet, slipped it on a hanger, and made sure all of it was in the garment bag before I zipped it up.

Ash had warned us that the skirt was made of some delicate material called tulle that would tear easily, and I didn't want to be the one who ruined a dress Posy loved.

Walking back into the bedroom once more, I saw the pups had gathered behind Lark's back, staring at her bra, although Topaz's eyes kept straying to her pert little ass. Judging by the tent in the front of his boxers, he needed a moment to calm down.

"Fetch a nightie for her," I told him as I stepped closer.

"Nightie, nothing. I'll get her one of my t-shirts."

And he trotted off to do just that.

"Bad to rip it," Gran said, still staring at her bra. "Ideas?"

I looked it over to see if I could figure out how to undo it. With enough time, I probably could, but I knew the pups would get impatient.

And we were all curious about the scars on her feet.

"Lark? Do you know how to work this hook thing?" I asked.

"Um, no." She squiggled around a bit. "But I can slip it over my head if I can get a boob free."

The pups tittered when she said 'boob.' I closed my eyes and counted to twenty.

"I help?" Gran asked a little *too* eagerly.

Without opening my eyes, I grabbed his shoulder and held him in place.

"I got it!" she said.

"That's good, sweetheart." Opening my eyes, I saw Topaz standing at my elbow with a t-shirt in his hand. "Paz is going to put a t-shirt on you, okay?"

"Wait." She wiggled around some more, then threw her bra onto the bed. "Whew! Okay. Ready."

I looked at Topaz, whose eyes were again locked on her bottom, and cleared my throat. He glanced over at me, and I jerked my head toward her and mimed putting the shirt over her head. He blinked a couple times, then his face grew serious and he nodded.

Holding the neck open, he lowered it over her head, careful of her fancy hairdo, then tugged it down to her hips and let it drop to her thighs. He whined, *actually whined*, when the gray fabric covered her ass, and I bit back a grin.

"You forgot arms, dummy," Gran laughed, and I looked to see Lark's arms pinned to her sides.

"I can do that," Lark told him. She got herself sorted, then looked over her shoulders at us. "Thank you, Paz. I love your shirts. They big and comfy and smell so good!"

"You're welcome, dearest."

"Lark, can we please see the bottoms of your feet now?" I asked.

With a nod, she dropped onto the bed, laid on her stomach, and kicked her feet up. The three of us immediately bent closer and studied the thick, dark scars that ran from the back of her heel to the middle of her arch. They looked exactly like Beta Tyler's scars, and I knew what had happened.

Someone had used a silver knife on them, and she'd been too weak or drained - or unconscious - to heal them properly.

"How you get these, my love?" Gran asked in a soft voice.

"We tried to run away. Alpha... Alpha caught us and dragged us back. He locked me in the dark room and said, 'It your fault, runt!' He left, but I knew he'd come back."

"You don't have to tell us, dearest." Topaz rubbed his hand up and down her back, but she ignored that and continued.

"Aiden's room was right next to mine. I heard alpha beat him. I get scared, really scared, because alpha never hurt brothers before. I heard things break and Aiden crying and crying, and I got even more scared."

Shaking hard, she knotted her little fists into the blanket. Figuring we'd seen what we'd wanted to see, I sat on the bed at the headboard, then pulled her onto my lap. She snuggled into my chest, and the pups cuddled her on either side.

"Lark, you don't need to tell us," Topaz tried to tell her again, but she shook her head.

219

She needs to talk, so let her, I linked my brothers. *We'll comfort her when she's done.*

"Then Agate told me, 'Go in your bathroom, Lark, and cover your ears and sing a song.' I did, but I still heard Aiden. His screams went on forever."

Goddess. How could a man do that to his own sons? I didn't even have one yet, but I knew I'd cut my own hand off before I used it to hurt my pup.

And I'd absolutely slaughter anyone else who tried to.

"When it got quiet, I left my bathroom. Outside my room, I heard James. He begged alpha not to punish me. 'My idea, not hers,' he said. He told alpha he'd do anything he wanted. 'Just leave her alone.' "

Fat tears rolled down her cheeks and her breathing picked up.

"Alpha didn't listen. Alpha made James hold me down while alpha cut my back feet."

Why he cut back feet? Gran linked me. *Why not front or all feet?*

Because, I said through clenched teeth, *when she shifted to human, Posy's hands would be fine to cook and clean for him, but her feet would bleed and hurt for days and days.*

Bastard, Topaz snarled, and a low growl rumbled out of Gran's chest.

Lark cried a little harder, and the pups let out empathetic whimpers. I wanted to comfort them, too, but our mate came first, and I knew they understood that.

"Oh, sweetheart." Rocking her back and forth, I pressed my lips to her forehead and kept them there as she cried. "Shh. We're here. You're not there anymore. He can't touch you."

She's okay, Gran. She's okay, Paz. She just needed to drain the poison from the wound.

Poison! Topaz yelped and ran his hands all over her, then picked up her feet and looked at the scars again.

Damn literal wolf.

I closed my eyes because, if I rolled them one more time tonight, they were going to roll right out of my head.

She doesn't have a wound and there's no poison, I sighed. *Her sharing what happened was **like** draining poison out of a wound.*

No poison? He narrowed his eyes at me.

No poison.

Letting out a heavy breath, he relaxed and slumped against her back, his arms wrapping around her waist and his face buried in her neck.

When her tears slowed to a stop, Gran got up, fetched a warm wet washcloth, and gently wiped her face. Topaz handed her a box of tissues - yes, the whole box - and I raised an eyebrow at him.

What good's one tissue at a time like this? he said with a shrug.

Sighing, I waited until she was finished blowing her nose, which did indeed take more than one tissue, and Topaz stuck his tongue out at me as he gathered up the pile and carried it to the trash can.

"Brothers not help you again?" Gran asked her before I could stop him.

"I not *let* them help me again. Alpha shut off my links. Banned me from talking to Slate or Agate. Alpha make brothers hurt me to punish them, so brothers moved out of alpha house."

"How do you know it was to punish them and not you?" I asked.

"Alpha said so. I hate to know they got hurt because of me."

"You want to talk to brothers, my love?" Gran kissed her cheek. "We call them?"

"Yes, please, but tomorrow. I so tired," she admitted.

And that was my cue to call it a day.

"As you should be since it's way past bedtime for all little wolves." I stood up and held her on my left arm as I pulled back the covers. I was about to lay her down when I remembered what Mason usually asked Posy before bed. "Do you need to pee?"

"Oh. Yeah. Brush teethies, too!"

Teethies, I cooed to myself.

So I carried her over to the bathroom door and set her on her feet.

Her small, scarred feet.

Stop it, I told myself as rage bubbled in my gut. *This is not the time or place. She needs calm right now.*

After a few minutes, she came out and looked up at me where I waited outside the door.

"Minty fresh!" She gave me a toothy smile, and I bit my lip to keep from chuckling at how she said fresh as 'fwesh.'

"Hmm. Let me see how minty fresh," I murmured and swooped down to kiss her plump lips.

She squealed in surprise, but threw her arms around my neck, making it easy for me to loop an arm under her bum and lift her up against my chest.

"You're right," I said while carrying her back to the bedroom. "Nice and fresh."

She giggled as I laid her in the center of the bed, where the pups piled on top of her. Granite cuddled tight against her right side

221

with his head on her breasts, and Topaz plopped between her legs with his arms around her hips and his face in her stomach. Chuckling at them, I climbed in on her left side and buried my face in her throat near her mate mark.

It was close to midnight, which explained why Gran and Topaz knocked out so quickly once we were lying down. After they'd been asleep for about ten minutes, Lark tapped my arm, and I raised my head to look at her.

"Was I right not to tell Posy?" she asked as soon as our eyes met.

"About Burnt Oil Man?" I clarified. When she nodded, I said, "Well, *I* think so, but what matters is what *you* think. What was your reason for doing so?"

"To protect her. Always to protect my girl."

"Then how could you be wrong?" Rolling to lay more fully on my side, I put my hand on top of hers and watched her silver eyes. "You hid a lot from her, didn't you? To protect her."

She shrugged, then nodded.

"You're so brave. So very brave." Drawing her hand to my mouth, I kissed her palm.

"Me? No. Not brave."

"You are so," I disagreed quietly. "You could have given up and faded back to the Moon Goddess. You could have lost your mind and yourself and left Posy all alone. But you didn't. You endured, and you encouraged your human to endure. Like King Julian said, you did what you set out to do, right?"

"I don't always know what to do, Garnet." A pained look flashed across her face, and an invisible fist clenched my heart in an iron grip. "I listen to my gut, but what if my gut is wrong?"

"It's been spot-on so far. Keep trusting it. But you know what, sweetheart?"

"What?"

"You have ten of us - me, my brothers, and our boys - all willing to help you whenever you need or want it." I moved her hand to my neck and pressed her fingertips to my mate mark, humming at the pleasure of her touch. "And don't forget your betas. Anyone of those wolves or their humans would lay their lives down for you, so don't be afraid to ask for their help, too. You will never have to make any kind of decision on your own if you don't want to."

"I— It's hard to trust," she admitted after a few seconds.

"I can't imagine how hard. And that's what makes you brave. Every day, you choose to trust us, despite the many times you were let down in your past. I don't know if I could be that brave after surviving what you did."

"Of course you're brave! You're brave and so strong. I admire you, Garnet."

She smiled a sunshine smile, complete with dimples, and that invisible fist squeezed my heart again, but for an entirely different reason this time.

"Well, thank you, sweetheart," I said gruffly, feeling heat steal across my cheekbones.

"It's the truth," she said, then hesitated before asking in a whisper, "Is Quartz mad at me?"

"Of course not. Why would he be?" I asked in surprise.

"I kept a secret. I promised him no more secrets."

"Oh, sweetheart, no. We're all furious that this happened to you, and that Burnt Oil Man is still alive, but no one is mad at you."

"But Quartz—"

"He understands. We all do." I realized something then. "Besides, you kind of forgot about it, didn't you? You've been so happy and felt so safe with us, you didn't really remember how Briggs got the wolfsbane."

"I only remembered Burnt Oil Man when I smelled him."

"That makes sense. Smells are powerful triggers when it comes to memory. Jay explained it to Mase once. Something about scents going straight to a certain part of the brain." I dropped a kiss on her forehead. "Lark, I know you already told the king no, but think really hard now. Are there any others you can remember who hurt you or caused you to be hurt?"

"No, I promise. Besides pack, Burnt Oil Man was the only one ever in alpha house. Oh! Until I smelled five wonderful scents that were my mates!"

I bent my head to kiss her, but she yawned suddenly, and my lips ended up on her cheek.

"Sleep, sweetheart," I chuckled.

"What about Sid and Quartz?"

"They'll be here soon," I crooned quietly. "Sleep now, and I'll stand watch. You don't need to worry or be scared anymore. All you need to do is sleep, Lark. Sleep and dream sweet dreams."

"No matter how sweet dreams are, real life is better now. I love you, Garnet," she whispered and closed her pretty silver eyes. "I love all my mates with all of my heart."

"We love you, too. You're our darling, our dearest, our love, our sweetheart, our little mate. And you always will be."

The words seemed so paltry, so minimal, to encompass the enormity of the feelings I had for her, but she seemed happy with them. With a contented sigh, she nestled her head against my chest as best she could with the pups' heavy weight on top of her.

223

Rolling my eyes for what I hoped was the last time tonight, I moved everyone around until she was curled up in the middle of the bed with a mate hugging her on either side.

Then I settled myself in front of them and kept my promise to stand guard as they slept.

19: Bad News, Good News, Best News

Cole

As our wolves got themselves and Lark ready for bed, we left Garnet to supervise them and checked in with Dad and Papa.

All's good here, but what happened with Posy and Lark? Papa asked.

Yeah. We almost had to chain your betas down to keep them from storming the palace, Dad added.

With a snort, Wyatt flashed us all the scene from *The Princess Bride* where Miracle Max says, "Have fun storming the castle!"

That movie was one of Mom's favorites, and she always seemed to have it playing whenever we hung out at Wyatt's house as kids. Even though none of us ever made it all the way through it in one sitting, we knew every line.

After a quick convo with my brothers, we linked the betas into the conversation, knowing they wouldn't settle until they had an update about their luna.

Long story short, Lark got scared when she smelled the bastard who supplied Kendall Briggs with wolfsbane, Wyatt told them. *The king has him in his cells for us to interrogate tomorrow while Posy has tea with the queen.*

Not even a heartbeat passed before Tyler said, *I respectfully request to help with the interrogation. I can drive through the night and be there by dawn.*

Pick me up before you leave, Emerson growled.

Me, too, Crew, Tristan, and Matthew said together.

I think the king has it under control, I said with an eye roll. *He's taken a personal interest in the matter, especially after discovering that Briggs' brother Calvin has been a royal staffer for two decades.*

And it's looking like Calvin Briggs is probably the one who hooked Briggs up with the wolfsbane supplier, Jay added.

What?! bellowed four of the five betas, making us wince.

He was covering his brother's crimes, wasn't he? Crew stayed calm, as usual.

As Mase explained everything we knew so far, my attention strayed to what our wolves were doing.

They stood in a cluster at Lark's back, trying to figure out how to get her bra off without destroying it, and I chuckled at their efforts.

Despite their years of experience running our human bodies, the pups still struggled with fine motor skills. Zippers, for example, always stymied Topaz. I couldn't count how many pairs of pants and jeans he'd ruined in frustration.

225

Ha ha ha! Wyatt giggled in the alpha link, and I realized he was tuned into the show now, too. *Look! Even Garnet is scratching his head!*

He's probably studying the mechanics of a clasp. I don't know that he's ever seen one before, I chuckled. *Guys clothes don't have any, and none of us ever undressed a girl before Posy came into our lives.*

Valid, he grinned. *Poor Lark isn't much help, either.*

Not surprising, I suppose. My amusement turned into a frown. *She was never allowed to control Posy's body at Green River. Hell, she was hardly allowed to shift into her own!*

Let it go, brother, Jay counseled. *All we can control is the here and now.*

So I grabbed my anger by the tail and locked it away again before tuning back into the conversation.

Who is the supplier? Papa asked.

Ezra Ikhlassi, Mase told him.

I was going to ask Gelo if he knows him, Ash mumbled.

My brothers and I looked at each other with wide eyes. Ash was on the verge of falling asleep, and his wolf was still roaming around outside somewhere. Any of our other wolves, we wouldn't have worried, but Sid had a special talent for getting into a hell of a lot of trouble when left on his own.

Ash, send Sid back here, Mase told him in the alpha link.

He's calmed down now, but he wants to— Ash's words slowed down until a snore cut him off, then he fell silent.

Yeah, this just keeps getting better and better, I thought to myself. *Quartz on a rampage and the baby running loose after him.*

Wait, wait, wait! Emerson yelped. *Who's going to be with luna bunny tomorrow while you're beating the hell out of Briggs' brother and this Ezra guy?*

*Dude, she'll be with the queen, who's guarded by two **royal** betas at all times.* Wyatt grinned. *She'll be well protected for tea drinking.*

Throwing no shade on betas Luke or Gisela, but they are there to protect the queen, Ty pointed out. *If it came down to it, they'd save her first, not our luna. We're coming.*

Ty, Dad and I need you here while the boys are away, Papa butted in. *The pack—*

Luna takes priority to all, Matthew and Crew said in sync.

I'll stay with them for tea. No one will get past me, let alone Quartz, Jay volunteered, and we all knew why.

If he went along with us tomorrow, unless the king intervened, Ikhlassi would be dead seconds after we entered the dungeon.

A few more minutes of arguing, and the betas finally - albeit begrudgingly - agreed to stay at Five Fangs and help Dad and Papa until we returned.

At least let us talk to our luna, Tristan said. *We need to hear from* her *that she's okay.*

Posy's sleeping. I smiled. *And Lark's currently in the human version of a puppy pile. Our wolves wanted to snuggle her.*

Wyatt sent them the image of the four of them cuddled up on the bed, and they all aww'ed. Lark must have felt the betas' intense concern through the bond, though, because her pretty silver eyes blinked open.

What is it? she murmured drowsily. *Why my beta wolves upset?*

They're worried about you, precious, Mase told her. *Can you tell them you're okay so they can calm down?*

I scared, she told them, *but I okay now. I safe. Nyx and king said so.*

Luna happy now? River purred as Tyler took a temporary backseat to his wolf. *Luna getting cuddles?*

Yep! Lark grinned happily. *My mates so warm and snuggly!*

Happy luna, crooned Arroyo, and Matthew rolled his eyes at him. *Happy luna, happy pack.*

We can be by your side in hours, luna. Bay forcefully shoved Crew aside to talk to her. *Link us anytime for anything.*

Even if you just want to chat or ask a question, added Creek as Tristan nodded in agreement.

Thank you, betas.

Sleep well, luna wolf, Cove murmured and Emerson echoed him.

You, too.

We said our goodbyes to the betas, and Lark went back to sleep almost immediately. We had a word with Dad and Papa about a couple of things and, right before we closed the link, Papa told us to check in with the gammas sometime soon.

Something wrong? I asked.

Oh, no. Quite the opposite, Papa chuckled. *I'm surprised the betas didn't spill the beans just now, but I suppose they were too worried about Posy and Lark. Anyway, link them and find out. Good night, boys.*

We chorused a variety of good-nights, then Mase suggested we contact Landry first, as he would be the most sensible, especially if the news was something exciting.

227

Alphas! You'll never guess what happened. He broke off to groan. *Stop teasing, angel! Hop on my dick now or I'll smack that round ass red!*

Yep, that's our most sensible gamma, I told Topaz, who giggled as I rolled my eyes.

Sorry, alphas. Landry was trying, but his mate obviously had his brain scrambled good and proper. *Finally! Now slide that tight little kitty all the way down to my balls.*

Landry, when you're mating Grace, don't answer the link unless we say it's an emergency! I growled as Mase's face and Jay's ears burned bright red. *You can't keep your thoughts separated from your mouth!*

I kind of like it, Wyatt smirked and wiggled his eyebrows. *It's like old-school phone sex.*

If Mase or I were in charge of our bodies, one of us - or both - would have slapped him upside the head.

Ask Rube, alphas, Landry gasped. *He can explain. Goddess, Grace! Just don't link Nick or Adam. Faster, angel! Faster! And probably not Rio, either. Oh, yeah, baby. Ride me hard. Just. Like. That.*

As Landry lost control, images and sounds started to seep into the link, and I slammed it closed before we saw something we shouldn't.

Oh, come on! Wyatt whined. *It was just getting good!*

Don't be disgusting, I muttered with a red face as Mase pinched the bridge of his nose. *You know he didn't mean for that to happen, and Grace would be mortified if she found out, so you better keep your mouth closed.*

Wyatt mimed zipping his lips and throwing away the key, and Jay giggled himself silly.

Jay, where are *you, anyway?* Mase asked.

Somewhere between the palace and the dungeon. Pumice is talking to Quartz, and Sid is waiting for him so they can walk back to the guest house together.

Oh, good. I'm glad they're together. I sighed in relief. *Q calming down?*

Slowly, Jay admitted, then changed topics. *Let's contact Rube. I want to know what happened.*

You want the good news, the bad news, or the best news first? Reuben asked as soon as he opened the link.

Bad news first, I said before anyone else could answer.

I still haven't found my mate.

Reuben's glum tone kind of clued us in that someone had found theirs, and I traded a look with my brothers.

Hundred bucks says it was Nick! Jay yipped.

No, Adam, Wyatt said.

You both win, Reuben grumbled. *That's the best news.*

*Wait. Nick **and** Adam?* I blinked in surprise.

Yep.

And Adam didn't run away? I asked. When Reuben said no, I scowled. *Well, hell! Now I owe Ash a hundred bucks! I bet him that Adam would run away when he found his mate.*

Not that I thought Adam was a coward or didn't deserve a mate or anything. Dude was a beast on the battlefield, and his conduct in the pack was above reproach. He was humble and kind and highly intelligent; he only graduated as salutatorian because Mase claimed the valedictorian spot that year.

To be fair, Papa bullied Mase to the top while Adam had a sincere love of learning.

For all his accolades, though, Adam was the textbook definition of an introvert, and his awkwardness around girls was next level. All of his confidence seemed to drain right out of him if a girl even looked his way, and he became downright bashful when one tried to talk to him.

No, he didn't run! Reuben smirked. *Tripped over his own tongue, but he didn't run.*

And Nick found his, too? Jay asked. *Were they together when they met them or something?*

Yep. They're twin sisters. Now there's just lonely me left.

Well, you'll find h— I stopped myself. Reuben was openly bi-sexual, so how could I know if his mate would be male or female? I settled with saying, *Your mate soon, too, Rube. Everyone else has, and the Moon Goddess won't leave you out.*

What are the sisters like? Wyatt asked before Reuben could respond.

They're fairies, Reuben said as casually as if telling us their hair color.

I blinked a couple of times, not believing my ears.

They're what? Wyatt sounded just as incredulous.

They're fairies!

What?

Fairies, alpha. Reuben rolled his eyes. *I know you know what they are, so stop saying what.*

They're—

Fairies, Wyatt! I growled impatiently. *Process it already!*

Sorry! I just never heard of a wolf mated to a fairy! he protested.

Ty said the same, Reuben chuckled. *He's going to look it up in the alpha library. Since you're there with the king, you could also ask*

229

him. We gammas had dinner with the betas tonight and I asked the witches. Ariel said there are many fairies mated with a variety of shifter species, including birds, so there probably are fairy-wolf pairings, just rarely. Oh, and I should mention that their wings look like a luna moth's.

My boys and I exchanged wide-eyed glances.

A gift from the Moon Goddess to honor their wolf mates? Mase suggested.

I wonder why Five Fangs is meriting all these odd pairings? I asked. *First bird shifters, who are also witches, then a fox, and now fairies. Plus, we have a higher than usual percentage of human mates in the pack.*

Can't be just a coincidence, right? Wyatt asked. *Maybe it's because the Moon Goddess trusts us to protect this pack of waifs and strays.*

A pack of waifs and strays? I chuckled and shook my head. *Sounds about right.*

#

Mason

Curious about our gammas' new mates, I asked Reuben when and where Nick and Adam met the fairies.

This morning, he said. *We gammas met for lunch yesterday, and Emmeline told Grace about this new cake shop that opened in Greenville a few weeks ago. It's called Fairy Cakes and—*

No way! Wyatt grinned. *They didn't name it that!*

Yeah, they did! Anyway, Emmeline talked it up so much yesterday that Adam decided he'd get his parents' anniversary cake from there. This morning, Nick tagged along with him to put in the order. By the moon, I wish we all had! I would have paid good money to see Adam tongue-tied and red-faced in front of his new mate!

As Wyatt and Jay snickered, I shushed them and asked Reuben to continue.

Anyway, Rio and Emmeline had a cookout this evening for the gammas and the betas, so we all got the chance to meet them. They're twenty years old and came here because they dreamed of opening this cake shop all their lives, but knew they'd never get enough business in the Woodland Realm. Alpha Jay, remember those pixies you and Gelo rescued from that prison?

Of course. Jay nodded. *I take it they went home and told the story of how Five Fangs wolves freed them?*

You know it, Reuben confirmed. *That led the twins to research Greenville and decide it was a large enough city to provide more than*

230

enough customers for the shop to be successful. Knowing there was a friendly wolf pack nearby was the icing on the cake.

Terrible pun, Rube-Cube. Wyatt rolled his eyes.

What are their names? I asked. *And who's mated to who?*

Georgina, who likes to be called Georgie, is Adam's mate. He sent us a picture of a lovely young lady with mint green hair, mahogany skin, and snapping black eyes. *She's full of energy and sass, and has a mischievous streak a mile wide. Ha ha ha! Matthew wouldn't stop teasing her about her pointed ears, so you know what she did? Gave him donkey ears and a tail!*

Posy is going to pee her pants when she hears that! Jay snorted.

Ty busted a gut laughing at him, too, Reuben continued with a broad grin. *Maria's been trying to reverse it, but fairy magic is very different from elemental magic, according to Ariel.*

Dude! Does he still have them? Wyatt asked.

Reuben sent an image through the link, and Jay and Wyatt howled with laughter as Cole and I chuckled.

Georgie told Adam they'll be gone by morning, Reuben said, *but no one's telling Matthew that.*

Sounds like Adam has his hands full. I was wary about this pairing, but trusted that the Moon Goddess had given our bashful gamma the mate he needed. *What about the other one? Nick's mate?*

Regina. She goes by Reggie. The picture he linked us was identical to Georgina's except this girl had lilac hair and calm, quiet eyes. *She's a female version of Adam. At first, I was worried that she was some haughty piece because she wouldn't look at any of us and didn't speak. Like, at all. It only took us a few minutes, though, to realize she has a crippling degree of shyness.*

Hmm. Do you think she suffered some sort of trauma? Jay wondered in the alpha link.

Shyness can be natural, Wyatt pointed out. *Look at Adam. He never had anything horrible happen in his life, and he's awkward as hell around most people, especially if they're females.*

It's not our business to ask, I reminded them both, then listened to what Reuben was saying.

—took about an hour for her to warm up to us and start talking, then it was easy to see how gentle and kind she is. Just like luna. Hmm. Now that I think about it, both of them are luna's height and size, too.

Posy will be happy to hear that. She gets touchy about always being the shortest, I said with a tiny smile.

Oh, I almost forgot! They have a pet chicken named Mrs. Featherstone. She's stunning, and I never thought I'd say that about a chicken! Her feathers are red-orange with dark blue edges and her under feathers, or whatever they're called, are light blue. You ever heard of a chicken like that?

Mrs. Featherstone? Jay raised an eyebrow. *Oh, no. Don't even tell me she was once a human!*

Georgie insists she's much happier as a chicken, Reuben said primly. *Since I myself have no desire to be a chicken, I did not inquire further.*

Reuben sounded a whole lot brighter than he had when we first linked him, for which I was thankful. It was going to be hard for him to be the only unmated one of the higher-ranking pack members. Even all our deltas had found their mates by now, and I made a note to tell everyone to help keep an eye on him.

After what he'd endured at Tall Pines, his mental health was already shaky, and the last thing we wanted was for him to fall into depression.

Wait, wait, wait! Wyatt shook his head and held up both hands. *How can they have a cake shop in a human city? They're fairies! I know humans are used to hair dyed in all colors, but surely even* they *are going to ask about pointed ears and skin that glitters. And what about their wings?*

Sara said they use something called a glamour. Makes humans not notice or look right past their unique features. As for their wings, wait until you see, alphas. It's fire! They have what looks like wings tattooed on their backs and unfurl them right out of their skin!

Dude! I can't wait to see that! Wyatt exclaimed.

Me, either, Jay said, just as excited. *Ash, too, when we tell him!*

Oh, my Goddess, Cole groaned as the thought struck him. *What are* their *pups going to look like?*

We're already looking at bird-wolves, fox-wolves, and potentially dragon-wolves if Konstantin finds a wolf mate. I shrugged. *Fairy-wolves will fit right in.*

Speaking of pups, Reuben said with a grin, *that's the good news.*

Who's pregnant? Jay caught it before the rest of us. *And don't even say Peri because I know she couldn't possibly have gone into heat yet.*

Emmeline. She found out yesterday and told Rio this morning. That's why they had the cookout, to officially announce it. Word spread from there and now pretty much the whole pack knows.

Wow. A pup. Rio was nineteen, two years younger than me, and he was going to be a dad. I couldn't even imagine taking that step yet. Then there was Emmeline, who was Posy's age and in her last year

232

of high school. How was she going to juggle a pup with homework and all the milestone activities that come with senior year?

I thought they wanted to wait until she graduated, I said, voicing my thoughts.

Well, they did, but Rio underestimated the number of condoms he'd go through while she was in heat.

Why didn't he link someone to bring him some more? I growled. *What was he thinking?*

After nearly three days of nonstop sex? Reuben deadpanned. *Probably not much.*

As Wyatt burst out laughing at that, Jay nudged the alpha link.

I think we'd better start stocking up on condoms now, he said with wide eyes.

Wyatt was too busy laughing his head off, but Cole's cheeks turned pink, and I knew his brain was stuck on the same thing mine and Jay's were.

Posy.

In heat.

Goddess have mercy on our souls, Cole whispered.

More like on our dicks, Wyatt smirked.

How many condoms do you think we're going to go through? I ignored him to ask. *Can you buy the damn things wholesale or in bulk?*

I don't know, but I'll find out, Wyatt promised with a wicked gleam in his eyes. *I think I better build us a condom closet somewhere in the house. Maybe in all that space downstairs, huh? Ooh! Better yet, what if I made us a little play room?*

My eyes widened as I contemplated that delicious thought.

Well, that's all the news here at the pack, alphas, Reuben said, innocently unaware of the sinful thoughts he'd interrupted. *Hope the rest of your trip goes well.*

Thanks, Rube. I cleared my throat. *I know Dad and Papa are there, but we're only ever a link away.*

We know that. Good night, alphas.

Good night, we chorused.

Our wolves were already asleep and snuggled up with our girl's soft body, so it was only a matter of moments before Cole, Wyatt, and I were crossing the border into dreamland, too.

Jay? I mumbled. *Please take care of Q and Sid.*

Don't worry. I'll bring them both home safe and sound. Good night, big brother.

Night, little brother, I yawned.

Knowing Garnet would stand watch until the errant duo returned, I finally let myself relax and fell into a dreamless sleep.

20: Dammit!

Quartz

Crouching low, I pushed off my back feet *hard* and launched forward like a missile. In seconds, I closed on my target and slammed into it with all of my strength. Repairing my dislocated shoulder and fractured vertebrae, I surveyed the undamaged steel door with a disgruntled huff.

Dammit! Didn't even dent it!

The intercom next to the door crackled to life, and I smirked. The royal guards had locked themselves inside as soon as they saw me coming.

As if that made the cowards any safer.

"Quartz, don't do this," one of them said. "I suggest you go home to Lark."

*DON'T YOU **DARE** TALK ABOUT MY MATE!* My vision went even redder. The audacity of this mongrel to have her name in his mouth! *OPEN THIS DOOR BEFORE I KILL YOU ALL!*

"The k-k-king g-g-gave orders."

Fine. The hard way, then.

Backing up, I hurtled forward and threw myself against the door again. The bang that echoed was louder than a firework going off, and I had to heal my ears along with half the bones on my left side as I staggered back. Shaking my head to clear it, I glanced at the door and frowned to see it unscathed.

Dammit!

"Q, you being dumb."

I whirled around to find Sid-in-Ash's-body walking toward me, Pumice trotting along at his elbow. Sid was wearing nothing but dark green shorts - ridiculously short shorts, might I add - with bright orange flip flops.

And he was casually eating popcorn from a brown bag darkened by butter stains.

I thought you were going to help me kill this bastard! I snarled in outrage at his nonchalance.

He reached into the bag, pulled out a big fistful of popcorn, and shoved it into his mouth. Looking like a chipmunk, he shrugged.

"King say no, so no," he said as he chewed.

Dammit! If he wasn't escalated, he would be no help at all!

"Pumice have clothes and flippy flops for you, too. I ate you popcorn, though." He pointed to a cloth bag hanging from Pumice's mouth. "Come on, Q. Just shift. Please? I wanna go cuddle mate."

Then go!

"Want you come, too. Please? Pretty please?"

I got to kill someone first.

"Q! King said no!" Sid shook his index finger at me. "You being a bad boy! You not listening! Time to go back to mate! Right now!"

I swung my whole body around to face him and stared at him without blinking.

Are you giving me orders, pup? I asked, my low tone a warning in itself.

"What you gonna do? You gonna hurt me? You gonna hurt little brother 'cause you mad?"

You should be mad, too! But no. Instead of cutting loose, you went back to being a baby—

Don't, Quartz, Jayden interrupted to warn me, and I ignored him.

—and you know why? Because you're a fucking sissy!

Sid's eyes narrowed as he threw the popcorn bag on the ground and clenched his fists.

"Don't say that word!" he bellowed. "Sid not a sissy!"

Stop pushing him, Jayden tried to tell me, but again I didn't listen.

Don't say what? Sissy? I sneered. *But you are. You're Sid the sissy.*

With a wild howl, he half shifted, and the beast that now stood before me was everything humans pictured when they heard the term werewolf: A furry man-shaped monster with pupils burning red with rage and his chest vibrating in a continuous snarl.

Half-shifted was our most dangerous form. It gave us all the best qualities of both bodies and none of the weaknesses - and Sid and Ash excelled at using it. Ash's extreme size and strength alone made them hard to beat; when Sid's inner berserker joined the party, he was all but impossible to take down.

Calm down, pup, Pumice leapt in front of him. *Like you said yourself, are you going to hurt your brother because you're mad?*

The words made no impact on Sid, who crouched in a fighting stance and howled his fury to the moonless sky.

*Okay, Q. **You** did this. **You** wanted his beast out.* Jayden sounded absolutely disgusted with me. *Now it is. What are **you** going to do about it?*

He was right.

He was right from the moment he told me to stop.

We all knew not to call Sid a sissy. Granite and Topaz had made that mistake a couple of times when we were younger, and each time they'd paid a grisly price. The first time, Ash got Sid back under

235

control before he did too much damage. The second time, though, Garnet and I had to intervene because Sid had gone to some dark place Ash couldn't reach and none of us ever wanted to see again.

Even knowing that, I *still* ignored my boy and positioned myself three feet in front of the dungeon door. Whirling to face Sid again, this time with a leer, I proved just how much of a cold-hearted bastard I was.

You're the biggest sissy I've ever met! I don't know how Lark can love a sissy like you!

QUARTZ! Jayden bellowed. *Apologize and yield control now!*

At the same time, Sid let out an incensed roar that raised the hair along my spine in a razor-edged ridge. He swatted Pumice out of the way, lowered his head, and charged. I was going to have to be fast if I didn't want to die...

Inches before he was on me, I threw myself to the side and rolled into Pumice, who was just crawling out of the bushes Sid had knocked him into.

You idiot! The old wolf snapped at me - literally - and I had to heal the gash across the top of my muzzle.

Sorry, sire. I didn't think he'd do that to you, I admitted.

I'm not the only one you need to apologize to! What were you thinking? What did you hope to accomplish?

It was a good thing I respected Alfred's wolf so much. Otherwise, he'd be missing his tongue for talking to me in that tone.

As it was, I only smirked as I pointed my bloody nose toward the dungeon door. Sid slumped against it, rubbing his head and moaning, but I was more interested in the huge dent in the steel.

That. Another few hits, and either the door will give in or the hinges will.

For the love of the Goddess, Quartz! Pumice growled.

Then Ash woke up in a panic, drawing our attention back to Sid.

Holy shit! What's wrong, buddy?

Sid mad! Sid so mad! Q call Sid the s word!

Calm down, okay? Just calm down. We'll sort this out. Breathe, buddy.

No! Q being bad! Q being a meanie!

Quartz, so help me, Jayden thundered, *if you don't stop this, I will tell Lark every detail of how you hurt Sid!*

Hurt him? I frowned in confusion. *I didn't hurt—*

You did! You called him a name that you knew would cut his heart, then used it to goad him into a rage! And don't think I missed why! You knew he could do more damage to that door than you could.

Dammit! Why did my boy have to be so smart all the time?

If you aren't ashamed of yourself yet, Jayden continued scolding me, *maybe you will be when you see how disappointed your mate is in you!*

Goddess, did this bitch know how to grab me by the balls! He may have promised to never cage me again, but my boy was clever enough to use my weaknesses to keep me on a chain.

Okay, okay! I growled. *Just... don't tell Lark.*

That depends entirely on what you do in the next sixty seconds!

You just want to kill Ikhlassi yourself tomorrow! I snapped, frustration strangling my anger.

For your information, I already volunteered us to stay with Posy during tea. Don't question my motives without knowing all the facts. Ha! Now that I think about it, telling Posy might be even more effective than telling Lark.

Dammit! If he did, I could kiss my ear rubs goodbye for the foreseeable future!

End this now, Q, Pumice added his two cents. *The king gave an order. Who are you to challenge it?*

He said not to kill Ikhlassi. The bastard doesn't need his legs to answer questions, I grumbled, *or his liver...*

Not helping, Jayden muttered.

Growling at the whole situation, I closed my eyes and drew in a deep breath. In the background, I could hear Sid and Ash arguing, although Ash wasn't doing too well in his sleep-muddled state. Tuning them out, I focused on clearing my mind and relaxing. I wasn't particularly good at either of those things, but I could try.

As I did, words I once said to Posy suddenly came back to haunt me: *I am sorry to say that there is a type of male in whom exists a need to brutally control everything and everyone, to destroy anything sweet and kind and gentle. Control without empathy. Destruction without sympathy.*

I'd promised her I'd never become such a wolf, yet was I not doing that very thing here tonight?

At the time I made that promise to Posy, I'd only been thinking of my treatment of her and Lark. However, I realized now that it applied to everyone. I wasn't much for self-reflection, but the truth was staring me in the face, and surely the Goddess herself would punish me if I was foolish enough to deny it.

Sid was not a tool to be used to achieve my own goals. He was my little brother. My baby cousin. The last of my blood family - and I'd hurt him in order to control him, to manipulate him into destroying something for me.

What a burden a conscience is, I grumbled to myself.

With an exasperated sigh, I shifted into our human body and went over to the bag of supplies Pumice had brought. Pulling out a pair of gray shorts, I yanked them on and slipped my feet into the black slides.

I called Sid's name, and his eyes instantly swung around to glare at me.

"I regret making you mad and hurting your feelings," I said. "I regret what I said. I didn't mean any of it. You're not a sissy, and Lark loves you just the way you are."

He bared his fangs at me, and a low snarl rippled through the air between us. Slowly, he got to his feet, shifted fully back to human form, and came toward me. I knew I deserved whatever he was about to do, so I simply stood and waited for it without lifting a hand to defend myself.

"You were a meanie, Q," he said as he towered over me.

"Yeah, I was."

"You not call Sid that again." He leaned down until his nose almost touched mine. "Never, ever again."

"I swear by the moon I won't," I vowed.

"And Sid knows Lark loves him." He gave me a smug smile. "You may be Daddy, but Sid is her big boy."

I do not need to be hearing this, Pumice muttered and used his teeth to pick up the cloth bag to take with him. *If you two are all right now, I'll be going.*

"Thank you for your help, sire," I told the former king with a curt nod.

"And for popcorn!" Sid crowed, which was all the proof I needed that he was back to normal.

Once Pumice disappeared into the night, we looked at each other.

"So, ah," I rubbed the back of my neck, "you want to punch me or...?"

"No, but you owe me popcorn. I dropped it when you made me mad."

"You said you ate my bag," I pointed out, "so technically, *you* owe *me* popcorn."

He blinked a few times, then he shook his head slowly.

"No, Q. I am right and you are wrong. You will get me more popcorn to say sorry."

"Sure. So you forgive me, right? I didn't mean to hurt you. I was so mad, I only saw you as a way to get what I wanted."

"I forgive you, Q." He lifted his arm and patted me on top of my head with his dinner-plate-sized hand. "But your words hurt my heart."

Dammit! Now *my* heart hurt. Felt like a freaking meat grinder going to town in my chest.

You have only yourself to blame, Jayden grunted.

Take your ass to sleep, I told him.

I'll see you both home safe and sound first. Well, just Sid really, because Ash is knocked out again and you're ... you.

Rolling my eyes, I brushed Sid's hand off my head and looked up at him.

"Thank you for forgiving me," I said.

"Welcome." He gave me a very serious nod, then raised his eyebrows hopefully. "My tummy saying, 'Munchie time!' We get popcorn now?"

"Sure." Knowing he wasn't allowed to use the microwave, I offered to make it for him when we got back to the house.

"Yes, yes, yes!" He did a little happy dance, and I shook my head.

"Why did Pumice get you popcorn, anyway?"

"I told him little wolves get hungry before sleepy time." With a devious cackle, he rubbed his hands together.

"I thought you were Lark's big boy," I teased. "You can't be a little wolf and a big boy at the same time."

"Yes, I can." His grin nearly split his face. "I am whatever Lark says I am because mate is always right. I am also a little wolf. Garnet and Mase say I will always be a little wolf even if I grow to seven feet tall!"

That was a lot of words and thought for his 'little wolf' brain, and I let a teeny smile flit across my lips.

"Thanks, Sid."

"For what?"

"For being you, I guess," I said gruffly.

"Who else would I be?" He tilted his head to the side with a confused frown.

I snorted, then slung an arm around his shoulder, pulling his head down several inches to accommodate our height difference.

"Let's go home to Lark."

"Yay!" He pulled out of my hold to punch his fists into the air. "Ashy said I can cuddle her as much as I want tonight."

"You'll have to pry her away from our brothers."

"They had their turn." He giggled. "Q?"

"Yeah?"

"I love you."

I didn't say those words very often to *anyone* except Lark and Posy, but after tonight, the words were the least I owed the pup.

"I love you, too, Sid."

239

With a squeal, he wrapped me up in a bear hug, lifted me clean off my feet, and swung me around. I rolled my eyes, but let him have his moment, hanging there in resignation and waiting for it to be over.

"I'm happy, Q!"

"Good. Now off." I made a shooing gesture with one hand, and he giggled as he set me down and dropped his arms.

As we set off, he prattled on and on about anything and everything that popped into his over-stimulated brain. He was so hyper and jacked up on adrenaline, it was going to take hours to calm him down. Thankfully, it was a long walk back to the guest house.

My ear was chewed off - *not* literally - by the time we reached the front walk, but at least he was winding down.

"Q?" he said as we went up the porch steps. "You 'member what you said, right?"

I'd said a lot of things tonight, but I knew which one was foremost in his mind right now.

"Yeah. Don't worry. I didn't forget your precious popcorn."

In his excitement, he jumped up and down, making the porch shake.

"But what about Lark?" I asked.

"She can have some, too." His big eyes shone with child-like innocence. "I will share with my darling."

Dammit! It isn't fair that he's so fucking pure and I'm...

You, Jayden filled in when I couldn't find the right word. *You're you. You're Quartz, and you have many good qualities.*

I know that! I hissed. *Not my fault everyone else is too blind to see them!*

Jayden chuckled, although it turned into a yawn.

Go to sleep, boy, I grumbled as I opened the door and ushered Sid inside. *See? Your baby is safe and sound now.*

And so are you, he murmured sleepily, then finally gave in and conked out.

"No, that's not what I meant," I explained to Sid as I led him into the kitchen. "I thought you were all hyped to cuddle her?"

"I am! I want to cuddle my darling!"

"But she's asleep right now, and you know the rule." Standing in front of the pantry, I found the box of popcorn, grabbed one of the bags out of it, and turned around. "No eating in bed."

"Aw! Come on, Q! One time!"

As I went over to the microwave, I saw he'd crossed his arms over his chest and his bottom lip was pushed out in a pout.

"Nope. You pups have made one too many messes in the bed. *Both* Mason and Garnet drew a line, and I'm not going to cross it just for your spoiled ass."

"They drew a line? In the bed? Like, with a marker?"

I closed my eyes for a second, torn between laughing and snarling, a frequent position for me when dealing with the pups. Sid and Topaz especially struggled with idioms. Granite wasn't far behind, but he could usually work his way around a metaphor. Well, if it was clear enough.

"It means they said no more eating in bed," I told him.

"Oh." Sid came closer and nudged my shoulder. "Pop pop, please."

"You know," I said as I opened the microwave door and threw in the brown packet, "you already ate one and a half bags. You really need more?"

"Yes. My tummy's saying, 'Growl! growl!' I will eat, then go cuddle Lark."

Closing the microwave door, I stared at it for a second. Good thing I could read since this model didn't have the popcorn symbol. I found the right button and pushed it, and Sid braced his hands on his knees to stare into the window and watch the action. He liked to see the bag puff up as the kernels popped.

Leaving him to his fun, I went to the sink and washed my hands and face, knowing I probably still had a little blood on me from where Pumice bit me. The delicious smell of buttery popcorn filled the kitchen, making my own tummy say, "Growl, growl," and I decided I'd make another bag while he was eating his.

I just finished drying off on a tea towel when the microwave dinged.

"It's done!" he crowed, bouncing up and down on his toes.

"Shh! The others are sleeping."

"It's done!" he whispered. "Hurry, Q!"

"Oh my Goddess," I muttered as I got it out for him. "Here!"

"Yippee!" He took it with another little dance, and I rolled my eyes as I tossed my own bag in the microwave. "Thanks, Q!"

"Sure, pup."

Once mine was made, I joined him at the kitchen island, where he sat on a bar stool and happily munched away. We ate in comfortable silence until I was tipping the last of the bag into my mouth and heard a gentle buzz coming from across the counter. Looking over, I saw Sid had finally crashed, one hand in the brown bag and the other dangling limply at his side.

"You're going to be pissed at yourself tomorrow," I smirked. "All this time you could have been cuddling your darling and you were down here stuffing your face instead."

Finishing up my snack, I threw away the empty bag, washed my hands again, and debated for a good two minutes whether or not to leave him there.

It's not like he's going to wake up for the next eight hours. And he's slept in worse places and positions.

However, I knew the others - especially Lark and Posy - would fuss at me, so I groaned and whipped the tea towel off of the oven handle again. Wetting it with warm water, I went to Sid, took his hand out of the bag, and wiped it clean. Then I did the same thing with his butter- and salt-stained face before I tossed the dirty tea towel on the counter.

One of the boys can deal with it in the morning.

Resigned to the inevitable, I slung his giant ass up in a fireman's carry and headed for the stairs, cursing with every step. It wasn't his weight that was the problem; I could carry ten bodies this heavy. His limbs were so long, though, that his hands and feet legit dragged on the floor alongside me, constantly knocking me off balance. After I jolted into the wall for the third time, I was sorely tempted to just drop him on the stairs, but I played nice and carried on.

Goddess, I hope our pups aren't this big!

Finally, we made it to the bedroom, and I pushed open the door with my foot only to blow out an irritated breath when I saw Garnet's eyes gleaming in the darkness.

"You son of a bitch," I groused in a whisper. "How long have you been awake?"

"Haven't been to sleep yet. Told Lark I'd stand watch until you two got home."

"Come get this big bastard."

"No, thanks. Looks like you got it under control." He closed his eyes and rolled over. "Good night."

"Asshole."

"So witty when you're tired and grumpy," he chuckled.

"I love how you state the obvious with such a tone of discovery." Dropping Sid on top of him, I grinned when I heard him groan.

"Listen to you! Trying to fit your entire vocabulary in one sentence," he snarked back as he wrestled out from under Sid.

"Your dick belongs in your pants, not your personality," I muttered half-heartedly.

"Why don't you slip into something more comfortable? Like a coma."

Snorting in appreciation at that one, I plopped down on the side of the bed and let my clasped hands dangle between my knees.

When I didn't respond, he came over and sat next to me.

"That bad of a night, huh?"

"I fucked up a bit," I admitted. "Garnet?"

"Yeah?"

"Don't let me—" Taking a deep breath, I let it out slowly. "Will you help me be a better brother?"

"Really bad night, then."

I just nodded.

"You know," he murmured, "that's the bravest thing I've ever heard you say. I'm proud of you, Q."

All at once, it hit me, how damn tired I was inside and out. And I didn't know what to do with all these messy feelings inside me. They were uncomfortable, twisting around inside me like snakes, and I wasn't prepared for any of them.

Which was probably why I did something that shocked us both. I leaned against him and laid my head on his shoulder. He froze for a second, but didn't move or push me away. He just sat there next to me for a few seconds, then his arm came around me in a tight hug.

"Give yourself some grace, Quartz. Leaving your comfort zone to grow is hard, but everything's going to be okay. I promise."

"How can you be so sure?" I whispered.

"Because I won't let it be anything else. I got you, little brother. Forever and always, I got you."

Dammit! Now my eyes were all wet!

The audacity of the little bitches, to betray me like that.

MASON ANDRE PRICE

Stats: 21 years old, 6'5" tall
Favorite candy: Snickers
Favorite drink: Coke
Favorite food: Bacon cheeseburgers
Favorite color: Red
Favorite game: Call of Duty (video), Life (board)
Birthday/Zodiac sign: May 2/Taurus
What I'd change about myself: Stop seeing myself through my father's eyes and holding myself to his standards instead of my own.
Guilty pleasure: Watching Posy when she doesn't know I am
Interests: Fishing, hiking, video games, cars
Things I'm good at: Fixing situations, organizing, keeping everyone on the straight and narrow, being tidy, not revealing what I'm thinking or feeling, and keeping my word
Song I'd dedicate to Posy: "Sidelines" by Phoebe Bridgers

COLE NATHANIEL BARLOW

Stats: 20 years old, 6'4" tall
Favorite candy: Skittles
Favorite drink: Orange Vanilla Coke
Favorite food: Pulled pork barbecue
Favorite color: Light blue
Favorite game: Call of Duty, billiards, chess, and poker
Birthday/Zodiac sign: February 23/Pisces
What I'd change about myself: Get better control of my temper
Guilty pleasure: Being lazy and ordering food instead of going out, then eating it in front of the TV
Interests: Playing chess and pool, card games, video games
Things I'm good at: Hand-to-hand combat, man-to-wolf combat, training our warriors, poker, and losing my temper
Song I'd dedicate to Posy: "Scars to Your Beautiful" by Alessia Cara

JAYDEN ELLIS CARSON

Stats: 19 years old, 6'3" tall
Favorite candy: Gummy bears
Favorite drink: Water
Favorite food: General Tso's chicken
Favorite color: Dark green
Favorite game: The Legend of Zelda (video), Monopoly (board)
Birthday/Zodiac sign: March 17/Pisces
What I'd change about myself: Be less boring
Guilty pleasure: Reading all day in a comfy chair
Interests: Reading, studying and learning, acoustic guitar
Things I'm good at: Researching, negotiating, being diplomatic, staying calm, making observations, and saying the right thing
Song I'd dedicate to Posy: "Pointless" by Lewis Capaldi

ASH LOTO MITCHELL

Stats: 18 years old, 6'10" tall
Favorite candy: Do brownies count as candy?
Favorite drink: Sweet iced tea
Favorite food: Steak and potatoes
Favorite color: Light pink
Favorite game: Call of Duty (video), Apples to Apples (card), Trouble (board)
Birthday/Zodiac sign: January 28/Aquarius
What I'd change about myself: Get a better handle on cooking. I'm sure I could do it if I focused hard enough...
Guilty pleasure: Binge-watching anime (try *Hell Girl, Ergo Proxy*, or *Gugure! Kokkuri-san* for some truly great ones that no one's ever heard of)
Interests: Sports, video games, cars, learning new hair styles, and fire. Like, watching fires, not starting them. Although I'm good at that, too. Real good.
Things I'm good at: Being loud, hitting my head on everything, forgetting things, getting dysregulated and distracted... Oh, you meant my strengths? Dude! Sports! Duh. And reaching things on the top shelf, fighting half-shifted, and keeping my bros and our girl looking sharp and in style.
Song I'd dedicate to Posy: "A Sky Full of Stars" by Coldplay

WYATT SHAWN BLACK

Stats: 18 years old, 6'0" tall
Favorite candy: Kit Kat
Favorite drink: Coffee
Favorite food: Burritos
Favorite color: Sky blue
Favorite game: Grand Theft Auto (video) and Battleship (board)
Birthday/Zodiac sign: April 5/Aries
What I'd change about myself: Stop going wolfy.
Guilty pleasure: Sleeping in late with our girl.
Interests: Drag racing, motorcycles, cars, sports, video games and art
Things I'm good at: Drawing, painting, carpentry, and fixing things
Song I'd dedicate to Posy: "I Don't Want to Miss a Thing" by Aerosmith

POSY ANNE EVERLEIGH BLACK

Stats: 18 years old; 5'0" tall
Favorite candy: Reese's peanut butter cups
Favorite drink: Chocolate milk or Pepsi
Favorite food: Chicken tenders
Favorite color: Purple
Favorite game: Uno
Birthday/Zodiac sign: June 19/Gemini
What I'd change about myself: Instantly know stuff I should already know so I don't have to keep asking my mates silly questions.
Guilty pleasure: Tricking the boys into agreeing with me (rubs hands together with an evil genius chuckle).
Interests: Flowers and learning, especially new words
Things I'm good at: Cooking and baking
Song I'd dedicate to my mates: Um, I don't have a huge knowledge about music, but Jayden is teaching me and introducing me to different kinds, and these songs said something to me about each of my mates.
Mason - "POV" by Arianna Grande
Cole - "Amazed" by Lonestar
Jayden - "You Matter" by Sara Bareilles
Ash - "Before You" by Benson Boone
Wyatt - "All of Me" by John Legend

THOREAU EZRA JONES

Stats: 15 years old; 5'4" tall
Favorite candy: Peanut butter cups
Favorite drink: Chocolate milk
Favorite food: Peabutter sammiches!
Favorite color: Pink
Favorite game: Tag
Birthday/Zodiac sign: March 14/Pisces
What I'd change about myself: I'd give anything to fix my brain.
Guilty pleasure: Sneaking ice cream without Mama Bubba finding out!
Interests: Fluffy animals, interesting bugs, 'sploring, wrestling with Papa Gelo, playing basketball with Leo, building my secret fort, riding dirt bikes with Way-Way and Chi-Chi, learning from Spring - he teaches me a lot! - and jigsaw puzzles
Things I'm good at: Everyone says they like my hugs, so I think I am a good hugger. Everyone laughs when I'm around, so I think I am good at making people happy.
Things I like about living at Five Fangs: Everything! Mama and Papa, of course, are number one. Then my besties, Spring, and Luna. Then the alphas, Gorgeous and Pretty and Poppy and Leo and Konnie and Dr. York and everyone! I like that I don't have a cage here. I like when Mama and Papa let me sleep with them when I have a bad dream. I like that no one yells at me or hits me here. I like eating anything I want, whenever I want with no punishment. I like riding dirt bikes with my besties and sleepovers at Dad Nathan and Mom Evie's house. I like playing basketball with Leo and doing archery with Papa and petting Poppy's fox. I like when Konnie shifts and Chime Karma takes me for a ride. We fly through the clouds! (I tried to eat them once, but I didn't taste anything.) I'm so happy Mama Bubba decided to keep me! I never, ever want to leave Five Fangs!

End of Book Four